continued . . .

Kansas Troubles
Nominated for an Agatha Award for Best Novel

"Mayhem, murder, chaos, and romance . . . well-paced mystery . . . fun reading." —*The Kansas Daily Reporter*

"A lot of fun to read. Fowler has a deft touch."
—*The Wichita Eagle*

Irish Chain

"Terrific. . . . The dialogue is intelligent and witty, the characters intensely human, and the tantalizing puzzle keeps the pages turning."
—Jean Hager, author of *The Redbird's Cry*

"This well-textured sequel . . . intricately blends social history and modern mystery." —*Publishers Weekly*

Fool's Puzzle
Nominated for an Agatha Award for Best First Mystery

"Characters come to full three-dimensional life, and her plot is satisfyingly complex."
—*The Jackson (MS) Clarion-Ledger*

"Breezy, humorous dialogue of the first order."
—*Chicago Sun-Times*

Berkley Prime Crime Books by Earlene Fowler

STEPS
TO THE
ALTAR

EARLENE FOWLER

BERKLEY PRIME CRIME, NEW YORK

STEPS TO THE ALTAR

A Berkley Prime Crime Book / published by arrangement with the author

PRINTING HISTORY
Berkley Prime Crime hardcover edition / April 2002
Berkley Prime Crime mass-market edition / April 2003

ISBN: 0-425-18944-9

For
Tina and Tom Davis

dear friends, brilliant webmasters, ardent supporters
my thanks for your sustaining help,
both emotional and culinary

and

For
Clare Bazley
Jo Ellen Heil
Sue Morrison

your friendship and loving encouragement
have been worth their weight in rubies

ACKNOWLEDGMENTS

As with all my books, there have been many kind souls who rendered me assistance. My sincerest appreciation to all of them for taking time out of their busy lives to help me.

Some trust in chariots and some in horses,
but we trust in the name of the Lord our God.
—Psalm 20:7

For help with spiritual questions and technical advice—Father Mark Stetz, AnnE Lorenzen, Father Jerry Kahler.

For help with police-related issues—Jim Gardiner, Chief, San Luis Obispo Police; Chris Rodgers, Investigator, San Luis Obispo District Attorney's Office; Burt Topham, Captain, San Luis Obispo Police.

For friendship and help in various areas—Joy and Lorna Fitzhugh, Jo Ellen Heil, Christine Hill, Karen and David Gray, Jo-Ann Mapson, Don and Lucille Rader.

For being a wonderful editor and friend—Judith Palais.

For their invaluable input on this book—my agent, Ellen Gieger, and my new editor, Christine Zika.

And always, my husband, Allen, whose daily courage, spirit, and generosity of heart continually amaze me.

The Steps to the Altar pattern most likely has its beginnings in things romantic, though there is a possibility that it also has a spiritual aspect. Before the twentieth century, marriage announced a major role shift in a woman's life. A gift of a quilt from her closest friends both honored this event and served as a reminder of her friends' love and support. The Steps to the Altar pattern is a fairly simple one using squares and triangles to make a block that is striking when contrasting fabrics are used. The name actually refers to at least three different patterns, some of which have their earliest origins in late-nineteenth-century Ohio and New York. It is also called Dish of Fruit, Flat Iron Patchwork, Strawberry Basket, Stairstep, Stairs of Illusion, English T Box, Jacob's Ladder, and Building Blocks.

1

GABE

LATE AT NIGHT when the dreams woke him, he would lie in the dark and try to forget the faces of the people he'd watched die. Memories of them exploded in his brain, popping and flaring like star shells launched from cannons. With a sick compulsion, he counted off their lives like a human rosary.

Vietnam was an old movie to him now, a videotape that allowed him to fast-forward through the unbearable parts. Except when he slept. In his dream world thumb-sized maggots burrowed into sweaty thighs, rancid jungles steamed like old garbage, the smell of foot rot gagged like a clump of gristle stuck fast in an esophagus narrowed by terror. His head filled with the sulfuric meaty stench of fresh blood and human entrails swarming with buzzing black flies. It was an uncontrollable roller coaster of terrifying peaks and valleys. Sometimes he cried out in his sleep, choking on his own salty bile, reactions that shamed him to his core and could have gotten him killed in country.

In 'Nam, his buddies, José Two, Willie M., and Clarence Earl, called him Stoneman because he never made a sound when he slept. It was a silly nickname, one given by adolescents. But of course, that's what they were. A bunch of boys sent to a jungle halfway around the world to fight some old men's pissing contest. That's the nature of war itself. At forty-four, Gabe understood that now, though he would protest in the streets and send his son to the Canadian back country before he'd let him serve in such a war.

When the dreams captured his mind and wouldn't let go, her voice brought him back.

"It's okay," her voice would call through the murky jungle of crimson sounds and smells that seemed so real they couldn't be mere products of his brain's electrical charges. Cool hands stroked his hair and face, coaxing him awake. "Friday, wake up now. It's okay. You're here with me. That's good, come on back now. Come on back."

It was the same voice she used with skittish horses and panicky new heifers delivering their first calves. It was a sweet, sure voice that he trusted like no other.

It was not lost on him that she was the only woman in his life with whom his subconscious had ever felt free enough to cry for help.

But still, it shamed him. He took pride in being able to compartmentalize his life. Take a long hot mental shower and scrub away the filthy parts. Vietnam and its brittle, grisly terrors in this corner. All the women he'd thoughtlessly used in that corner. His first wife, Lydia, and his inability to love her here. His son, Sam, and how he failed him there. He wrapped all the street stories together in one filthy bundle: dead babies in plastic bags, women beaten until their faces resembled rotten plums, needle-scarred heroin addicts lying in their own shit, little girls ripped apart by their fathers' uncontrollable lust. Take all those sad human stories and shove them in a room and padlock the door. It worked perfectly. Until he went to sleep and the padlock was snapped as easily as a child's forearm.

When he came to San Celina, he'd planned only to help out his old partner, Aaron, to hold his place as police chief until he could return. He was merely looking for a stopover, a place to regroup and think about where he wanted to go. To find a place where the images could fade. He knew the faces would never go away. He knew that the past couldn't be changed. He only wanted moments of peace. That was all he hoped for. But he expected nothing.

He never expected Aaron to die. He never expected to fall in love. He never expected to find grace.

2

BENNI

I WAS AFRAID to move.

One unlucky stumble or shift in weight and it appeared to me that I could bring Miss Christine's whole knickknack-filled teahouse down around my mud-caked boots.

As much as I loved Miss Christine, a former Vegas show girl who was rumored to have once been a mobster's girlfriend, only one thing could entice me into this garden of girlish delight. Too many clichés flitted through my mind: fish out of water, square peg in a round hole, and the most appropriate, the infamous bull in a china shop.

But it was this or having my best friend, Elvia Aragon's, wedding shower, a shower I'd waited to give since we were both second graders trading my pimento-cheese sandwiches for her homemade burritos, in my own cramped Spanish-style bungalow. I wasn't the only one who'd waited a good many years for this momentous event. When the shower's guest list hit forty, I started panicking. After moaning about the problem to my friend, Amanda Landry, expert quilter and pro bono attorney for the Josiah Sinclair Folk Art Museum, where I was curator and head bottle washer, she suggested I rent Miss Christine's Tea and Sympathy Parlor for the whole afternoon and let someone else do most of the work.

Relieved, I jumped at her advice and called two weeks ago. Thanks to Miss Christine, most of the preparations were ready to go and we were in the final phase—selecting the menu. Amanda, a good ole Southern girl raised by a rich society mama in Alabama, was having the time of her life.

"I'd forgotten how fun showers are," she said, giving me her wide, white-as-new-cotton grin. Anticipation brightened her smooth-cheeked, ivory complexion as she peered toward the kitchen where Miss Christine and her chef, José, were working on sample trays of sandwiches, scones, and other teatime treats.

Trying to avoid what could be a small but very costly disaster, I carefully crossed my legs, resting my ankle on the knee of my slightly grimy Wranglers. I'd forgotten how crowded this place was with English china, silver, and Victorian geegaws. I'd come straight from the ranch, where I'd helped Daddy and Sam, my stepson, stack a ton of hay bales. My shoulders, unused these last few years to the manual labor, were already starting to ache. At that moment a couple of aspirin washed down with a Coke sounded more appetizing to me than chicken salad sandwiches.

"I still think A. J. Spurs Restaurant would have been better," I grumbled.

"Sure, if we were wanting steak sandwiches for you and a bunch of your ranch women friends at a Cattlewomen's luncheon," Amanda said, flipping back her thick, auburn hair. "But this is *Elvia* we're talking about. She's waited a good long while for this wedding shower. I'll bet she's attended a lakeful of them in her thirty-five years on this earth and it's payback time, babydoll."

I sighed and said, "You're right. If anyone deserves the best, it's Elvia. I'm just always afraid I'm going to trip and break a million dollars' worth of china in these places."

Amanda laughed. "This isn't Tiffany's and I promise I'll pay for whatever you break."

I was picking at a piece of oat hay stuck in my jeans when Miss Christine, wearing a dress that appeared to be made of a hundred black-and-red silk scarves, came floating out of the kitchen followed by a short, thick-chested Hispanic man in a spotless white chef's coat. He carried an ornate silver tray the size of a tractor seat.

"Ladies, thank you so much for being patient," Miss Christine said. "I can assure you, it will be worth the wait. My José is a genius with petit fours and his honey-walnut scones." She rolled kohl-lined green eyes and fanned herself with elegant fingers that seemed to be made to dangle an ivory cigarette holder between their crimson tips. "Paradise on your tongues."

The sober-faced, middle-aged man set the tray on the linen-covered table in front of us. Amanda and Miss Christine sighed simultaneously as they surveyed the tiny, crustless sandwiches and other colorful treats.

Turning my head slightly, I peeked at José's hand, trying to see if the rumors were true. Yep, there it was. SC 13 tattooed in dark green between his thumb and forefinger. Gabe had told me that the chef here was once quite high in one of our local gangs. He'd gone to prison for armed robbery, studied there in a special program under a San Francisco pastry chef, and recently emerged from incarceration with a skill much more in demand than driving a getaway car. Somehow, Miss Christine managed to snag him out from under the five other gourmet restaurants vying for his prestigious talents.

He saw where I was looking and gave me an amused wink. I felt my face grow warm and pretended intense interest in the food he'd prepared. My identity as the police chief's wife here in San Celina, a medium-sized college and retirement town on the Central Coast of California, was not much of a secret, even though I didn't look like the typical police chief's wife. I did my best, wearing dresses whenever appropriate and making small talk at political shindigs and charity events, but my heart just wasn't in it. I was a country girl, reluctantly moved to town by the death of my first husband and the loss of our ranch a few years back. I still managed to get out to my gramma Dove and Daddy's ranch a few times a week, but my life these days included more afternoons punching computer keys down at the folk art museum than punching cattle. Not to mention, as my beloved second husband would point out, getting way too involved in the criminal affairs of San Celina County.

Or how my cousin Emory, Elvia's fiancée and a journalist with the *San Celina Tribune*, would most likely say in his sexy, Arkansas drawl, sticking my snout where it shouldn't be sticking. It did me no good to insist that all the homicides I'd been involved with were only because I happened to be unlucky enough to be in the crime's vicinity.

"That's okay, sweetcakes," Emory had said a few days ago, his even-featured, handsome face giving me a loopy grin. These days, drunk on the idea of finally achieving his life's dream, marrying Elvia, every expression he wore looked a bit goofy and amazed. "Without you, the chief's life would be incredibly pedestrian."

I gave a decidedly unladylike snort. "I'll remember to mention that the next time I get involved in a murder. *Not* that there's going to be a next time."

"Pay attention, cowgirl," Amanda said, smacking my knee. A tiny puff of chaff dust exploded and she waved it away like unwanted cigarette smoke. "What do you think of watercress, chicken salad, cucumber, and this lovely nutty-tasting spread for the sandwiches?"

I popped one of the crustless, star-shaped sandwiches in my mouth. It tasted like walnuts, mayonnaise, grape, and some other flavors I couldn't put my finger on. "It's all okay with me, though I vote thumbs-down on the watercress."

"Why?" Miss Christine and José blurted out simultaneously. The hurt look on José's craggy face made me instantly explain.

"It's not the sandwiches. I'm sure they're wonderful. It's just that watercress and I have a tumultuous history." I didn't want to go into detail about the first homicide I'd become involved with, the incident where Gabe and I met. Right before I discovered the body, I'd eaten watercress sandwiches at one of Elvia's book-signing events at her store, Blind Harry's. Later that night, I'd retasted the watercress in a not-so-pleasant manner. "Really, the watercress is fine."

José's face softened in relief. Miss Christine straightened her spine and asked, "What about everything else?"

I glanced over the pastel-colored cakes and cookies and tiny scones and croissants. "It's all perfect. I think we should have a bit of everything you have here. Enough for forty, no, make that forty-five people. What do you think, Amanda?"

She popped another strawberry-and-cream-filled miniature croissant in her mouth. "I agree. And we'll have Lady Grey tea and a lovely mint lemonade."

"Very good," Miss Christine said. "We'll see you all here this Sunday afternoon then."

"Wearing clean boots and underwear," I said.

Amanda kicked me under the table, grinning as she did. "I wish I could have inflicted you on my dear sweet mama before she passed on to that great tea party in the sky. She so loved a challenge."

José laughed out loud, a masculine rumble that was wonderfully at odds with the ultrafeminine decor. Miss Christine bestowed upon me a tentative, but brave smile, not quite certain if I was joking.

Outside the tea parlor, Amanda asked, "What about the cake?"

"Ordered it a week ago," I said. "I'm dropping by Stern's Bakery with the check this afternoon. I need to talk with Sally about Dove's shower cake. This is not the only shower meeting I had on my schedule today, you know. I'm due at the historical museum in"—I checked my dependable Daffy Duck watch—"an hour to discuss Dove's wedding shower."

My gramma, who had raised me since I was six years old when my mother died of cancer, had, after some thirty-odd years of widowhood, decided to get married. Her fiancée, the world-renowned photographer Isaac Lyons, had entered our lives a year and a half ago when he'd come to San Celina to investigate his granddaughter's mysterious death. He and I solved the case and in the process he fell head-over-boot-heels in love with my gramma. A man of impeccable taste if you wanted my unbiased opinion.

"That is so great," Amanda said, leaning against one of San Celina's black wrought iron lampposts. They were decorated on this cool, February morning with emerald green, royal purple, and bright gold streamers advertising this week's Mardi Gras festivities. "Dove gettin' married at seventy-seven after all those years being a widow. How's your daddy takin' it? Is he feelin' threatened by Isaac becomin' his stepdaddy?"

"Are you kidding? He is so thrilled to have someone *else* getting all Dove's attention and nagging he's been telling his cronies down at the Farm Supply that he's got the shotgun loaded in case Isaac tries to back out."

Amanda gave a delighted laugh. "Not much chance of that, I'll just bet. Isaac is downright besotted, far as I can see."

"Yeah, he and Emory could be January and February for a Men Crazy in Love calendar."

"Where're Dove and Isaac plannin' on living?"

"Out at the ranch. It's got four bedrooms and three bathrooms. Daddy says one more place at the table sure doesn't bother him."

"Have they set a date?" Amanda asked.

"Tentatively. It's after Elvia's for sure. Dove's thinking three weeks."

"Are you involved in the planning?"

I shook my head no. "Trying not to be. She hasn't decided yet what kind of wedding she wants and she's been driving me crazy with her suggestions. She wants it to be memorable, she says. Since Isaac's been married five times, she wants this one to stand out."

As if on cue, my new cell phone rang. "Happy Trails" reverberated from deep inside my leather backpack, and it took a few minutes for me to find the phone and answer it.

"Yes? Hello?" I said in that loud tin-cans-tied-with-a-string voice that none of us seems to be able to stop using with cell phones.

"Medieval," Dove yelled back at me. She must have been using her new cell phone too. "I could wear one of them pointy hats like Maid Marian. Make Mac dress up like Friar Tuck. We could serve chicken and fruit and eat it with our hands."

"That would certainly save on dishwashing," I said noncommittally. However this wedding of hers and Isaac's turned out, I was determined not to be the person blamed for any mishaps, so I was agreeing with everything.

"Think I could talk your daddy into wearing tights?"

I held back my laughter. "Uh . . . if anyone could, you could." Not unless he'd just drunk a gallon of moonshine, I was actually thinking.

"I don't know," she yelled. "I don't look that great in pointy hats. Call you later." The phone went dead.

"What's the news?" Amanda's face was curious. Being an only child, she envied the complications my extended family brought into my life.

"I think we just narrowly missed a Robin Hood wedding."

"I loved Kevin Costner in that movie no matter what anyone said."

"Well, Dove doesn't look good in pointy hats."

"Who does?"

We hugged, said our goodbyes, and agreed to meet at Miss Christine's this Sunday an hour before the shower to set out the party favors and do a little decorating. Amanda, bless her Martha Stewart heart, was planning all the shower games. All I had to do was buy the prizes and my own shower gift for Elvia. That meant a trip to Angelina's Attic, a local lingerie store.

February was one of my favorite months in San Celina. The air was cool and clean-tasting, like water from a deep, rock-lined well. Cal Poly students had lost the frenetic gotta-try-it-all edge they sported at the beginning of the school year and hadn't yet acquired the end-of-the-year hysteria that would come in a few months. Except for the tinge of excitement brought on by the coming Mardi Gras festival and parade that San Celina proudly touted as being the biggest ones west of the Mississippi, the town had a calm, peaceful air to its tree-lined streets. I walked down Lopez Street toward Stern's Bakery, my mind wandering, thinking about the blissful time a month from now when both Elvia and Dove's weddings were over and life was back to normal.

At Stern's Hometown Bakery, a jingle of sleigh bells announced my entry into the almond-scented place. Sally, a handsome, white-haired woman who'd owned the bakery since I was a kindergartner, sat at a round glass-topped table thumbing through a photograph album of cakes with two older ladies. She lifted up a finger to let me know she'd be with me in a moment. I poured a cup of their strong dark coffee, picked a cherry-topped cookie from the tray of freebies, and sat down in a white wicker chair.

After Sally had taken the ladies' order and pressed upon them a free half dozen of her famous poppy seed cookies, she poured herself a cup of coffee and joined me.

"Hello, Mrs. Chief-of-Police," she said. "How're the dual shower plans progressing?"

"Just came from Miss Christine's Tea and Sympathy," I said. "It was brilliant of Amanda to suggest letting someone else do all the work. All I have to do is buy the prizes,

Elvia's shower present, and write a check. And speaking of checks, that's why I'm here." I pulled my checkbook and a copy of the bakery bill out of my backpack. "I want to settle up my accounts for both cakes so I can mark one more thing off my list."

"I'm always amenable to accepting money," she said, tucking a strand of loose hair back into her bun. "The cakes will be ready when you are. Sunday and Wednesday, right?"

"Right. I'll pick up Elvia's cake about ten A.M. Sunday and Dove's about noon on Wednesday." I handed her the check.

"So, are you about ready to go nuts?" she asked, taking the check and standing up. "Want some more coffee?"

"No, thanks, I'll just have to find a bathroom, and from what I hear, the one over at the historical museum has been on the blink."

"What's going on over at the museum?" she asked, walking behind the counter and punching the keys to the cash register.

"Final preparations for Dove's shower."

"She is one brave woman, getting married again after all these years. How's she holding up?"

I grinned. "*She's* doing fine. Now Isaac . . ."

Sally laughed. "He should be used to it. Hasn't he been married a few times?"

"Five, to be exact. But *never* to a Ramsey woman."

Sally nodded, her pink cheeks shiny under the bright fluorescent light. "He needs to consult with the chief."

"Not if we can help it," I said, laughing. "We want this marriage to take place."

"Well, I'm so happy for both Dove and Elvia. I'll be at both showers."

"See you then." I snagged one more cookie and headed toward the historical museum.

The San Celina County Historical Museum was located one street over from Lopez Street in the old brick Carnegie Library building. As a child, before they built the new library out by Laguna Lake, I'd spent many long, lazy afternoons here in the children's department reading Curious George and Big Red books. When I was fifteen years old, I received my first adult kiss under the pepper tree on the patio from Jack Harper, my late first husband who'd died in a car wreck three years ago this month. Walking under the stone archway into the old library never ceased to fill me with a sweet, sad longing for times past. When the building came to house the historical remnants of San Celina County and its citizens, I'd spent even more endless afternoons as an adult helping Dove catalog and organize donated items. As a thirty-year member of the historical society, she knew every piece of clothing, jewelry, tools, and needlework by heart.

Inside the cool entry hall, I spotted June Rae Gates, one of Dove's oldest friends, behind the gift shop counter.

"Hi, June Rae," I said. "Everyone present and accounted for?"

"Yes, ma'am," she said, locking the cash register and slipping the key in the pocket of her wraparound denim skirt. She taped a hand-printed sign to the register that stated if anyone wanted to buy something, to come find her at the back of the museum. "We need to make it quick because Elmo's cat has an appointment for a CAT scan and my college helper canceled out on me. I think she has a new boyfriend."

"His cat is getting a CAT scan?" I couldn't stop the giggle that fell from my lips.

She patted her peppery hair. "I know, it does sound funny. The poor thing's got arthritis so bad it can barely walk. I don't think a CAT scan will show much but that it's as old as the rest of us, but Elmo'd sell his new Cadillac for Inkspot."

I nodded, feeling sympathy for Elmo. I'd probably be just as insistent when it came to my dog, Scout, a chocolate Lab–German shepherd mix. I followed her toward the circle of folding chairs. The rest of the Dove Ramsey Wedding Shower Committee was already in place, munching away on some of Maria Ramirez's chocolate cinnamon cookies. I grabbed one with pink icing and slid into an empty chair. The air was a sugary mixture of lavender- and magnolia-scented colognes, the bitter scent of store brand coffee, and the dusty, comfortable smell of a building that had survived two World Wars and more than a few broken hearts.

After a brief report by all the members, we agreed that everything was on schedule and ready to go. June Rae went back up to the counter and I was standing around the coffeepot listening to Elmo Ritter's diatribe about the sad state of veterinary medicine (he'd been through four vets looking for the one who could give him the impossible—the fountain of youth for Inkspot) when Edna McClun, another of Dove's friends, grabbed my forearm and exclaimed, "You're just the person I was looking for!"

Why is it those words never fail to fill me with trepidation?

My response was automatic. "I didn't do it and I didn't see a thing."

"Oh, you," she said, patting my shoulder lightly. "You're such a card. Seriously, I have something I think you'll really be interested in."

Another statement warning me there was work involved.

I contemplated my half-eaten cookie, then looked back at her cajoling smile and said, "Okay, I'll bite."

"You know I'm on the committee to restore the Sullivan house."

"No, I didn't," I said, popping the rest of the cookie in my mouth, figuring I'd need the carbohydrates for whatever task she was wanting me to take on.

"Have you been reading about it in the historical society newsletter?"

"Yes, and congratulations on finally getting it declared an historical landmark." The Sullivan house, a Queen Anne Victorian on the far edge of San Celina's city limits, had been in a state of decay as long as I could remember. I had vague memories of someone saying the Sullivan family had died out and the house was repossessed for back taxes. I also vaguely remembered buying raffle tickets for a quilt made to raise funds to buy the property. I assumed the historical society must have succeeded when I read a few months back about the house being declared an historical landmark. On the property there was also another unusual structure, an octagonal barn, one of only two in California.

"Acquiring it wasn't easy, but generations to come will be glad we did," she continued. "The Sullivans were a very prominent family in San Celina County during the early part of the century. Arthur Sullivan and his son, Garvey, owned many of the best grain fields and the largest beef cattle herd in the county. They were also smart enough to build huge grain storage silos in the thirties, which they rented out to other farmers during the war when the farmers had to switch from bags to bulk because the government needed the jute for the war effort. The Sullivans also owned a good bit of downtown and were very involved with the building of Camp Riley up near San Miguel."

I glanced at my watch. Though normally I enjoyed hearing oral history from someone who'd lived during that time, I had a lunch date with Gabe in fifteen minutes. "So, what are you trying to rope me into doing, Edna? You know I've got a pretty full plate these days so it can't take too much time."

"Oh, it's something you can do at your leisure. It's about Maple Bennett Sullivan."

The name sounded familiar but I couldn't put my finger on how. "Maple Bennett Sullivan?"

"I'm sure you must have heard about the tragedy with her and her husband, Garvey."

I shrugged. The history of this county was rife with nefarious shenanigans usually involving land ownership, cattle rustling, and water rights. Every old family had its share of misfortune and sad stories. "Can't recall anything offhand."

"I don't see how you can't remember this one, my dear. It's right up your alley." Her watery blue eyes twinkled behind her round plastic eyeglasses.

"Why's that?"

"She murdered her husband, my dear girl."

3

BENNI

"SHE WHAT?" I exclaimed.

"She murdered her husband," Edna repeated. "Surely you've heard the story."

I started to shake my head no, then a shadowy, childhood memory came back to me. "You know, I do think I remember hearing it mentioned sometime when I was a kid." Dove and I had gone riding at her friend's ranch, which bordered the Sullivan property. Dove's friend, a red-faced woman named Lucie who raised Appaloosas, pointed out the house, in disrepair even then, and called it the murderess's house. I was seven at the time and remember asking Dove when we were unsaddling the horses what a murderess was. She told me in her usual blunt way that it was a woman who killed someone because she was angry or wanted to get something the person owned. That seemed to have appeased me because I never thought about it again even though I'd passed by that house dozens of times in my life.

"Why did she kill him?" I asked.

She flipped her palm up in a who-knows gesture. "It was quite the scandal back in the forties. 'Forty-four, I think it was. The war was still going on and there weren't many young men left here on the Central Coast. They were all off fighting somewhere. We lost too many of our boys during that time." Her orange-painted mouth turned straight. "It was a bad time."

"How did she do it?" I couldn't resist asking, though I suspected my showing of interest would probably add work to my already overloaded schedule.

"Shot him in the head." She put a finger gun up to her own blue-veined temple. "The rumor swirling around town was she was pregnant with another man's child and wanted to run away with him. The story goes that she told Garvey about the baby, they had a horrible fight, she shot him, and then fled. They never found hide nor hair of her."

"What about the man she had the affair with?"

"He disappeared too." Her penciled eyebrows rose high on her pale forehead. "He was a local boy also. They both worked at the paper together. Did I mention she wrote a column for the *San Celina Tribune*? Human interest, women's affairs, and such. I think she even did some articles on quilting. That would be right up your alley too. At any rate, no one heard from either of them again, so that tells it all, doesn't it? Garvey's father, Arthur, lived a few years after the war. Died in the early fifties, I think. Garvey's mother died when he was a baby. Since Garvey had no heirs, his estate eventually went to some distant relatives back East, who apparently spent all the money and let the house and property be foreclosed for back taxes."

"That's an interesting story," I said, wiping my hands on a napkin. "But I'm not clear on how it concerns me."

"There are four trunks filled with her belongings and we need someone to catalog—"

I held up my hands to interrupt her request. "I can't, Edna. As fascinating as it sounds, I'm just too busy."

"There's no time limit on when it needs to be done," she said. Her voice took on a cajoling tone I knew would

eventually wear me down. "Please, Benni. We need someone we can trust and someone who appreciates history,
even the history of a murderess."

"Why in the world would you think that I'm the person
most suited for this project?" I rolled the small white napkin into a ball and started squeezing it like one of those
rubber stress toys so popular at Elvia's bookstore.

She patted my arm again with her cool, dry hand. "Because, my dear, you have a historian's mind, a detective's
tenacity, and your grandma's compassionate heart."

Oh, Lord, how could I answer that? Or even think of
saying no to her request? "You would have made a great
used car salesperson, Edna McClun," I grumbled.

She gave a tinkly laugh. "You are not the first person
to tell me that. Shall I have the trunks delivered to your
house or the museum?"

"The museum. I don't know if Dove told you, but Gabe
and I finally bought a house and we're half in one, half
in the other. Escrow closes in two weeks, but the owners
are letting us move in early since the house is empty. The
trunks would be less likely to get misplaced at the museum." Besides, I thought, there was no way I was doing
this at home. I had enough of my own unpacking and
sorting to do. I'd somehow squeeze it into my workday
at the museum. "I can't believe I let you talk me into
this."

"Oh, you'll enjoy it," she said, reaching into her skirt
pocket and handing me a key ring with four old-fashioned
keys. "Like I said, it's right up your alley, her being a
murderess and all."

Before I could protest that this husband killer and I
were not psychic cohorts, she told me that one of the
restoration volunteers would deliver the trunks in the next
few days and thanked me profusely for doing this wonderful, generous thing for the historical preservation of an
interesting if tarnished part of San Celina history.

"Remember," she said. "No time limit on this. Just do
it at your leisure."

Leisure? What was that? On the way to Antonio's Italian Restaurant, where I'd agreed to meet Gabe for lunch to sign yet more papers pertaining to the three-bedroom California bungalow house we'd bought in downtown San Celina just four blocks over from Elvia's store, I mentally berated myself for allowing someone to talk me into taking on another project. Though a part of me was curious about this woman and her, to say the least, troubled past, right now the thought of digging through four trunks of anyone's belongings, including my own, just seemed tiring.

At Antonio's, Gabe had already ordered for us and was flipping through a stack of official-looking documents. He'd taken off his jacket and rolled up the sleeves of his crisp white dress shirt, revealing one of my favorite parts of him, hard, corded forearms covered with coarse black hair.

"You're late," he said, standing up to kiss me.

"I was at a historical society meeting. You want to know what Edna McClun wants me to do?"

"Hold that comment," he said. "I need to have you sign these papers for the house before we get distracted."

After signing where he indicated, our lunches came— vegetarian lasagna for him, beef ravioli for me. I picked at my meal, not really hungry.

"What's wrong?" He pointed at my plate with his fork.

"Ate too many cookies this morning."

He shook his head in reproach and began a story about a new rookie who had injured himself when he'd been on the job only three weeks and was now trying to sue the city. I half listened, thinking about what else I had to do this afternoon, until he rapped on my water glass with his knife.

"Dispatch to Benni," he said. "What's got your attention? It's certainly not me." He smiled that devastatingly sexy smile of his—white, white teeth against tanned olive skin. A smile that could stop most women in midsentence and make them imagine physical pleasures that they'd never confess to even their closest girlfriends.

I smiled back, not as seduced as I would have been two and a half years ago when we first met, but warmed by it because I saw the self-mocking twinkle in his eye. "Friday," I said, using my favorite nickname for him, based on his adherence to the original Joe Friday's straight-and-narrow view of life. "I love you with all my heart and you are the sexiest male thing walking on two legs, but sometimes I'm just busy with my own thoughts, and hard as this is for you to believe, they don't *always* include you."

His laugh rumbled deep in his chest. "*Te amo mucho, querida.* You are good for my ego."

"And a great and mighty ego it is, *Papacito,*" I said, toasting him with my water.

"See you around six," he said. "Guess dinner is Big Top Pizza again."

"Since all our pots and pans are packed in a box that *someone* forgot to label, that's a good and safe bet."

He grinned, not fazed by my criticism. "We'll find them eventually. Just think, once we move into this house, we'll never have to move again. The only boxes coming out of that house will be pine ones with us in them."

"And on that cheery thought, my dear Sergeant Friday, I'll make my exit."

We kissed goodbye, both lightened by our midday break together, an unusual occurrence, given both our hectic schedules. I was excited that we'd finally found the perfect house. It felt like we were officially starting our life together even though we'd been married two years ago this coming Sunday. This was only the second thing we'd bought together, the first being my new Ford Ranger pickup truck, a two-month-old purchase I was still being razzed about by Daddy and all my ranching friends.

For one thing, it was a Ford. A dirty word among most ranchers on the Central Coast, who were diehard, Mom and Apple Pie, Chevy-till-I-die fanatics.

And it was purple.

The official color was listed as sapphire blue, but it was blue with a clear top coat of red that, any way you looked at it, made purple. Since this was my truck, Gabe said the color choice was up to me. There were white, brown, red, turquoise, and purple ones on the lot.

I don't know what came over me, but the purple one just called my name. And I'd been the butt of every grape, eggplant, and Barney joke that every rancher I knew could think up.

Gabe said he liked it because it was easier to keep an eye on me, something I certainly hadn't considered when we bought the truck. Nevertheless, it ran like a dream, had air-conditioning, a working tape deck, and an extended cab with enough room for my backpack, my dog, and my horse tack. And it could haul hay bales with the best of any full-size Chevy pickup. All a woman really needed.

Right at that moment, walking down the sunny street toward my best friend's bookstore to harass her about her pending nuptials, I felt content and happy. Feelings I was learning to savor when they came in this unpredictable life. After bugging her, I would go shopping for her shower gift, stop off at the mall to buy the game prizes, and head home, where Gabe and I would spend another evening moving stuff to our new house.

Blind Harry's Bookstore was right in the heart of downtown San Celina. The redbrick building felt like a second home to me since Elvia started managing and slowly buying it five years ago. As one of the last surviving independent bookstores in San Celina County, it had become one of the most popular spots in town for both locals and tourists. I paused in front of her large glass window and studied this month's display. Though I nagged her to make it a wedding motif in honor of her and Emory, she'd remained firm and stuck with the always popular Mardi Gras theme. This year's theme was Masked Madness. At least fifty masks filled the window—including antique ones with faded feathers and still bright rhinestones; dime store varieties with their rainbow-colored feathers and cheap glitter; and elaborate one-of-a-kind creations made with large face-framing plumes, hundreds of sequins, and price tags that moved them from merely masks to pieces of art. Her window designer, an ex–Cal Poly art student who, though she no longer worked for Elvia but for a local interior design firm, still loved doing Blind Harry's windows.

Inside the bookstore, the mood was subdued, not unusual for a Wednesday afternoon. Things usually started picking up in the early evening when the students, done with their classes and looking for fun, started hanging out in the coffeehouse downstairs. The only activity going on right now was an after-school story hour presented by one of Elvia's student employees, a girl majoring in early childhood education. She was reading *The Tortilla Quilt* picture book, one of my own personal favorites, to a group of fidgety five-year-olds. Elvia had the colorful quilt made from the pattern in the book hanging above the small storytelling stage.

"Where's the boss lady?" I asked the clerk at the counter. She had burgundy hair in two thick farm girl braids and a diamond stud in her nose.

"Downstairs with Mr. GQ," she said, smiling big. She made elaborate kissing noises. Since Elvia's engagement last September, her employees, a mixture of senior citizens and college students, had taken great pleasure in teasing her about finally screwing up her courage to jump over the marriage broom. She allowed them a little fun, then when the enormity of this life change became overwhelming, went into her upstairs office and slammed the door. That was when everyone knew to leave her alone. If she was downstairs, she was obviously in an amiable mood.

"Thanks," I said, heading for the wooden stairs. She was in the back of the used-book-lined coffeehouse (her system of borrow a book and replace it with another had been a hit from its inception) sitting at a round oak table sharing a cranberry scone with my dearly beloved fifth cousin Emory.

"Hey, kids," I said. "Are you ready to stomp on the wineglass?"

"I'm glad you're here," Elvia said, standing up. "You can entertain the poultry baron while I get back to work and earn a real living."

Emory worked at the local newspaper though he was, in fact, filthy rich from his father's smoked chicken business in Arkansas. He gave me yet another wide, goofy grin. His bright green eyes glowed as if he were on some kind of very potent, possibly illegal drug.

"Oh, geeze," I said, sitting down next to him. "If I have to gaze upon his canary-eating grin one more minute, I'm going to puke."

"You and me both," Elvia said, rolling her black eyes.

"Ladies," Emory said, his smile not losing one kilowatt. "Why can't you just let a man be happy? Y'all complain if we're sad and complain if we're happy. What is it y'all want?"

Elvia and I both laughed.

"That, my dear boy," I said, reaching over and patting his hand, "is a secret women are sworn to keep from the minute they learn it at their mama's knee." I looked over at Elvia. "Right, *mi amiga*?"

Elvia just laughed again, kissed Emory quickly, and headed back upstairs. "Your tux is ready," she called over her shoulder. "We'll need to go pick it up tonight."

He watched her walk up the stairs, lovesick amazement on his face.

When he could no longer see her, he turned back to me. "Well, sweetcakes, how are things going on the move?"

"Slow but sure. We're moving some of our clothes over tonight. It's nice having a few extra weeks to do it in."

"I'll bet. I want to find a house as soon as we get back from our honeymoon. Both our condos are full to bursting. I've had a real estate agent out scouting. There's a

real nice Victorian down on the corner of Second and
Heron Streets I think Elvia might love."

"That gray-and-white one? With the pink petunias in
front?"

"Yes, ma'am."

"It's only two blocks from me and Gabe!"

He grinned. "Yes, ma'am."

I leaned over and hugged him. "Oh, cousin, that would
be so perfect. You and me living so close. Did you ever
think when we were eleven and twelve something like this
would happen?"

That summer, back in 1970, when he'd come from Arkansas to stay at our ranch because his mother had just
died and his father had gone quietly crazy for three
months, had started our deep, lifelong friendship. Since
I'd lost my mother when I was six, I understood what
he was going through, and in long afternoons down by
the creek or up in the airy lofts of our haybarn, we discussed life, death, and the odd world of grown-ups, con-
fiding in each other all the scary things kids feel about
those subjects, but never told the adults in their lives. He
went home in September, but we'd kept up a correspon-
dence that cemented our new friendship. He was my best
friend and the only person in the world related to me on
both sides of my family—his grandfather and my dad's
grandfather were first cousins by marriage and his father,
Boone Littleton, married my mother's third cousin, Er-
valean.

"I'm happy as a new tick on a fat dog," he said, heaving
a big sigh.

"Gee, I couldn't tell," I said, grabbing his cup of latte
and taking a sip. "How are the plans for the bachelor
blowout going? I'd better warn you, we've got spies.
There'd better not be any naked ladies."

"No chance on that," he said, leaning back in the old
wooden library chair. "I'm not about to do anything that
would cause Elvia to back out. No, it's going to be a
classy event down at the Jamestown Tavern. I've rented
the upper room and we're going to have a bourbon tasting,

play low-stakes poker, eat high-fat appetizers, smoke illegal Cuban cigars, and watch crazy police chase videos that your hubby is providing."

"When?"

"Next Wednesday night. This Saturday's out because of the Mardi Gras parade and costume ball at Constance Sinclair's. And we don't want to do it too close to the wedding because I want everyone hangover-free, including myself."

"That's the night of Dove's shower! Maybe we'll run into each other. Well, just be careful driving home."

"Already taken care of, my dear worrisome girl. I've hired a passel of college students to drive the inebriated safely home."

"Remember, alcohol kills brain cells."

"Ha, health advice from a woman who eats banana Moonpies for breakfast and calls them a serving of fruit."

"Untrue!" I slapped his hand. "For lunch maybe . . ."

He grabbed my hand and squeezed it gently. "Don't strike me too hard, sweetcakes. I might wake up and find out like Dorothy that this is all a dream."

I lay my other hand on top of his, tears itching the back of my eyes. "It's not, Emory. I promise."

After a few minutes up in Elvia's office receiving my instructions about our last bridesmaid dress fitting this Friday, I headed down the street to Angelina's Attic.

Once there, I threw myself on the mercy of the salesclerk, who knew Elvia's taste intimately since my friend kept a running tab at the store and we settled on a café-au-lait silk and satin peignoir set that cost me a hundred twenty bucks. That done and safely away from the girly, rose-scented store, I headed out to the mall, where at a Gottschalk's Department Store I picked up more smelly, girl-type prizes for the shower. After a quick trip to the feed store to pick up dog food and get my weekly ration of Barney jokes about my truck from the old guys behind the counter, I started toward home. When I drove past the police department, I spotted Gabe's sky blue '68 Corvette still in its space. I parked in a visitor's spot next to a new dark green Porsche and my twenty-year-old stepson, Sam's, primer gray Chevy Malibu. Gabe and Sam had been slowly restoring the car and just as slowly working on their loving, though often volatile, relationship.

The front desk clerk, Kaneesha, a young African-American woman with tiny, perfect cornrows, was just starting to lock the lobby door when I walked up.

"Is *El Patrón* back in his office?" I asked her.

She nodded and smiled. "Sam is ahead of you by five minutes." Her dark eyes took on a luminous glow I'd grown used to seeing when Sam's name was spoken. Gabe's only child was an extremely attractive young man with a pleasing, cheerful personality who was adept at the kind of respectful flirting that could have only come from being raised by a loving but feminist mother. He and I had an easy relationship that was not fraught with the emotional mine fields of blood relatives. We shared a love for maple bars, Little Rascals movies, Dodger baseball, and his enigmatic father. The order of those loves was often subject to change.

As I walked down the corridor toward Gabe's office, I met Sam coming the opposite way.

"Hey, Sam," I said. "What's up?"

"Hey," he said, giving me a quick nod. His dark coppery-olive skin was a few shades deeper than Gabe's, but other than that and his black-brown eyes, he was a twenty-year-old version of his father. Gabe's slate blue eyes were a product of his Anglo Kansas mother, where as Sam's mother, Gabe's first wife, Lydia, was full-blooded Mexican-American. Though Sam looked like his father, there couldn't be two more opposite personalities on this earth. My husband was an intense, hardworking, follow-the-rules, straight-arrow sort of man. A credit to his Midwestern roots. Sam was the quintessential California suburb–raised child of divorced parents who, to the frustration of his father, could talk coconuts out of a tree. People adored Sam and they respected Gabe. And those two still couldn't see how they envied the other's position. The only things these two men had in common were a love for surfing, old cars, and each other.

But right now, Sam's normally genial face was void of his heart-dropping smile.

"What's wrong?" I said, stopping for a moment. "What are you and your dad fighting about now?"

"Nothing," he said, his baritone voice low and strained. "Yet."

"Oh, Sam, did you tell him you wanted to switch majors?" He'd been contemplating a change from agriculture, which Gabe had only just grown comfortable with, to culinary arts. His latest career plans were to become a chef, something he'd confided in me and no one else.

"No," he said, not elaborating.

That instantly made me suspicious. Sam had never had trouble whining and complaining to me about his father.

"I need to phone my mom," he said, brushing past me without another word of explanation. "See you later, Benni."

I started to call after him, then decided that perhaps it would be better if he vented to Lydia rather than me. She was, after all, his mother. And though her job as a criminal defense attorney in a prestigious firm in Santa Barbara and her striking beauty were still things that left me feeling a tad inferior, I respected and liked her, to a degree. We'd formed a tentative if a bit awkward relationship last year when Sam had gone through some hard times.

Who knew what was going on in my usually easygoing stepson's mind? He was a man. Who ever knew what went on in their minds?

Gabe's office door was closed and his assistant, Maggie, already gone for the day so I sat down behind her desk and dialed his extension.

"Chief Ortiz," his voice answered.

"I have a complaint to lodge with the police department. My husband is spending way too much time at work and not enough time getting naked with me."

His laugh could be heard through the thick oak door. "Sweetheart, where are you?"

"At Maggie's desk. Will your meeting take long? Let's ditch moving tonight and I'll treat you to kung pao chicken at Ling's if you can wrap it up in the next five minutes. I'll even let you peek at my fortune cookie."

"That is an offer no sane and healthy man would turn down. Get in here. It's not a business meeting. Del's an old LAPD friend I've been wanting you to meet. One of my ex-partners, as a matter of fact."

"Great, then he can join us for dinner and I'll ransack his memories for stories of your dastardly deeds during your twenty years in L.A. I've always wanted to know more about that time of your life." His years as an undercover narcotics officer were something he rarely talked about, much like his time in Vietnam. Sometimes it felt like there was a whole portion of this man that I didn't know.

"Just for the record, I deny everything," he said, still laughing. He sounded relaxed and happy, something that had grown increasingly rare in the last few months. The town of San Celina had grown substantially in the last year or so with the influx of retirees from both Southern California and the San Francisco Bay Area, not to mention the rise in enrollment at the college and the statewide rise in gang violence. His department had been strained to the point of breaking and he'd felt the stress of that pulling in the last few months.

When I opened the door, he had already moved around his desk to greet me. "Benni, this is Del. One of the best cops I've ever had the pleasure working with."

The tall blond woman stood up and held out her hand. "Del Hernandez. It's so nice to finally meet. Gabe has told me so much about you."

I think I successfully hid my surprise. At least, I think I managed to close my mouth after about five seconds.

"Benni Harper," I answered, shaking her hand and thinking, *Wish I could say the same.*

4

BENNI

HER HANDSHAKE WAS dry and firm, self-assured, but not pushy.

She had honey blond hair pulled back with a hammered copper clip, milk chocolate eyes, and brown skin a shade or two lighter than Gabe's. She was not particularly pretty, but more the type of woman who'd be described as handsome. But there was something else about her, a seductive aura that she gave off that told me that men would flutter around her like drunken moths.

She was dressed in a conservative navy blazer, red blouse, dark blue jeans, and was at least five-ten, with an inseam that had to be thirty-eight inches. I mean, this woman could mount a eighteen-hand horse without a block.

I ran my damp palms down the sides of my own short legs and instantly hated her.

She gave me a shy, hesitant smile and I felt a stab of guilt for my quick judgment. I didn't even know this woman, for cryin' out loud. So Gabe had failed to mention that he'd once had a female partner. So what? He'd had a lot of partners during his twenty years in the LAPD.

Well, not a lot, but some. The fact that he didn't tell me that one of them was female was just a sign of his liberated sensibilities. A cop is a cop. Sex didn't matter.

Yeah, right, Benni.

"You ladies up for some dinner?" he said, reaching for his coat behind the door. "Benni said she'd treat us to Chinese at Ling's. You still crazy over sweet and sour pork, Lupe?"

"*Absolutamente,* Gilberto," she said with a perfect Spanish accent.

"Gilberto?" I said, confused. "Lupe?"

"Our undercover names," he said, pulling at his cuffs. They exchanged an amused look that made me feel as if I weren't in the room.

"Oh," I said. Undercover names? I didn't like the sound of that. I shifted my leather backpack to my other shoulder, feeling a bit lost as to what to say or do. I had seen Gabe with one of his ex-partners, Aaron Davidson, San Celina's former chief of police, who'd died a year or so ago of liver cancer. Rachel, Aaron's wife, and I used to tease them about the similarities of their partner relationship with that of a marriage. A cop's partner was someone he literally trusted with his life so it followed that the relationship would have an intimacy not seen in most other friendships or even some marriages.

Was it the same when the partner was a woman? As we walked out to our respective cars, Sam's agitated expression came back to me. Did he know something about Gabe and Del's relationship that caused that anger? As much as I wanted to call and ask him, I admonished myself to stay calm and just observe. For once, I wasn't going to jump in and make a fool of myself without knowing all the facts.

The new Porsche parked next to my purple truck ended up belonging to Del. What a surprise.

"Cute truck," she said, nodding at my Ranger. "Guess you can find that real easy in a mall parking lot."

"Yep," I said.

"Yin and yang," Gabe said with a smug smile. His comment grated on my nerves like knuckles across a brick wall. Forget being an understanding, liberated woman, I was going to jump his bones the minute we were alone and demand to know why he'd told his female ex-partner about *me* and failed to tell me about *her*.

"I'll go on over and get us a table," I said stiffly.

"Great," he said, not picking up on my irritation. "I'll give Del directions."

I slowly pulled out of the parking lot and watched them through my rearview mirror. There was nothing in their body language that suggested that they'd been anything but partners in the most innocent definition of the word. His hands pointed and explained, telling her directions to Ling's out by the Amtrak station. She listened attentively, asked a question, then nodded. He put a hand on her shoulder in the same way I'd seen him do hundreds of times with male police officers.

I let out a deep breath and, while I drove to the restaurant, gave myself a lecture about seeing things that weren't there. Only six months ago I'd gone through this same situation with his ex-wife, Lydia. Though she had been flirting with the idea of her and Gabe resuming some kind of relationship, he eventually realized, with a little help from my protective and very verbal cousin Emory, that he had hurt my feelings by paying too much attention to her while trying to assuage an ego that had been damaged when she left him years before. He'd apologized, I'd accepted his apology, and we'd moved on. After all, neither of us had come into this middle-aged second marriage without baggage, though there was no doubt he lugged around a few more suitcases than me. I believed in grace and forgiveness so I was trying to keep all my judgmental stones in my pockets. We'd have dinner with his old partner tonight. I'd suffer through their numerous "Remember the time . . ." and "Whatever happened to . . ." stories and I'd go home, make love with my husband, and be thankful we ended up together.

At Ling's the evening progressed as I'd predicted with story after story about the trials and tribulations for working for the LAPD. The restaurant was busy for a Wednesday night, and being a favorite of many police officers, they stopped by our table to greet Gabe as they waited for their take-out. Del was warmly welcomed into the law enforcement fraternity by virtue of her credentials. I picked at my kung pao chicken in silence wishing I'd gone straight home. When you're not a cop, you can only listen to so many "And then the dirtbag said . . ." stories before wanting to scream or die of boredom. I was interested in Gabe's job, when he chose to talk to me about the cases they were working on or ones he'd worked on in the past, but "war stories" that often took on an "us against them" sameness grew wearisome after a while. Kind of like me telling Gabe about a particularly complicated calving and going into graphic detail about twisted umbilical cords, breech births, and torn uteruses.

When it hit seven-thirty and we'd been there two hours, I leaned over to Gabe and whispered, "I'm going on home. I've got a million things to do."

"Okay, sweetheart," he said, kissing me on the forehead. "I'll be along shortly."

I nodded at the three detectives sitting at our table drinking Chinese beer and said to Del, "Nice meeting you. Have a good trip." It had been mentioned during the evening that she was driving up the coast to Seattle, where her two brothers lived.

"Likewise," she said, standing up.

At home I fed Scout, giving him an extra portion for being so patient. After my shower and one last quick call to check on Elvia and her emotional state, which was in a calm holding pattern tonight, I crawled into bed and waited for Gabe. I dozed over the novel I was rereading— Wallace Stegner's *Angle of Repose*. Its complicated two-layer story line never failed to amaze me, the interweaving of the past and the present as the man in the story researched the secret in his grandmother's past while dealing with his own marriage problems and mortality, trying to discover his own angle of repose.

My bedside phone rang.

"On horseback," Dove said. "Up on Sweetheart Hill." The hill behind our ranch had a two-hundred-year-old oak tree with a knot hole in the shape of a heart. At one point, when Jack and I were engaged, we'd discussed getting married up there where all of the Ramsey and Harper ranch land could be seen. It was a good hour-and-a-half horseback ride from the ranch house, though, and not an easy one, so the logistics convinced us to abandon the idea.

"How will your friends get up there?" I asked, laying my book across my knees. Then I cursed myself. Dang, there goes my plan to stay noncommittal. Still, Sweetheart Hill? It was a stretch considering the age of most of her guests.

She contemplated that for a moment. "Helicopters?"

"Two at a time? With how many friends you have, we'd be transporting them for ten hours."

"Well, fine, what do *you* think I should do?"

"I have no idea. Maybe . . . here's a radical thought . . . your church?"

"A lot of help you are, missy." She hung up with a loud click. I laid the phone back in the cradle, glad it was her in a tizzy and not me. How nice to be the one settled and happy for a change.

Gabe came in about an hour later, startling me awake. "Did you have a good time?" I asked, my voice groggy. My book slipped down onto the floor next to our pine four-poster bed. It hit the wooden floor with a loud clump.

He shrugged out of his gray suit jacket and unbuttoned his cuffs, his face thoughtful. "It was good to see Del again. Shortly after you left, so did everyone else, and she and I were able to talk privately."

I sat up in bed, instantly awake. "About what?"

He shook his head and finished undressing, hanging his pants and jacket up in the closet and tossing the rest of his clothes, like the neat ex-Marine he was, into the wicker hamper. "Things aren't going so good for her right now. She's taking some personal time off from the department."

"Why?"

"Her dad died about a month ago. Heart attack. They were close."

I wrapped my arms around my raised knees, feeling ashamed that I'd not been more congenial during dinner. "That's too bad. Did you know him?"

Gabe nodded, deep lines forming next to his mouth. "He was on the job when it happened. Desk sergeant. Good man."

"How old was he?"

He walked into the bathroom and turned on the shower. "Around your dad's age, late fifties." He stuck his head through the doorway.

"How old is she?"

"Same as you. Thirty-six," Gabe said and then his voice disappeared into the shower's running water. When he emerged fifteen minutes later, I was standing in the doorway. The steam from his hot shower slowly floated across the small bathroom and dampened my bare legs.

"What's Del stand for?" I asked, watching him dry the slick, black hair on his chest.

He grinned. "Delilah. But don't ever call her that. She hates her name. It was her Indiana grandma's and she's never forgiven her mother for giving it to her."

"I can relate." My given name, Albenia, was not my preferred title either. "So, how's her mother doing?"

"Her mother died when she was ten. Her dad raised her and her two brothers alone. Heck of a guy, Rudy. Real family man."

It dawned on me. "*That* was the funeral you went to last month."

He'd spent the night in Los Angeles and had come home quiet and pensive for a few days afterward. I hadn't pressed him about details, having learned that this very private husband of mine would reveal them to me when he felt ready.

He nodded. "Rudy Hernandez. He was one of my instructors when I joined the LAPD. I remember Del when she was just a skinny fifteen-year-old girl. Always wanted to be a cop just like her dad. She's a lieutenant now. We worked undercover narcotics together for two years."

"Oh," I said, feeling a twinge of apprehension, but forcing it back. For pity's sake, I told myself, the woman had just lost her father. It was natural she'd drop by and see Gabe on her way up north. Old friends are often the most comforting when you're grieving. It was not any different from me going to Elvia when I had a problem.

Remembering her long legs and rich brown eyes, I thought, well, a little different. I rubbed the dampness off the backs of my legs before crawling under our flannel-covered comforter.

"Did you ever mention Del being your partner to me?" I asked as casually as I could manage. What I really wanted to ask . . . accuse . . . was did you ever mention her being a *woman* to me? Of course, I knew the answer, which was no. I'd have remembered that little fact, I'm absolutely certain.

He slipped under the covers and settled down next to me. The heat from his body smelled a soapy, musky clean.

"I'm sure I did. She wasn't exactly a partner like Aaron was. We didn't ride in a car together. But she and I worked a lot of busts. They liked pairing us because the Mexicans trusted us and would sell us dope. In East L.A. the dealers didn't always trust the white guys. Usually made them for cops right off. So she and I were more often out making buys rather than sitting in the surveillance van."

"With her blond hair?"

"She used to dye it brown. She's half Anglo, half Mexican, like me." He chuckled and folded his arms behind his head. "We always got a kick out of that, how similar our backgrounds were. Mexican dads and Midwestern Anglo moms."

"So, she's leaving for her brother's house tomorrow? Was it Seattle where he lives?"

"He's a fire fighter up there. She's feeling a bit out of sorts so she's taking some time off. Wants to be near family."

"I can understand that."

"Her other brother's up there too. An insurance guy, or something like that. She likes his wife, so she's looking forward to seeing her."

Okay, Benni, I told myself. Crisis averted. She's just passing through on her way to her family up north. So what if he forgot to mention her to you? Nothing to worry about.

"She's decided to stay in San Celina for a few days, see the sights before going up to Seattle. I'm giving her a tour of the station tomorrow. She thinks it's hilarious that I'm a suit now. To be honest, I just think she needs to talk about Rudy."

I didn't answer. She was staying for a few days. Not with us, I hoped.

Before I could ask, he said, "She's over at the Embassy Suites."

"That's nice," I murmured. I had enough to worry about without entertaining some woman who might know my husband in some ways better than me.

"So, how was the rest of your day?" he asked.

Glad to be discussing something else besides Del, I told him about what I had bought for Elvia's shower, Dove's quandary about her wedding, and about Edna McClun's request about cataloging Maple Bennett Sullivan's personal effects.

"Killed her husband, huh?" he said, his voice slowing down and lowering in pitch as he neared sleep. "Nice woman."

"Allegedly," I said, feeling irrationally defensive about Maple Sullivan.

"I'd say a fifty-year disappearance of her and her lover might be a good indication of guilt."

"I suppose. Anyway, there's no time limit, thank goodness, because it feels like I've got every hour in the next three weeks booked solid. Which reminds me, did you go get fitted for your tux?" Gabe was best man to my matron of honor at both weddings.

"Yes, I did, *querida*. And I dropped my navy suit at the cleaners in preparation for the Ramsey-Lyons nuptials though it sounds like we're not certain what we'll be wearing yet. I've also thought about toasts for each wedding and have my department on call to chase down any and all nervous, runaway grooms. I'm organized and ready for both happy events."

"I'm impressed," I said, turning on my side and smiling at him. "But I'm feeling a bit displaced. What do you need me for?"

He slipped his hand under my T-shirt, caressing me with an experienced hand. Instinctively, I moved toward him.

"I can think of a few things," he said.

5

BENNI

THE PHONE RANG the next morning while Gabe was out jogging.

"Benni?" Del's crisp, businesslike voice was already familiar to me.

"Oh, hi."

"Is Gabe there?"

Luckily I'd had two cups of coffee so my voice was semipleasant. "He's out jogging. Want me to have him call you back?"

There was a slight hesitation in her voice. "No, that's all right. I was just going to check to see if his offer for a tour of the department today was still on, but knowing Gabe, he wouldn't have suggested it if he had something more important planned."

"I'm sure you're right." This time I hesitated, then said, "I'm sorry about your dad. Gabe said you were very close."

"Yes," she whispered. "We were. Thank you."

A half a minute passed in silence. "Well, I'll tell him you called."

"Thank you, Benni. Really, thank you."

"You're welcome."

As I put a chocolate iced Pop-Tart into the toaster, I discussed our short, but awkward conversation with the other important male in my life.

"What do you make of that?" I asked my dog, Scout.

His German shepherd ear perked up jaunty as a beauty queen's wave. A low rumble in the back of his throat told me he'd tell me anything I wanted to hear for a piece of my Pop-Tart. I reached into a glass jar on the counter and threw him a dog biscuit instead.

"I think I'm being paranoid." His tail beat the tiled floor in agreement . . . or in enjoyment of his biscuit. "You know, it's a pain in the butt to be married to such a good-looking man."

Scout swallowed his biscuit and lifted one paw, begging for another.

"Not a chance, Scooby-Doo," I said, juggling my hot Pop-Tart back and forth before dumping it on a plate.

I was halfway through my third cup of coffee and my toaster pastry when Gabe came in, all sweaty and slick from his run. I smiled a good morning and continued eating. Scout trotted over to the biscuit jar, his ocher eyes hopeful.

"Don't fall for it," I said. "He's scored his morning biscuit already."

"Hope springs eternal in a dog's heart," he said, kissing the top of my head. "Is that your breakfast?" His bottom lip tightened in disapproval.

"You get your vitamins your way, I'll get them mine," I replied, unperturbed. My eating habits were a constant source of irritation for my health-obsessed husband. I conceded to his concerns by taking the plate of vitamins he left out every day, but that was as much control as I would allow him.

"You know, an orange once in a while wouldn't kill you," he said, reaching for one in the glass bowl next to the bread box. "I bought these at Farmer's Market last week. They're incredible."

I blew him a kiss and popped the rest of the disputed pastry in my mouth. "Umm, umm, good."

He just shook his head and laughed, efficiently peeling the orange. The sweet, mouth-watering scent of citrus groves filled our warm kitchen.

"Here," he said, taking a slice and rubbing it across my lips. I opened them and took the fruit, licking his fingers as I did.

"That really is pretty good," I said.

"Told you so."

I grinned at him. "Yeah, and the orange was all right too."

After he'd taken a shower and was dressing for work, I told him Del called. I sat on the bed, my legs crossed underneath me.

The subtle brightening of his face did not make me happy, but remembering my worries a couple of months ago about Lydia and how they came to nothing, I pushed them away. I was going to trust my husband. That was all there was to it.

"What did she want?" he asked.

"Just to make sure everything was still on with your tour today."

He nodded, turning to the long mirror to fix his subtly printed maroon necktie and button his cuffs. In the lightly starched white shirts he always wore, his dark skin looked wonderful. How could I blame any woman for looking twice at this man?

Just so long as he didn't look back.

"Luckily, she chose to visit on a day I have only one meeting," he said, critically eying his Windsor knot, then pulling it apart to retie it. "I expect to get lots of teasing today."

"Why would the guys tease you about her?"

"Not the guys, *her*. Don't forget, she's never seen me in a 'suit' position. She's used to a whole other side of me. A definitely wilder side."

I silently contemplated the meaning of his words.

After he left, I straightened up the kitchen, threw back the comforter on the bed, and dressed in my everyday working clothes of a plaid flannel shirt and faded Wranglers. As I cleaned my muddy boots in the bathtub, I worried his relationship with Del like a dog with a marrow-filled bone.

Let it go, I commanded myself while drying my boots with an old towel. You knew this man had a very complicated personal life before he met you, so grow up and accept it. Quit being such a small-town girl. You have shower gifts to wrap, paperwork to do, a multitude of problems to be solved at the museum. Besides, she'll be gone soon. *Get over it.*

After that lecture, I called to Scout. He jumped into the back of the truck and I sat down in the driver's seat, enjoying for a moment the still new car smell. To force myself into a more amiable mood, I slipped a Tish Hinojosa cassette into my new truck's player and sang along with "La Rancherita"—"The Little Ranch Girl." Its buoyant melody and touching love story never failed to make me smile.

My mood was much cheerier when I pulled into the folk art museum's parking lot. The museum had become truly a home away from home for me. I knew every inch of its white-washed adobe interior as well as I did my rented bungalow. Better maybe. I parked under my favorite spot at the back of the lot, under an initial-scarred oak tree, where I noted with consternation a fresh carving—RICHARD LOVES KATHY. (Though I wished he'd found a different place to show his love, I also wished the couple well in their relationship.) The museum looked warm and welcoming under the gray February sky.

Once a ranchero for the Sinclair family, deeded to them by the then ruling Spanish government, the two-story adobe house and attached stables with their dusky red-tiled roofs now housed a constantly changing crew of folk artists and volunteer docents. Constance Sinclair, our own personal patron, donated the hacienda to the historical society about ten years ago and still helped out by hosting the occasional fund raiser and by paying my salary. But the museum and the artists' co-op affiliated with it were supposed to be self-sustaining. Which meant I spent a lot of time writing grant proposals, figuring out fund raisers, and begging money from rich, hopefully folk-art-loving people. Now that Isaac Lyons was about to become my stepgrandpa, I was finding it much easier to acquire funds from people wanting to meet and mingle with him. At first I was hesitant to cash in on my relationship with him until he told me in no uncertain terms that we were going to be family and that he was more than happy to use any influence he had over people's pocketbooks to help the museum.

"Frankly, Benni, I'd be supporting this museum even if you weren't involved, so take advantage of me. Please." He punctuated that last word with a huge bear hug, which was not just a cliché with him but a reality, seeing as he was six-four and large-boned as a grizzly.

That was why, even though he was to be married in three weeks, he was the main attraction at the Mardi Gras Costume Ball that Constance was holding at her mansion in Cambria, a small, affluent town north of Morro Bay. It was *the* social event of the season with a price tag that irked me a bit . . . three hundred dollars a person. It limited the people who could attend, giving it an exclusivity that pricked at my egalitarian sensibilities. But as Elvia pointed out with logical pragmaticism, the whole point of the event was to make money for the museum so it made sense to appeal to people who had most of the green stuff.

Of course, that meant I had to attend also . . . in costume. A costume I still had to pick up at Costume Capers downtown, a store owned by an old friend of mine. Cathy Gustavson and I had attended San Celina High School together and had shared not only the giggly experience of dissecting a sheep's eye in sophomore biology (she held, I cut), but the wonderful agony of a crush on a young, bearded psychology teacher who didn't know either of us existed. My time being so tight these last few weeks, I'd given her full authority to choose my costume with the only stipulation that I not be a cowgirl (too predictable) and it not be low cut. She knew me well enough to know that comfort was my main criteria for a costume so I was secure in the knowledge that a Mae West dress or skin-tight Cat Woman jumpsuit was not in my immediate future.

Inside the museum itself, it was quiet, since the doors didn't officially open until 10 A.M. Behind the counter of our gift shop, Edna McClun was cleaning the glass counter top with a solution that, by the smell, contained a large amount of vinegar.

"Hey, Edna." I walked behind the counter and checked my mail tray. Two letters and a catalog for leatherworking supplies. "We're running into each other everywhere these days."

"It's because I've got too much on my plate," she said. "The trunks are being brought over today by one of our young men volunteers. He's a real sweetie. Been working every weekend on the octagonal barn. Real talented carpenter, this boy."

"Trunks?" I said.

She reached over and thumped the top of my head. "Anyone home? Remember yesterday? Maple Sullivan's trunks. The murderess. You said you'd catalog the contents."

"Oh, those trunks," I said, shaking my head. "I'd already forgotten about them."

"Like I said, we aren't in any hurry, but the sooner you do them, the sooner I can mark them off my list." She gave me an encouraging smile and rubbed vigorously at a stubborn spot on the counter. I felt sorry for the spot.

"I'll do my best," I said, trying not to heave a big sigh. What difference did it make *when* this woman's last effects got cataloged? She'd probably been dead for years. For a moment, I pondered on where she and her lover might have gone after she killed her husband and how she'd managed to stay uncaught all these years. The historian in me, the person who had irrationally decided to major in history in college and minor in agriculture rather than the other way around, couldn't help wondering about her life before she came to San Celina, what drove her to murder her husband, a man, I assumed, she'd once loved.

No time for speculation, I told myself, sticking the mail in my back pocket and saying over my shoulder to Edna, "Just have your talented carpenter boy put them in my office. No, have him check with me first. My office is pretty small. I'll have to find someplace else to work on them."

"He said he can come by around noon. Is that okay?"

"That's fine. Just send him back to my office."

I walked through the current exhibits, both upstairs and down, making sure everything was in place and noting any repairs that I'd need to report to my very capable, senior citizen assistant, D-Daddy Boudreaux, a retired commercial fisherman from Louisiana. In theory and on paper, his work schedule was three days a week, two hours a day, because that was all the museum could afford. In reality, he worked many more hours than that and claimed he was paid in the joy of being needed.

The current exhibits were of local wedding and anniversary quilts and samplers. The samplers were upstairs, the quilts downstairs. There were many traditional Double Wedding Ring patterns, most of them in the pastel prints popular in the thirties when that pattern was in its heyday, but there were other more unpredictable patterns like Alaska Territory made for a local woman's grandmother who married a man from Alaska whom she met through the mail, Bachelor's Puzzle for a woman who'd been engaged for ten years before marrying another man she'd known only three days, and Steps to the Altar done in gold and white made for a woman who married the Church by becoming a nun. That was the pattern Dove and I had decided to make for Elvia and Emory's wedding quilt, though we chose dark green, maroon, and off-white, the colors of her bedroom.

My favorite quilt was a story quilt made by a local artist who also taught women's history at Cal Poly, our local university. In its colorful story squares it incorporated many of the folk sayings and superstitions about quilting:

> If you're the last to place a stitch in the quilt, you'll have the next baby. Always make a deliberate error in your quilt to avoid bad luck. Don't let your son or daughter sleep under a Drunkard's Path quilt or they'll turn to drink. The first person to sleep under a quilt just off the quilting frame will have their dreams come true. If you break a needle while quilting, you will have the next baby. If you begin a quilt on Friday, you will never live to finish it.

That last one gave me pause. What day *did* Dove and I start Elvia's quilt?

All was well among the exhibits, which according to our daily head count, had been our most popular one so far, so I headed through the back, under the thick canopy of honeysuckle vines toward the old stables that now held the co-op workshops and my office. It was quiet for a weekday. No quilt guild was meeting here today to stitch a quilt, and even the wood shop held only one lone carver sitting on a stool hand-sanding to the sound of a classical music station.

Scout settled down on his rug and I was in the middle of writing the short speech I'd have to give at the Mardi Gras ball thanking everyone for their generous support of the folk art museum, when from the doorway, there came the sound of a clearing voice. I turned my head toward the sound and resisted the urge to groan out loud.

Lydia, Gabe's ex-wife, stood in the doorway in a dark green suit looking gorgeous and a little embarrassed.

My first thought was, *Dang it all, what does she want?*

6

GABE

HE POURED HIMSELF a cup of coffee and took it back to his desk. Del would be here any minute. His heart sounded like a drum in his ears.

He'd never expected to see her again after Rudy's funeral. There was so much going on then, so many people, they had only a few minutes to speak. Long enough for him to say how sorry he was, what a great guy Rudy was, how much he would be missed. He remembered the look in her eyes, a fear he'd never seen before, not in all the dangerous situations they'd encountered. Like a wild cat he'd caught once in a trap back in Kansas. That same glossy, panicked look.

"I'm sorry," he'd said. "Del, I'm so sorry."

She'd grabbed his hand with both of hers for a second, her look as intense as a lover's, and for a moment, he remembered those hands on his naked back and his brain sizzled in his skull.

He didn't go to the house afterward, though her brothers had invited him. He was smart enough, wise enough, he thought, to avoid that situation. He loved Benni. She possessed his heart like no woman ever had. He had no business dwelling in a past he wasn't especially proud of.

But seeing Del brought back memories of a time when he was young, when he felt powerful, invincible. When the only thing that meant anything was the cat-and-mouse game of undercover narcotics, the feint and jab of psychological fencing between buyer and seller, between bad guy and good guy, when sometimes you almost couldn't tell who was who and all that mattered was the game of "gotcha."

When Del had walked into his office yesterday, a flood of physical memories had hit him in the stomach like a fist. Of nights that he'd long since relegated to the dark corners of his brain. Nights only half remembered, of the drive back to her place and later his, after Lydia had left taking Sam; half remembered because they were punctuated with that crazy, hysterical euphoria brought on by a successful buy and the "choir practice" they attended afterward in bar after bar, drink after drink, all running into each other like one long highway of blurred neon signs. Lydia could take him stumbling in drunk and exhausted at 4 A.M. for only so long. He couldn't blame her. But he also couldn't explain to her how alive he felt after a successful buy, how it brought back the adrenaline high of combat, which he inexplicably missed. He could never tell her how narcotics work felt like a war, the planning of a buy like the planning of a battle. And like Vietnam, it didn't seem to matter who won and who didn't. How, at the moment he was doing it, when the buys went down, the sellers in cuffs, and he survived, it felt like he would live forever.

And Del was a big part of that. She was just as crazy, maybe crazier, than the rest of them. Would try anything, go anywhere. No matter how many times her tits and ass were grabbed by the sellers, no matter how crude their remarks, she never lost her cool. Practically every buy she and Gabe made were good ones. Yes, Del Hernandez was as crazy and committed as they come. Would not back down for anyone. And they all loved her for it. Gabe, most of all.

Everyone knew she was his from the moment she joined the squad. She made that clear to any guy who hit on her. She'd waited a long time for Gabe and wasn't about to waste a second with anyone else.

He leaned back in his chair and glanced at the clock on his desk. She would be here any moment. He closed his eyes, feeling for a moment as if the world were tilting. He wondered what Benni was doing, felt irrationally guilty for a past that did not include her, did not even touch the life they had now. An image of the pale, downy skin on the back of Benni's neck came to him and his heart felt enlarged and throbbing. There was so much about him she didn't know, so much he never wanted her to know. He wanted to remain in her eyes as she first saw him, in control and strong, a man of integrity, a man to be admired.

Like he remembered his father. For some unexplainable reason, he had started thinking about him a lot this last year or so, though he'd been dead for twenty-eight years. Every time Gabe looked into Sam's face, he missed his own father with an ache inside that felt almost physical.

He glanced at the clock again. Only ten minutes before Del arrived. She would be on time. She was always good about that. He would give her a tour, brag a little, endure her teasing. They'd have lunch in a public place . . . they had nothing to hide . . . and she'd be on her way. No talk of the past. He would make sure of that. He leaned back and closed his eyes. Think about something else, he commanded his brain. Think about the master's thesis you still haven't finished. Philosophy. What had possessed him to contemplate getting a master's degree in philosophy? Who did he think he was? What did he ever expect to do with it? Time was running out. He needed to finish it.

He locked his fingers behind his head. The back of his neck was damp with perspiration. A flash of a remembered image. Del's long legs wrapped around his waist . . .

Think about something else.

He forced himself to remember what he'd read last week. Kierkegaard had claimed that Providence watched over each man's wandering through life and in the process provided two guides. One called forward to the good, the other called backward from evil. The philosopher believed that both guides were needed, that to make the journey of life secure, one must continually look forward and backward. That without remorse, a man traveled too lightly into the future, that he did not use his experience and repentance to wisely live in his new life.

Oh God, Gabe thought, an almost earnest prayer, when Del walked into the room. Desire coursed through his veins hot as the coffee he'd poured and didn't drink. He stood up and came around the desk, Kierkegaard and all his agonizing wisdom pushed aside as Gabe's almost forgotten past moved swiftly toward him.

7

BENNI

"Hi, Benni," Lydia said. "Do you have a few minutes?"

Scout, familiar with my husband's ex-wife, trotted over to her, tail wagging.

"Hello, sweet boy." She bent down and scratched under his chin. She looked up at me, her attractive, copper-colored face friendly and calm. "I was hoping we could go to lunch or something. I . . ." She stopped for a moment, faltering, her dark brown eyes, the beautiful eyes she'd passed down to her son, Sam, widened slightly and I caught a nervous twitch under one of them. That surprised me. She was a prominent defense attorney in Santa Barbara, a piranha in the courtroom, I'd been told, and she had always slightly intimidated me with her self-assurance. She was dressed for court in a dark green tailored suit. Though my jeans and plaid flannel shirt were clean, next to her magazine perfection, I felt like I'd just come in from mucking stalls.

I straightened my spine, hearing Dove's voice inside me reminding me that I was a Ramsey and Ramseys weren't no less than no one else, thank you very much.

"What can I do for you?" I said, rescuing her from her

unusual lapse into wordlessness. That alone made me feel a little more in control. "Is everything okay with Sam?"

He was the common denominator that had formed the fledgling relationship between us. She loved Sam, Gabe loved Sam, and I loved Sam. On that we all could agree. And she was secure enough as a parent to know that a person could never have too many people caring about them. If she was jealous of my friendship with her son, she never showed it to him or me. For that, I had a great respect for her.

She nodded over at one of my visitor chairs. "May I . . ."

I jumped up saying, "Where are my manners? Please, sit down."

I closed the door behind her and, instead of retreating behind my desk, sat in the visitor's chair next to her. Her face visibly relaxed at my equalizing gesture.

"Would you like some coffee?" I asked. "Or a soft drink?"

"No, I'm fine," she said, smiling at me gratefully. "And I know it's only ten-thirty, too early for lunch. That was just . . . I'm just trying to break the ice. I need to talk to you."

I leaned back in the chair, my stomach rumbling in anxiety. Was there something wrong with Sam? "Is Sam—"

She broke into my sentence. "It's not Sam, don't worry. Well, it concerns him, but it concerns you more. He called me last night."

I nodded. "I saw him at the station yesterday. He seemed agitated. Was it about school?"

"We're okay on that," she said, settling into the chair, her stiff posture relaxing slightly. "He told me about changing his major. As far as I'm concerned, if he's happy, not on drugs, and still in school, I don't care what he studies."

"Good," I said. "He was afraid . . ." I stopped, suddenly realizing that I'd revealed that he'd talked to me about it before her or Gabe. I bit my lip, feeling like a fool.

She laughed and touched my arm. "Don't worry, Benni. I know he talks to you about these things before me and Gabe. That used to bother me, but these days he's so happy, so *all right,* how can I be angry?"

My respect for her was growing by the minute. "So, what brings you up to San Celina?"

This time, she bit the corner of her lip. Lydia disconcerted. That was something I'm sure not many people saw. "Actually, it's you. I'm . . . we're . . . that is, me and Sam, are concerned about you."

I jerked my head back. "Me?"

"Yes."

"Why?" I asked the question even though I suspected I knew what she was about to say.

"It's Del Hernandez. Sam told me she's back in Gabe's life."

I stared at her dumbly for a moment, a little annoyed that she and Sam would get involved in what was definitely none of their business, but also curious. This Delilah Hernandez was obviously someone more than just Gabe's ex-partner. And here was a person who would probably know more about that than anyone. The question was, how much did I really want to know?

I looked down at my nails, picked at a hangnail before looking back at Lydia. "They were lovers, weren't they?" I asked bluntly, wanting and not wanting to know the answer.

She nodded, her face sad, obviously recalling painful memories. "More than that. She was the reason I left Gabe."

I contemplated that piece of information. Though I'd known that Lydia had left Gabe, I'd never known why. I just assumed from the hints he'd dropped that she couldn't live with the wild, unpredictable life of an undercover cop, that at the time, he had aspired to be nothing else and that she'd wanted a man who fit better into her idea of a successful, upper-middle-class lifestyle.

Another woman had never been mentioned. I could feel

my heart start to beat rapidly—the flight-or-fight response.

"We were having problems before he met her," Lydia said, her voice low and even. "I don't want to imply she came in and broke up a good marriage. We might have—probably would have—split up anyway. But she set her eyes on him from the time she was teenager at the police department picnics, and the first opportunity she had to seduce him, she took. *That's* the kind of woman she is. I just wanted you to know it."

Her face blushed a deep red under her coppery skin. This was hard for her, this intimate woman-to-woman confessional talk, and I thought it spoke a lot of her integrity to attempt it.

I licked my suddenly dry lips, wishing I had some Chapstick on me. "I appreciate you telling me," I said, not certain if that was entirely truthful. "But I'm not clear about what you think I should do about it. I mean, I knew Gabe had a life before he came to San Celina and that sometimes that life overflows into ours, but I trust him."

"Benni, I know how much Gabe loves you. I see it every time he looks at you. I feel really foolish coming to you like this, but Sam was so upset that I felt I had to do something. And trust me, I'm not being all that noble. I don't want her anywhere near my son, and frankly, I'd rather you have Gabe than *her*." She didn't hide her bitterness on that last word.

I waited for a moment. An uncomfortable silence hung heavy between us. Were her motives really that above-board? Or was she trying to get back at Gabe by ruining his happiness with me? She'd just gone through another painful divorce and there was one thing I'd learned in my short years on this earth, that there were some people who, when they were in the midst of bad times, did everything they could to bring you down with them. Was Lydia one of those people?

The apologetic, embarrassed expression on her face led me to believe she wasn't. This time, I chose to believe that she was sincere.

"Thanks for telling me this. I do appreciate it and I'll keep an eye on the situation. Please assure Sam that I'll be okay."

She nodded, her luminous eyes still troubled. Then, as if some unseen puppeteer had pulled her strings, she stood up, back as straight as a two-by-four, transformed back into the controlled, every-vowel-in-its-place attorney who could intimidate a prosecution's witness with one cynical, dark-eyed glance.

"I have an appointment in three hours," she said. "I just thought this was a situation better dealt with in person."

"Thank you," I said again, just wishing she'd leave now so I could mull over what I'd just learned.

"You're welcome." She held out a hand and we solemnly shook.

"Take care," I said, not knowing what was the appropriate goodbye to your husband's ex-wife who was warning you about his ex-girlfriend. Did Miss Manners have a chapter covering this modern situation?

"You too," she replied.

I sat for a moment in the visitor's chair, scratching behind Scout's ears, a bit dazed at what had just taken place. As if I didn't have enough to worry about with two showers, two weddings, and the Mardi Gras ball, I now had this uncomfortable situation with Gabe's past. He and I would definitely have to talk about it tonight, something I wasn't anticipating with any pleasure, but knew was necessary if we wanted to keep our still fragile relationship from imploding.

Scout picked up a tennis ball he'd hidden in his bed and dropped it in front of me, making me laugh out loud.

"Ball? You want to play ball at a time like this?"

His tail thumped on the braided rug in front of my desk. He picked up the ball and dropped it again. It's *always* a good time to play ball, he informed me.

I picked it up and led him out into the big, still empty main room, where I tossed the ball across the wide floor, bouncing it off the cabinets and tables. When no one was working in here, there was nothing in this room that could be harmed, and Scout and I had many lively games of ball here. I sent a grounder that he missed and it rolled under an oak credenza one of the woodworkers had made for the quilters to store their extra supplies.

After laughing at Scout's unsuccessful attempts to try to squeeze under it, I gave in to his whining and got on my hands and knees and reached for it myself, hoping that D-Daddy had recently sprayed for spiders and complaining out loud to Scout that he needed to take up Frisbee tossing. I was in that compromising position when from behind me came a great, booming laugh then a low wolf whistle.

"My sweet mama in Dallas," he said. "It is so good to see you again, Benni Harper."

8

BENNI

OH, GREAT, I thought, immediately abandoning the ball and scrambling up to face my visitor in the most dignified way I could manage. How long had he been standing there?

Detective Ford Hudson of the San Celina Sheriff's Department grinned at me with his ingratiating Tom Sawyer smile, no doubt thrilled to the tips of his garish Texas boots at having grabbed the upper hand so quickly. "Have you been working out? You look great. Especially the part you were waving at me."

"What do *you* want?" I asked more than a tad ungraciously because I'd been caught in such an embarrassing position and because he was crass enough to mention it. Next to me, Scout wagged his tail, his canine memory never faltering once a person was deemed a friend by me, a reluctant concession I'd given to this man a few months ago when he and I had, unwillingly on my part, worked together on a homicide case. We'd fought and thrown barbs like it was a rodeo event with a silver belt buckle prize and, in the end, agreed to disagree on what we thought would happen to the suspect in the crime.

He was loud, cocky, flamboyant, and as Daddy would say, full of Texas piss and vinegar, which according to Texans is, of course, stronger and better than anyone else's. A Houston native who claimed to be half Cajun, he'd moved out here after his divorce to be near his five-year-old daughter.

"Now is that any way to greet your ole buddy?" he said, his Texas drawl still thick as homemade banana pudding. "Aren't you just as thrilled to see me as I am you?" He rested his hands on his hips. "I'm crushed."

The grin got bigger, assuring me he knew he was entirely full of bull pucky and enjoying every minute of it. He wore beat-up Wranglers, a dark green plaid flannel shirt similar to mine, and plain tobacco brown Ropers. We could have posed for a Shepler's Western wear ad.

I stared for a moment at his boots, determined to keep my cool around him, something he never made easy. He normally wore expensive cowboy boots made of exotic leathers and hides, more often than not in what I called "white trash" colors. He claimed to have twenty-five pair. A girl collection if I ever heard of one.

"What's with the plain boots?" I asked, ignoring his question.

"I'm working," he said.

Before I could ask him at what, Edna came into the room.

"Benni! I see you've met Hud. He's the boy I was telling you about. A real genius with wood. I bet if you talked real nice to him, he might make those cabinets you've been wanting. And guess what? After he heard how busy you were and how long it would take you to get to it, he's very graciously agreed to help you catalog the contents of the murderess's trunks. It's kind of up his alley too, since he's a crack detective with the sheriff's department. He's a very busy man, but he says he always has time to help out the historical society. Isn't he just the sweetest thing in the world?"

I narrowed my eyes. "Just the sweetest," I managed to

say, then added, "You know, Edna, as much as I appreciate the offer of help, I've managed to clear some time—"

"No, no, no, my dear girl," she said, shaking her head. "It was thoughtless of me to ask you to take on that job when you're so busy. Hud says he has plenty of free time and all you have to do is show him how you want it cataloged. He's a pretty sharp cookie, this one." She gazed up at his tanned, boy-next-door face with grandmotherly adoration.

"Sharp as a Mallomar," I said, my sarcasm wasted on her. "But really, I've already worked it into my schedule."

"Not another word," she said, clapping her hands together sharply to shut me up. "He's your assistant and that's that. Now, I'm off to see about your gramma's shower. We've rented the upper room at Baxter's Bungalow."

"You didn't tell me *that* at the meeting," I said. Baxter's was a popular and often rowdy college bar downtown. Not at all the place I'd expected a senior citizen wedding shower to be held. Apprehension scratched at my insides. "Why are you having it there?"

She looked at me as if I had suddenly grown antennas. "Because it's got a karaoke machine, of course."

Before I could ask more, she had breezed through the door, calling to us to stay in touch and let her know if we found anything interesting in Maple Sullivan's trunks.

"So, boss, where do you want the trunks?" Detective Hudson asked.

"Detective," I said, making my voice as firm as I could. "As much as I enjoyed working together with you a few months ago . . ."

He broke into my lie with a huge guffaw.

I glared at him. "Okay, who are we kidding? You bug the crap out of me and I don't want to work with you. I can't even guess *why* you'd suggest it to Edna."

"Hey, what do I have to do to get you to call me Hud? And maybe I missed you." His dark brown eyes twinkled.

Before I could comment, he continued, "Look, you haven't even seen the trunks. Take a look at them and then decide. There's a lot of stuff there and two people could get it sorted and cataloged faster than one." He closed the distance between us with two long strides and said in a low, conspiratorial voice, "And I don't have to be telling you what a nag Miz McClun can be. If you really are that busy, you should be grateful for my help. There's nothin' says we have to work on it at the same time."

Thinking about the two weddings, two showers, the Mardi Gras ball, and that somehow I was going to have to deal with the fact that my husband's ex-girlfriend was sniffing around did tempt me into accepting his help. He was right, we didn't have to work on it at the same time. I could teach him the cataloging method, give him a key to the folk art museum—he was a sheriff's deputy, after all, I could trust him not to steal the silver—and he could work on it when he could. Maybe this would work out and I could get Edna off my back that much sooner.

"How many trunks are there?" I asked.

His grin returned, as if he had heard my thoughts and knew he'd won out. "Four. I've got them in the back of my truck. Where do you want them?"

I sighed. "Over in the corner there." I pointed at the far end of the room, next to the oak credenza that still held Scout's ball captive. "I'll show you how we catalog things for the museum and we'll divide up the trunks. After we're through, we'll go over each other's lists to double-check that everything's been properly cataloged. Also, we'll wrap any linens, quilts, and clothes in acid-free paper to preserve them better. I'll show you how."

He nodded, his face turning serious. "I'm fascinated by this Maple Sullivan's life and I'm bettin' you are too."

"I'm too busy to be fascinated," I snapped. "So the woman killed her husband. *So what?* I'm sick of a society that finds murderers and criminals more fascinating than people who go through life not giving in to their baser instincts."

"I don't know," he said, shrugging. "People givin' in to their baser instincts is what puts gas in my truck."

"Just go get the trunks," I answered, not wanting to get into any kind of philosophical discussion with him.

He came into my office about a half hour later, his sleeves rolled back and his face rosy with perspiration. "Thanks for the help," he said, flopping down in one of my visitor's chairs without asking.

"You forget, I'm the brains, you're the brawn. I've been working in here getting the forms ready." I held up four file folders labeled MAPLE SULLIVAN, TRUNK NUMBER ONE, TWO, THREE, FOUR. Each held some photocopied cataloging forms that listed the item, description, shape it was in, and its approximate value.

"Wow, I bet you're exhausted," he said, grabbing my half-full can of Coke and drinking it in two gulps. "Fillin' out labels is real thirsty work."

"Hey, that was mine!"

"And it was the last one, I noticed," he said. "Real hospitable of you, Mrs. Harper."

"This isn't a tea party. So, when can you get started?"

He crushed the empty can, tossed it toward my trash can, and missed. Then he didn't bother to get up and throw it away. What a jerk.

"Not today. I promised Maisie I'd take her to the Atascadero Zoo. She never gets tired of that place."

I scooted my chair over and picked up the can, giving him an irritated look as I tossed it in the trash. "How is your daughter?"

His face relaxed and lost that edgy, out-to-get-you look cops seem to develop after years on the job. "She's real fine. Growin' like a California weed, but pretty as a Texas bluebonnet." He stood up abruptly. "Well, gotta go. Show me real quick what you want me to do."

I pulled out a form and went over it with him, emphasizing the importance of describing each piece as thoroughly as possible. We would eventually take pictures of everything, but the written account was just as important.

He listened attentively, without interrupting, obviously interested in the process. My judgment of his facile personality altered just slightly.

"How did you become interested in the historical society?" I asked, giving him a key to the co-op building and showing him where in my desk I would keep the trunk keys.

He shrugged. "One of the guys in Robbery told me about how they were having trouble finding workers to fix up the Sullivan place. I went down with him one afternoon and had a great time paintin' and sawin'. Learned that stuff from my mama's daddy, my pawpaw Gautreaux down in Beaumont, Texas. He built the house he and Mawmaw Gautreaux lived in from the day they were wed to the day she died of cancer last year. My mama was born in a bed he carved. Kinda made me feel closer to him." He raised his eyebrows. "Besides, felt like I had to do something with my useless history major."

"You majored in history? So did I!"

"And did it help you grow better cows?" he asked solemnly.

"No, the agriculture minor did that. Does it help you catch criminals quicker?"

He rolled down his sleeves and buttoned the cuffs. "Maybe. It taught me how to be patient when I'm looking for something. Also taught me that folks do the same ole crazy-ass things they've always done. Ain't nothing all that new and creative about a criminal mind."

"So I've heard Gabe say." I looked over at my black-and-white schoolhouse wall clock. "You'd better get going or Maisie will have your hide."

His eyes crinkled in pleasure, thinking about his daughter. "Amen to that. She's a real little whip-cracker." He stood in the doorway, leaning against the frame. "I'll leave my finished forms on your desk. That okay?"

I nodded. "I'll leave the file folder on the credenza."

"Oh and one more thing."

I waited expectantly, feeling a bit friendlier toward him now. Maybe he wasn't as big a jerk as I thought.

"I was standin' there watchin' you for two long, glorious minutes and I'd have givin' a hundred bucks straight out of my pocket for two more."

"Get out, you freak," I said.

9

BENNI

AFTER DETECTIVE HUDSON left, I decided to take a quick look at the contents of each trunk and try to assess how much time this job might take. I was annoyed that he'd finagled his way into this project and even more annoyed at the way he could still jerk my chain.

Three of the trunks, of obviously good quality, were made by the same manufacturer. They were a shiny black with pale wood trimming and slightly tarnished brass hardware. The fourth was much older and more cheaply made—dark green metal with rusty hinges and a silver-colored padlock that had, I would guess, been added later. Using the keys Edna had given me yesterday, I opened the one closest to me, one of the more expensive-looking black ones. A sweet, musty scent wafted up, like the smell of dried rose petals. The top tray contained a tangle of costume jewelry, fake jewels that winked and glittered under the harsh, overhead lights. Under the tray were neatly folded clothes, tissue paper stained gold with age carefully placed between the wool suits and linen dresses.

I lifted out a stiff, narrow-collared navy gabardine jacket. Underneath it was a matching skirt. It looked like something Katherine Hepburn would wear playing a wise-cracking lawyer in the movies. A business suit? Edna said Maple Sullivan had worked as a writer for the *Tribune* so that made sense. I made a note to stop by the library and look up some of her work on microfilm. Would there be any indication in her writing of the horrible crime she would eventually commit? I'd check the stories on the murder too. How difficult it must have been for her col-leagues to have to report on a crime committed by one of their fellow writers. I folded the suit and carefully placed it back in the trunk.

The other three trunks were just as full and emanated that same sweet, potpourri smell. The second one held mostly household linens. Stitched by her or by friends and fam-ily? A set of dishtowels caught my eye and I pulled them out. In her cedar trunk, Dove had a set of these towels made during the war years when, because of gas rationing, inexpensive, stay-at-home hobbies like needlework were popular. Maple's towels were made of that same lintless, flour sack cotton which was more decorative than useful when it came to drying dishes. Dove's, like many others I'd seen in antique stores, had the days of the week em-broidered in bright cotton thread—MONDAY—WASH DAY, TUESDAY—IRON DAY, WEDNESDAY—MEND DAY, all the way to Sunday, which usually showed the housewife sit-ting in a rocking chair reading her Bible.

Maple's dishtowels revealed a side of her I couldn't help liking. Like so many other women during that time, she had embroidered a set of tea towels. But hers showed the woman sitting in the rocking chair reading every day, with the titles of the books she was reading embroidered across the bottom of each towel: MONDAY—WINDSWEPT, TUESDAY—FOR WHOM THE BELL TOLLS, then the rest of the week, MILDRED PIERCE, THE ROBBER BRIDEGROOM, VALLEY OF DECISION, CROSS CREEK, and the one that made me smile at its sheer audacity, that forbidden yet widely read book, SUNDAY—FOREVER AMBER. The tow-els looked brand new and I wondered if she'd ever shown them to anyone or kept them to herself as a secret amusement.

"Maple Bennett Sullivan," I said out loud. "You were a caution."

The third was full of small knickknacks and mismatched pieces of china. It appeared she collected teacups. There were also some hats, trimmed with netting and miniature artificial flowers. Small, tight hats that would cling closely to her head, held on by the sharp combs inside, neat and as trouble-free as a hat could be. Though I didn't know what she looked like yet, I could picture her in the navy suit, one of the hats attractively cupped to her head, strolling purposefully down Lopez Street, enjoying the admiring glances of the flocks of servicemen who crowded the streets of San Celina, off duty from Camp Riley, north of the grade, up near San Miguel. She would acknowledge their respectful wolf whistles with an indulgent smile, her stride never faltering. She'd be on the way back to the *Tribune*'s offices. During the war they'd been located in a building across from the courthouse. It was a red brick building with carved stone curlicues above the oak doors that was now a bar and restaurant called The Twisted Tort Cafe popular with deputy DAs and defense attorneys who needed a quick bite before or after court.

I smiled to myself, amused at my own imagination. I was already giving this woman a life and a personality when all I really knew about her was she was married to the only son of a once-prominent San Celina ranching family, worked for a time as a journalist, and had killed her husband. And remembering the tea towels, she definitely had a mind of her own.

Allegedly killed her husband, the small voice inside me insisted.

Projecting undocumented feelings and possible scenarios into the lives of the people I was studying was one of the biggest problems, Russell Hill, my old history professor and mentor at Cal Poly, could find in my research

papers. He once suggested that perhaps I should be mi-
noring in creative writing and not agriculture and make
my living writing historical fiction. This was all said in a
gentle and amused manner as I was unabashedly one of
his favorite students. I'd have to pay Professor Hill a long
overdue visit in the next few weeks and see what he knew
about Maple Sullivan. He had been born and raised in
San Celina County and its history was his passion.

The fourth trunk, the older, cheaper one, was one that
I would not trust to Detective Hudson's inexperience. It
held books, files of papers that appeared to be the original
drafts of her stories, scrapbooks, including one that contained brittle yellowed clippings from the *Tribune* showing Maple Bennett Sullivan's bylines. She had saved me
from a lot of tedious research at the library. All I'd have
to do was read this scrapbook. I pulled out one clipping
and read her human-interest story about a man in a ranch
outside of Cambria, back before rich people discovered
the town, who had braided a rawhide riata for a war bonds
drive. She described how he scraped the hair off the rawhide, cutting the strings from the full hide, beveling the
strings so they would lay straight, and finally braiding the
rawhide.

"It's hard on the hands," Abbott Fitzhugh, the cowboy
artisan, said. "Even with hands as tough as these old paws.
You get blisters and the muscles get real tired. You have
to be careful to pull each string evenly so you don't have
a lumpy riata or it doesn't pull itself into a circle."

It was auctioned off for two hundred dollars to a Standard Oil executive. Fitzhugh, whose picture showed a man
of lean handsomeness with thin, taciturn lips, had worked
full-time as a wrangler up at the Hearst ranch, where he'd
ridden for the rich newspaper man five days a week, then
come home on the weekends and worked his own ranch.
He was proud, he said, to help his country and had willingly and joyfully braided this rawhide riata in his spare
time.

"And when, pray tell, would that be?" Maple Bennett

Sullivan added in an authorial aside at the end of the piece.

Just that line alone made me like her. It told me she understood how hard this man worked and how precious his time was.

I picked up a packet of letters tied with a red ribbon. The top one was addressed to Garvey Sullivan, 112 Firefly Lane, San Celina, California. The return address was Maple Bennett, Mercy Ridge, Kentucky. Courting letters between Maple and Garvey? So, she was obviously a Southern girl, another thing that endeared her to me, seeing as I was technically born in Arkansas even if I had lived most of my life in California. I took the letters and the scrapbook of newspaper clippings to read when I found the time.

Underneath the packet of letters, in a tarnished silver frame, was a black-and-white photograph of a man and a woman. The engraving on the frame said MAPLE AND GARVEY—MAY 1, 1942. She had a sturdy thinness that suggested her tough, rural upbringing and a simple face with even, pleasing features. Her dark hair was shoulder-length cut in a modified Veronica Lake pageboy. Her eyes were also dark. In the black-and-white photograph, her red lipstick appeared the same color as her eyes. She wore a simple dark suit with a light-colored blouse pinned with a corsage of roses. He wore a dark suit with a small handkerchief tucked in the chest pocket. His hair was combed straight back from a high forehead. She smiled shyly at the camera while his face held a steady, solemn gaze.

Back in my office, I left a note on the front of the file containing the log sheets for the trunks.

"Leave the fourth trunk (the older one with the books and stuff) for me. And put everything back in the trunks *just like you found them.*" I underlined the last five words twice. Someone a long time ago had taken the time to pack her things neatly in her trunks and I didn't want to dishonor that act. Of course, storing some of her things in the trunks might not be the best way, but I'd have to consult with Edna to see if she wanted to store them any other way . . . or even perhaps display them. There was a forties section of the historical museum where Maple's things would fit in. On the other hand, some of the members of the society were probably put off by the fact that she was a criminal and didn't want to celebrate that piece of San Celina history.

Alleged criminal, the voice corrected me again.

I sighed and left the file and note for Detective Hudson on the corner of my credenza where he couldn't miss them. I was definitely going to have to find out more about this Maple Bennett Sullivan if for no other reason than to convince the skeptical little voice that there was no mystery here. A dead man, a rumored affair and pregnancy, a wife who disappeared leaving everything behind. Sounded just like what it was, a sordid mess of human emotion and pain, the breakdown of love between two people who couldn't imagine that ever happening—a domestic disturbance that got out of hand—the stuff that patrol cops see every day of their lives. Today, the whole story would be dissected on a daytime talk show and the couple would be given their fifteen minutes of tacky fame before becoming another statistic.

Hunger pangs were telling me it was lunchtime, so I headed for my truck. It was past one o'clock, and on the way out, I met a couple of potters. Behind them trailed a group of quilters carrying an array of colorful bags containing supplies they didn't store here. The co-op studios were always busier in the afternoons and evenings because many of the artists worked as housecleaners or other service-type jobs that were best done in the morning. That's why I tried to go to the museum and get my work done before noon. When the co-op was full of artists, if I was in my office, it became the social and complaint center of the building, which I mostly enjoyed, but it also kept me from getting any real work done.

"Are you all ready for the Mardi Gras festival this Saturday?" I asked Manuel, this year's co-op president. He was a leather worker who combined his talent with wood-working. He made very unique and popular leather and oakwood coffee and end tables.

"Everything's on schedule and ready to go," he said. "I'll be down there early to set up the booths. I've got Bob and Jared and Ricardo helping so it shouldn't take too long." We were going all out and renting three booths this year. At a hundred bucks a booth, it was a gamble for the co-op since the money came out of our always meager budget. The deal was that everyone gave ten per-cent of what they sold back to the co-op. That meant we'd have to sell at least three thousand dollars of merchandise for the co-op to just make its booth rental back. A couple of big sales like Manuel's tables would help, but most of the artists did well if they sold three or four hundred dol-lars' worth of merchandise.

"I'll be in the booth a good part of the day," I said. "We've got to move that merchandise, so I'll be donning my 'Let's Make a Deal' personality. I will have to leave the cleanup for you all, though, as I have to be in Cambria by six to see to the last-minute preparations for the charity ball."

"No problem, *chiquita*," he said, flashing me a white, outrageously flirtatious smile that never failed to make me laugh. "You just be your *muy bonita* self and the art we make, it will fly into the people's hands."

"Manny," I said. "You are nothing but a big ole flirt and I think you'll have a better time talking women out of their hard-earned cash than I will."

He shook his head, his smile still teasing. "Any sacri-fice for the co-op . . ."

Ten minutes later I pulled into Liddie's parking lot, Manuel's reminder causing me to contemplate another an-niversary. Gabe's and my second anniversary was this Sunday and I hadn't thought of a thing to buy him. Which traditional present was it for the second anyway—paper was first, then was it wood or brass? Did anyone follow those rules anymore? Besides, after Lydia's visit and her revelation about Del, I wasn't sure what kind of celebration Gabe and I would be having. I tried to ignore the mental picture of Gabe and Del laughing together, working together, not to mention other even more disturbing pictures of them together. Every time I thought of sitting last night at dinner with them being completely ignorant of the situation, I became angrier.

Liddie's Cafe was, thankfully, in one of its slow times. A twenty-four-hour restaurant that served huge portions of good home-style food, it was a Central Coast landmark beloved by locals, students, and tourists alike. Its lobby harked back to the fifties with a glass counter packed with Wrigley's chewing gum, Hershey bars, Necco wafers, and cinnamon toothpicks. A new hand-lettered sign next to the cash register admonished cash-strapped students and frugal senior citizens: TIPPING IS NOT A GAME PLAYED WITH LIVESTOCK. Nadine's doing, no doubt. As head waitress, she ruled the roost of this particular chicken coop.

After calling hello to Jake, the fry cook, I slid into a red vinyl booth in back. I gazed out the window and mentally tried to organize the next week. After a few minutes, I gave up and fiddled with the salt and pepper shakers, trying not to think of what Gabe and Del might be doing right now.

"What do you want?" Nadine's screechy-tire voice demanded.

She startled me into dropping the salt shaker, spilling a thin layer of salt across the dark brown Formica table.

"And quit making a mess." She yelled over at Monica, one of the buspersons, to come over and wipe down the table.

Nadine was also a local landmark. Though she kept her age a secret, she had to be in her mid-seventies, though you'd never be able to tell it from her energy level. In her pink waitress uniform and teased beehive hairdo dyed a shade of pinkish-tan never seen on any Miss Clairol box, she ruled the roost at Liddie's. She and I had a loving, if prickly, relationship. She'd known me since I was, as she liked to say, "little biddy." Once in a while, when she was in a good mood, she called me "Lil Bid." Today was obviously not a "Lil Bid" day.

"You'd better comb that tangled hair of yours," Nadine said, "and put on some rouge."

Monica wiped down my table, glancing up apprehensively at Nadine. She was obviously a new hire from the college and hadn't learned yet that Nadine barked more than she bit. Usually. I gave the girl an encouraging smile before she hurried away.

"And why is that, Nadine?"

"I seen that old friend of Gabe's and she's after your man sure as my name is Nadine Maeleen Johnson."

I sat back in the booth, keeping my elbows away from the still wet table. "Your middle name is Maeleen? I didn't know that. Nadine Maeleen. Lovely cadence." I made myself smile. There was no way I was getting into this with her or anyone else. At least not before I talked to Gabe.

She smacked the top of my head with her order pad, then slid into the bench seat across from me.

My mouth dropped open in surprise. In all the years I'd know Nadine, I'd never seen her sit down on the job. Even when she had an appendix attack about ten years ago, she refused to sit down until the paramedics came and forced her to lie down on the gurney.

"Close your mouth," she said. "It looks cheap." She tested the table top for dryness, then rested her age-spotted elbows on it and leaned close to me.

"Now me and your gramma go way back. You're like one of my own grandbabies, and I just got to tell you, that woman friend of Gabe's is big trouble. You got to get rid of her quick." She smacked her hands flat on the table in emphasis.

I was so surprised by this I didn't know what to say. When, after a minute or so, my speech came back, naturally it was a smart remark, my first response in all situations too confusing for me to handle.

"Uh, my husband's the chief of police. Having a wife who murders his ex-partner might hurt his next merit raise and we were counting on it to pay for our new house."

She glared at me from behind her pointy fifties-style eyeglasses, her brown eyes bulging like a blow fish. "Don't say I didn't warn you, Miss Smarty Mouth. See if I care if you rattle around that fancy new house all by yourself." She slid out from the seat. From behind the front counter, Monica and Jake were staring over at us, as surprised as I was at Nadine's sudden change of habit.

"Nadine, wait. I'm sorry. I didn't mean to sass you." I didn't want her mad at me, especially since I hadn't ordered yet and didn't want to wait an extra half hour for my food.

Her well-traveled face softened slightly . . . I think. Then again, it could have just been the early afternoon sun shifting.

"I'm not teasing you now," she said, her gravelly voice low and serious. "I think you got real problems on your hands. They ate lunch here and your husband was laughing."

"They're old partners. They worked together. They know a lot of the same people." Nadine was trying to help in her own way, but I didn't need anyone ringing a warning bell for me. It was already clanging loudly enough on its own.

"They was laughing *too much*, Lil Bid." Her eyes were truly worried.

"Thanks, Nadine," I said softly. "I'm aware of the situation. Don't you worry now. I swear, I have it under control." I gestured over at the seat. "Now, sit back down because I have a question for you."

She slid back across from me and nodded, assuming it was about Gabe and Del. On some level, I appreciated her concern, but I was determined to deal with this situation on my own. Though I suspected that might prove impossible in a town where everyone knew us. But since I had her sitting down, I could pick her brain about some other gossip, gossip going a little farther back in San Celina history and that didn't concern me.

"Tell me about Maple Bennett Sullivan," I said.

Her face froze, her bottom lip, painted the same cotton candy pink as her nails, narrow to a thin, bright slit. "Why?"

"I'm cataloging her trunks for the historical society. They couldn't get anyone else to do it because of, well, you know . . . her alleged crime. I figured you were around back then and I wondered if you'd heard about it."

She closed one dark brown eye, as if readying to shoot a rifle. "Alleged crime, my aunt Sadie. Of course I heard about it. She killed her sweet husband in cold blood, shot him in the head and ran away with her lover. What else do you need to know?"

"It was never proved that she actually did it," I said, still not understanding why I felt so protective of this woman whom I actually knew nothing about. Maybe if I did find out more about her, I'd be as convinced of her guilt as everyone else.

"My girl, who else would have done it? Garvey Sullivan was one of the most respected and loved men in this county. Didn't have one single enemy far as I know. And the man that Maple Sullivan was spooning with was gone same time as her. Neither were ever heard from again. His best friend and his wife. What an old, sad story." She closed her eyes briefly and shook his head.

"The man she supposedly had an affair with was Garvey Sullivan's best friend?" Edna hadn't told me *that*. Their life was beginning to sound like one of those afternoon talk shows . . . or a soap opera.

"Name was Mitchell Warner. We called him Mitch."

I stared at her. "As in the sporting goods store Warners?" The Warner family had owned a sporting goods store downtown for over sixty years. They were a prominent local family who spanned five generations. One of the Warner boys, Frankie, was my age. He and I danced to every song at our junior high school graduation dance. He'd gone into the Navy after high school, become a SEAL, then after ten years decided to join the family business. Last I heard, he worked at one of their new stores up in Paso Robles.

"That's the ones. Mitch was Micah's younger brother."

"Micah's the oldest, right?" Micah was Frankie's father.

"Yep, he's still going strong too, I hear. Works at the store in Paso Robles twice a week. Turned eighty-seven last month. Mitch was ten years younger than him. There was six of them, all boys. Mitch was the baby, which is probably why he stole someone's wife."

I protested her cock-eyed psychology. "Wait a minute, Nadine. I believe somewhat in the study of birth order, but I don't think being the youngest makes him more prone to adultery."

"Spoiled rotten, he was. I ought to know, went to school with him clean through the twelfth grade. Always got what he wanted, and as I heard it, he wanted Maple Sullivan. There you go."

"Okay, so the rumor was that Mitch and Maple were lovers. Is there any proof?"

"They say she was pregnant when she ran away right after she killed Garvey. Had to be Mitch's."

I didn't add "allegedly" except in my mind. "Who is 'they'? And why did it have to be Mitch's? It could have been her husband's."

She patted the left side of her stiff hair. "Jemima Smith. She worked for old Doc Goldstein until his business fell off so bad during the war. His wife was pure German from Germany. They moved away about 1944. Winter, I think it was. Just up and left his office and Jemima had to pack it all up without a lick of help. Have to say, though, he did send her some money after the war was over. From Canada, I hear."

"So she told you Maple Sullivan was pregnant."

"Yes, ma'am. It was right there in her file. She wasn't too far along."

So much for doctor-patient confidentiality, I thought.

"Then that hussy ups, shoots her husband dead, and runs away. Now, why would she do that if it was his? Guess we know where she'll be spending eternity, that one." Nadine's eyes glistened with anger.

I wasn't about to start discussing eternal justice with Nadine when she was so worked up. I was curious, though, about why this made her so angry.

"Did you know Garvey very well?" I asked.

Her spine straightened just a centimeter. "He ate lunch here every day. Tuna salad and a dill pickle. Iced tea and pie of the day. He liked raspberry best, but would eat anything but rhubarb. Sometimes he ate dinner here too, when his wife was too busy writing away at those stories of hers to be bothered to cook."

"You remember what he ordered? His favorite pies?"

Her face turned a dull red beneath her pink face powder when she slipped out of the booth for a second time. "I remember what you eat every day too, young woman. I do all my regulars because I'm a good waitress. Now if you're done badgering me, I'll get that cheeseburger, fries, and vanilla Coke ready for you." Her eyes challenged me to say anything more about Garvey Sullivan.

"Thanks, Nadine," I said and left it at that.

She'd had a crush on Garvey Sullivan, I'd bet my truck on it. That meant I couldn't believe half of what she told me about Maple Sullivan. I needed to find a more objective source. Of course, with what she'd been accused of doing, killing the town's favorite son, that might prove difficult.

When Nadine brought me my late lunch, I asked, "Is Jemima Smith still alive?"

She slapped my bill down on the table. "No, why?"

I shrugged. "Just trying to figure out Maple Sullivan's story. I thought Mrs. Smith might be able to shed some light on it."

"Sometimes the past is best left in the past," Nadine said.

"I'm a history major," I said, opening my hamburger and grabbing the ketchup bottle. I hit the bottom of the bottle and sent a huge surge of ketchup over my steaming patty. "I believe in studying the past."

"Some things don't need studying. They are what they are."

"I don't agree. Sometimes things aren't at all what they appear to be. And if something is wrong, if we can understand how it happened, maybe we can keep it from happening again." But my words, the words of every student who studied history and sociology, even sounded lame and clichéd to me.

She sniffed audibly, letting me know what she thought of my theory. "I'm a lot older than you and I'll tell you this. There ain't no figuring out why folks do mean things. It's just in some of them to do it. She was a selfish, self-centered woman who wanted what she wanted with no regard to anyone else. I think you'd best leave it all alone."

"Well, I'd like to, except Edna McClun has talked me into cataloging Maple's personal effects, so as long as I'm stuck doing that, I'm going to do a little research. I think I'll go to the library after I eat."

She shook her head and stuck her order pad in the pocket of her pink polyester dress. "You're as stubborn as a clingstone peach pit."

"Which reminds me, is there any peach cobbler today?"

"I'll wrap it up to go," she said, turning to walk away.

"That's okay, I have plenty of time."

"No, you don't. You're due over at Beckah's Bridal Shop for a fitting at three o'clock. Then you have to go to Costume Carnival to pick up your outfit for the dance Saturday night. And they close at six today because Cathy's going down to Santa Barbara to fetch some costumes she's borrowing from her sister. Better eat quick."

"Shoot," I said, staring after her. I'd completely forgotten about both appointments. There went my leisurely afternoon in the library. I didn't even bother to ask Nadine how she knew my schedule. That was like asking someone to paint a picture of the wind.

I pulled my date book out of my purse just to double-check. It was right there in my handwriting if I'd bothered to check it this morning. I managed to eat half my burger and take a few gulps of Coke before dashing back through the cafe. I handed a twenty-dollar bill to Nadine, grabbed my papersack of cobbler, and yelled out, "Keep the change." An eight-dollar tip. That ought to buy me back into her good graces.

I was only ten minutes late to Beckah's. Elvia was already in her wedding gown, standing in front of the three-way mirror, looking so gorgeous she could have posed for a fashion layout.

"You're late!" she wailed. Her wedding preparations had acquired the overtones of boot camp and I was, no doubt, her most unresponsive grunt. Next to her in an overstuffed pink brocade armchair, her mother, Señora Aragon, glowed. The bridal consultant, Tia, smiled at me and continued fluffing out Elvia's full skirt.

I blew my nervous friend a kiss, then went over to hug her mother. *"Buenas tardes, Mama Aragon. Como estas?"* I flopped down in the armless chair next to hers upholstered in the same stomach-cramping pink. I shifted from one cheek to the other, trying to find a comfortable spot. I'd sat on concrete curbs that were more forgiving.

"Muy bien, Benni, *muy, muy bien,"* Señora Aragon said. "Isn't she *preciosa? Mi bella niña* is finally going to be a bride. Thanks to the Virgin." She crossed herself, her dark eyes welling up with tears.

"Oh, Mama, don't start crying again," Elvia said, swirling around in her dress to pat her mother's hand. It had a tightly fitted pearl-embroidered bodice, tiny cap sleeves, and billowing layers of netting under the thin chiffon-covered skirt. I wanted to tell her she looked just like a perfect little Latina Barbie doll, except I knew she'd kill me. Emory was going to pass out from joy when he saw her float down the aisle.

"She's going to be the most beautiful bride that old Mission has ever seen," I said, shifting again in my uncomfortable chair.

"Oh, you two just stop it," Elvia said, blushing with pleasure. She took her shoulder-length black hair, twisted it, and held it on top of her head. "I've decided on wearing my hair up. What do you think?"

Mama Aragon just wiped away the tears running down her wrinkled brown cheeks and nodded.

"I think that's a great idea," I said for at least the hundredth time. She'd waffled back and forth between wanting her hair upswept or down for the last two months. Like a good matron of honor, I agreed with whatever she said.

"Okay, Benni, your turn now," Tia said. She took my gray silk bridesmaid dress out of its off-white garment bag and handed it to me. It was a gorgeous dress, form-fitting, but comfortable with a V neckline with just a touch of lace and cap sleeves that matched Elvia's. She wanted each of us to wear silver jewelry that reflected our tastes and personalities. I was still thinking about what to wear.

"I forgot my slip and my heels," I said. When Elvia glared at me, I made a goofy face, trying to make her laugh.

"No problem," Tia said, her easygoing smile telling me she'd been through this numerous times. "I have a slip in the dressing room and we keep sample shoes here just for that reason. What size shoe and what heel height?"

"Six and two," I said, grateful to the bottom of my boots. I turned back to Elvia. "*Lo siento mucho, mi amiga,* but I've had a crazy day. I get points for making it here, don't I?"

She tried to look mad, but didn't succeed. She was just too happy. "It's all right. I know you have a lot going on right now besides my wedding. We'll have coffee afterward and you can fill me in on Dove's wedding and everything else that's been happening. It seems like I've been in a fog these last few months."

"Wish I could, but I have to pick up my costume for the Mardi Gras ball Saturday night and Cathy closes early tonight."

"How are things progressing with the ball? I should have helped you. Is there anything you need done?"

"Everything's fine," I assured her. "You've got more important things to worry about. Just show up with Emory and have a good time. And don't forget your shower this Sunday. Two o'clock at Miss Christine's."

"I won't forget," she said, stepping down from the pedestal and waving at me to go try on my dress.

"Has everyone else been fitted?" I called over to the next dressing room, where she was taking off her dress. Though Elvia had no sisters, only six brothers, she'd ended up having ten bridesmaids, not counting me, because she had so many cousins and sisters-in-law who'd waited for this day.

"You're the last," she called back. "As usual."

"Hey, Miss Better-late-than-never. I wouldn't throw any sharp stones if'n I were you. I'm still two marriages ahead."

Her uncustomary giggle caused me to smile at myself in the mirror. This was the happiest I'd ever seen her.

During my fitting, one of her brothers, Miguel, came by to pick up Señora Aragon. He was younger than us by ten years and had been a San Celina police officer for over four years now. It was a fact I still had a hard time comprehending. Right now, he was off duty and dressed in Levi's and a eye-popping blue-and-purple Hawaiian shirt decorated with palm trees and forties-style pinup girls.

"Groovy shirt, Officer Aragon," I said, turning when Tia told me to turn. "Real Hawaii Five-oh. Book 'em, Dano."

"Huh?" he said, his square, young face confused.

I made a face at Elvia and Señora Aragon. "I'm too old."

After my fitting and two reminders from Elvia about our hair and facial appointments tomorrow, we were finally finished. As Elvia and her mother settled some last details with Tia, I joined Miguel out on the sidewalk, where he leaned against his black Camaro.

"How're things at work?" I asked.

He shrugged his thick, muscled shoulders. "Okay, I guess." He glanced sideways at me. "Met your husband's old partner today." He grinned. "Wish I'd get a partner like her. Man, she's really hot."

I leaned next to him and stared at our reflections in the bridal shop window. "Gee, thanks for pointing that out to me, Miguel."

He quickly backpedaled. "Sorry, Benni, I didn't mean it the way it sounds. I mean . . . she's okay . . . I just meant . . ." He cleared his throat. His dark spaniel eyes wore the same troubled glow he'd had when he came to me as a little boy after breaking one of his mother's dishes.

"It's okay, Miguel."

His face looked only slightly relieved. "I'm sorry. Really."

"Forget it." I wasn't about to let one of my husband's employees, not to mention a kid I'd once baby-sat, see just exactly how much it did bother me. "Have you been fitted for your tux yet?"

He nodded with more enthusiasm than the question warranted, anxious to change the subject. "Yeah, and I'm all set for the bachelor party too. It should be a blast, even if there aren't going to be any girls there."

Before I could answer, his mother and Elvia came out of the bridal shop. After settling his mother in the passenger seat and hugging his sister, he gave me an apologetic wave before he climbed into the driver's seat.

I stared after his car for a long moment.

"What's wrong?" Elvia said, digging through her purse

for her cell phone. "You look worried." She punched a number on automatic dial.

"It's . . ." I started.

She held up her hand and said into the phone, "I received a message that there's some problem with my wedding napkins. Yes, I can hold, but not for long." She tapped her foot on the concrete sidewalk and asked again, "I'm sorry. What did you say you were worried about?"

"Not a thing," I said, not wanting to burden her with such a mundane marriage irritation during the last week before her wedding. "Not a doggone thing."

10

BENNI

At Costume Carnival it was exactly that, a carnival. With everyone getting ready for Mardi Gras, I had to wait twenty minutes just to reach the front of the line.

"Oh, hi, Benni," Cathy said, her pale blond hair disheveled, her china blue eyes already glassy with fatigue. "Your costume's all ready. I hope you like it. It's one of my new ones." She called out my name to one of her assistants, who checked it on a computer printout. Two minutes later, she held two plastic maroon garment bags across the counter. "Here's yours and Gabe's too. Want to try yours on?"

"No time. I trust your measurements. It's not a cowgirl outfit, right?"

"Nope, and it's very comfortable, I promise."

"Then it's perfect. Thanks a lot."

I paid, wished her luck with the next few crazy days, and started for my truck. My watch said four o'clock. Since I didn't have to worry about cooking dinner and Gabe rarely made it home before six o'clock these days, I decided to find a quiet place to look through Maple Sullivan's scrapbook.

The library was definitely the quietest and warmest place to do some uninterrupted reading. Besides, I could do a little research while I was there. This was just what I needed to get my mind off Gabe, Del, and the confrontation I knew for a fact he and I were going to have tonight.

I went by the old house to drop off the costumes, feed Scout, and pick up my heavier, wool-lined Levi's jacket. The air had a distinct chill, and an army of dark gray, rain-fat clouds had marched in and halted right over San Celina. I wouldn't be surprised if we saw a downpour in the next couple of hours. Scout whined when he saw I was heading back out the door.

"I'm sorry, boy," I said, giving his broad chest a good scratching. "But I'm going to the library and they won't let you in there. I'll be home in a couple of hours. Guard the house."

My cell phone sang "Happy Trails" when I pulled out of the driveway. The display told me it was Gabe.

"Hi," I said, trying to keep my voice neutral.

"Question. What's on for dinner tonight?"

"Your guess is as good as mine. Taco Bell?"

"Over my plugged-up arteries. Actually, I was thinking, since Del's still here, maybe we should take her out to McClintock's. Give her a taste of some local cuisine."

"Oh, wasn't she leaving today?" I said, still trying to sound casual.

"She thinks she might stick around for a week or so," he replied, his tone matching mine.

"Why?"

I could imagine his nonchalant shrug. "Just needs to talk. About her dad, what she wants to do with her career. Things aren't working out that well for her in L.A. I jokingly told her if she stayed too long, I'd have to put her to work."

I was silent, thinking, buddy-boy, those house plans aren't even on the drawing board.

"You know," I said, not believing I was saying it even

as I did. "I've got a lot of work to do with the Mardi Gras festival so why don't you two go on without me. I'll meet you at home later." I couldn't spend another night looking at her face, knowing what I knew now. Was that smugness in her expression last night? Now I wondered.

Are you out of your mind, girl? Nadine's voice screamed inside my head. Miguel's words echoed behind hers. *Man, she's hot.*

I have to trust my husband, I told the voices. And myself.

"Are you sure?" Gabe said. "She said she really enjoyed talking to you last night. She wants to get to know you better."

That sealed it. My good intentions flew right out the truck window. "You know, on second thought, I'm not sure it's all that great an idea for you to be spending so much time with a former lover, do you?"

His silence lasted for a long minute. "Where did you hear that?"

At least he wasn't trying to deny it.

"Doesn't matter. The point is, I'm not sure her intentions are as pure and innocent as she would have you believe."

His voice went stiff. "You're being unfair. Try to have some compassion. She's going through a tough time."

"Gabe, I don't think she's here to just cry on your shoulder."

"And I think I know her better than you."

"Yes, we've established that little fact already, haven't we?"

A longer silence passed while we both waited for the other to pass or deal.

He dealt. "You knew when you married me that you weren't the first woman in my life." He paused a moment, then said, "Just like I wasn't the first man in yours. And if I recall, we've had a few of your old loves pop up in our lives."

"One," I countered. "And that was before we were married. And it was a *high school* boyfriend. *Big* difference."

"There's no place for this conversation to go," he said in a cold voice.

"I disagree. There's plenty of places for it to go."

"I'll only ask one more time. Do you want to join us for dinner?"

"No." I disconnected and stuck my cell phone in my backpack. When it rang again and I saw it was Gabe on the display, I ignored it.

I hit the steering wheel in frustration. What was I going to do about this? Ignore it, fight about it, take out a contract on Del Hernandez? The last one sounded the most satisfying, even though I knew it was more than just her involved. Was it possible to take a contract out on his feelings for her?

I thought I knew this man. We'd shared a lot, been through a lot, in the last two years, both emotionally and physically. I'd held him in my arms time after time when his terrifying nightmares woke him in a cold sweat. He'd held me in his during my own bad times. I trusted him . . . or had . . . like no one else on earth. But now I had to wonder if it had all been an illusion on my part. I'd once read in an article on relationships that two years was the outside time limit for romantic love. After that, it had to move on to something else, what the author called "authentic love" or die. Some people went through their lives just reliving the same two years over and over with different partners. Was that Gabe? Did I really have any idea who this man was . . . or is?

"Happy second anniversary, Benni Harper," I said out loud, tasting salt in the back of my throat.

As I was pulling into the library parking lot, my cell phone rang again and I was really beginning to regret having one. The display read DOVE, so I answered.

"Hey, Dove. What's new?"

"Water."

"What?"

"I want to get married on water. I was thinking maybe

on a yacht. We could serve seafood appetizers. Play fish music."

"Fish music?" I pictured Charlie the Tuna singing into a microphone.

"You know, those tapes of whales and dolphins talking. I've heard some real pretty ones with violins and flutes in the background. I think it was downtown at that hippie store that smells like it needs a good cleaning with Lysol. That would be a wedding to remember, don't you think? I'm sure Isaac has never been married on a yacht."

"With fish music," I added.

"Right. So, what do you think?"

"Wouldn't that cost a lot of money? I mean, the helicopters were bad enough . . ."

"Oh, *pshaw* on the money. I've got plenty of money. I've been waiting thirty-three years for this wedding. I want what I want."

"But, Dove, we talking thousands and thousands of dollars."

"So?"

"So, do you think Isaac wants to spend that much?"

"Whatever gave you the idea he was paying for this? Missy, I'm paying for my own wedding. And I told you, I have plenty of liquid assets. I've been saving my chicken money."

"But, Dove, we're talking a lot more than chicken money. We're—"

She interrupted me. "I've got one hundred thousand dollars. You figure it would take any more than that?"

I held out my phone and looked at it, certain I'd heard wrong. "Did you say one hundred thousand?"

"Yes."

"Dollars?"

"Well, it ain't eggs. Though eggs was how I got it."

"You're telling me you've sold a hundred thousand dollars' worth of eggs?"

"Well, I've been selling them a long time, honeybun. And I've worked at growing it. Me and Auburn, that is."

"Who's Auburn?"

"My broker. Auburn T. Jones. The T doesn't stand for anything. He just thinks it sounds more brokerish. Lives in San Francisco and drives a Ferrari I helped pay for, if you want to know the truth. I tell him what stocks to buy and he does. We squabble sometimes because he thinks I'm too adventuresome, but we do okay. He sometimes calls me for advice. Says I got a real feel for picking winners."

I was speechless. My gramma had a whole financial life I knew nothing about. Just goes to show you, we *don't* know everything, even about the people we love the most. My thoughts flashed back to Gabe. What was I going to do?

"If you want water, Gramma," I said, suddenly feeling too emotional to talk any longer. "I say go for it. Just don't make me wear a mermaid costume."

"I'm not *that* nutty," she said, her cheerful cackle over the phone making me smile through the haze in my eyes. "Nothing's for sure yet. I'm still working on it. I'll keep you posted."

"You do that," I said, but she'd already turned off her phone.

I sat in the truck for a few minutes, looking out over Laguna Lake. The San Celina Library, which sat on a large bluff overlooking the lake, was a large, forbidding-looking building with all the appeal of a federal prison. What had caused the change in architecture from the beautiful, artistic buildings of the thirties and forties to our modern-day, functional, all-purpose buildings? It was as if sometime in the fifties, buildings had lost their souls and become mere depositories for information and data. Were they the canaries in the coal mines? Did our buildings reflect what was happening in our society or foretell what was coming?

In the deepening dusk, I watched the mallard ducks dunk for food until the only thing I could see were the white feathers of the pencil-legged egrets. My mind was a turmoil of feelings and worries, all so jumbled I couldn't untangle them. What I needed was a distraction, at least for a few hours. Sometimes, things became clearer when you let your subconscious do the work.

The library was so warm that the first thing I did was remove my jacket. It was quiet for a Thursday so I assumed term papers were not due at Cal Poly or any other local school. At the reference desk, I found out where the microfilm drawers for the *San Celina Tribune* were located and I picked out three reels—October through December 1941, April through June 1943, and January through March 1945. I wanted to get a feel for the time period before I read Maple's letters or looked through her scrapbook.

It was easy to get caught up in reading the old newspapers. They reported a world that was so foreign to me it could have been on another planet—rationing, war bond drives, USO dances, serial stories. The prices of things amused me, as I'm sure the prices of the late twentieth century will amuse someone fifty years from now: coffee—one-pound tin, thirty-one cents; Ovaltine—large tin, sixty-one cents; string beans—two No. 2 tins, thirty-five cents; catsup—fourteen-ounce bottle, fifteen cents. And in the middle of every page of food advertisements: YOU TOO CAN SERVE BY SAVING! BUY DEFENSE BONDS AND STAMPS!

My quest was for articles about Garvey or Maple Sullivan, but a few times I couldn't resist reading the articles.

**CAROLE LANDIS, JACK BENNY
CHEER PACIFIC SERVICEMEN
SPOKANE GIRL WEDS
JAPANESE-AMERICAN**

**4 BOYS IN FAMILY DIE
IN BATTLE;
5TH MAY COME HOME**

GERMAN PRISONER HANGED
IN CAMP

I scanned the bylines looking for any mention of Maple's name or an article with her byline. Most of the stories were written by men and had to do with what was happening overseas. Then I concentrated on the society pages to see what they revealed about what the women were doing while the men were off fighting and because of whom she'd married, there might be a chance I'd see something about Maple. Articles told of Valentine theme contract bridge parties hosted by generals' wives, afternoon classes in first aid at the local Red Cross hosted by the Elks Club, and dances scheduled at the local USO canteens in San Celina and Paso Robles, but though they listed many names of the participants, some last names that were even familiar to me, there was no mention of Maple Sullivan. For someone who was married to such a prominent man, her name was surprisingly absent from the society pages.

I finally found an article written by her in January 1944 on the stories behind some quilt patterns' names. Whether she knew it or not, she was an early quilt historian.

> Quilt patterns often derive their names from many fascinating places and take into account religious traditions, geographical fauna and wildlife, local customs and historical and political beliefs. A good example according to Ruth Finley, author of *Old Patchwork Quilts and the Women Who Made Them*, is the pattern Bear's Paw. The four-pointed, tulip-like pattern was popular under that name in western Pennsylvania and Ohio since the 1800's. The exact same pattern has been called Duck's Foot in the Mud in Long Island, where ducks were more prevalent than bears and Hand of Friendship

by Pennsylvania Quakers who are known for their gentle hospitality.

The difficult pattern known as Drunkard's Path has also been called, before 1849, Rocky Road to Dublin suggesting that Irish immigrant women might have utilized the design and Rocky Road to California which would have certainly been the case for many pioneer women on the trail West. It was also known for reasons personal to the quilter herself as Fool's Puzzle, Falling Timbers and Country Husband. It is a Robbing Peter to Pay Paul pattern which also suggests how much folk sayings and wisdom played in the naming of patterns. No child, according to quilt lore, should be allowed to sleep under a Wandering Foot quilt or they would grow up with an unstable, seeking life. It is not a pattern that a bride would want in her dowry of quilts.

Some patterns name origins are obvious from nature such as Streak-of-Lightning, Rail Fence and Pickle Dish while others are more mysterious like Sugar Loaf and Blindman's Fancy. My own favorite pattern, Secret Drawer, a spool-like pattern has also been called Arkansas Traveler though there is nothing in the history books to suggest why. Political quilts have always been popular, showing that women felt a real interest in their country's affairs. Burgoyne Surrounded immortalized British General John Burgoyne who in 1777 led a poorly equipped army in the Saratoga Campaign of the American Revolution and eventually surrendered. Lincoln's Platform and Madison's Patch celebrated sitting presidents. I wouldn't be a bit surprised if some quilter now is fashioning her own pattern which might be called Victory Over the Axis or Bring Our Boys Home.

After a few minutes trying to figure out the copying mechanism attached to the microfilm machine, I made a copy of the article for our library at the museum. I continued to run through the pages looking for more articles by her or any story about the Sullivans.

The tragedy of her husband's death was reported on February 10, 1945. Exactly fifty years ago this month. It was not a headline I could miss.

PROMINENT RANCHER,
BUSINESSMAN FOUND SHOT TO
DEATH IN HOME

The article gave the barest details. Garvey Sullivan was found in the attic of his Victorian house by a housekeeper. There was one gunshot to the temple. No weapon was recovered. His wife was absent at the time and is being sought for questioning. There was no mention of Mitch Warner.

I looked for follow-up stories in the days afterward. There were only three. San Celina police were vague about details, saying only they were working on the case. Then it disappeared among the always dramatic war news.

I found the funeral announcement a few minutes later.

February 15, 1945

MASS SCHEDULED FOR
MR. GARVEY SULLIVAN

A requiem high mass for beloved local rancher and businessman, Garvey Sullivan, will be celebrated at the Santa Celine Mission Friday at 9:00 A.M. He died at his home in San Celina.

Vault entombment will be made in the family plot in the Catholic cemetery under the direction of R. G. Thomlinson Funeral Home.

Recitation of the rosary will take place this Thursday at 8:00 P.M. at 112 Firefly Lane. Mr. Sul-

livan was a native of San Celina. He leaves his
father, Arthur Sullivan, and many friends and col-
leagues.

No mention of Maple. No mention of how Garvey died.
I could guess by the announcement that his father, like so
many others, had pronounced her guilty already.

Rubbing the back of my aching neck, I glanced up at
the clock over the reference desk. Seven-forty. I had less
than an hour and a half before the library closed and I
wanted to read her letters.

In the library's no-talking reading room, which was oc-
cupied only by one older man dozing over a book, I settled into a chair in the corner, setting the scrapbook down
on the floor next to me. I untied the red ribbon around
Maple and Garvey's letters. Maybe there'd be something
I could trace in their relationship from the beginning that
pointed to the way it ended up.

Flipping through the letters, I realized I'd only see one
side of the relationship tonight. These letters were written
by her to him. Did she save his letters? Were they in her
trunks or somewhere else? Another mystery to look into.

The letters themselves were so touching and hopeful, it
was hard to imagine this woman taking a gun and in cold
blood shooting this man she obviously adored.

March 7, 1942
Louisville, Kentucky

My dear, sweet Garvey,

*How thrilled I was when I came back to the
boarding house and found this letter from you. (My
nosy landlady, Mrs. Palmer, tried to read it through
the envelope, I just know it. Poor old soul, all of the
girls who live here confide in her about their love
lives except for me. I refuse to share our glorious
love with anyone. It is too precious to me.) How*

*many times have I wondered in the last week
whether you were merely a figment of my romantic
imagination? How can I have found true love in just
three days? Your proposal took me by surprise and
I'm sorry if I didn't believe you were serious. Now I
know it is true. You are the man of my dreams and
you do love me as I so desperately love you. As I go
to work at the cafe every day and watch the people
come and go in the train station, I wish upon every
star in the sky that one of those trains would bring
you back to me. What a wonderful, beautiful chance
our meeting was! If you had not had the urge for a
cup of coffee right at that moment, if I'd taken my
break or called in sick that day, our lives would be
so different. For me, the days would have sped along
one long, dull highway, always longing for the one
person who could fulfill this empty feeling that I have
always carried deep in my soul. You, only you, my
dear, sweet boy, you who have kidnapped my heart
and captured my soul in the prison of your sad eyes.
Yes, yes, yes, I will marry you! We will marry and
live as only two who have committed themselves to
their one true love can, always and forever together.
I will feed you grapes from my own fingers, my love,
and pour your sherry for you every night until the
day I die. I will wipe away your sorrows with my
bare hands. I thank God and all His saints in
heaven, all those marvelous saints and angels so
dear to your heart, for your long-awaited and
anticipated love. Take good care, oh my love and
life, until we can be together again and forever and
you will never be sad again. I cannot wait to see you
again and kiss your sweet lips goodnight.*

Your only love, Maple

There were twelve letters in all. They all sounded the
same, optimistic and lovesick, letters only a young woman

in love could write. The last one was dated April 22, 1942.

Dearest Garvey,

This will be my last letter until I am in your arms! It was so wonderful hearing your voice last night, if only for a too short ten minutes. Thank you, thank you for the beautiful silver locket! I will treasure it as long as I live and wear it over my heart. I look forward with great joy to the sound of your voice everyday for the balance of my life. I promise, once we're married you'll never be sad again! My single trunk has been sent ahead. I fear I do not bring much to this marriage but that of my great love for you. Mama is naturally saddened by the fact that I will live so far away but is happy for me. Daddy is only worried about the crops, as he always is and about how to buy shoes for my brothers. Will and Lyle are naturally curious about my new life in California. I've promised to send them an orange tree. Is that possible? I hope once this war is finally over and that terrible man, Hitler, is put rightfully in prison where he belongs, I will be able to have my family out to California to visit us. If Mama can pull Daddy away from his land, of course. Though he is only leasing, he thinks of it as his. Maybe someday it actually will be. Oh, I miss you so much, darling! The time cannot fly quickly enough to bring me to your side. I look forward to meeting all your friends and being the caring wife you so deserve. Look for me soon, my love. My train, with God's good timing, will arrive on Thursday, as I told you on the telephone. I'll be wearing the ring you gave me and the smile you have, alone, put on my face. I love you so!

Always and forever your, Maple

I folded up the last letter and stuck it back into the yellowed envelope. How had such love and hope turned to murder a mere three years later? I wanted to like Maple Sullivan, wanted so much for this relationship to work out. Her life, or the little bits I could discern from these letters, didn't sound easy. I guessed that she had come to the big city of Louisville from her daddy's farm in Mercy Ridge when the war started to waitress in a cafe. From my history studies and Dove's stories, I knew a lot of women went to work during those times because so many men had joined the war. In Maple's case, it might have been out of necessity too. Tenant farms were not known for making people rich. Marriage to a wealthy California rancher would have been an unbelievable opportunity to anyone in Maple's financial position.

So did she really love him or just saw him as a way out of poverty and a dead-end future in Kentucky? Her articles and letters told me she was an articulate woman for being raised in the hills, which led me to believe she had a gifted intelligence. Or a gift for words, anyway. Did she get to California, decided she liked the life but not the man? Did she kill him to get his money? She wouldn't have been the first woman to attempt that.

I tied the letters back together and picked up the scrapbook. A chill ran down my back and I looked up to see through the darkness outside that a heavy rain had started. I slipped on my jacket and opened the scrapbook.

The first page showed the start of their lives as reported by the *San Celina Tribune*.

SAN CELINA TRIBUNE
SAN CELINA, CALIFORNIA
May 1, 1942

COUPLE SAY PLEDGES AT
SANTA CELINE MISSION

A whirlwind courtship that had its beginnings two months ago in Louisville, Kentucky, when the groom met the bride in a local dining establishment, was successfully culminated when Garvey Michael Sullivan, local rancher and prominent businessman, made Miss Maple Bennett, of Mercy Ridge, Kentucky, his bride.

The couple exchanged their vows at 5 P.M. at Santa Celine Mission with Father Joseph O'Malley as the officiant. Mrs. Maude Crawford, church secretary, and Arthur Sullivan, the groom's father, were the sole attendants. Miss Bennett was dressed in a navy blue gabardine suit with an ecru chiffon blouse and a matching close-fitting feather hat with a veil. She had ecru accessories and wore a corsage of pink rosebuds.

Mr. Sullivan, the son of former San Celina mayor, Arthur Sullivan, is a city council member, president of the Cattlemen's Association, owner of many local businesses and a possible candidate for State Senator. He was educated at Stanford University in business and agriculture, then spent a year abroad completing his education.

Miss Bennett is the daughter of Mercy Ridge, Kentucky, farmer, John Bennett and his wife, Raylene.

After a short honeymoon in San Francisco, the couple will make their home at the Sullivan house on Firefly Lane.

I studied the announcement. Something about it bothered me, something that seemed a little off, but I couldn't put my finger on it. I read it three more times. Then it occurred to me. First, all the information was about him and what he'd accomplished. Second, his life was listed first. I'd read and reread Elvia's announcement enough times before she sent it to the newspaper to know that traditionally the woman's life is acknowledged first. Maple Bennett was already being told by San Celina society where she rated in importance.

Page after page of her scrapbook were clippings of articles where Garvey was mentioned, more often than not accompanied by a photograph—Garvey handing out a prize to the child who'd collected the most tin cans for the war effort, Garvey auctioning off a painting for a USO benefit, Garvey heading a war bonds drive in San Celina, Garvey breaking ground on a new hospital maternity wing being built to accommodate the influx of service men and their wives in San Celina County. All of them portrayed the same tall, smoothly handsome man with dark, brooding eyes and a sad smile I first saw in his wedding photo. I studied the photos closely. If he wasn't forty, then he was close to it, which would have made him too old for the draft. And most likely, with his large cattle ranch to oversee, with much of the meat going to soldiers, he was probably considered a necessity on the home front. I knew there'd been some industries labeled ESSENTIAL TO THE WAR EFFORT by the government and the men running them were left to do just that. Many of those men made a small fortune during the war. Getting married and having a child also helped keep men from the war, though even that eventually wasn't enough deferment on its own. Did he marry her just to stay out of the war? On her part, there was definitely love, but I hadn't read anything written by him yet. I needed to find his letters.

A professional photograph of the both of them was stuck inside one set of pages. I was struck again by how young she appeared. I would guess her at no more than twenty. Like the other photograph, the black-and-white photograph didn't reveal much. She stood behind him resting one hand on his shoulder. Her dark eyes and smile seemed tentative now to me. How long after their wedding had this picture been taken? What happened to the hopeful smile from her wedding portrait? His face was still sober, his eyes staring at something beyond the camera.

I flipped quickly through the rest of the scrapbook. Toward the end there were clippings of her stories, including the quilt history one I'd just read and other human-interest stories similar to the one about Abbott Fitzhugh. There was even one about Ernie Pyle, the famous journalist and war correspondent. She interviewed him when he came through the Central Coast on his way to see John Steinbeck over in Monterey. What a thrill that must have been for her. And how unusual.

I knew enough about the forties to know it was not the norm for women to be given such literary privileges. All the other female bylines were relegated to the society pages and consisted of reporting what subjects were discussed at women's clubs meetings, how best to stretch those precious pounds of rationed sugar, and what was going on at the various USO clubs around the county. How had Maple, a stranger from Kentucky whose last job was obviously being a waitress, broken such a barrier?

I suspected that Garvey's political and monetary influence probably had something to do with it.

I set the scrapbook down and decided to make a list of what steps I needed to take, what people I should see, a game plan as my old history professor used to call it. I was already on the second page of my notebook when a voice over the library's speaker system announced that it was a quarter to nine—the library would be closing in fifteen minutes.

By the time I'd gathered up my belongings, the rain was falling harder. I stood under the library's outside awning and contemplated the distance to my truck. The letters could fit in my backpack but the scrapbook was too big so I took off my jacket and wrapped it around the book. I could survive getting wet better than these old newspaper clippings. By the time I had reached my truck, my hair and flannel shirt were soaked, but the scrapbook was dry.

On the drive home I kept thinking about Garvey's letters to Maple. I wouldn't rest tonight until I saw if they were in her trunks. Knowing that I was deliberately avoiding the emotional mess waiting for me at home, I turned the truck toward the folk art museum. When I was almost there, I'd already talked myself into waiting until tomorrow. The museum was isolated on this long stretch of road it shared with the Coastal Valley Farm Supply, the San Celina Feed and Grain Co-op, and other smaller businesses housed in prefab metal buildings. Stopping here by myself this late at night was foolish even if I did suspect that most criminals would not venture out in weather like this. Not to mention it was against our co-op's rules. When I reached the museum, I'd talked myself out of stopping and instead going straight home to resolve this problem with my husband.

The vehicle parked next to the museum's entrance changed my mind. Everyone affliated with the co-op knew the rules. I pulled in for a closer look.

Then I recognized the red Dodge Ram pickup. Detective Hudson, who was obviously here working on the trunks. I parked next to him and dashed around the museum toward the studios. Underneath the canopy of honeysuckle and ivy, the still pouring rain dripped through the heavy foliage. Knowing how jumpy cops can be, I carefully opened the studio door and, before sticking my head in, called out in a loud voice, "It's me, Detective. Benni Harper."

He was sitting on the floor next to the first trunk, objects neatly lined up on the floor around him. He faced me, his right hand behind his back. Where he kept his gun, no doubt.

"Leaving that door unlocked is really stupid," I said, walking into the icy room. "You're just setting yourself up for an ambush."

"Bobbie Lee said she would lock it when she left," he said, bringing his hand back around and resting it on his knee.

Bobbie Lee was one of our artists, a brilliant landscape painter whom I wouldn't trust to take out the trash, much less lock up after me. "Bobbie Lee has to be reminded to take a leak, Detective. She's a bit, shall we say, absent-minded."

"How was I supposed to know that?" he asked peevishly. He was dressed in an off-white Irish cable knit sweater whose dry warmth I envied right now. My Levi's jacket was still damp and clammy from its use as a protective cover for Maple Sullivan's scrapbook.

"I guess you couldn't." But I couldn't help poking fun at him. "You know, I would have thought your superior detecting abilities would have clued you in to her flaky nature."

"She's real pretty," he said, grinning. "Sometimes that interferes with my brilliant detective's radar."

I shook my head. "You're a hound dog, Detective Hudson. A real hound dog."

"I've been called worse. Speaking of stupid, what are *you* doing here alone this late at night? Being a police chief's wife, I would assume you would understand the possibilities of robbery, assault, and rape that coming here alone might engender."

"Not that it's any of your business, I'd already decided that coming by here to pick up something wasn't too smart and was going to drive on by until I saw your truck. Maybe I forgot to tell you, but we have a rule that no one can work up here past nine o'clock. Because of its isolated location, the co-op board decided it was too dangerous."

"Hey, don't vote me out yet. I didn't know, and besides, I didn't realize how late it was. When I started at six, there was a whole crowd of people here. Before I knew it, it was nine-thirty."

I couldn't help smiling because I understood the feeling. Only someone who was fascinated by history and the past could get that lost in time when surrounded by old teacups, pocket watches, magazines, and fountain pens. Time had just flown by for me in a similar way at the library.

"So, how's it going?" I asked, picking up an ivory-backed hairbrush. A few dark hairs still clung to the bristles. Hard to believe they were still there after fifty years.

"It's taking longer than I thought," he admitted. "I've only finished one page." He held up a cataloging page where twenty items had been listed. I took it from him and read his first entry.

Dark brown kidskin women's gloves. Eight leather five-petal daisy-like flowers on each cuff. Size six and a half. Made in Paris. (Markings inside right glove) Aris of Paris. (Markings inside left glove) Real Kid.

I handed it back to him. "Very thorough. I'm impressed."

"Well, my mama owned an antique store for a while when I was a boy—"

"Stop it!" I said sharply, holding up my hand. "We're not going to start on the phony mother stories again." He'd driven me crazy the last time we'd worked together with all the things his mother had supposedly done or worked at—an interior decorator, a Cajun restaurant owner, a wedding photographer who'd once worked for *Life* magazine. He even claimed she'd been a clown with the circus. Tonight particularly, I was in no mood for any kind of lying from *any* man.

"You think I'm lyin'?" he asked, his face amiable.

"I think you think it's funny and it's not."

"I swear everything I told you was true. Swear it on the Alamo."

"You need to get all this put away. You can't stay here."

"Okay," he said, getting up slowly, watching my face with a curiosity. "As my pawpaw Boudreaux would say, what's got you all het up?"

"Nothing. Just get that stuff put away. And remember you can't stay here after nine o'clock. You got it?"

"Yes, ma'am," he said in a slow, sarcastic drawl. "I

definitely got it. So, havin' a little trouble down at the ranch house with the big boss?"

"Why don't you just shut up?" I snapped, annoyed that he'd zeroed in on exactly what was bothering me. I walked past him to the trunk that had held Maple's scrapbook to look for Garvey's letters.

"Well, no need to sharpen your claws on *my* balls, Miz Harper," he said. "Bein' divorced and all, I reckon I've experienced that particular pleasure already."

Ignoring him, I dug through the trunk of old *Life* and *Look* magazines and novels that were obviously hers—all of them matched the titles on the embroidered tea towels. There was no packet of letters from Garvey. Maybe, when she left, she took them with her. Now that would be odd. Murder your husband and then take his love letters with you. What a crazy thing to do.

If, the little voice said, she murdered him.

What I really needed to see was the police file on Garvey Sullivan's murder. And the newspaper stories. I knew it was wishful thinking, but I wanted Maple and Garvey's love to have been real, not just some marriage of convenience because of the war or her desire to escape Appalachian poverty.

But first I had to go home and fight with my husband.

I inhaled deeply, wishing like heck that Del Hernandez had never shown up.

And I was feeling a bit guilty for snapping at Detective Hudson. He was annoying with his mother stories, but he didn't deserve the brunt of my anger at Gabe.

I turned to apologize just as I saw him folding up a small quilt.

"Wait," I said. "Let me see that before you put it away."

"It was at the bottom of the trunk," he said. "Wrapped in paper. But the paper just disintegrated when I took it out so we'd better get some of that acid paper you were talking about."

"Acid-free," I corrected, taking the quilt out of his hands. It was a baby quilt. Exquisitely hand quilted, the stitches almost perfect. It was an unusual pattern for a crib quilt—bow tie. And unusual colors, red and green striped print fabric used on the bow ties with an overall white background. Individualistic and bold. Uncaring of convention. I knew it had to have been made by Maple herself.

"Oh, Maple," I murmured, running my hand over the stitches. "You always had to be different."

Why didn't she take it with her? If she'd been pregnant, that would have made sense. But then, nothing about the scenario around her disappearance made sense. Definitely tomorrow I was going to visit my old history professor Russell Hill and not only get his take on the Sullivans, but perhaps find out whom I could talk to who knew them back then and had more impartial memories than Nadine.

I carefully folded it and handed it back to the detective.

"I do that with my murder victims," he said, placing the quilt back in the trunk, then shutting it.

"Do what?"

"Talk to them. It's kinda weird, I know. But it helps me remember they were real living human beings, not just a name in a police report."

We looked at each other for a long ten seconds. His deep brown eyes were pink-rimmed with fatigue and so dark I couldn't see his pupils. Eyes so dark they didn't tell you anything about the man. Eyes that fit more with my husband's black hair than Detective Hudson's brownish-blond. I broke away before he did, suddenly feeling disoriented.

"I have to get home," I said. "Let's get these trunks locked."

Outside, the rain had slowed down to a heavy mist.

"Good luck back at the ranch," he said as I climbed into my truck.

I didn't answer or even glance at him in my rearview mirror as I pulled out of the parking lot and headed toward the unavoidable conflict I knew was waiting for me at home.

11

BENNI

"WHERE HAVE YOU been?" Gabe demanded the minute I walked through the door. "It's past ten o'clock. I called your cell phone three times and you never answered."

"I turned it off," I said, setting down Maple's scrapbook and bending down to scratch behind Scout's ears.

"Why?"

"Because I wasn't in the mood to talk to you. Besides, I thought you'd be plenty busy being a big broad shoulder for Del-li-lah to cry on."

"We were finished with dinner by eight o'clock."

"You say that like I'm supposed to give you a medal. Gee, I'm *so* proud of you, Gabe. You only managed to spend two hours comforting your ex-lover. What a good husband you are. I guess I should thank you for not spending the whole night holding her hand. Or whatever." I peeled off my damp jacket, threw it on the sofa, and headed for the bedroom to take off my wet shirt and jeans.

"You're being childish," he said, following me.

"Just call me silly and immature, but not wanting my husband to date an ex-lover while we're married is just one of my childish little demands."

"How many times do I have to tell you we're just friends."

"Men and women can't be just friends."

"*You* have male friends."

"Not ones who've seen me naked."

We glared at each other, both too angry to go on.

He broke the impasse, inhaled deeply, and said, "Look, I know this is hard for you to understand, but Del and I . . . we . . . it's a cop thing. We were partners. She saved my ass more times than I can remember. For pity's sakes, Benni, I've known her since she was fifteen. Her dad died and she's depressed. There is nothing happening between us except talk. Can't you be a little more understanding? Please?" He held out his hand.

I stared at him a minute, ignoring his outstretched hand. Was I being unreasonable? Or was I being the most naive wife in San Celina? Heaven knows, I wanted to believe him. But the memory of them sitting there last night at Ling's laughing and teasing each other, *knowing* their history while I sat ignorant and smiling, was like eating a mouthful of clay.

"You should have told me your history with her before we went to dinner. I feel like a fool."

"When was I supposed to do that? Right after I introduced you in my office? Benni, meet Del, my ex-partner who will be joining us for dinner. Oh, by the way, I've also made love to her. Any questions before we order our sweet and sour pork?"

His words struck with the force of an axe blow. How I wished he would have used "had sex" or "slept with" or even any of the cruder terms to describe the act. Saying he made love to her told me something about them I didn't want to know.

"I can't talk about this anymore," I said, choking on the words. "Let's discuss it tomorrow."

He shrugged. "I don't see what there is to discuss. As far as I'm concerned, you are overreacting."

I bit back my response, knowing that there was no point

in fighting about this anymore tonight. We'd just have to go to bed angry at each other. Not, I'm sure, a therapist's preferred method to resolving marriage conflicts. How many times had I heard and read that couples should never go to bed angry? I guess those people had never had jobs and lives they had to see to the next day. Sometimes things just looked better in the morning . . . or at least easier. We went to sleep with our backs to each other, the storm beating hard outside, rattling the thin glass of our bedroom window.

I woke up earlier than usual after a restless night full of dreams I couldn't recall in detail. It took a moment after my eyes opened to remember why I felt so sad and abandoned. The storm had passed and the sun was shining through the pale lacy curtains. Snowflake patterns fluttered across the oak floor. Next to me, Gabe's side was empty and cool.

He was sitting at the kitchen table reading the newspaper, his T-shirt and shorts still damp from his run.

"Hi," I mumbled, heading straight for the coffeepot.

"Good morning." He didn't look up from the paper.

We didn't exchange more than a few more words before he stood up and went into the bedroom to shower and dress for work.

"What're our plans for dinner tonight?" he asked, coming back into the kitchen carrying his leather briefcase. He checked his tie in the toaster's reflection.

"I have a dinner date with Elvia," I lied. "So you're on your own. I might be late. We're going over wedding stuff so I won't have any time to pack or move anything tonight. Are you free to move some stuff?"

He shrugged and didn't answer my question. "Guess I'll see you when I see you then."

"Yep." Fine, I thought. We'll just leave it all to the last minute.

He gave Scout a pat on the head and left without another word.

Well, fine, I thought. That was sure smart of you, Benni

Harper. Give him another night free so he can see Del.

Oh, can it, the cynical side of me said. You can't *make* someone want to be with you. Or love you.

"Enough whining," I said out loud, abruptly pushing back my chair and standing up. Scout jumped up, hoping for a biscuit or a trip.

"We're getting on with business, Scooby-Doo," I told him, picking up the breakfast dishes and dumping them in the sink. "This is just a bump in the road. I'll just hold on and wait for her to leave." He barked in response.

I quickly pulled on clean black Wranglers, a sage green handknit sweater that always brought me compliments, and shined my black boots. I would look good even if I felt like crap. "We've got a lot to do today, my boy. And it's your lucky day because you're coming with me."

He ran over to the sofa, stuck his nose under the cushions, and brought out a shocking pink tennis ball, dropping it at my feet.

I scratched under his chin. "No time for ball today, my friend."

We started off at the folk art museum, where at eight o'clock things were already busy as a Christmas Eve bus station. The frantic catastrophes were something I welcomed. Anything was preferable to thinking about my own problems. I managed to solve everyone's immediate dilemmas and was back out the door by 10 A.M. I called Russell Hill and he said he had a free period from eleven to one and to meet him at his office. I was anxious to pick his brain about Garvey and Maple Sullivan. I left Scout in D-Daddy's capable care and promised I'd be back in a couple of hours.

"I'll be here all day, *chère*," he replied.

"Hey, Benni," Bobbie Lee called as I walked through the museum on my way out. "Met your buddy the Cajun cop yesterday."

"Part Cajun," I said. "Or so he claims. I wouldn't take anything he says real seriously, if I were you. He's kind of a bullshitter."

"Be that as it may, he's a cutie," she said. "If I wasn't already romantically attached, I'd go for him myself."

"You girls talking about that sheriff's detective in here yesterday?" Ruth Gibson said. "The one combing through those trunks?" She was the president of the Wandering Foot Quilt Guild in Los Osos. A snowy-haired woman with a bawdy sense of humor, she'd raised four sons and one daughter, all attorneys, so she was never without an opinion. "Can't be shy after raising that group," she'd always say.

"I like him," she said, elbowing me in the side. "That husband of yours is a good-looking man, but I'd leave him in a New York minute for that sheriff's detective." She snapped her fingers for emphasis.

"Well, Ruth, wait'll you get to know him a little better before making any plans to leave your husband," I said, glancing at my watch. I didn't want to be late for Professor Hill so he could tease me about how *some things* never change. It became a real joke between us by my senior year, my inability to make it to any of his classes on time. "He gets more annoying with time."

"Oh, sweetie, you'll learn when you're my age that kind of annoying's fun," she said laughing. "Keeps you on your toes."

"I'm spending more than enough time on my toes these days. You can have him."

Walking through the Cal Poly campus always made me feel young again. Because of its agricultural roots it seemed to have a homier feel to me than other college campuses I'd visited. Being able to buy milk and ice cream in the student store produced by the Ag Department's cows gave it a connection with our country's rural roots that most other California universities had long lost.

Professor Hill was already in his cramped, book-lined office even though I'd arrived fifteen minutes before our scheduled appointment.

"I can come back if you're busy," I said, poking my head through the open door.

"You're early!" He stood up behind his beige metal desk, brushing crumbs off the front of his dark blue wide-wale corduroy slacks. "What a surprise! Cookie? My granddaughter made them." He held out a tin of oatmeal cookies. "Would you like some coffee?"

"Thanks," I said, taking a cookie. "And yes, coffee would be nice. Cream and sugar and I *am* known to be on time once in a while. When the company deserves it."

"Sit down, sit down." He gestured at the chair next to his desks. While he fixed my coffee, I nibbled on the moist cookie, the first thing I'd had to eat all day, savoring its sharp cinnamon taste.

"It's so good seeing you, my dear," he said, setting the steaming mug next to me. His neat salt-and-pepper goatee and kind gray eyes seemed unchanged from seventeen years ago when I'd been a student in his classes. "How's married life treating you? I must admit, the missus and I get quite the kick out of seeing your picture every so often in the society pages. Wearing a dress yet." His eyes twinkled with amusement.

I gave a half smile. "The sacrifices one makes for love."

"And is love treating you well?" He settled back in his chair, stroking his goatee. His voice, as even and calm as his gray eyes, beckoned confidences I wasn't willing to give.

"Pretty good," I said, trying to keep my face neutral.

His shaggy gray eyebrows lowered in question.

"Gabe's a handful," I admitted. "But we're doing fine. Really."

He nodded his head, watching me over tented fingers. I could tell he didn't believe me. Was my life that much of an open book? How did people acquire a poker face? If there were classes, I needed to sign up.

"I'm here to ask you some historical questions," I said, putting down my cookie and reaching inside my backpack for a notebook. "About an old San Celina family."

"You know there is nothing I love better than pontificating on the foibles of our local historical figures," he said cheerfully. He leaned forward, resting his elbows on his knees. "Fire away."

"Maple and Garvey Sullivan."

His pale lips turned up into a small, sad smile. "Ah, yes, San Celina's infamous murderess."

"Alleged murderess," I said.

He nodded his head in approval. "You are technically correct, my dear. They never actually proved she killed her husband. But even I, who have a fondness for soiled doves, and for her in particular, must admit the evidence points overwhelmingly in her direction." He picked up his chipped mug which was printed with the saying DON'T KNOW MUCH ABOUT HERSTORY. . . . , and took a sip. "What's brought Maple Sullivan to your attention?"

"I was asked by the historical society to catalog her belongings."

"Part of the Sullivan house reconstruction, no doubt."

I nodded. "When I started going through her things, I just became interested in the crime. I read her love letters to Garvey and they've made me suspect that she's innocent."

He sat back in his chair and rested his hands over his small belly. "Fair enough. So, convince me."

That had always been his method as a teacher and was one that worked well with history students. He taught us that history was more than just recorded facts, that history was also the remembered past. That people's memories, oral history, whether written or verbal, was as accurate, if not more accurate, than the facts found in newspapers and other official historical documents.

"Memory is more than just a function of electrical currents in your brain," he would lecture us in his soft, monotone voice. The voice that would often lull many of his students into a dreamlike stupor on warm spring days. I, fascinated by the whole concept of memory and time and how the past and the present blend every second into one, never dozed in his classes. "Remember, humans are the only animals that know that we live at the same time we actually live. What a gift that is." He'd clasp his hands together in wonder.

"Well," I said slowly, trying to collect my thoughts and present a concise, believable reason why I thought she might be innocent. "I don't so much believe she didn't kill Garvey as that maybe the whole story wasn't told. I think, no, make that *sense*, that maybe she didn't, but I know for sure that we don't know the whole story." I sat forward, trying to convince my former teacher's noncommittal face. "I know, I'm not being clear. But it's her letters to him. They were so ... loving and hopeful ... that I can't imagine her falling in love with another man and plotting with him to kill her husband. Not so quickly. I mean, it was only three years after they met that this happened." I threw up my hands in exasperation. "When I say it out loud, I *know* how ridiculous it sounds. I know letters can lie. I know that even the most sincere love can go sour."

I heard my voice catch with that statement and continued quickly, trying to cover it. "I also know that back during the war there were lots of marriages of convenience as well as those done on the spur of the moment, and it appears that Maple and Garvey's might have been one of those. But it just seems to me that everyone assumed she killed him without looking deeper into it. I mean, maybe the guy she was supposedly having an affair with did it. He disappeared too, from what I hear."

"Mitchell Warner," he said. "Worked as a reporter for the *San Celina Tribune* during the war years. Part of the sporting goods store Warners." He scratched the side of his nose with a finger. "So, have you questioned any of the Warner family yet?"

I shook my head no. "I decided to start with picking your brain and go from there. This is my game plan." I opened my notebook and read off to him the list I had made at the library last night.

"One, see Professor Hill." I smiled at him. "Two, find out if police file for Sullivan murder is still available. Get copy. Three, read old newspaper accounts of the crime. Four, interview Warner family members about Mitchell Warner. Five, check Internet for whereabouts of Maple Sullivan and Mitchell Warner." I glanced up at him. "That's a long shot, I know. They most likely took on new identities, but you should never leave off doing something just because it seems obvious. Some teacher told me that."

His eyes crinkled in approval. "Good girl."

I continued reading him my list. "Six, find out where historical society keeps Garvey's belongings and go through them. Seven, question people alive during war years about the crime." I looked up from my notebook. "I'm hoping to find a cop that worked on the case, though that's probably expecting the impossible." I flipped to a clean page. "That's it so far, though I'm hoping you'll give me some more directions."

"Sounds like you're doing just fine on your own, my dear. You learned your lessons well. What does your husband think of your investigation?"

I chewed on my bottom lip for a moment, then said, "I haven't talked much with him about it. He's pretty busy with modern-day crime these days though I imagine he'd be glad to know I was working on something that has a very low danger level."

Russell chuckled and stroked his goatee. "I would imagine so. Your exploits have put him in the hot seat a few times, I'd venture to guess."

I grimaced. "Your guess would be accurate. Anyway, what do you remember about the incident? If I recall correctly, you were in your early teens at the beginning of the war. And your father was mayor, right?"

"Good memory. That's right, he ousted Garvey Sullivan's father, Arthur, though Arthur wasn't too upset about it. Arthur Sullivan didn't have time for politics during those years, he was too busy making money. During the war the Sullivans grew even wealthier than they already were raising beef for the military, overseeing the construc-

tion on Camp Riley as well as owning quite a few of the
other businesses in town that served the military and their
families. He and Brady O'Hara competed neck and neck
in the department store wars. It was a joke among the
locals about which Irishman was going to win out. My
mother preferred Sullivan's. She said their selection was
better, but I suspect it had more to do with the store being
five blocks closer to our house. Arthur and Garvey were
busy men during those years."

"Why wasn't Garvey in the service?"

"Age. He turned forty shortly after the war started."

I nodded, my guess verified. "How old was Maple? I
can't seem to find that anywhere."

"A lot younger than Garvey. Early twenties, I'd guess."

"Quite a difference."

"Yes, and it caused some talk, if I remember correctly."

"Did you ever cross paths with them?"

"Saw Garvey lots of times. His father, Arthur, was very
helpful to my father when he was taking over the may-
orship. Father used to take me to lunch with Arthur and
Garvey Sullivan and I'd listen to them talk about budgets
and working with the city council. It mostly bored me
until the conversation turned to wrangling bulls and cattle
drives. I had brief dreams of being a cowboy then, when
I wasn't dreaming of being a fighter pilot and shooting
down Messerschmidts for God, the flag, and Franklin
Roosevelt."

I laughed at the picture of my intellectual, soft-spoken
teacher being either a cowboy or a fighter pilot. "What
did you think of Garvey?"

He pulled at the side of his cheek. "He didn't talk
much. Wasn't at all like his father, who was one of those
Irishmen who had a story for every occasion. My father,
who was quite garrulous himself, often said that Arthur
was a hard act to follow. Arthur drew people to him like
crows to a ripe cornfield. The man loved to laugh, as they
say. And as genetics is wont to do, Garvey was the polar
opposite. He was quiet and thoughtful. He always handed

me a quarter after lunch and told me to buy myself some comics, that the laughs were on him. But he never smiled when he said it."

"He sounded like a nice man."

"Yes, that's exactly what Garvey was. A nice man. Nothing bold or loud or special, at least in the way the world calls special. I never saw him say a bad word or snap at anyone. He was meticulous and careful. That's the best word I would describe him as, careful. As personable as his father was, he also had a firecracker temper that was legend among his employees."

"Maybe that's why Garvey was so quiet and careful," I said.

"Could be."

After jotting a few lines down in my notebook I said, "So, what about Maple? Did you ever meet her? What were your impressions of her?"

He leaned farther back in his chair, a look of almost adoration smoothing out his fine wrinkles. "Ah, Maple Bennett Sullivan. I have a confession to make."

I raised my eyebrows. "Don't forget, I'm married to the police chief. I'm morally obligated to report any crime to him."

He chuckled. "My dear, if people were arrested for this, our jails would be a thousand times more crowded than they currently are. She was my first crush. And oh, what a crush it was."

"You sly devil," I said, slapping his knee. "Tell me all about her. Not that any of it will be accurate now, seeing as you viewed her through the cheesecloth of a teenage boy's lust."

"She was simply the most beautiful woman I'd ever seen," he said, reaching over and picking up his mug of coffee. "Not counting Marie, of course."

"Good thing you added that because I was going to rat on you."

"Wouldn't have to. Marie knows everything about me,

I promise. You can't be married forty-three years and hide much."

"So, about Maple."

"Maple Sullivan was the first woman who treated me like I was something besides a gangly adolescent even when I still was one. She had a way of listening to you that made you feel as if whatever you were telling her was worthy of a book. I'm sure I bored her to tears with my thirteen-year-old opinions on Hitler and Mussolini, but she listened and asked questions as if she were going to write a feature article for *Life*. That's probably what made her such a crackerjack reporter."

"I was going to ask you about that. Wasn't it pretty unusual for a woman to be a newspaper reporter in the forties? I looked through some old *Tribunes* yesterday at the library, and except for the society pages, all the by-lines were given to men."

"Women were taking over a lot of men's jobs back then, but you're right, it was unusual. Maple was a very good writer and it didn't hurt that her father-in-law owned the newspaper."

I flipped a page over on my notebook and wrote that down. "Yes, that probably helped. I haven't found out much about her. I've figured out through her letters and their wedding announcement that they met in Kentucky when she was working as a waitress. That was the beginning of March 1942. It appears they had a fast three-day courtship and he asked her to marry him. They exchanged twelve letters, at least that's how many she wrote him. Two months later on May first, they were married at the Santa Celine Mission. The announcement said her father and mother were Kentucky farmers. Her letters indicated that her father didn't own the land he farmed so I assumed he was either a tenant farmer or a sharecropper. Not a society girl by any means."

"That she wasn't," Russell agreed. "That's what was so refreshing about her, I think. She never mentioned her life before coming to San Celina, at least not in my young presence, but I remember when she joined us for lunch a few times, she always waited until the men had started out and she went back and added money to the tip. As an idealistic youth, I found that utterly charming. As I do even more now. That small act certainly substantiates her background." He leaned back in his chair and stared at a child's painting of Laguna Lake on his wall. His eyes grew dreamy behind his tortoiseshell glasses. "She had the most beautiful, wavy dark brown hair. The color of bittersweet chocolate."

I hated interrupting his memories, but the color of her hair and his remembered adolescent longings really didn't tell me much about the woman. "Russell, tell me the truth, do you think she killed her husband?"

His eyes focused again and he looked at me thoughtfully. "Well, she was a young woman full of life. Always happy and busy, interested in what was going on around her. Only went through the eighth grade, but you'd never know it. I'd venture to say if they'd tested her IQ, she would have been close to a genius. But there wasn't a single snobbish air about her even though her husband was one of the most prominent men on the Central Coast, indeed, in California."

"So," I said, smiling. "You didn't answer my question. Do you think she had an affair and killed her husband to be with her lover?"

He inhaled deeply, letting it out in an even deeper sigh. "My girl, with all his prominence and education, Garvey was no match for her. As I said, he was a rather sober individual. I can't even imagine what those two would have had to talk about when they were alone. And he was so much older than her . . ."

"So you're saying that it's not inconceivable that she'd look for fun somewhere else. Like with another reporter at work."

He nodded, his face miserable. He obviously didn't like thinking about his first crush being so human as to have a tawdry affair with a fellow employee. "Mitchell Warner would have been a real attraction to any young woman. Smart, rich, fun, closer to her own age."

"Why wasn't he in the service?"

"Some medical reason, I imagine. That was the only reason a man was let out of the draft during the war. He played football during his college years so he was fit at one time. But who knows? He was the baby in the family, the apple of his mother's eye. It wouldn't be the first time some political strings had been pulled to keep some mother's son out of a war."

"So he worked for the Sullivans at the *Tribune*. Why didn't he work in his father's sporting goods store?"

"The *Tribune* was only partially owned by the Sullivans. The Warner family owned the other half."

"Those prominent families back then had all these interesting connections."

"Not unlike today, my dear. Oh, and one last bit of information. Mitchell and Garvey were best friends even though there was a fifteen-year difference in their ages. Both loved to hunt and fish."

"That verifies what Nadine told me." I sighed and leaned back in my chair. "My belief in Maple's innocence is getting a little rocky, I must admit."

He ran his fingers through his graying mop of hair. "No one would love it better than me for you to find out that Maple wasn't involved with the death of Garvey Sullivan, but I must admit, it's a long shot."

I closed my notebook and stood up. "It certainly can't hurt me to ask a few questions and do a little research." Besides, I thought, it'll keep me busy while Del is hanging around. Better my imagination run wild with a past affair than a possible current one. My stomach churned when I actually thought the word I'd been conciously avoiding.

"Finding out more about the past only helps us prepare better for the future," Russell said, standing up and holding out his hands to me. "That is, if we heed and learn the lessons from the past."

I took his hands and squeezed them. "Well said, Professor Hill."

Outside, the sunny day was already waning. Storm clouds hovered over the tops of the hills surrounding San Celina, threatening another downpour. This unpredictable weather so close to the Mardi Gras festival and parade was making everyone involved skittish. Twice in the past the festival and parade had to be called off because of stormy weather, and a lot of people were disappointed because a year's worth of work was for nothing. Hopefully, the clouds would just hang out and look menacing until after Saturday.

I stood next to my truck in the parking lot trying to decide my next move. Though I knew I had a lot of things I should be doing instead of this probably futile investigation of a crime that no one cared about anymore, something in me wouldn't let up. I dialed D-Daddy at the museum on my cell phone to check on Scout.

"He's doing fine, *ange*," D-Daddy said. "He's havin' him a good ole time with me, him."

"I'm going up to Paso Robles so I'll be back later than I thought. How long do you plan on staying there?"

"Don't you worry now. I'll keep the pooch until I'm done, then if you're not back, I'll drop him off at your house. Put him in the backyard."

"D-Daddy, you are a sweetheart. Thanks."

"Anything for you. By the way, your fella, he called."

"Oh, what did Gabe want?" Usually, these days, he dialed my cell phone because it was the only sure way to reach me.

"Not Gabe, your other fella."

Why would Daddy call me at the museum? He never used the phone unless it was an emergency. "Is Dove all right?"

"I guess she is," D-Daddy said, chuckling. "But I wouldn't know. I mean your *other* fella, Hud."

I tried not to growl into the phone. "D-Daddy, that's not funny. And he's not my fella."

"Tell *him* that. He wanted to know where you were, what you were up to. I told him you was off investigating a murder."

I groaned. "I wish you hadn't told him that. He's supposed to be helping me catalog the contents of Maple Sullivan's trunks and nothing else. I don't want him involved in . . . this other thing."

"Sorry," D-Daddy said, his rough voice contrite. "Didn't know what you was doing was a secret."

"It's not. I just . . . oh, forget it. I'll tell him myself. Thanks for taking care of Scout. I'll see you at the festival tomorrow."

"Good hunting," he said.

Before I could even put my key in the ignition, my cell phone rang. I checked the display. It was Elvia.

"Hey, Mrs. Littleton-to-Be, what's new?"

"Aragon-Littleton," she replied. "And I just wanted to remind you of our appointment tomorrow morning."

I was quiet for a moment, frantically searching my memory. Appointment? I didn't remember any appointment for Saturday morning. The Mardi Gras festival was tomorrow and then I had the charity costume ball that evening. What had I forgotten?

"At Jamaica You Beautiful," Elvia said, exasperated. "Facials and manicures and a trial run on my hair for the wedding." Her voice paused dramatically. "You forgot, didn't you?"

"No, no, I didn't . . ." I started, then gave up and said, "Shoot, yeah I did. What time are we supposed to be there?"

"Eight A.M. We specifically made it that early so you could get to the craft booths by ten. Benni, what is wrong with you these days? I'm the one who should be distracted, not you."

"I'm fine. I just left my date book at home. So, what are you and Emory going as to the costume ball?"

"Elizabeth Bennet and Mr. Darcy." I could imagine her smile over the phone.

"Of course, who else?" I said, laughing. *Pride and Prejudice*. I couldn't think of a more appropriate story to describe Elvia and Emory's relationship.

"What about you and Gabe?"

"I have no idea."

"What? Don't tell me you haven't got a costume yet! It's too late to get anything—"

I interrupted her. "Don't worry, *mi amiga buena*, I have a costume. Cathy picked one out for me. I just haven't looked at it yet. I'll be there in full costumed glory, I assure you. I trust Cathy, it'll be a good one."

"Good. Have to go. One of my clerks is motioning at me in panic. Looks like Bill the pickpocket is back."

I laughed. Bill was a homeless man who had a bad habit of stealing pencils and paper from Elvia's bookstore. Not a lot, just enough to continue his rambling diary. She'd explained to him many times she'd be happy to *give* him all the paper and pencils he needed, but he just enjoyed stealing them more. "Good luck and see you tomorrow."

I had just driven off Cal Poly's campus and was on my way to the freeway, when my cell phone rang again. I was beginning to wonder if the convenience of this new technology was worth the loss of peace and quiet.

"Hello?"

"Black and white," Dove said.

"Huh?"

"A black-and-white wedding. The wedding party wears white and everyone else wears black. Very elegant."

"And you could serve licorice and marshmallows for appetizers," I said. "Blackened fish and white rice for the main dish. You could walk down the aisle to Paul McCartney and Micheal Jackson singing 'Ebony and Ivory.' "

"I'm serious," she said, not laughing. "What do you really think?"

I gave up trying to be impartial. "Let me rephrase and shorten my comments . . . yuck?"

"Fine." The phone went dead.

Weddings and marriage and all the tumultuous feelings between men and women tangled in my mind on my drive over Rosita Pass to Paso Robles. I was so wrapped up in my thoughts that I was only vaguely aware of the lush green hills and young calves butting their mamas' sides, something I usually loved to watch. Early spring on the Central Coast is its most physically beautiful time, a season of renewal and hope. But in my life, early spring had become a mixture of upheaval and confusion, sorrow and joy. Jack and I were married in early spring. Fifteen years later, Jack died in early spring. Then a year after that, Gabe and I were married in early spring.

Warner's Sporting Goods was located on River Avenue, the main street that bisected the center of Paso Robles. It was in an old brick building catty-corner from the city park, a square of green lawn and mature trees that was a popular meeting place for Paso Roblans from birth to ninety. According to the MidState Bank's electronic thermometer, the temperature was seventy degrees, ten degrees warmer than San Celina, so I pulled off my jacket and shoved it behind my seat. I parked across the street and waited ten minutes before the traffic slowed enough for me to cross. Paso Robles was going through an even more radical change than San Celina. More and more city people from the Bay area and Los Angeles were discovering this longtime ranching community. Housing developments and the inevitable chain stores and businesses that followed were turning this once small, traditional Western town into a sometimes uncomfortable mix of affluent retirees, new young families who worked at the mushrooming businesses, and oldtime ranching and Hispanic residents.

A young man, about fifteen or sixteen, with a flat-top haircut was the only person behind the counter. He had what appeared to be a schoolbook open in his lap but he was talking on the phone. The guilty expression that flitted across his freckled face when I walked up told me it was probably his girlfriend.

"Gotta go. I have a customer." He hung up quickly and gave me a wide smile. His front tooth had a small chip out of it, giving him a mischievous look. He looked so much like Frankie, it had to be his son. "Can I help you?" he asked politely.

"I was wondering if Frankie . . . uh, Frank Warner is around."

He held up one nail-bitten finger and picked up the phone. "Dad, some lady's looking for you." He listened for a moment. "I don't know. She called you Frankie." He looked over at me. "Uh . . . who are you?" Then I heard a voice over the phone snap his name. "Sorry," he said to me, his expression twisted in chagrin. "May I tell him who's asking?"

I smiled, remembering when Frankie had been as awkward as his son. "Tell him it's Benni and that he'd better get his two left feet out here now." I said it loud enough that his son didn't have to repeat it.

The young man grinned at me. "He said he'd be right out."

Minutes later, Frankie Warner came out of a door in the back of the store. "Benni Harper!" he called across the barbells and bicycle helmets. "It's been a million years since I've seen you, old girl. When was that anyway?" When he reached the front of the store, he caught me up in a spine-crushing hug. For a moment, my feet actually left solid earth.

Laughing, I hugged him back. "Now put me down, you big ole bull. It has been almost three years. At Jack's funeral. You look great."

He let me down gently, but still kept hold of one hand, his face sad for a moment. He and Jack had played high school football together. Jack was a quarterback; Frankie a defensive tackle. He turned to his son. "Hey, Bryan, this is an old, old friend of mine. Benni Harper. We go way back."

"Let's delete one of those olds, okay?" I said, patting his hand. I let go and held a hand out to his son. "Nice to meet you. Your dad and I went to school together from the first grade on."

"Cool," he said, shaking my hand. He glanced back over at the phone. Old school friends of his father's weren't nearly as interesting as the girl he'd had to hang up on so unceremoniously.

I turned back to Frank. "Do you have an office where we can talk in private? I've got a couple of questions for you."

"Sure," he said, taking my elbow and guiding me toward the door in the back. "Watch the store, Bryan."

"Sure thing, Dad." When I glanced back, he was already dialing the phone.

After settling down in Frank's spacious office and asking the requisite "Have you seen" and "Whatever happened to" questions, Frank settled his still linebacker-size body into his chair, linked his fingers behind his head, and said, "So, what questions do you have for me?"

I shifted in the padded office chair, feeling a bit embarrassed now by my investigation. "This may sound silly to you, but hear me out, okay?"

"Fire away."

It took me about twenty minutes to tell the condensed version of who and what I was investigating and why. During my explanation, he'd unlocked his hands and sat forward in his chair, resting his thick blond forearms on his desk.

"So, what I was wondering was this," I said. "What do you know about your great-uncle Mitch and do you think your grandpa would talk to me about it?"

He patted the side of his blond crew cut. "When I was growing up, things were whispered about Uncle Mitch. We kids knew he'd done something awful, that he'd brought disgrace to the family, but it was never talked about openly."

"I know how that goes," I said, nodding.

"So I never pursued it. You know me, if it didn't have something to do with sports, it didn't interest me. Now Rosie was different." Rosie was his only sister, older than us by ten years. "She inhaled all those Nancy Drew books when she was a kid. Thought herself quite the detective. Decided to find out the real story." He leaned back in his chair and chuckled.

"So, did she?"

"I guess. Though all I know is what you already know. That Great-Uncle Mitch ran off with this Maple Sullivan after she killed her husband."

"Why does everyone assume she did it?" I asked. "I mean, no offense, but couldn't your uncle have just as easily pulled the trigger?"

He shrugged and leaned forward, reaching for a Roledex on the corner of his desk. "I agree with you. Frankly, I have no idea why he wasn't suspected. There must have been some evidence that pointed to her." He started flipping through the Roledex. "I'll give you Rosie's number and you can call her. After her divorce, she built a new place up here outside Paso. Gramps is living with her now in a guest house out back of her stables. She breeds Arabians."

"Do you think he'd talk to me?"

The corners of his lips moved downward and he shook his head. "Doubt it. He's of that age, you know. Past best left in the past, yadda, yadda." He dialed Rosie's number and, after a quick explanation, handed the phone to me.

"Hi, Rosie," I said. "Benni Harper."

"Nice talking to you again. Congratulations on your marriage even if I'm a tad late." Her voice was a rich alto with a slight roughness that overtakes some women's vocal cords when they reach middle age.

"Thanks," I said abruptly. "I'm sorry to interrupt your day . . ."

"Not a problem," she said, laughing. "I take care of ten horses, two dogs, a tortoise, three ducks, my new grandson and Gramps. Any distraction from the real world is welcome." There was a slight pause. "Sorry, putting out my cigarette." That explained her husky voice. "Look, why don't you come on out. I'm only about fifteen minutes from the store. This would be easier to talk about in person. I mean, if you have time."

"Sure," I said. "That would be great."

Frank drew me a map to her place on a piece of Warner's Sporting Goods stationery. After shooting the breeze with him a few more minutes, I drove out of town on a highway going east. Twenty minutes and many twists and turns later, after passing too many twenty-acre ranchettes with homes that looked like something out of *Architectural Digest,* I found Appleman Way. I turned down the narrow road marked by a plain black mailbox with WARNER ARABIANS painted in neat red letters. Frank had told me that she'd taken back her maiden name after the divorce. The road was lined with leafy, full-grown shade trees that must have cost a small fortune to plant. The concrete circle driveway was surrounded by thick hedges five feet tall. I parked directly in front of the house.

Rosie was waiting for me on the wraparound porch of a new two-story farm-style house. She sat in a wicker rocker that matched the navy blue trimming on the white clapboard house. A cigarette dangled from her lips, which she stubbed out in a large ashtray on the floor next to her.

"Good seeing you again, Benni," she said, reaching out a dry, weather-worn hand that had obviously picked more than a few horses' hooves in its lifetime. She was long-legged and strong-looking with shoulder-length, reddish hair streaked with white. Beneath her pale-lashed gray eyes there were bluish half circles. She was dressed in a clean gray T-shirt and faded, dirt-stained Wranglers.

"Likewise," I said, shaking her hand.

"Join me." She nodded over at a matching chair. "Gramps and my grandson, Trace, are both taking naps and nothing else on the spread needs my attention right this moment, so I'm yours. Would you like something to drink?" She nodded at a small wicker table that held the makings of gin and tonics.

"No, thanks. I'm fine."

"Mind if I do?"

I shook my head. "Not at all." Actually, it could work in my favor. A little liquor always did loosen people's tongues, a sad but true fact that I suspected all investigators knew and took advantage of when they could.

As she mixed a drink, obviously not her first, she talked to me over her shoulder. "So, you're looking into Great-Uncle Mitch's little indiscretion. Well, good luck to you, girl. Hope you find out more than I did."

My heart sank a little. Great, she probably didn't know any more than I did and just wanted some company. I sighed inwardly and settled deeper into the wicker chair, prepared to listen to the rambling of a bored, semidrunk woman. The next hour would be wasted, but then, what else did I have to do?

She sat down next to me, held up her pack of Winstons with a question on her face.

"No, thanks, but go right ahead," I said.

She lit up another cigarette, thoughtfully holding it to the side away from me, and took a sip of her drink. "Okay, now," she finally said. "Great-Uncle Mitch. He worked with Maple Sullivan on the paper. He was their sports reporter, of course." She gave a small wet cough. "He and Maple had an affair and then Maple killed her husband, Garvey, whose family was as prominent as ours, then they both headed for Mexico to live out their lives drinking margaritas and writing love sonnets to each other."

"They went to Mexico?" I said, sitting forward. "How did you find that out?"

She brought her cigarette to her pale, unpainted lips and inhaled deeply, blowing a crooked smoke ring. "Sorry, that's just my facetious little story. Actually, I have no idea where they went. To be honest, I don't know much more than you, and after doing some research back in the eighties when I was really into genealogy, I even hired a private detective to try and find any trace of them. Nothing. Nada. He was the one who told me they most likely went to a foreign country, which would make them almost impossible to find. Especially after such a long time and especially if they changed their names, which they most likely did."

"What about your grampa? Would he ever talk to you about the incident?"

She frowned, picking a piece of tobacco off her lip and wiping it on the edge of her gray T-shirt. "Like Frankie probably told you, that was the one big black blot on the Warner family history book. Gramps wouldn't even allow Mitch's name to be spoken. Though when my grammy was alive, she used to tell us that Mitch was not a killer, nor would he help someone who had killed, to not believe everything that was whispered about Uncle Mitch. She told us that we should never talk about it to anyone, but that we shouldn't believe what was said or written. She said Mitch was a fine, decent man. A good Catholic. And Grammy didn't bestow that kind of praise lightly. She was a six-day-a-week Catholic. She believed in her brother-in-law in a way that his own brother never did. I always wondered about that, why she defended him to us kids. I thought at the time that maybe she was in love with him or something. I was twenty at the time and thought love— that is, sexual love—was behind every motivation. Thinking about it later, I realized that Uncle Mitch was only ten when Gramps and Grammy got married, and Grammy being an only child, she probably really thought of him as her little brother."

"So your grandpa didn't agree with her. About Mitch's innocence, I mean."

She took another drag from her cigarette. A red-and-white corgi with one blind eye bounded up the three steps to the porch and, after a quick sniff at my legs, settled down in front of Rosie. She stretched out a bare foot and stroked his back. "I didn't say that. I think that maybe he did agree with her. He never said his brother did it. He just wouldn't talk about it. I think there's more to the story than he's telling and Grammy knew it."

"That's exactly how I feel," I said eagerly. "That there's more to the story."

"Well," she said in a lazy voice. "If you find out anything, clue me in. I hit nothing but brick walls." She gave a sly smile. "But then again, I didn't have your official police connections or expertise in winnowing out the truth."

"Don't believe everything you read," I said, giving an uncomfortable laugh. My few stumblings into crime had, unfortunately, been reported in the same paper Maple and Mitch had worked for.

"I think it's a hoot," she said. "And I appreciate your interest. I'd honestly love to see Uncle Mitch's name cleared."

"And Maple's," I reminded her.

"Right." Rosie's unconcern for Maple and her reputation made me feel even more protective toward her. It wasn't fair that, even after all these years, it was the prominent local boy who had people caring about whether his name was cleared and not the young Kentucky farm girl who had come to San Celina armed only with her starry-eyed love and one meager trunkful of possessions.

Inside the house, a small child started crying. The corgi jumped up and barked twice.

"Okay, okay," Rosie said, slowly putting out her cigarette in the half-filled ashtray. "I'm coming. Sorry I couldn't be of more help. Good luck."

"Thanks," I said.

A louder wail caused her to roll her eyes. "Thought I was through this part of my life." She gave me a wave goodbye, then opened the screen door. "I'm coming, baby boy. Just hold on." The corgi dashed through the open door in front of her.

I was opening the door to my truck when a grizzled, old man's voice said behind me, "She's full of crap, you know."

Startled, I jerked around to face the man. He seemed to have appeared from nowhere, but I realized after a moment, that he had probably been lurking behind the hedges listening to every word we said. He appeared to be in his eighties and was dressed in new blue Levi's rolled up with large cuffs and a pale blue Western shirt. His face was red and peeling, as if he'd just had a bad sunburn, though most of it was hidden under his expensive white Stetson cowboy hat. I assumed him to be Frank and Rosie's grampa Micah.

"Excuse me?" I said.

"Crap," he repeated. "Full of it. You and her both. There ain't no more story to Mitch and that Sullivan woman and you'd best be leaving it at that. Hear me now." He poked a ragged-nailed finger at me, punctuating each word. "Hear me?"

"You must be Micah Warner," I said, unnerved by his aggressiveness, but wanting to keep him talking as long as I could. Maybe some vital piece of information would slip. "I'm Benni Harper. I'm just doing a little research for the historical society."

He didn't acknowledge my statement. "Mitch was my baby brother," he said. "I'm sick and tired of people dragging him through the mud."

"That's not my intention, Mr. Warner. I just want to know the truth."

He grabbed my forearm with an iron grip that spoke of a man who'd spent many years roping cattle. I could feel his horn-sharp calluses through my shirtsleeve. "Young woman, I know about you and I don't want you nosing about my family's business. I'm telling you to leave Mitch alone. Let his soul rest in peace."

He made the statement with such authority.

"He's dead?" I asked, trying to pull my arm from his strong grip without actually jerking it away. "How do you know that? Have you heard from him in the last fifty years?"

He released my arm abruptly, giving me a slight push. I fell awkwardly against the side of my truck. He stared at me a long minute, then said, his voice less harsh, but still tinged with anger, "What he did or didn't do is between him and his God. Do everyone a favor. Stay out of it." He turned and started back around the house.

Trembling slightly, I gave the house one last look and got into my truck, wondering if Rosie had seen my encounter with Micah. There was no doubt he knew more than he was telling and also no doubt that he was not willing to share it with me.

"Okay, Mr. Warner," I said, maneuvering the truck down the long tree-lined driveway back to the main road. "I'll just have to find out on my own."

It was seven o'clock and already dark by the time I got back to San Celina. I cruised by our old house and noted that Gabe's Corvette was gone. Obviously off drying the tears of the beautiful, yet deeply troubled Delilah Hernandez.

I pulled into the driveway and went inside. The house had that sad, pocked-wall look of a place in transition. I sent up a quick prayer that the next person who lived in this house would not have as much emotion-filled upheaval as I'd had in the time I'd lived here.

I let Scout in from the backyard, which told me Gabe had never come home. I fed him, hid a couple of biscuits in his toy box for him to root around and find later, then headed back out. Neither house in their half-empty–half-filled states felt enough like a home for me to settle down. What an odd and sad coincidence that Del would show up right at the time when I felt like Gabe and I were finally starting a real life together.

Restless and disturbed by the small bit of information Micah had let out about his brother, I wanted something to do that would completely occupy my mind. What I really wanted to do was run this whole situation with Gabe and Del by someone I trusted. Normally I'd go to either Elvia or Emory with a crisis like this, but it was only a week before their wedding and I was not going to lay any kind of marriage woes on them now. The same with Dove, who didn't need one more distraction in her harried life.

"So it's time to solve your own problems, Benni Harper," I said out loud. But darned if I could figure out what to do. Wait and see what would happen—that seemed my only mature option. My other option was shooting Del in the heart, which would certainly only add to my problems.

I drove through McDonald's and drank a chocolate shake while listening to the radio and watching teenage kids loiter in the parking lot, moving from car to car, talking and laughing. I sat there until nine o'clock, my mind hopping from Maple's situation to my own, not allowing myself to cry even though my chest grew tight and hard begging for the release. I wouldn't give Gabe or Del that power over me. At nine-twenty, I still didn't want to go home. I was determined to stay out longer than Gabe, though I had no idea why I thought that would prove anything.

Needing to kill more time, I decided to drive by the Sullivan house and take a look at it.

The last half-mile stretch before the house was lit only by my headlights, city streetlights not reaching this far out. As I turned a sharp corner, the work light shining in the octagonal barn next to the house was like a beacon. There were obviously some people up there working. When I pulled into the gravel driveway and saw who it was, I put the brakes on and threw the transmission in reverse. But not before he saw me.

I watched Detective Hudson slip his hammer into his leather toolbelt and start down the little slope toward my idling truck. He waved a hand in recognition. If I pulled away now, I'd look even sillier than I already did. I reluctantly rolled down my truck window.

"What are you doing here so late?" he asked, his dark eyes sympathetic as if he knew exactly what I'd been doing the last two hours.

12

❖ ❖ ❖

GABE

WHAT IS WRONG with her, Gabe thought for the fifth time as he stared at the unfinished paperwork on his desk. He'd been irritated by Benni's stubborn refusal to understand his relationship with Del since he'd first walked in this morning. Maggie, his assistant, had noted his mood from the moment he passed her desk hours earlier.

She'd silently handed him his mail, raised her dark eyebrows, and gestured at the full coffeepot on the credenza next to her. "Would you like a cup?"

"Yes, please," he said. "Black."

"Morning's problems haven't even started yet, boss," she murmured, pouring him a cup. On good days, he took cream and sugar.

"On the contrary," he'd replied, without elaborating. He mumbled his thanks and went into his office, closing the heavy oak door behind him.

He'd attended his morning meetings and said the appropriate things, trying not to think about Benni's words. But their persistent points kept intruding into his thoughts.

Was he wrong in not telling her about his and Del's personal relationship? Should he have pulled her aside and whispered a confession to her before they had dinner? The thought seemed ridiculous to him. What would he have said? What would that dinner have been like had she known? Women were so irrational about that sort of thing. He wasn't forcing details about her love life with Jack out of her, was he?

He knew her so well, he could almost hear her tart voice. *Yeah, well, he's not sitting at our dinner table either.*

It was late afternoon now and he rested his hand in his chin, too weary after his restless night to contemplate all these figures and facts spread out in front of him. He let his mind wander back to a time in his career when paperwork didn't encompass ninety percent of his time. He missed the drama of the street, the adrenaline of a good bust, even the crazy people he'd met and grown to like, the snitches and the liquor store owners, the pawn shop men with their hungry eyes, the fast-talking prostitutes who were there one day, gone the next, like a whisper of fog. He never felt more alive than when he worked the streets.

Except for Vietnam. There, each morning he woke still living, all his parts still attached, was a gift gladly accepted, unquestionably taken. He tried not to think too long about all the guys who didn't receive it, but instead were surprised by death with a bouncing Betty or the exploding burst of a sniper's bullet.

His phone rang, and after three rings, he reluctantly picked it up. He should have told Maggie to hold his calls. The late afternoon sun coming through his window warmed the back of his neck.

"Hey, Chief Ortiz," Del's voice said in a mocking tone. "How many paper cuts have you survived in the last hour?"

"Screw you," he said good-naturedly, glad it was her voice and not Benni's on the phone. At least with Del he didn't have to explain or apologize. She never asked and he never offered. It was so easy to fall back into their joking, easy partner relationship.

"Been there, done that," she said, giving a rumbling, deep laugh.

It was a laugh that brought back more memories, a low, cynical laugh that always connected with something broken and angry inside him. That laugh had always made him feel she understood, as much as any woman could, the edge he walked, the edge all men walked.

"Are you busy after work?" she asked, her voice flippant, but with that sadness he recognized. During dinner last night, she'd cried for her father, for the emptiness in her life. When she ran out the door, he followed her to the dark, empty parking lot and he'd held her for a moment, fearful yet excited by the quickening of his blood when he caught the sweet coconut scent of her hair.

He glanced at his wall clock. Four-thirty. "Actually, I was thinking about leaving early."

"I'm free for dinner," she said.

"Great. How about Italian?"

"Sounds wonderful. Will Benni be joining us?"

He pressed the phone closer to his ear, listening for any artifice in her voice, for the duplicity of Benni's accusations. In his mind, there were none. Only the sound of a friend asking for some of his time. If she were a man, this wouldn't even be a problem between him and Benni.

"No," he said. "She sends her regrets, but she's in the middle of wedding preparations with her best friend. She'll be really busy the next week or so."

"Oh, that's too bad," Del said. "I guess I'll have to help you kill time so you don't get lonely."

He laughed, aware of every movement of his body. He picked up a metal paper clip and bent it into tangles with one hand.

"So," she continued. "Let's not eat in town tonight, what do you say? I'm a little embarrassed about making a fool of myself in one of your local restaurants last night.

Is there anyplace we can go where we can talk without being so scrutinized?"

"Sure. There are plenty of restaurants between here and Santa Barbara."

"Thanks, Gabe. You don't know how much it means to me, you taking the time to talk. I really hope Benni doesn't mind me borrowing you for a little while."

"No problem," he said. "Absolutely no problem."

13

BENNI

I TOOK A few seconds to answer Detective Hudson, not knowing exactly what to say.

He bent down and rested his elbows on the truck's window frame. "Want to come up and see what we're doing to the barn?"

I hesitated for a moment, then said, "Sure."

He opened my door and swept his hand out in front of him. "After you, Mrs. Harper."

I walked up the rough driveway, gravel crunching like hard-packed snow under my boots, acutely aware of his presence behind me. When I reached the barn door, I stepped inside and stood for a moment, looking around. This barn was a local landmark, one I'd driven by hundreds of times. I was glad one of the groups of people in San Celina who cared about preserving San Celina heritage had decided this was worth saving. Too many of our old buildings were being torn down in the name of progress.

"We're working on the framing first," the detective said, coming up beside me. He pushed up the sleeves of his gray sweatshirt and pointed toward the barn rafters.

"Another year or so, this baby would have tumbled to the ground, the wood was so rotten. That would have been a shame."

"Yes, it would," I said, my eyes following his finger to the newly replaced framing inside the weathered structure. There were gaps in the roof wide enough to see the stars, visible now that the storm clouds had moved south. A chilly wind blew through the barn, causing me to shiver inside my flannel-lined jacket.

"Hey, I've got some hot coffee here," he said, stepping over a pile of lumber and picking up a large red thermos. "There's only one cup, but I swear I don't have any infectious diseases."

"On your mawmaw's grave?" I asked.

He laughed and untwisted the cap. "Absolutely. On my mama's good name too."

I shook my head and frowned. "Please, Detective, let's not even get into the mother thing or I'm outta here."

He held out a steaming cup of coffee. "Could you please do me one favor? Call me Hud. I think we've known each other long enough for first names, don't you?"

I took the cup and brought it up to my lips. "I suppose." One swallow of the strong, black coffee caused me to gasp, "Geeze Louise, this isn't coffee! It's hot mud."

He threw back his head and laughed. "None of that Starbucks dishwater for this Cajun boy. That there's Community brand coffee. Best on earth. Guaranteed to put hair on your chest . . . or wherever you want it."

"It's terrible," I said, handing the cup back to him.

He took it, drank after me, then said, "Say it."

"What?"

"Say my name. I won't believe you until you say it."

"Oh, for cryin' out loud . . ."

"Say it."

"You're nuts."

"Say it or I'll make you finish this coffee." He thrust the cup back into my hand.

"Okay, okay," I said, setting the cup down on a make-shift table of plywood and two sawhorses. "Hud. Hud - not - the - government - agency. Hud - like - the - movie. Hud - who - doesn't - look - at - all - like - Paul - Newman." I looked directly in his eyes. "Are you happy now?"

He gave a slow, thoughtful smile. "Ecstatic."

I cleared my throat and said, "Actually, the reason I drove by—"

"Was because you're investigating this murder of Garvey Sullivan and wanted to see the murder scene. You've decided Maple's innocent, haven't you?"

I didn't answer. It was annoying that he could read me so well.

"You hate it that I know what's going on inside you, don't you?" he said, still smiling. "Drives you crazy."

"You don't know squat," I snapped.

He shrugged. "My mistake. I was going to offer to let you inside the house, but if you're not interested . . ."

I bit the inside of my cheek, thinking. I did want to go inside the house, not necessarily to see the murder scene but to see if I could find any of Garvey's letters to Maple or anything that told me something about his side of the relationship. Something that would either confirm or disprove Maple's guilt. I didn't particularly want Hud involved. This was a personal quest for me and I didn't want to share it with anyone.

"Why do you have access to the house?" I asked, sticking my hands deep into the pockets of my denim jacket. The temperature had dropped at least another ten degrees in the last hour, and irritating husband or not, my warm bed was looking better and better.

"I'm kind of the unofficial caretaker," he replied. He picked up a flashlight sitting on the ground and switched it on, motioning me to follow him. We left the barn and started up the sloping gravel driveway toward the Victorian house, towering dark and menacing ahead of us. Wisps of fog were already starting to form and drift around the house, and the overgrown oak trees around it gave it a traditional haunted house look. His police issue flashlight was a single white beacon up the dark path. Feeling the sudden urge to grab the back of his belt, it occurred to me that coming back tomorrow in daylight might be a better idea.

"I live here, as a matter of fact," he said over his shoulder.

"In the house?" It was definitely in the middle stages of restoration so I couldn't imagine anyone living there. It couldn't possibly have working plumbing or safe electricity. Not to mention it would creep out anyone with an ounce of imagination.

"Not in the big house," he replied. "There." He pointed behind the barn toward a wooden clapboard house whose windows shined yellow bright and comforting in the dark hazy night. "Old caretaker's house. It's not huge, but it's great for a divorced guy who only has his daughter every other weekend. Maisie loves coming out here. She's become quite a little nail banger."

"Doesn't it get lonely?" I couldn't help asking.

He stopped at the Sullivan house's steps and turned to look at me. I couldn't see his eyes in the smoky black shadows. "Sometimes. But I don't mind. Contrary to my party-loving demeanor, I'm actually quite a loner."

"Why?" The question popped out of my lips before I could stop it.

His smile was sad as his left shoulder lifted in an almost imperceptible shrug. "Guess you'd have to ask my mama. She's the psychology expert."

I blew out an angry breath. "She probably studied under Sigmund Freud too."

His laugh was softened by the rapidly thickening fog. "She'd scalp you if she heard you say that. Not only is it an insult to her age, she never did cotton to Freudian theory."

"And she'd know the proper way to scalp me, right?" I said. "Because she's half Cherokee and learned how to scalp the white man at her own mama's knee."

He grinned. "You been peekin' in our windows, ranch girl?"

"Let's just see the house," I said, annoyed that my sarcasm didn't even faze him.

"There's a lot to see," he said, walking up the steps. "Careful now, some of these aren't nailed down too good. What are you exactly looking for?"

I hesitated, not wanting him to know any more than he had to. But if I wanted to find out anything tonight, he was the only one available to ask. Unfortunately, patience has never been my strong suit. "Actually, I was interested in looking at some of Garvey's things. I'm kinda looking for some letters . . . or something like that."

"His love letters to her," Hud said, unlocking the elaborately carved front door. It was in the mid-stages of restoration, the bottom half painstakingly hand-sanded. When this house was in its prime, it must have been incredible. What a lifestyle change for little Maple Bennett of Mercy Ridge, Kentucky.

I didn't answer him, not wanting to verify what I was trying to do.

"You want to see if he loved her as much as she professed to love him," Hud said softly, holding the door open for me.

I ignored his comment and stepped over the threshold. The spacious entry hall smelled of a mixture of sweet mildew and grainy sawdust. I caught the faint scent of a skunk and wondered just how neglected this house had become before the historical society claimed it. I swallowed hard, a deep sadness coming over me. Her hope-filled letters were such a contrast to how their lives eventually turned out.

He waved the flashlight around the entry hall so I could see the carved moldings and the hammered copper ceiling. "You really can appreciate it more in daylight. Want to see where it happened?"

"Yes," I said, feeling unexplainably pulled to the spot. But what did I think it would tell me?

"It's up in the attic. Watch yourself on the stairway. It's not carpeted and kind of slippery."

I followed him up the steep stairway, feeling the wood creak and give with the pressure of each step. Halfway up, I stumbled and fell to one knee.

"Dang it!" I exclaimed, rubbing my throbbing knee.

"I told you to be careful," he called over his shoulder.

"I'm fine," I mumbled, scrambling to keep up with him and his flashlight. The stairs up to the third floor were just as steep, but I managed to maneuver them without a mishap.

A door closed off the attic to the third-floor hallway. He opened it and shined the light up the stairs. These were enclosed and I felt like I was suffocating when I followed him up.

The attic was empty except for one old metal trunk.

He nodded at the trunk. "There's nothing in it."

I gazed around the room. There was nothing special about it except for the weirdness of seeing it in the shadowing frame of Hud's police-issue flashlight.

I expected to feel something—a leftover sadness, violence, *something*—that verified that a tragedy had happened here. That a life . . . no, more than one life . . . had ended here fifty years ago.

But things like that only happened in cheesy horror novels and cable TV movies. All I felt was the cold dampness of an empty room in an old house. Whatever feelings that had taken place in this room fifty years ago were not soaked into this wooden floor.

"Where did it actually happen?" I whispered, though I wasn't sure why. Who was I afraid would hear me?

"I have no idea," Hud said, turning the flashlight square on me.

I held my hand up to shield my face from its brightness. He pointed it down at our feet. "Sorry."

"I wonder if I could find out." It seemed an important fact to know.

"This is technically within city limits. It was fifty years ago so that depends on whether the San Celina Police Department keeps murder books that long. You certainly have the resources to find out."

"I'll ask Gabe," I murmured. I gazed around the room and then back at Hud. "Don't you find it odd she would shoot him up here?"

He tilted his head, jiggling the flashlight in his hand in a nervous gesture. "Not especially. People kill people in the strangest places. There's no real logic to domestic murders. Most of the time, it's just an unplanned moment of anger. In my opinion, we all walk that edge in our relationships. Any of us could pull the trigger given the right circumstance."

"You really think so?"

His face was grim in the shadowy light. "Yes, I do."

"So do I."

His eyebrows shot up in surprise. "Now, I didn't expect that coming from *you*."

"Shows that you don't know all that much about me then, doesn't it?" I said coolly. "But I still don't buy her shooting him up here. If what you said is true, I would have expected her to have shot him in the bedroom . . . or the kitchen. That's where people fight. It just doesn't make sense up here."

"Like I said, domestic homicides hardly ever make sense."

I shook my head. "Not make sense, maybe, but most people do things in a basically logical way. I mean why would they be up here? I bet this was the maid's quarters back then . . . or storage. What reason would he have to come up here and what reason would she have to follow him? If they were arguing about some other man, it would probably have taken place downstairs."

"That's the most convoluted reasoning I've ever heard and it is just pure speculation on your part. Not an ounce of *logic* in it. Besides, there's no way to find out now."

"Maybe there is, maybe there isn't." After seeing the place where she'd supposedly shot and killed her husband—aided, some believed, by her lover—I was more convinced that there was more to their story than we knew. "I'm going to try and find out, though."

"How?"

"I've got some ideas."

"Need help? I have plenty—"

"No," I interrupted, turning to leave. "Let's get out of here. What I want isn't up here, but thanks for showing it to me."

We didn't talk again until he'd locked the front door and we were walking back toward my truck. A breeze had come up, swirling the fog around us. The setting was so perfect for the story, it could have been a movie set.

"You know, they don't keep any of his possessions in the house," he finally said.

"So I guessed."

"I know where they are."

I stopped and turned to glared at him, fully annoyed. "Why didn't you tell me?"

"You didn't actually ask."

"But you knew that's what I wanted!"

"You wanted to see the scene of the crime too, didn't you?"

He had me there. It just made me mad that he'd withheld information he knew I wanted until *he* felt like revealing it to me.

"So, where are they?" I asked, still irritated.

He pointed over at the caretaker's house. "Some of his things are in the garage behind my house. Some are kept at the historical museum. Some are at the college."

"What about written things?"

"Like his letters, you mean." He smirked at me.

I was sorely tempted to smack his face. "Yes, his letters. Do you know where they are?"

He started walking toward his house. I followed after

him, stumbling once on the rough path when his flash-light's beam got too far ahead of me.

"Be careful," he called cheerfully over his shoulder.

"Eat dirt," I mumbled.

Inside the caretaker's house, it was warm and yeasty smelling, like someone had just baked bread. From the living room, where the decor could be called early bach-elor since it consisted of a sofa, recliner, a couple of plain tables, a wall clock, and a stereo, I could see into the small yellow-and-white kitchen. On the gray formica counter sat two round loaves of freshly baked bread covered by plain white tea towels.

"Baking bread relaxes me," he said, noting my obser-vation.

"*You* baked it?" I couldn't help laughing. Somehow the thought of Hud up to his elbows in bread dough struck me as funny.

"I make great bread," he said, his face turning a bright pink.

"I'm sure you do, Martha," I teased, gratified to see him disconcerted for once. "Where are the letters?"

He pointed to the hallway. "First door on your right."

Inside the room were a couple of long folding tables with papers laid out on them in colorful stacks, an old rolltop desk, and dozens of pasteboard boxes labeled GARVEY SULLIVAN. I opened one and it contained letters, accounting books, and piles of papers.

"Are they all like this?" I asked.

He nodded. "I'm going through them slowly. A little bit every night."

"You're sorting Garvey Sullivan's papers?" That sur-prised me.

"What's so weird about that? I told you my major in college was history. It's a great hobby. And one that has some benefit to the community. He was one of your county's most prominent citizens. He's a fascinating man. Ahead of his time in a lot of his thinking about preserving the environment, things like not letting cattle graze an area until it was bare, but moving them around on a rotating basis and letting the land renew itself naturally."

"Holistic ranching," I said.

"Exactly. And it was very radical thinking back then. If he'd lived until the fifties, he probably would have been called a socialist. And he was an extremely well-read man, if his collection of books tells anything and I think they do. He liked biographies, was especially fascinated by Lincoln. Had a dozen books about him, a lot of them rare. There're a lot of first editions in his collection. They look well read and he refers to them in letters to friends and in many of the newspaper articles about him."

"You're more involved in this restoration . . . in the Sullivan lives . . . than I thought."

He gave me a level, unrevealing look. "Got involved before you did."

He was right about that. So he did have some sort of stake in finding out what happened between Garvey and Maple that day.

"So," I said. "If you've been learning about him, what do you think? Do you think she killed him?"

He leaned against the paneled wall. "I'm reserving judgment until I know more. That's why I offered to help you with the trunks."

"You mean until I find out more."

"Do you have any reason why I shouldn't know what you find out?"

Except for the fact that he personally irritated me and I was beginning to suspect that hanging around him might not be the wisest thing for me to do when my own marriage was at this bumpy spot, I couldn't think of one.

"Let me read his letters to Maple and I'll see," I hedged.

"Just what I'd expect you to answer," he said, amused at my reluctance. "Benni, these people are dead. The case has been gathering dust for a long time. What harm would it be for me to know what you find out? As one history buff to another?"

He was right, I was being a dog in the manger. "Okay,"

I conceded reluctantly. "But I don't know much yet. Only that Mitch's older brother, Micah, is very bitter about Maple Sullivan and wants me to stay out of their past."

"You talked to Mitch Warner's brother?" he asked, his eyes widening in interest.

I quickly told him about my connection to the family and my encounter with them today.

"Interesting," Hud said. "So you're convinced he knows more than he's telling."

"Absolutely. I mean, the comment about letting Mitch's soul rest in peace reveals a lot. That perhaps he knows his brother is dead and that he must have had contact with him after Garvey was killed and Maple and Mitch disappeared."

"I agree. What's your next move?"

"Read Garvey's letters to Maple and . . ." I paused. "And then I don't know." I did, but I just didn't want to tell him.

"Aren't any," he said.

"What?"

"After I started on Maple's trunks, I came back here and did a quick look through. There isn't one letter from him to her in all of his papers."

"See!" I said, excited. "She probably took them with her! That means she didn't kill him. She wouldn't have taken his love letters if she was in love with another man."

"Or in a fit of anger or hatred, she could have destroyed them," he said.

I brushed his comment away, not willing to be swayed though his counterpoint was justified. "I know I'm right. If what you said was true, she would have destroyed her letters too. I think she took his with her so she could remember him."

"Why wouldn't she have taken hers too? Not to mention her scrapbook about him. Their marriage certificate. The jewelry he gave her. All these things were left behind."

I had to admit he was right, but I was sure there was

an explanation for all that. "She *didn't* kill him."

His country boy face remained skeptical. "That remains to be seen."

Out in the living room, a clock struck once for the half hour. I glanced at my watch. "Dang it, it's ten-thirty," I said. "I have to go."

"Past curfew, huh?" he said. His lips turned up in a mocking smile. "Hope the big Kahuna doesn't restrict you for being late."

"Oh, shut up," I said and headed toward the front door. He would have to end the night on a sarcastic note.

"Wait," he said.

I ignored him and kept on going right through the open door.

He caught up with me when I was opening my truck's door. He held out something wrapped in a white paper bag. "I'm sorry for my smart-ass remark. Please take a loaf of bread in apology. You and the chief enjoy it."

I looked at him for a long moment, reluctant to take his gift.

"Please," he said. "I was a jerk and I'm trying to make amends. Don't your religious beliefs say that you're supposed to forgive people?"

"You don't know anything about my religious beliefs," I said.

"I know you're not a person who holds a grudge," he said, holding out the bread. "I know you have a kind heart."

A sharp wind blew through at that moment, causing a shiver to run down my spine. He shoved the package in my hands. "I promise, it's great bread. Sourdough from my mama's own starter. She once owned a bakery in Beaumont."

I started to open my mouth to squawk a protest. He reached over and laid a finger on my lips. I froze at his touch. His finger was warm and I felt a shock run through me.

"I swear," he said, his dark eyes solemn. "She really

did own a bakery, but I learned to make bread from my ex-wife."

He tapped his finger lightly on my lips, then turned and started toward his house. "I'll let you know if I learn anything new about Garvey that supports your theory," he called.

I arrived home at ten forty-five. Gabe's Corvette was in the driveway. I laid my hand on the hood. It was still hot, telling me that he'd not been home long himself.

The minute I walked through the door he said, "I was getting ready to go out and look for you." The air inside the house was freezing, though I could hear the heater running. Another clue that he'd just come in.

Scout bounded up to me demanding attention. I walked into the kitchen and laid the bread on the counter. Then I knelt down and gave my dog a thorough chest scratching. His tail thumped the tiled floor in pleasure. Gabe followed us and stood there waiting, his breathing slow and measured. I didn't have to look at his face to know he was annoyed.

"Why would you do that?" I finally asked, still not looking at him.

"I was worried. I called Elvia. She said she hadn't seen you all night."

"Couldn't have been too worried since you obviously just got home yourself."

I stood up and looked into his face. Annoyance had been replaced by another expression, guilt, fear? I couldn't tell. His deep-set eyes seemed the color of frosty steel.

"Where were you?" he asked, his voice controlled and as chilly as his eyes.

Deliberately taking my time to answer, I hung my still damp jacket over the back of a pine kitchen chair, unwrapped Hud's bread, and slipped it in a large plastic bag so it would stay fresh. "You know, unless both of us want to give a detailed reports on our respective evenings, perhaps it might be better if we just go to bed."

"I had dinner with Del. I haven't done anything wrong. You have to just trust me with this, Benni."

"Likewise, Chief," I replied, walking out of the kitchen and switching off the light.

I lay in bed a long time unable to sleep. The parallels between my marriage and Maple's were not wasted on me. She married a man she barely knew though she was certainly braver than me—she actually picked up her whole life and moved cross-country to be with him. Would I do that for love? Gabe had asked me once if I'd leave my family, our ranch, my roots, to follow him somewhere else. I had to admit, a part of me rebelled against it, that giving up of everything for a person. Was that what love was all about? Total surrender? Maybe I didn't love anyone enough to do that. Or maybe, unlike Maple, I had a lot more to lose. Maybe her family wasn't much to leave behind. If you hated your life, had no strong connections to your family, then creating a new life wouldn't be a struggle, it would be a blessing. In my case, I wasn't looking for a new life when Gabe had come into it. I was perfectly happy before he blew into town.

Well, not perfectly happy, a small voice inside reminded me. You were still mourning Jack. You were just getting through each day with no hope that happiness would ever touch your life again.

Gabe did change that. He did bring joy back into my life.

And now, it appeared, he was going to take it away.

14

BENNI

GABE AND I didn't say much to each other the next morning. We were painstakingly polite, which saddened me more than a screaming fight. It was like talking to a stranger.

"I'll be at the hairdresser until ten," I said, picking up my backpack. Gabe, still in sweats and a T-shirt from his run, sipped coffee at the kitchen table. His sharp cheekbones seemed stretched across his olive skin. Was his night as restless as mine? It didn't seem so to me. Every time I woke up, he seemed to be sleeping fine. "Then I'm at the Mardi Gras carnival. Then the parade, then the charity ball at Constance's."

He bit a piece of toasted sourdough bread. "I'm meeting with my department heads to check on parade control. Do you want to go to the ball together?"

"I have to be there early. I'm not staying through the whole parade." Scout nudged my leg. I stooped down and scrubbed behind his ears. "Not this time, Scooby-Doo. I've got too many places to go to worry about you."

"We'll meet there then. I'll probably be a little late depending on what kinds of problems we run into at the parade." He took another bite of bread. "Is there a new bakery in town? This bread is great."

"A friend gave it to me yesterday," I said, trying not to move a muscle on my face. I had to admit, it gave me a tiny bit of pleasure for him to rave over Hud's bread. If he knew who made it, it would irritate him to no end.

"Tell her it's wonderful."

I gave a half smile. "Okay."

At the door, I stopped and turned back to face him. "Oh, one question. Do you keep crime files as far back at the forties?"

He set his bread down. "I'm not sure, why?"

"This project I'm working on for the historical museum. The Sullivan restoration."

He nodded, comprehending. "We might have kept an unsolved homicide, but all other 1940s cases would likely be long gone. We have some old photos, I think, and some booking logs, but I'm not sure about any other documentation."

"You mean, they didn't microfilm old files like the library does old newspapers?"

"Nope. I imagine they didn't have the manpower or the money. Captain Joan Sackett is our unofficial department historian. You met her at the last picnic. She played shortstop."

"I remember. She works as a docent at the Mission."

"That's her. You could call and ask her next week. She works eight to five Monday through Friday."

"Okay, thanks. I'll call her on Monday."

We kissed politely and said goodbye.

"Aren't we just being so adult about this," I muttered as I pulled out of the driveway. Somehow, the fact that we weren't yelling at each other made our situation feel even more hopeless.

I arrived at Jamaica You Beautiful at five minutes to eight. It was located in a bright lavender-and-white clapboard house on Lopez Street about five blocks from Elvia's bookstore. I stood on the porch for a few minutes, attempting to rearrange my despairing mood before seeing Elvia. This was the most exciting week of her life and I was determined not to wreck it with my marital problems.

Female laughter and the sharp, grassy scent of clean wet hair and hair spray bombarded me when I walked inside. Elvia was already reigning in chair number one, her shoulder-length black hair being arranged in an elaborate hairstyle of curls and braids. Her wedding veil and pearl-encrusted headpiece sat in a clear hatbox on the table next to her.

"Hey, Benni," Teresa called over at me. She was the shop owner and Elvia was one of her best customers. "Zelda is ready anytime you are."

Zelda was their skin expert. Elvia said my face needed a good cleaning and vacuuming. I couldn't help picturing a small Hoover upright moving across the bridge of my nose.

"Okay, I'm here. Vacuum me," I said.

Elvia rolled her eyes. "You'll be amazed at how much better you look after Zelda is through with you. And it's very relaxing. Besides, I'm paying for it and you promised you would do whatever I asked with this wedding. An inch trimmed off your hair and your nails done."

"And I always keep my promises," I said, going over and giving her a pat on the knee. "My body is yours for the next"—I checked my watch—"one hour and fifty-five minutes. I have to be at the festival booths by ten o'clock or my artists will think I'm deserting them."

"You'll be a new person," Teresa promised.

That, I thought, might not be a bad idea these days. Maybe *that* was the way to keep my husband.

Zelda, the woman who would attempt to restore youth and vigor to my face, was a tall, red-headed woman with slanted green eyes and sharp features. She settled me down on a table that was not unlike a doctor's exam table and went to work on my face. The room was warm and had a woodsy scent. Gentle, nature-like music played from a hidden stereo somewhere. After a fifteen-minute massage with oils, when I'd almost fallen asleep from the mesmerizing stroking of her strong, thin fingers, she covered my eyes with small plastic cups and flipped on a bright light. For the next fifteen minutes she scrutinized and cleaned my face with a variety of probes and potions.

So, I thought, as she poked at something on my forehead, basically a facial is when you pay someone else large amounts of money to pick your zits.

"Very funny," Elvia said, turning her chair around to face me after I had whispered my revelation to her. Teresa had gone to get us both cappuccinos from their new copper espresso machine. "It's much more involved than that. Zelda is the most sought after skin specialist in the county. I had to bribe her with a fifty-dollar gift certificate to the store to work you in today. Your skin looks years younger."

"It was wonderful," I admitted, running a hand over my cheeks. They did feel softer and smoother.

"I told you she was good. Now Angie is waiting for you. What do you think?" She pointed to her upswept elaborate hairdo of curls and braids. It was a miraculous piece of hair art. Fit for a magazine cover. It could win awards at a competition. And it didn't look at all like my best friend.

"Honest answer?"

She hesitated, then nodded.

"I think you'd look the most beautiful with your hair down in its usual way. That's the Elvia who Emory loves. That's the Elvia we all love. We want to see you walking down the aisle, not your hairstyle."

She sat dead silent, her smooth brown face expressionless. I lambasted myself for giving my opinion when I swore I'd just go along with whatever she wanted.

Then she smiled. "You're right, Benni. I was getting so wrapped up in what everything will look like in the photographs that I was forgetting what this was truly about. Me and Emory getting married." Her black eyes grew shiny. "Thank you for reminding me of that." She grabbed my hand and squeezed it.

I leaned down and hugged her. "And you guys are going to live happily ever after."

She laughed. "Just like you and Gabe."

I looked over her shoulder. In the mirror, my freshly vacuumed face glowed healthy and clean, but it was still me. Not a new person, just one with a few less impurities in her pores. "Yes," I said softly, feeling like a fraud. "Just like me and Gabe."

Angie, Teresa's daughter, who was scheduled to trim my hair, was a short, chesty girl with a diamond in her nose, a long line of pierced earrings up both ears, and a gorgeous head of dark brown hair that cascaded in natural curls around her shoulders. She herself had a delightful, tinkly laugh that reminded me of puppies barking. She herself was like a puppy, cuddly and cute and full of life.

"So," she said as she trimmed the back of my hair. "Did you enjoy the French restaurant last night?"

"What?" I said, confused.

"Diamanta's in Santa Barbara. Jenny, a friend of mine, said she saw you and the chief there. She absolutely loved those leather pants you were wearing. Where did you get them? I just love French food, don't you? Especially their bread. Was it good? What did you have? Jenny says that place is *so* romantic. You're so lucky." She gave a big sigh.

My face felt numb, but I managed to say, "Do I know your friend Jenny?" My throat felt thick, like I'd swallowed an ice cube.

She gave a cheery giggle. "Oh, no, you've never met. That's why she didn't say anything. She only knew it was Gabe because her boyfriend is a new officer at the station and she went to his swearing-in a few months ago. But she said he was with a cool-looking blond lady and I said that must be you. So, was it good?"

I tried to swallow over the icy lump in my throat. "Fine," I croaked. "Could I have some water, please?"

"Sparkling or regular?"

"Doesn't matter." An intimate French restaurant in Santa Barbara. That was more than taking an old friend to dinner in town. That was the beginning of an affair.

When she came back with the water, fortunately she started telling me about her latest boyfriend, a trumpet player in a jazz band. "He's totally wicked," she said. "When he plays that horn, I swear I would follow him anywhere, do anything he asks. Have you ever felt like that about someone?"

Luckily, I figured out that she was a compulsive talker and didn't really expect answers to any of her questions. I just made pseudo-interested sounds in the back of my throat and that seemed to satisfy her. After my trim, I was steered toward the manicurist, who clucked over my ragged cuticles. The whole time the shop grew busier and the noise louder until I thought I was going to scream. While everyone around me chattered about dates and Mardi Gras and weddings, I mentally was watching my life swirl down the drain like gray dishwater.

"You look great," Elvia said when our beauty regime was finally over and we walked toward our cars.

"My skin does feel better," I said, trying to sound enthusiastic. I clutched her wedding veil hat box against my chest, wanting to hold on to something, anything.

She turned to look at me, her face concerned. "*Hermana,* are you okay? You look funny."

It's hard to hide your emotions from someone who's known you since second grade. But I was determined not to rain one drop on her parade, not one single drop.

"Cramps," I lied, falling back on that old standby.

She nodded sympathetically. "*Tía Roja* always seems to pay a visit when we're the busiest, doesn't she?"

I just nodded and readjusted my arms around the clear hatbox.

"See you tonight," she said when we had reached our cars.

"With bells on," I said, with as much fake cheer as I

could muster. "Well, actually I have no idea what I'll have on, but I'll be there."

She laughed and hugged me. "See you there."

At the Mission Plaza, where they'd moved the Mardi Gras festival since it had outgrown its original Garden Street location, the crowds were already dancing and eating jambalaya and gumbo at 10 A.M. There were twice as many booths this year and three times as many people. The Mardi Gras committee was trying to make the festival more family oriented to counteract the sometimes bad press the parade usually garnered where scanty costumes and drunken revelry were turning it more like the New Orleans celebration than a lot of people had initially intended. This year there were face-painting booths, coloring contests, a children's costume parade, and a balloon animal clown for kids. There were also three bands—Zippy's Zydeco Kings, Alfonse Balfa and his Cajun Cozzins, and Valerie Johnson and the Blues Doctors, a blues band Gabe and I particularly enjoyed. They were regular performers at Iry's Creole Cafe down near the police station.

The folk art museum booths were three deep with customers so I jumped right in and started helping, thankful for something to occupy my mind. For the next four hours I sold quilts and pots, stained glass wind chimes, and handmade Mardi Gras masks, only occasionally thinking about Angie's troubling words.

At two o'clock, Bobbi Lee pushed me out from behind the counter. "Go look at the booths," she said. "Get yourself some gumbo and relax. You've put in your time hawking our wares. Have some fun."

So I was reluctantly cast adrift in the happy crowd, carrying a plastic bowl of gumbo that was probably wonderful, but had no appeal for me. I tried to get interested in the booths selling masks, sparkling beads and fake tattoos showing a grinning alligator wearing a jester's hat, but all I could think about was Del in leather pants sharing a crème brûlé with my husband.

As if thinking about him conjured up his presence, I spotted Gabe over near the front of the Mission. Confront him now, a voice inside me demanded. Run the other way, another countered. After a minute of arguing, I decided now was as good a time as any. I pushed my way through the dancing crowd and caught up with him. He was deep in conversation with a deputy district attorney he knew.

"I need to talk to you," I said, not even excusing myself before butting into their conversation.

"Sure," Gabe said, his face confused and a little irritated. "I'll catch you later, Sean."

The man nodded and walked away.

"What's going on?" Gabe said.

I glanced around. It was too crowded here so I said, "Let's walk."

He followed me out of the Mission Plaza and around the corner to the historical museum.

"Let's talk in the garden," I said. "We can get in the back way. It's closed for a few weeks while they're working on the watering system."

In the privacy of the old Carnegie Library Garden, where underneath an ancient pepper tree I'd received my first real grown-up kiss from Jack, I confronted Gabe with what I'd learned about his dinner with Del.

"What's the big deal?" Gabe said, his voice rising in anger, telling me I was smart to find a private place for us to have this conversation. "Don't people in this pathetic little town have anything better to do than gossip about innocent dinners between old partners?"

"Innocent dinners take place where people can see them."

"Benni, I'm telling you, *nothing* happened."

"Yet."

He glared at me, his eyes a blazing blue against his brown skin. "Is that what you think of me? That I'm a person with so little self-control?"

I stared up at him, silent for a moment, then said, "Just tell me one thing. Are you still in love with her?"

His face looked shocked for a moment, then grew still. Not a muscle moved. Around us a mockingbird flew from the pepper tree to the edge of the museum's roof to an old Martha Washington rosebush that was taller than me. His song was filled with distress and territorial anger and, I knew, a little bit of fear.

Finally Gabe said in a voice low, rough, agonized, "I don't know."

Heat exploded through my body so quickly I felt like throwing up. I closed my eyes for a moment, chanting silently to myself, *Don't cry, don't cry, don't cry.*

"*Querida,*" he started.

I opened my eyes and said, "Don't call me that." Then I turned and walked out of the garden, slamming the gate behind me.

He didn't come after me, which was good. At that moment, I knew I could not trust myself, at that moment I knew I would say things I'd regret later, hit below the belt, thrusting at vulnerable spots as only a lover and a wife could. Places only I knew about.

Or at least thought only I knew. Really, what did I know about what he'd revealed to the other women he'd had in his life? I could just be another in a long chain of conquests. One that took a little more work because he had to marry me to sleep with me. But marriages were easy enough to dissolve these days. I was a little more trouble to get in his bed, but not much. I'd fallen just as quickly as any of the others.

I didn't pay attention to where I was walking, I just wanted to lose myself in the crowd, get somewhere where he couldn't find me. Before I realized it, I was back in the midst of the Mardi Gras festival.

"Hey, Benni!"

I turned at the sound of my name. Over at the children's face-painting booth, Joan Sackett waved over the crowd. I weaved my way around a group of people dressed like sparkly green cockroaches and sidestepped a woman carrying a dachshund wearing the identical green-and-purple fool's hat as her owner, a round-faced, frizzy-haired woman who contradicted the adage that people chose dogs that looked like themselves.

"Hey, Joan," I said when I finally made it up to the booth. Four people were busy painting butterflies, rainbows, and turtles on the smooth cheeks of children. "How'd you get roped into this?"

She jerked her head over at a woman in her early twenties who had Joan's tall, muscular frame and freckled complexion. "My daughter's working for the recreation department now," she said, dipping her brush into a muffin tin filled with fluorescent oranges, greens, and blues. "Pull up a stool and keep me company. Gabe was by a few hours ago. Said you were wondering about old records." She bent close to a ten-year-old girl and continued working on the half-finished parrot framing her right eye. "Close your eye, honey. I don't want to get paint in it."

At the mention of his name, my stomach rolled and churned. I prayed with all my being that my normally open face hid at least a modicum of the pain I felt. For not the first time in my life I wished I lived in a huge, impersonal city where your world could crumble like old concrete without the benefit of a curious audience.

"I'm looking into the Sullivan murder. Well, not officially looking into it, more like curious about it." I was glad for a chance to avoid my terrified thoughts and concentrate on a relationship that had been over for fifty years.

She nodded and stroked a long cobalt blue bird tail down the girl's cheek. "That's quite an interesting story. But Gabe was right when he told you we don't have much left from that time. What's weird is we have all the records from the late nineteenth century. Back then the arrest ledgers were also the crime files. They wrote everything down right where they logged in the suspect's name so we actually have great records from then."

"Nothing from the forties?"

"Nope. From what I can tell, the department didn't start

keeping accurate records until the late fifties. The forties were an especially hard time in the San Celina PD. Right at the beginning of the war they brought up a new chief from Los Angeles." She grinned. "Sound familiar? Except then they did it to sort of clean things up."

"There was corruption in the police department?" I wondered if that had any significance in the Sullivan investigation.

She finished the parrot by giving it a bright purple eye and said, "There you go, honey. Have a ball."

"Thanks, Mrs. Sackett," the girl said and jumped up to gaze at her face in the plastic hand mirror. She and her friends squealed in delight at Joan's artwork.

Joan smiled at them indulgently. "Wish my rookies were as enthusiastic about my evaluation reports." She turned back to me. "There wasn't really corruption back then. It was more that everything was so small town. Kind of unprofessional. Until the war when Camp Riley was built and so many military men were shipped in to train here on the Central Coast, the county did not have a whole lot of serious crime. A few rancher squabbles about fence lines, a little cattle rustling, but nothing that required a big-city approach. The war changed this area permanently. Anyway, the new chief implemented a lot of improvements, kind of cleaned out the old timers, the ones not willing to change and try new techniques. He was the one who opened the police pistol range and started a program for regular firearms qualification."

All of her information was interesting, but it wasn't giving me what I wanted. "So, what about the Sullivan investigation?"

She stretched her long arms above her head and rolled her neck. "I've been doing this three hours straight. Didn't know there were so many kids in San Celina. The Sullivan murder was never actually officially solved, as you probably already know. It's pretty obvious what happened, but even though it was still an open case, no one saw fit to save any of the records or evidence." She shrugged. "Too bad. Cold cases are being solved quite regularly now that we have so much advanced technology. Some departments even have special cold case detectives. Guess we'll never know what really happened with Garvey and Maple Sullivan.".

"Is it possible that anyone who was a police officer then would still be around? Maybe he could tell me something about it."

"It's possible. Best I could do is ask some of the old timers in the department, see if they're in touch with any of the retired officers. I'll ask around on Monday."

"Thanks, I appreciate it."

"Another customer, Mom," her daughter said, pointing at a small, redheaded girl wearing a puffy pink ski jacket, black leggings, a pink skirt, and Beauty and the Beast sneakers. She looked about five or six years old and stared up at Joan with apprehensive brown eyes.

"So, what's your favorite color, honey?" she asked, stooping down to the child's level. Though I'd seen Joan in her professional personality when she could scare any cocky punk or mouthy rookie into terrified silence with a mere look, this Joan was as gentle as a cookie-baking grandma.

"Pink," the girl whispered. "Then purple."

"Then how about a pink-and-purple butterfly on your cheek?" Joan asked.

The girl smiled and nodded, more relaxed now. "My daddy's over there. He says to tell you that sheriffs are better than police."

We both looked up and saw Hud sitting on a stone fence ten feet away. He touched two fingers to his brown Stetson.

Joan laughed and showed a fist to Hud. "Honey, you tell your daddy that he's a very nice, but ill-informed man."

"Ill formed?" the girl said, her brown eyes wide.

Joan and I both laughed at her word choice.

"Good enough," Joan said. "Though his form is actually quite fine." She turned to me. "You know Hud? He's quite a character. He and I became acquainted at a workday for the octagonal barn. I joined the historical society a while back though I never can seem to make it to a meeting. He's good people, even if he is a sheriff's deputy."

"We've met," I said, glancing up at his smirking face. "Thanks for the information, Joan. You saved me a trip down to the station to hunt you down."

"No problem," she said, settling Hud's daughter on the stool. "I'll call you as soon as I get a name."

I went around the booth and walked over to Hud, who was sipping some kind of coffee drink with whipped cream floating on top.

"Having fun?" I said.

"Maisie is. My fun's later."

I raised my eyebrows. "What's later?"

"The Masked Ball. You'll love my costume."

Assuming he meant the open-to-the-public ball at the Forum downtown, I said, "Well, too bad I won't see it. I'll be in Cambria at a fundraiser."

"I know. That's the one I meant. I'll see you there."

"*You're* going to the ball at Constance Sinclair's house?" I didn't even try to hide my surprise.

"Don't be such a snob. Is there any rule that says only the upper-crust society of San Celina can support the folk art museum?"

"No, it's not . . . I mean I didn't . . . You're more than . . ." I stammered in my embarrassment at my obviously elitist attitude. What kind of person was I turning into? "I'm sorry," I finally just said, feeling like bursting into tears.

He grinned at me. "Well, I don't know if I can forgive you."

At that moment Gabe's voice, his words, echoed in my head.

"I don't know."

How could three little words turn my whole world so

completely around? What was a little squabble about an old girlfriend had turned into something that was life changing.

"I don't know."

Could I ever hear those words again and not remember this day?

My head suddenly felt fuzzy, and I knew if I didn't get away, I would start sobbing right there in the middle of three thousand people. I willed myself to maintain a calm exterior.

Apparently I failed because Hud's normally smart-ass expression turned gentle and concerned. "Hey, it's all right. I was just kidding. You're forgiven."

"Okay," I said, still feeling disoriented. "I guess I'll see you there." I turned to walk away when he grabbed my upper arm.

"Sit down," he said, steering me over to the stone wall. "You look like you're ready to pass out."

"I'm fine," I said, but let him lead me to a spot a few feet away.

"I'd say you're not, only you're likely to bite my head off at the shoulders," he said, pressing a warm paper cup into my hands. "Drink some of my cappuccino."

I did as he said, grateful for a moment just to follow directions. I sipped at the hot drink, trying to hold back the trembling that was threatening to overcome my body.

"What's wrong?" he asked, studying my face intently. "Did you get some bad news?"

I handed back his drink and stood up. "Nothing," I said, irritated at myself for my momentary loss of control and how quickly I would let a man comfort me. "Thanks for the drink. I'll see you later."

"Wait," he said, setting the cup down on the wall. "If you need to talk—"

"I don't."

He stepped closer, his face inches from mine. "Really, I'm a good listener. I know what it's like—"

I didn't let him finish. "Look, Detective, you gave me

a sip of your coffee. That doesn't entitle you to a stroll through my psyche."

"Wait," he said again, reaching out to me.

I walked right past him, ignoring his outstretched hand. When I reached my truck, I'd already made up my mind. There was no way I would live with Gabe while he was going through this crisis of . . . whatever. And luckily there was a way we could live separately that no one would suspect. At least for two weeks until our lease was up on our rented house. At the old house, I packed a suitcase, cleared my personal supplies out of our small bathroom, and left him a note on the kitchen table.

> *Gabe, I think it would be better if for the time being I stay at the new house and you stay here. Don't call me or come by. I'm not ready to talk yet. I'm taking Scout.*

Then finally, I let myself cry.

15

GABE

HE STOOD IN the garden of the historical museum and watched Benni walk away. And with her the sanity and peace he'd always known would only be temporary. Above him a mockingbird perched on a pepper tree branch and screamed an insane melody.

Why had he answered Benni that way? Was he really still in love with Del, or was it just something he'd lashed out with to hurt his wife, to hurt the person he loved more than his own life, a person he loved more than he could imagine loving anyone except his son. He didn't know. It had just fallen off his lips like broken glass, leaving his mouth tasting of blood and bitter salt.

He closed his eyes, felt the February breeze cool the burning heat on the back of his neck. Del's face swam before him in the darkness, her honey-colored hair bright as a lighthouse beacon.

"Why did you get married?" she'd asked him last night over the bottle of cabernet he had ordered. "You swore to me you'd never get married again." Her voice had been slightly accusing.

He'd looked at his glass a moment, seeing his reflection

in the deep red color. Guilt was a sharp knife dividing his ribs.

"How's John B?" he'd asked, changing the subject. "Does he still eat fried chicken for breakfast?"

He stood in the empty garden wishing he could go back in time a half hour, snatch back the words that had stained his wife's cheeks as surely as if he'd physically slapped her. Though he wasn't sure how he felt about Del, he didn't want to lose Benni. As sick as it was, he wanted them both.

He went through the gate, not bothering to close it behind him. Around him people talked and laughed, the smell of fishy gumbo floated through the air along with the tinny, cheerful sound of zydeco music. Someone greeted him and he heard himself respond through the sound of cicadas in his ears. Except this wasn't Kansas. There were no cicadas in California. And it was February. He gritted his teeth and willed the buzzing away.

Minutes later, he found himself inside the Mission Church, crowded and noisy with visitors, their hard shoes obscenely loud on the painted cement floors. He stood in the cold dim light and mentally willed the tourists away. He wanted to scream at them—show some respect, lower your voices, let this place be what it is supposed to be, a sanctuary for those seeking peace.

He walked through the crowds to the front, past the paint-peeled wooden statue of the crucified Christ, and without kneeling or crossing himself, turned right. Only one of the two confessional booths was free, the small red light above it dark, so he ducked inside and stood there in the dimly lit room, not caring if a priest was there or not, just wanting to find some quiet, impossible in the packed church where people snapped pictures with disposable cameras and snuck bites of candied apples held low in their hands.

A shuffling, then a soft cough came from the priest's side. Gabe froze for a moment, feeling like a boy caught stealing a pack of baseball cards. Why had he come here?

Out of habit, because it was either this or flee, he knelt down on the padded kneeler in front of the curtained half wall, made the Sign of the Cross, and said automatically, his voice scratched and torn, "Bless me, Father, for I have sinned." He searched his memory. "It's been . . ." He faltered, unable to remember exactly the last time he'd been to confession. "I don't know how long it's been . . ."

"That's all right," murmured a low masculine voice. "God knows. Go ahead."

Gabe leaned forward, trying to swallow and speak over the rawness in his throat. His heart felt burnt, like a black cinder in the middle of his chest.

Neither of them spoke for two minutes. It stretched into three, four, then five.

Finally, the priest said in a normal tone, "Gabe, you want to go get some pasta? I'm starving."

"Father Mark?" Gabe said, relief and embarrassment making him laugh. Sweat pooled under his breastbone.

The tall, muscular man wearing a priest's collar opened the wooden door separating them.

"Sounds to me like you're not quite ready to confess," Father Mark Dominguez said. He was as tall as Gabe though thicker in the chest, with upper arms that could bench-press two hundred sixty pounds. His handsome, acne-rough face and penetrating brown eyes gave him a dangerous look that not only helped when dealing with sullen teenage boys down at the Youth Authority where he volunteered, but had caused more than one female parishioner to attend Mass often enough to make her husband suspicious.

"I didn't realize it was you," Gabe said, unable to look the priest in the eye. "Where's Father Leo?"

Mark was a friend, a person he'd jogged with occasionally and spotted at the gym. They originally met when Gabe joined the gym the first months he'd lived in San Celina, before he knew Benni. At first meeting, Gabe had been certain that Mark was a gang member . . . or at least a former one. His years working narcotics in East L.A.

had taught him how to spot homeboys immediately, even if their tattoos weren't obvious, that quick gaze about the room to check it out, the tendency to choose the gym equipment where your back is to the wall, unexposed. He was either a gang member or a cop, and Gabe knew he was no cop.

He'd been right, which he'd found out after he'd shared a round of workouts. Before he'd joined the priesthood, Mark had been connected to the 16th Street Amigos, one of the most brutal California Hispanic gangs.

"Father Leo's down with the flu," Mark said. "I'm taking his shift with the sinners." He gave a broad wink. "And my shift is over unless there was somebody after you or you change your mind . . ." His eyebrows rose in question.

"No, pasta sounds great," Gabe said quickly, thankful he'd been rescued from having to face his feelings.

"Then let me see if there's anyone else. If not, then I can take off this dog collar and get into something more comfortable," Mark said.

When he saw there was no one else waiting to confess, he said, "Let's go to my office."

In his book-filled office, Mark pulled off his vestments and put on a black T-shirt with white lettering that said, THERE'S NO FEAR IN JESUS.

"How about Antonio's?" Mark said. "They've got a shrimp fettuccine I've been lusting after for the last three hours."

"Sure," Gabe said.

In the restaurant, they talked of the Mardi Gras celebration and how it had grown, how Gabe was faring with the latest city council, which had members who annoyed both Gabe and Mark, the vacation Mark would be taking to Greece in December.

"How's Benni?" Mark asked, spearing a plump, buttery shrimp.

"Fine." Gabe bit down on the word and dropped his gaze down to his pasta primavera.

Mark chewed the shrimp slowly, nodding his head. "What's up, *mano*? You and Benni having problems?"

Gabe looked up at the priest, feeling himself stiffen. He didn't want to tell Mark about Benni and Del. Confessing to a faceless priest behind a screen was one thing; facing Mark's discerning eyes and priestly judgment was another. He set his fork down and took a sip of wine. "I said we're fine."

Mark nodded again, his face friendly and open. Around them, the sounds of the restaurant grew louder and more intense. A waiter dropped a tray of glasses and everyone in the restaurant applauded.

Mark speared another shrimp. "Did I ever tell you that before I became a priest, I was married?"

Gabe tried not to look surprised. Though he could picture Mark in baggy, gangster clothes selling crack on a filthy street corner, he could not imagine him with a wife.

Mark's brown eyes bore directly into Gabe's. "Had a little girl too. Marisol. Both were killed in a drive-by."

Gabe's heart twitched, then hardened. "I'm sorry, but I guess that's part of the life." He felt like an asshole for being so cold, but he knew what Mark was trying to do and he refused to become vulnerable.

Mark's sharp eyes didn't move from Gabe's. "All I'm trying to tell you, my stubborn friend, is that death is the only irreversible problem we creatures down here on earth have. Whatever's going on between you and Benni can be fixed. If you love each other." He picked up a glass of water, still watching Gabe. "Do you love her?"

Gabe nodded, unable to speak.

"Talk to me then. As a friend. And I will bestow upon you my best Solomonic advice." He gazed at him solemnly and sipped the water. "Or preach you some home-boy bullshit, whichever you prefer."

Gabe couldn't keep back a small smile. In the next half hour, he told Mark the whole story.

"So," Mark said, when Gabe had finished. "I'll ask you again. Do you love Benni?"

"Of course I do." Gabe felt the heat of anger rise in his chest. Maybe he shouldn't have said anything to Mark. The guy could be a complacent jerk sometimes.

"Okay, this Del. Do you really love her or—"

Gabe snapped, "I told you I don't know how I feel about her."

Mark's face didn't react to Gabe's irritation. "Fair enough. We'll agree you feel something. Unfortunately, that something is causing you to step out of the circle of love that you've established with your wife. What do you think you should do about that?"

Gabe looked around, trying to figure out a polite way to escape from this situation. He should have kept this to himself or waited until Father Leo was well and confess to the old priest, who'd give him his penance but not want to delve into his psyche. He turned back to the priest. "Look, I know I should just send Del on her way. I *know* that. But it's not that easy. You don't understand . . ." He felt himself flush.

Mark threw back his head and gave a hearty laugh. "How much you want to sleep with this woman? You're wrong there, my friend. When I put on a collar, I didn't take off my dick."

Gabe stared at him, not certain how he should react.

"Look, Gabe, I'm not trying to put you on the spot," Mark said, pushing his half-eaten pasta aside. "It just seems to me that the sacred is missing from your struggle. How would you act with all this if you brought the sacred into it?"

"It's not that simple." Heat burned inside his chest. He should have refused this lunch with the priest.

Mark's face remained calm and expressionless. "Gabe," he said so softly that Gabe was tempted to lean closer. "What are you so afraid of?"

Gabe stiffened his bottom lip. He stared at the priest, not answering.

Mark's voice remained soft. "You know what's so funny and sad about us human beings?" He didn't wait for Gabe to answer. "We are constantly torn between the all-consuming desire to be loved and the terrifying fear of being known. Deep inside we don't believe the two things can exist together, that if anyone really knew us, they would surely never love us, so we spend our whole lives concocting this wonderful, plastic shell that we fight like madmen to keep pristine. But eventually the plastic cracks and falls away and what is inside is a raw, quivering mass of imperfect humanity that has always been lovely and precious enough for God Himself to love. Don't be afraid of that love. Or of Benni's."

Gabe folded his napkin and set it on his plate. He pulled out his wallet and threw two twenties on the table. "Lunch is on me. Thanks for your help, Father. I have to get over to the parade route and check on things."

Mark stood up and held out his large-boned hand. "Come back and talk to me again, Gabe. If I didn't do so well advising you this time, give me another chance. I'm new at this priest gig. I need practice."

Gabe, irritated as he was, couldn't help liking the man. He was honest and sincere. He just didn't understand how complex this situation was. "Sure, Father Mark. Take it easy."

"You too, Gabriel. Take it easy and take it slow."

16

BENNI

AFTER FIFTEEN MINUTES of crying that didn't make me feel one bit better, I loaded my suitcase, Scout's food and water dishes, and a sleeping bag and pillow into my truck. I turned to look at the small Spanish bungalow that had been my home since I'd left the Harper ranch after Jack died. When I came here to live, I had no idea what my future held. Now, it appeared I was back at that same place.

The new house was cold and lonely; the oakwood floors echoed with emptiness. But I didn't mind. They mimicked what I felt, the chilling heaviness weighting my heart. The walnut mantel clock chimed five o'clock. The Mardi Gras parade started at four fifty-seven and I'd promised Elvia I'd take pictures of her employees and their well-rehearsed and very popular "March of the Banned Books." I'd also promised Constance I'd be at her house before the party started at seven to supervise the caterers' setup. At least I'd be busy tonight, hopefully too busy to contemplate the disintegration of my marriage.

As I walked through the rooms that had so delighted us both when we first saw this gray-and-blue California bungalow, my heart throbbed in my chest. The large picture window looking out over a huge old rosebush, red ones the realtor had promised, the tiny alcoves and built-in bookshelves, the natural stone fireplace in the living room, all seemed to echo with a mocking sound. I had pictured the Mission-style furniture I wanted to buy, the soft rugs I wanted to put on the shiny oak floors, the lacy curtains on the four-pane windows. I had imagined us growing old together in this house. I had imagined us making love in every room.

Now I could only wonder if we'd be able to sell it easily. And wonder where I would live then. My throat tightened as if someone were choking me.

Upstairs, the master bedroom had new, double-padded plush carpet in a soothing honey beige. I unrolled my sleeping bag, hung the garment bag containing my costume in the walk-in closet, and set up the bathroom with minimal grooming supplies. I took a quick, hot shower even though it meant I had to rush to put on my costume.

Wrapped in my terry bathrobe, I unzipped the garment bag, then moaned out loud.

A flapper?

I held the off-white dress in front of me and shook it, the rows of pale pink fringe shimmering in the soft multicolored glow of the Tiffany floor lamp Emory had bought us for a housewarming gift.

Cathy hadn't lied. It wasn't low cut and it wasn't a cowgirl outfit, but it was very, very short. And a little snug.

I slipped it on and jumped up and down a few times trying to see myself in the bathroom mirror. The fringe went wild.

"Oh, geeze," I said. "I look ridiculous."

Scout just beat his tail on the floor and stared at me in curiosity, no doubt wondering what sort of new game this was.

"You don't know how lucky you are to be a dog," I said to him, sitting on the closed toilet lid and pulling on the stockings and thick-heeled strapped shoes that came with the costume. At least they'd be easy to walk in. I grabbed the head-hugging hat or whatever it was called, put on my wool-lined trench coat, and fed Scout down in the box-filled kitchen.

After reminding him about the doggy door in the kitchen that led out to the fenced backyard, I kissed the top of his head and promised I'd be home as soon as I could manage.

Home, I thought grimly, pulling out of the wide, short driveway. Would this be my home? I couldn't picture living here alone. Not to mention I couldn't afford the mortgage payments on my part-time curator salary. No, if we split up, we'd definitely have to put this house on the market . . . before we'd even lived a day in it together.

You're washing the pie plate before you've even rolled out the crust, Dove's voice reverberated in my head. My heart beat faster. Dove. How would I ever break the news to her about me and Gabe? Her hurt and disappointed look was something I wasn't sure I could survive.

I parked on a side street near the end of the parade route for an easy getaway, sitting for a moment with my head resting on the cold steering wheel. I wanted so badly to find Dove and beg her to tell me what to do. But I was determined to deal with this on my own. I wasn't a child and she had her own life and impending marriage to worry about.

As if she'd sensed my worry in the wind, my cell phone rang and Dove's voice blared out from the palm-sized instrument.

"Cosmic Cavern!" she yelled, her voice broken by static.

"What?"

"In Berryville, Arkansas. They got a room there called Silent Splendor that you can get married in. The brochure says there's a trout there in Mystery Lake that's the size of a six-year-old child."

"You want to get married in a cave?"

"Bet Isaac would remember *that*."

"No doubt."

"You don't sound very enthusiastic," she said in an accusing tone.

I couldn't help myself, "Dove, a cave? A *cave*?"

"It's God's creation," she said, her voice getting huffy in that way that told me I was tap dancing on thin ice. "It would be special."

"And damp," I couldn't help adding.

"You have no imagination."

I sighed. The thought of traveling back to Arkansas to go to a cave wedding sounded less inviting than walking all night with a colicky horse.

Then an idea flashed in my head like a cartoon light bulb. "Well, since it's in Arkansas, I imagine Aunt Garnet will insist on taking my place as matron of honor. She'll probably want to help you with the reception too. And don't pick out a dress yet. I'm sure she'll want to help with that."

The line grew silent except for pops of static. "I forgot about Garnet."

"She'll be *thrilled* about it being in Arkansas."

"You know, I don't even know if Isaac is claustrophobic," Dove said. "Let me get back to you."

"Over and out," I said.

Clutching my camera, I made my way to a spot next to the section reserved for the elderly and handicapped. It wasn't as crowded here as at the parade's beginning, where college students and rowdier Mardi Gras revelers liked to carry on and act outrageously, yelling the traditional "Throw me some beads, mister," begging for the colorful plastic beads and metal Mardi Gras coins stamped with this year's date and theme. I found an empty place behind the three-foot chain link barriers lining the parade route, a safety precaution Gabe had just implemented this year, and wiggled my toes in my twenties flapper shoes, wishing I'd thought to wear wool socks and boots. By the time the parade made its way down here, my feet would be popsicles. But I'd also be less likely to run into Gabe, who would probably be wandering around the section that held the most potential problems.

Up and down the parade route rode San Celina bicycle officers and Parks and Recreation officers. At each corner stood uniformed sheriff's deputies and San Celina patrol officers. I knew that Gabe had arranged for twice the number of officers this year owing to the near riot that had occurred after last year's parade.

"Hey, Benni!" A helmeted police officer stopped his bike in front of me. When I looked closer, I realized it was Joan Sackett.

"Hey, yourself," I said. "You really are a Jill-of-all-trades today."

She grinned and grabbed the fence next to me, keeping herself balanced and upright. "Hey, rank does pull some privileges. It's a lot easier riding this bike than walking."

"I bet."

"I'm glad I saw you. I've got some information about that Sullivan murder. Talk about serendipity. Matt, one of our former sergeants, came by the booth with his granddaughter shortly after you did. He just retired six months ago. Anyway, I told him about your quest and he said he was still in contact with some old guy who was an officer here back in the forties. Said the guy lived up around Jolon, was kind of a loner. His name is Bob Weston. Matt didn't have his phone number on him but he's going to call me on Monday. I'll give you a ring when I get it."

"Thanks, Joan," I said. "Let me give you my cell phone because I'm in and out of both houses so much I might miss your call." I copied it on one of Elvia's business cards I found floating around the bottom of my purse.

Joan stuck it inside her knee-length sock. "I heard you and the chief bought a new house. Good for you. Bet you're really excited."

I nodded, unable to make a sound for fear I'd start crying again.

"Hey, moving's the pits," she said, her voice sympathetic, mistaking my obviously troubled expression for stress. "But it'll be over before you know it."

"I know." Her words and their possible double meaning tore at my heart. "Thanks, Joan. I'll be waiting for your call."

"No problem, Benni. You enjoy the parade now. And be careful."

It took a long time for the parade to reach where I was standing, and the numbness I'd felt inside since that moment with Gabe so many hours ago was beginning to be matched by a real physical numbness in my hands and feet.

Belly dancers slunk by, people dressed as sparkling playing cards weaved in and out of each other in some rehearsed formation, masked people in animal print tights cavorted and preened, throwing beads and coins at the surging crowds. I gripped the chain link fence, determined not to lose my spot so I could snap as many pictures of Elvia's Krewe as possible.

My mind was only vaguely on the parade when I looked up and noticed a man in an Old West frock coat, tall white cowboy hat, knee-length boots, and revolvers strapped to his legs coming toward me. A shiny gold six-pointed star glittered on his chest. Around him, girls dressed in saloon girl outfits smiled and threw beads, every so often doing a short can-can dance. Behind him, a man in a black outfit with a rubber Simon Lagree mask skulked and mimed shooting him in the back.

The man in the white hat walked slowly toward me, his face completely covered by a Clint Eastwood mask. He held out a strand of shiny purple beads.

I watched him approach, mesmerized by his intense and obvious focus on me. Around me the crowd pushed me into the fence, a huge roar like one voice surrounded me, "Throw me some beads, mister! Hey mister, hey mister, throw me some beads!"

He was two feet from me now, close enough for me to see his dark eyes peering out of the mask. Eyes the color of French roast coffee beans. I held out my hand for the beads.

He pulled them back, holding them just out of my reach. He pointed at his mouth and shook the beads. Without a word, he was telling me the price I'd have to pay for them.

I leaned toward him, unable to stop myself, thinking, why not? He moved closer. I reached out and grasped the beads. His face was close enough for me to see the clear white around his brown eyes.

Then, at the last moment, I turned my head and let the mouth of his mask touch my cheek.

The man gave a low laugh, took the beads, and solemnly placed them around my neck. Then he turned and strode back to the cavorting saloon girls.

I stood there for a moment, breathing hard, staring at the shiny purple beads in my hand. What was I thinking? I shook my head, amazed and a bit irritated at how the frenzy of Mardi Gras could cause me to almost kiss a stranger. Or maybe someone who wasn't exactly a stranger, a voice inside chided me.

"Tell me the truth," a voice behind me said next to my ear. "Were you tempted to kiss him because you thought it was me?"

I whirled around and faced Hud's grinning face. I glanced back at the masked sheriff, who had already been replaced by some dancing giraffes and a pirate ship from Krewe Creole.

"You wish," I muttered, my neck hot as an iron.

"See you later," he said and melted back into the crowd.

After I took twenty-four shots of Elvia's dancing books, I pushed my way back out of the crowd and headed toward my truck. The drive to Cambria was not long enough for my taste and I was at Constance Sinclair's huge Julia Morgan–designed Craftsman-style mansion before I wanted. It sat on a hill high above all the other expensive newer homes built on land that had once been only pine trees. I gave my keys to the parking attendant and went inside the brightly lit foyer. People dressed in black-and-white tuxes bustled around like ants on a collapsed anthill.

I grabbed the arm of a young man with a red goatee and said, "Excuse me, but do you know where Mrs. Sinclair is?"

The skin around his eyes turned white. He pointed upstairs. "Better watch your step," he whispered. "She's *not* a happy camper."

"Don't worry," I said, patting his arm. "That's her normal state of being. Just nod and agree with whatever she says and you'll be fine."

He gave me a tentative smile, but didn't look convinced.

I found Constance up in her sitting room drinking a glass of champagne. Constance Sinclair, thin as a greyhound and just as overbred, had been born into one of San Celina's oldest families. She could trace her lineage back to the days when the Spanish owned most of San Celina County, which made her the closest thing to royalty that San Celina had. She used to scare the stuffing out of me until I learned how to deal with her. Which was let her do whatever she wanted and clean up her mistakes behind her.

She and Dove were good buddies, a friendship that defied explanation but certainly made it easier for me to work with her. Constance never got away with the queenly act around Dove and I think that's why Constance respected and liked her.

"How are you, Constance?" I said, putting a large spoonful of fake sympathy in my voice.

"Exhausted," she said, sipping her champagne. A bottle of Dom Perignon sat on the Chippendale table next to her brocade chair. Her silver-white hair looked like a mound of glittery cotton candy under the soft yellow light of a fringed twenties-era lamp. She was dressed in a long off-white gown that probably cost as much as my truck. On the delicate table lay an elaborate black-and-white sequinned Mardi Gras mask, her one concession to the party's theme. "I'm so glad you're here. Please check to see that the caterers have done everything they're paid to do. I need a few moments to gather my wits before my guests arrive."

"Don't worry," I said. "I'll make sure everything's okay."

"Thank you, dear." She drained her glass and closed her eyes. I wondered how much of that bottle of champagne she'd consumed in the last hour or so. Constance had been known to enjoy her champagne, especially under stressful circumstances. And she got more uninhibited with her comments when she did, which was obviously what had panicked the young man downstairs.

I watched her fluttery eyelids for a moment. Constance had most certainly been around in the forties when the Sullivan murder had taken place. She could be an invaluable source of information. And this was my only chance to talk with her privately. Once her guests had arrived, I'd most likely not catch her alone for the rest of the night.

"Constance, did you know Maple and Garvey Sullivan?"

Her eyes flew open, their pale blue depths impaling me with some emotion I couldn't decipher. "Why?" Her voice cracked like a broken branch.

Surprised by the angry tone in her voice, I stuttered, "I . . . I'm . . . doing some research on them. I'm cataloging—"

She interrupted me with a wave of her hand. "Of course I knew him. Garvey's father and mine worked on many of the same projects. Garvey and I attended high school together. He was a fine man. Until that cheap . . . until Maple Bennett turned his head." She struggled up, using the end table as a crutch, and pointed a long finger at me. "Why are you asking about Garvey and . . . that woman?"

"I'm cataloging the contents of Maple Sullivan's trunks for the historical society and I just became interested in the story of their life. I want to try and understand why she might have wanted to kill him." I reached down and pulled at one droopy stocking. "I mean, if she really did kill him."

"Oh, she did, all right," Constance said. "I told him when he brought her out from that Kentucky backwoods he found her in that no good would come of it. But he was crazy in love with her." Her blue eyes turned narrow and mean. "Or maybe he was just crazy."

"So, do you think that she and Mitch Warner were having an affair? That they killed him so they could run away together?"

"No! Absolutely not!" Her bony shoulders stiffened.

Her strong reaction caused a small thrill inside me. She knew something and I was determined to find out what. "Why not?"

"She was a low-class nobody who ended up showing her true colors once she got what she wanted, Garvey's money and good name."

"So," I said carefully, not wanting to stop the flow of information. "She didn't fit in very well with Garvey's crowd. *You* didn't like her."

She looked directly in my eyes. "Maple Sullivan murdered him just as sure as I'm standing here. That's all you need to know. Now please go check on the caterers."

I knew I was risking her wrath, but something in me caused me to keep pushing. "But it just as easily could have been Mitch who killed him. Why does everyone assume it was her?"

Her voice turned into a quiet hiss. "Mitch Warner was a fool, but he didn't kill Garvey Sullivan." She stated it with absolute certainty.

"How do you know?"

"He was a good Catholic man. He wouldn't murder and he wouldn't commit adultery."

"Even good men sometimes do wrong things," I said, swallowing over the lump in my throat.

She paused for a moment, hesitating.

I could tell she was torn between telling me to get out and wanting to defend Mitch Warner. I stood my ground, determined to find out as much information as I could. Constance Sinclair's snobbery had always annoyed me, and after hearing what she said about Maple, I was tempted to leave this party completely, but she had information I wanted. More than ever I was certain that Maple hadn't killed her husband and that the elite of this county was covering something up.

She finally said, "I know he didn't kill Garvey because he told me so."

I drew in a surprised breath. "You were in contact with him after Garvey was killed?"

She nodded.

"Why . . . why didn't you go to the police?"

Her blue eyes turned glassy and sad. "Because he asked me not to."

"Where was he?"

"He didn't say. He just wanted to let me know he was all right. That . . . that it was . . . it had nothing to do with us. He said she was innocent. *That* was a lie. There wasn't an innocent bone in her body. But he told me that he and Maple . . . they weren't together. He swore . . ." She sat down heavily on the brocade chair. "I never heard from him again." By the stricken look on her face, I realized why she'd jumped to his defense. Constance had been in love with Mitch Warner and he'd put the welfare, maybe even the love, of another woman before her. I felt ashamed for bringing up such a painful part of her past. Still, after all these years, she defended him. Without a doubt, we women were a pitiful lot sometimes.

"I'm sorry," I said softly. "I'll go see to the caterers."

She remained in the brocade chair, staring at her hands, when I backed out of the room.

By nine o'clock the party was in full swing and all the guests had arrived. Constance, like the true diva she was, had set our conversation aside and resumed her role as queen of the Mardi Gras ball. I purposely avoided her, spending most of my time in the kitchen making sure the food and drinks were flowing smoothly. I knew that tomorrow, when the effects of the champagne had worn off, she'd regret telling me about her and Mitch Warner. I still felt ashamed for bringing it up, but it had also given me another piece in the Sullivan puzzle. Could I trust Mitch's implication to Constance that he wasn't protecting Maple because they were in love? Or was that just what he'd said to let her down easy and to keep her from calling the police?

Then why call her at all? That was the conundrum. If he'd helped Maple kill Garvey or even did it himself, why call Constance at all?

I worried over the new information as I studiously tried to ignore the feelings of anxiety about my own troubled relationship. I'd fretted about what I'd say to Gabe when he came to the ball, but then realized by eight-thirty that he had probably decided not to attend. Part of me was glad. Another part of me despaired that he'd honored my request and not tried to talk to me. Though I knew we'd only fight, I wanted him to care enough to pursue me.

I was killing time in Constance's huge kitchen re-arranging some canapés on a large silver tray when a warm hand squeezed the back of my neck.

"Why are you hiding out in here?" Isaac asked. "You should be out dancing. And where's that husband of yours?"

I turned to look up at my future stepgrandpa and smiled. He was dressed as the Lone Ranger. The Lone Ranger with a long white braid and an earring. "I'm working tonight, Isaac. My fun will come when I go home, take off this ridiculous dress, and make myself some cocoa. And I imagine Gabe probably ended up having to deal with some crisis downtown. He wasn't sure if he was going to make it." The lie sounded convincing even to me.

"I think you look cute as a bug's ear, but I am a little biased. You sound a little under the weather. Might better add some rum to the cocoa tonight," he said, his dark raisin eyes crinkling.

"Might better," I agreed. "So, how are things with the great wedding site search? Is it just me Dove's been harassing or have you been getting daily updates too?"

He leaned against the tiled counter and sighed. "I wish she'd quit worrying so much about it. I just want to get married and start living our life. Neither of us have that much time to ponder over the styles of print on our wedding napkins."

I pushed shrimp-topped crackers around on the tray. "She wants to be special to you. She wants this wedding to be unique."

He reached up and scratched the side of his broad nose. "Benni, she *is* special. How can she not know that? She doesn't need a wedding in a glass-bottomed boat to prove that she's special."

"A glass-bottomed boat? I haven't heard about that one yet. I'm still bowled over by the cave."

His eyes widened. "Cave? I hadn't heard anything about a cave. I'm not crazy about being underground until I actually am forced to be."

I laughed and held out the silver platter. "To be honest, I don't think you have to worry about it. It was in Arkansas, and after pointing out Garnet would most likely be involved, she nixed it."

"Thank you, Lord," Isaac said. He took a canapé and popped it into his mouth. "Could you talk to her? Tell her she doesn't need to prove anything to me."

I was still apprehensive about getting involved, but unable to say no to this man I cared so much about. "Sure, Isaac. I'll talk to her. I'm not certain it'll do any good, but I'll try."

He leaned down and kissed my forehead. "Thank you. You don't realize how much she respects your opinion. She'll listen to you."

The door of the kitchen flew open and Constance's shrill voice called out, "Isaac, darling, what are you doing in here with the help? People want to meet you. That's what they came for." She glanced over at me, her eyes locking with mine for a moment, their message indecipherable.

"Is everything going well, Benni?" she asked stiffly.

"Just fine, Constance. I'm just helping the caterers get more food out to the guests. A couple of their helpers didn't show up." I picked up the silver tray of stuffed mushrooms.

Her nose quivered like she'd smelled something bad. "Probably off drunk somewhere. Then again, what can you expect with those sort of people."

I felt anger heat up my chest. Those sort of people? Like *working people*? Her tone was the same as when she'd been talking about Maple Sullivan. I'd held my tongue then, but I wasn't about to now.

"*Those* sort of people, Constance, are what make *your* sort of people able to have parties like this."

"Young lady!" she said, pulling herself straight. "You'd better watch your tone. I'm paying good money—"

"Canapés coming right up," Isaac interrupted, taking the tray out of my hands. He said in an aside to me, "Go get some air, kiddo."

I frowned at him, annoyed he was taking her side.

"Constance, we'll be with you in a minute," he called across the kitchen.

She glared at me before giving him a flirtatious look. "Of course, dear Isaac, I'll let you handle it."

After she'd left, I growled at Isaac, "Why did you stop me?"

"Because that fire coming out of your eyes tells me you'd be better off thinking before speaking right now. Now Constance has said worse things than that around you before. You know you can't change attitudes like hers. Why is it bothering you tonight?"

I inhaled deeply, not wanting to go into the whole story about Maple Sullivan one more time. "I'm just tired. You're right, I shouldn't let her get my goat. Thanks for stopping me before I blasted her."

He laughed and held out the tray. "Not that I wouldn't

have thoroughly enjoyed seeing you argue the rights of the working class with her, I just felt that you'd be the one who ended up suffering more."

I took a mushroom and popped it in my mouth. "I think I will go out to the garden and get some air."

"And I'll soothe the snapping greyhound for you," he said.

His comment made me giggle. "I thought I was the only one who thought she looked like one."

"That's better."

"Thanks, Pops. You're the best."

"And you're the Tower of Pisa."

Outside, it was cool enough that I had the garden to myself. The quiet, green-scented pathways were just what I needed. At the back of the garden, I found a cold marble bench and sat down, staring back at the lit-up house. The hum of the party, in full swing now, filtered through the thick trees. No one would miss me at the ball. I could probably sit out here until it ended and I had to supervise the catering crew's cleanup.

I closed my eyes, my mind completely blank for one glorious moment.

"That is some kinda dress, darlin'. You know, every time I see you, I have to rearrange my fantasies. The way that fringe moves when you walk away . . . why, it's a true gift from the gods."

Hud stood in front of me wearing a pin-striped twenties-style suit complete with a fedora and two-toned shoes. He looked like a bad imitation of F. Scott Fitzgerald. There was no way it could have been a coincidence.

"Like my costume?" he said, giving me a wide smile. "Wanna do the Charleston?"

"You are a royal jerk," I said.

"Hey, that's better than a common one. And I may be a jerk, but baby, I'm a jerk who has something you want." He wiggled his eyebrows.

"*You* couldn't possibly have anything I want." I contemplated getting up and leaving, then decided I was here first and *he* needed to leave. "Go away, Hud. I'm truly not in the mood to banter with you right now."

He ignored my request and sat down beside me, his face suddenly sober. "You're upset about something."

"Go away. I mean it. I don't want to talk to anyone right now."

"Where's your husband? You two on the outs?"

I turned, put my hands on his chest, and shoved as hard as I could, knocking him off the bench. "I said get lost!"

He lay awkwardly on the ground, his face comical in shock. I almost laughed, but knew that would only encourage him. His shocked look slowly turned into a grin. Geeze Louise, I thought, doesn't this guy ever get a clue?

"My pawpaw Gautreaux always said the feisty ones were the ones who'd last. Bet you live to be a hundred and five." He stood up, brushing leaves and dirt off his suit. "If there're any stains, I'm sending you the bill."

"Turn blue," I said, getting up to leave.

"I wasn't lyin' when I said I have something you want."

"And I said you have nothing I want. Not now, not next week, not next year, not ever. Clear enough, *Detective Hudson*?" I started walking toward the house.

"Are we back to formal names again?" he said, moaning. "After we made so much progress. Guess I'll just put this diary back where I found it."

I stopped dead and turned around to face his smirk. "Diary?"

He pulled a small bound book from inside his suit coat. "Whose diary?"

"One Maple Bennett Sullivan's."

17

BENNI

"GIVE IT TO me!" I dashed across the brick walkway, holding out my hand. When I reached him, he held the thin book above his head.

"Not so fast. I want an apology first for your unnecessary rudeness and unfriendly demeanor."

Instead I slammed my fist into his stomach.

He anticipated me this time and my fist hit clenched muscle. I pulled it back, rubbing my throbbing knuckles.

"Ha!" he said. "Outfoxed for once. All you have to do is be nice and I'll give it to you. I swear, darlin', I'd give you anything you want if you'd just sweeten that sour attitude a little."

I stood back and glared at him. He was lucky I didn't have a gun because I swore at that moment I'd shoot him right in the heart without one ounce of regret.

He threw back his head and laughed. "That's murder I read in those pretty hazel eyes. Pawpaw would just plumb love you to death. I may have to fly him out from Baton Rouge just so you two can meet."

Forget the gun. I wanted him to dangle at the end of a

rope. For a long, painful time. Then have wolves chew the meat off his bones.

"Here, take it." He held out the cracked leather journal. "Found it this morning inside a box of old books. Can't believe nobody found it in all these years. I haven't read it, I swear. I knew you'd want to be the first."

I searched his dark eyes. He wasn't lying. Just when I wanted to leave his carcass to the buzzards, he did something incredibly thoughtful. I took the diary and held it against my chest. "Thanks."

He stuck his hands deep into his pants pockets. "One favor? Let me know if you find anything interesting in there?"

"Sure," I said, then shivered.

"You'd better get inside. You can't solve a fifty-year-old murder mystery if you've got pneumonia."

Back inside, I put the diary in my leather backpack, wishing this party were over and I could rush home and read Maple's journal. Would the answer to the tragedy be there in her own words?

Dove and I eventually crossed paths over the punch bowl. She was dressed as a pioneer woman in a full calico dress and sun bonnet, which was now dangling down her back much in the same way it probably would have if she'd actually been a pioneer woman.

"Hey, honeybun," she said. "What in the world did you do to get Constance's dander up?"

I leaned my head down and rested it a moment on Dove's shoulder. "She was just being a snob and I called her on it."

Dove patted my back. "What else?"

I straightened up and reached for a crystal punch glass. "What do you mean?"

"She told me to reel you in. That you were sticking your nose in old business that was better left alone." She took my glass, filled it full of punch, and handed it to me. "What's she talking about?"

Knowing better than to try and hide anything from

Dove, I quickly told her the story of Maple and Garvey Sullivan, why I was involved, and what had taken place between Constance and me.

Dove clucked her tongue when I was through. "Always knew there were shenanigans in ole Connie's background. Her fancy act never fooled me."

"So, are you telling me to back off?"

Dove looked at me thoughtfully, fingering the ties of her bonnet. "Honeybun, you just do what you have to do and don't pay no never mind to Constance Sinclair. Whatever was going on between her and Mitch Warner fifty years ago doesn't change the fact that she withheld information that should have been told to someone in authority. What's your next move?"

Sipping the punch, I told her about the possible link to the retired cop Bob Weston.

"Sounds like you've got things covered. Speaking of covered, how's Elvia's shower doing?"

"Everything's ready to go for tomorrow," I said, setting down my empty glass. It suddenly struck me at that moment that tomorrow was not only Elvia's shower, it was also my second anniversary.

She gave me a sharp look. "Is everything okay?"

I knew I wouldn't be able to hide our separation forever, but I was not ready to talk about it yet. I held her watchful gaze. "Fine."

"I'd go see Mac if I was you."

I froze for a moment. Why should I go see our minister? Did she know about Gabe and me? How could she know already?

"Why?" I said, trying to keep my voice from shaking.

"He could probably find out something from Oralee. I wasn't around these parts back then, but I'll gander she was part of that crowd. She's got to know something, but the strokes have made her kind of stubborn. Mac's about the only person can get her to do anything."

"Good idea," I said quickly. "I'll talk to the other ladies

in my quilt group at Oak Terrace Retirement Home. They might know something too."

She searched my face another moment, then kissed my cheek. "Give my love to Gabriel. I'm assuming he's still cleaning up the streets of San Celina."

"Probably so," I said, hugging her.

I spent a few more hours mingling, including some time spent with Emory and Elvia, where I excused Gabe's absence with the explanation I'd given to everyone else.

"He really should learn to delegate," Emory said, refilling my punch glass.

"You know him," I just said.

After checking with the catering staff and being assured that they'd attend to the cleanup detail, I was ready to go home.

Finally, by 1 A.M. I was unlocking the door to the new house. I spent a few minutes petting Scout, then peeled off my costume, tossed it over a pasteboard box, and pulled on thick, warm sweats. With a cup of instant cocoa, I settled down in the bedroom in my sleeping bag with Scout stretched out next to me and opened up Maple's diary. I flipped through it quickly to get an overview of the time it covered. The first entry was in June when she'd been married only a few weeks. The last entry was a month before Garvey was killed. She didn't keep it up on any sort of regular schedule, but seemed to write when the mood struck. I punched my pillow so it supported my neck, then started reading in the yellowish-orange light from the Tiffany floor lamp.

June 30, 1942

Everything is so beautiful here! I am especially charmed by the smell and long-limbed beauty of the eucalyptus trees, something I'd never seen before coming West. Someone told me that whenever you see a row of them there had once been a field or a homestead, that the pioneers used them for windbreaks. People here complain about their sharp, medicine-like smell but I find them exotic and fascinating. The adobes that dot this county are equally fascinating to me. I picture Spanish señoras waiting on their wide verandas for their dashing husbands with their tall leather boots and handlebar mustaches to ride up on a wild black stallion. Sometimes when I spin my tales I can even make my dear husband smile. He doesn't smile very often these days. He has so much to worry about with the building of Camp Riley. It was a very wet winter and construction was halted many times due to rain. Garvey and I have settled down in his family home. Its extraordinary elegance leaves me feeling more than a little like a country bumpkin. I've not much to do as there are people who clean and a woman who cooks our meals. Though there is rationing, we seem to want for nothing, which bothers me. I've spent a lot of time sitting on the front porch reading and watching the green hills turn a soft, caramel brown. I've written Mama and Daddy twice and have not gotten a response. Without me to come home once a month to read and answer their mail, I wonder what they do now.

September 9, 1942

A letter from home arrived today. Brother Perimon at the church wrote it for them. Mama said it was a hard summer and the tobacco crop has not done well. They are further in debt than ever. Daddy has even taken to hiring out to other farmers though there isn't even much field work to go around. It makes me feel so selfish and privileged to enjoy fresh milk and butter whenever I desire. I've mentioned to Garvey that it didn't seem quite fair for us to have so much when others had so little. He looked at me with such bemusement. Has he never been without in his life? Perhaps not. He gave it over to me to do what I see fit with our rationing stamps. I have informed our cook to heed the recipes in the newspaper that use little from rationed food and to give the rest of the stamps to me. I'll find some family with children who need them worse than we do.

Perhaps someone who works for Garvey on the ranch. I'll speak to him about it tonight. And I'll try to send money to Mama again though I know Daddy will make her send it back if he finds out. I miss Mama so much these days.

October 3, 1942

California is not at all what I imagined, though I must confess I didn't have any idea what to expect. The people aren't as welcoming as I had hoped. Though Garvey has many friends, not many of them have taken to me though I have done my best to be pleasant and interested in their lives. There is a large group of his old school chums who have made it clear that I am not of their class. I am lonely sometimes. Garvey is still very busy with all the building projects because of the war and with the cattle ranch in the north county. He was sweet enough to find me a job at the Tribune. Though many of the people there are only nice to me because I am the wife of one of the paper's owners, they are starting to warm up to me. I brought in a batch of my molasses cookies and one of the women who writes for the society column actually asked me for the recipe! I want so badly to make a good life for Garvey, be the best wife he could imagine having, not have him regret one moment that he plucked me out of a train station cafe. I love him so much! But sometimes, I can't help wondering why he chose me. He goes away without me for weeks at a time to the ranch even though I have begged to go along. He says it is no place for a lady. I even talked Mitch Warner into giving me horseback riding lessons in secret so I can surprise Garvey with my ability to ride. Maybe then I can share that part of his life.

December 25, 1942

I am sad and utterly without hope. Our first Christmas together and Garvey disappeared three days ago without telling me anything more than he was going up to the ranch. I begged and begged to go along with him but Garvey in-

*sists on going alone. Is this normal for a man to spend
half his time away from his wife? I had no one to ask
about it since I have no friends here. When I casually
brought it up to the woman who asked me for my cookie
recipe, Lois Hartman, she said it sounded like he might
have a little on the side, if I wanted her honest opinion. I
was so shocked by her words that I left and went straight
home. I refused to believe that about Garvey who is as de-
vout a Catholic as I've ever seen. A man who attends Mass
faithfully twice a week when he is here in town would not
do the thing that Lois suggested. Oh, am I being naive?
What do I know about men? What do I know about their
needs? Am I a good enough wife for him? If I was, why
does he need to leave me so often? What am I to do?*

I read through all thirty entries. She told about writing
her columns, the few times women would ask her to
lunch, dates she prepared for and worried over as if they
were her wedding day. None of them ever asked her
again, apparently their duty fulfilled. Garvey was such a
powerful man that I'd guessed that the wives of San Celina local society had been requested by their husbands to
include Maple Sullivan. But you can't force friendship on
people. Or love, for that matter. Her loneliness and the
isolation she must have felt brought tears to my eyes. The
only thing that kept her going was her job at the paper
and her growing friendship with Mitch Warner.

July 12, 1944

*Garvey gone again. He says he is going to San Francisco
on business but I fear it is more than that. I have no proof,
of course, but I fear I have lost him long ago to a faceless
woman there. When he comes back from the city, he never
comes to our home but goes to the ranch. Mitch tells me
not to worry, that Garvey loves me, wants to protect me,
but as kind as Mitch is trying to be covering up for his
friend, I have long realized the truth, that it was a mistake*

for us to marry. But he is Catholic and now I am too so I know he will honor our marriage, at least on paper. Mitch has been a good friend. He makes me laugh, a rare occurrence these days. We went for a ride last Sunday afternoon and I saw a bald eagle! His majestic wing span left me open-mouthed with wonder which Mitch has not let me forget. He's such a tease but it's nice to have someone to pal around with. I spend a lot of time at the Red Cross these days as they are in continuous need of volunteers and I've a new project, writing down the stories of local women and how the war has affected their lives. Maybe that will be my life's work, a recorder of women's history. It has amazed me the willing sacrifice that the average woman has given to support the war. It needs to be remembered. My work and my faith are all I have left.

January 10, 1945

Mitch and I rode again today. He says I am becoming quite the cowgirl. It is so easy to talk to him. How I wish that Garvey and I had the friendship Mitch and I enjoy. But that is not to be. I do love my husband. For all his silences and his deceptions, there are times when he becomes the man I met in that train station cafe back home, a gentle, listening man whom I trusted enough to leave my family and like a pioneer lady, come West. I laugh at myself for comparing my situation to the real dangers those women faced, their true bravery. I took a train across the country to become the wife of a rich man while they fought disease and snakes and bears and starvation to come West to their men. How I wish I could have talked to some of them. When I look at some of their quilts displayed down at the Carnegie Library I am amazed that they could find enough joy in their bleak lives to create such perfection. What have I done in the three years I've lived in San Celina, wrote a few stories, typed some letters at the Red Cross, served doughnuts at the USO. I do have my ladies histories, though. Of all I own, next to the letters Garvey

wrote me which I still read to recapture the feelings I
know he had for me, those histories are my treasure. Must
finish now, I hear Mitch downstairs kidding with Garvey.
Sometimes he is the only person who can make him smile.
I should hate Mitch for that, but instead, I am grateful.
Their friendship is a life saver for both of us. He is a trea-
sure, without a doubt, one richer than rubies.

That was the last entry. A month later to the day, Garvey was dead and Maple and Mitch had disappeared.

I lay there in the glow of the lamplight, tears streaming
down my face. What had happened among the three of
them? I didn't want to believe that Mitch and Maple did
what everyone assumed. I wanted to believe that their
friendship was just that and that eventually everything
worked out between Garvey and Maple. But of course, it
didn't. Garvey was killed, Maple and Mitch disappeared,
the war ended, and the Sullivan dynasty was another small
footnote in history. Still, deep in my heart, I felt the real
story had never been known. And maybe never would be.
And really, what did it matter? Everyone in this sad tale
had probably been dead for years, their secrets along with
them.

Next to me, Scout stood up and started whining. My
stomach twisted slightly in apprehension. I was normally
not an easily frightened person but this house was still
unfamiliar to me and empty enough to cause a small echo
when I said to Scout, "What is it, boy?"

He stood up and trotted over to the window that over-
looked the street. In the hollow quiet of the house, I could
hear the mantel clock downstairs chime three times. I'd
been reading for two hours straight. I crawled out from
my sleeping bag and followed Scout to the window. He
put his front paws up on the window seat, the window
seat that was the one single thing that had sold me completely on this house. I had imagined sitting in it and
watching my husband stroll up the walk from work.

The street was empty. A half moon seeped through the

treetops, making black lacy squares on the sidewalks.

Scout whined again and pressed his nose against the cold glass.

"No one's out there, boy," I said, scratching behind his left ear. "Everyone's asleep except for us."

I sat down in the window seat for a moment, looking out on the desolate-looking street, wishing I were back at the other house, curled up next to my husband, hearing his sleepy murmurings and surrounded by his nighttime scent. I closed the shade, turned off the Tiffany lamp, and crawled back into my sleeping bag, feeling at that moment more alone than I'd ever felt in my life.

Then the doorbell rang.

18

GABE

HE STOOD IN the shadows across the street from the house and watched Benni's ghostly face in the window, wanting to go to her as badly as he lusted for Del. He'd been walking for the last hour, since leaving his senior officers to take care of the last of the Mardi Gras revelers as they straggled out of the Lopez Street bars. It was almost 3 A.M. and he was tired, but he couldn't face going back to the Spanish bungalow across town, where he would lie in their empty bed under quilts made by her aunt and gramma feeling like his life had ended.

So, *mano loco*, go to her, a voice inside him said. A voice that sounded suspiciously like Father Mark's. But he couldn't. If he went to his wife, they would have to talk and he wasn't sure yet what to say. He was still confused about his feelings for Del. They'd eaten dinner together again tonight and she had come right out and asked him back to her hotel room.

"What's the big deal, Gabe?" she said, laying her hand over his. The warmth caused his stomach to tighten in anticipation. "For old times' sake. I'm not looking for a diamond ring and a picket fence. Just someone to hold me for tonight. What could it hurt?"

He pulled his hand from under hers and reached for his wineglass. He hesitated, then chose the water glass instead. "Not tonight."

She laughed, a throaty sound that seared right through him. "You always did like to play hard to get. That's part of the reason women want you so bad."

He looked over his glass at her, hating that she laughed at him, but still wanting her so badly he could imagine the feel of her slippery lipstick on his throat. "I have to go. I'll call you tomorrow."

"I'll sit by the phone in anticipation," she said, her chocolate eyes shiny with amusement. She reached over and tapped a long-nailed finger on the back of his hand. "But hear this, Gilberto, I won't wait for very long."

He focused again on the house's second floor. Sometime in his musing, Benni had moved away from the window. What had caused her to gaze out to the dark street at three in the morning? Did she sense his presence out here? Like him, was she unable to sleep?

Go to her, the voice said and he recognized it this time as his father's. How ashamed his father would be of him. Like that was something new. He had spent his life doing things that would have shamed his father. He knew if Rogelio Ortiz were standing here next to him, he would have called him foolish, would have scolded him in his strong Spanish-accented English.

"*Mijo,*" his father would have said, shaking an oil-stained finger at Gabe, a gesture that even remembering it to this day made him feel as sullen and stubborn as an adolescent. "*You can never serve too many meals a friend. Or tell a woman too much you love her. Women need tu corazon.*" He would tap the blackened finger to his chest, marking his gray workshirt with a smeared finger. "Your heart," he'd repeat in English, so Gabe could not fake misunderstanding. "No matter what your mistakes, they will hold you in their arms when you are dying if you give to them your heart."

His heart. An organ that had never failed to bring him trouble. It beat fast and hard in his cold chest, feeling twice, three times its size.

"Go to her, *mijo*," his father's voice insisted and he knew he had no choice but to obey the command, even if he had no idea how she would receive him.

He rang the unfamiliar doorbell once, then waited. After a minute or so, she opened the door.

They stared at each other for a long, silent moment.

"What do you want?" she finally asked. Her red-blond hair was wild and tangled in that way that drove her nuts, but always caused a ribbon of desire to course through his body. It reminded him of the first time he'd seen her standing outside the folk art museum throwing pebbles at a San Celina patrol car, her hair full and damp and wind-whipped, her face pale with fear and fatigue. He had wanted to take her in his arms that night, hold her to his chest, sink his face into all that hair, take her home to his bed.

He'd never told her that, how he'd fallen in love with her the first moment they met.

"What do you want?" she asked, the words coming out with a small stutter. Next to her, Scout whined, his tail moving slowly in a tentative wag.

"To talk."

"I think you've said enough. More than enough."

Anger bubbled in his chest. "Is that all you think of our marriage? You won't even let me try to explain?"

Without a word, she turned and walked away, leaving the door open. He came inside and watched her go up the stairs. He shut the door quietly behind him, wishing he had some kind of script about what to say and do next.

The living room was filled with boxes. The only touch of hominess was the mantel clock, which chimed the half hour. Three-thirty. In another three hours he will have been up twenty-four hours and his body was beginning to feel it. The back of his eyes sizzled with fatigue.

He found Benni upstairs in their future bedroom. She sat under the multicolor glow of the Tiffany lamp, her chin resting on her drawn-up knees. He shut the door of the room, leaving a whining Scout on the other side.

"Querida," he said. "Hear me out."

She didn't look up. "I told you not to call me that."

"You're being ridiculous."

She turned her face up to look at him. "Ridiculous? Just because someone doesn't see things exactly how you do, Gabe, doesn't mean they're stupid."

"I didn't say you were stupid."

She jumped up, pointed a finger at him. "It's your attitude. If someone doesn't agree with you, you give them that look."

He felt heat on the back of his neck. "What look?"

"That superior look. That look that says you know best, that your way is the only way. You discount other people's opinions and feelings. You make them . . . you make *me* . . . feel like I don't matter."

He started to say again that was ridiculous, then caught himself. "Why are you turning this into something so complicated?"

She stared at him in amazement. "How can you not see how complicated it is?"

He knew she was right, but he didn't know how to explain to her how he longed for the safety and reality of their love and yet was still undeniably drawn to the danger and excitement of Del and everything she represented.

He crossed the room until he was inches away from her. He took her face in his hands, his thumbs caressing the softness of her cheeks, and looked deep into her tear-filled eyes.

"Querida," he whispered, deliberately ignoring her request to stop using the endearment. He kissed her softly, then with more insistence, forcing her mouth open to accept his tongue. If they could just make love, he knew

this would all blow over. He could put Del and those memories behind him.

She moaned deep in her throat in protest, but he knew her desires, knew how to seduce this woman. He'd spent two years learning her vulnerable spots, finding the way around her heart. He moved his hands down her neck, down the front of her, along her hips, tracing the shape of her body, this body he knew almost better than his own.

"Mi corazon esta llen dear amor por ti. Mi amor, mi amor . . . Desde el dia que to conoci supe que eras alguien especial . . . Te amo, carina, te amo . . ."

She pulled away with a jerk, her hazel eyes glossy with desire. He was slightly ashamed of the triumph he felt.

"No words," she said, her voice cool, emotionless. "I don't really want to hear your voice."

He froze for a moment, her statement an unexpected splash of cold water. With those words, she'd somehow managed to snatch back the control he'd had . . . or thought he had. This woman never failed to surprise him. Desire exploded in his gut and he lowered his head, taking her lips with a desperation that surprised him.

They made love in silence, though he fought the urge to cry out in Spanish, the language in which he'd always made love. A small part of him felt rejected, but he admired her show of pride. It was something he might have done.

Afterward, while she lay on her back with her eyes closed, he studied her naked body. She still wore the platinum horseshoe necklace he'd given her for their first anniversary. Surely she would not still be wearing it if she intended for their marriage to be over.

She was so physically different from Del, from most of the women he'd taken as lovers. He'd always been attracted to tall women with long legs, full breasts. Benni was compact and wiry with short, strong legs, muscled arms. She was as agile as a gymnast, with an energy and openness that delighted him from the first time they made love. But it was the softness of her skin that never failed to crack his heart and the rich, deep, sweet-apple scent of her hair. Hair that now lay in a fan around her head. Everything would be okay now. She'd made love with him. They were back. The foolish words he'd spoken this afternoon erased.

"Benni," he murmured.

Her eyes opened and she turned her head slightly to look at him.

"Will you come back with me tonight?" He laughed softly. "I mean this morning. All my clothes are at the other house."

Without answering, she stood up and started gathering her clothes. He watched her pull on her underwear, sweatshirt, sweatpants. When she was dressed, she faced him, looking down at him with an unreadable expression.

"This doesn't change what you said in the library garden."

He jumped up, his chest tight with anger. "What do you mean?"

"Are you in love with Del Hernandez?" she asked, her face still expressionless.

He hesitated, still not certain about his feelings toward his ex-partner. "I don't want to talk about that anymore."

She narrowed her eyes. "That pretty much answers my question. Please lock the front door when you leave."

The warm feelings he'd had only moments before turned cold as a winter stream. He'd never allowed any woman to dictate his feelings, his actions, and he wasn't about to start now.

"At least she lets me be who I am," he said, pulling on his jeans, grabbing his shirt from where it had been tossed on the floor.

"And who would that be? A fickle man who uses women like tissue or a man too cowardly to make a real commitment to another human being?"

"If you think so little of me, why in the world did you marry me?"

"That, Ortiz, is certainly the question of the hour, isn't it?"

19

BENNI

HE SLAMMED THE door on his way out. The sound echoed through the semi-empty house with a reverberating sadness.

I sank down on the glossy living room floor in such despair I couldn't even cry. What had I expected when I let him in? That we'd somehow talk this out, reason away his feelings for Del, make some kind of list as if our emotions were chores that we could split and take responsibility for?

I was angry at myself and humiliated for allowing him to seduce me so easily. What did I think that would accomplish? Did I think it was like some kind of stupid country song, make love to your man so thoroughly, so expertly, that you wipe away his lust for the other woman? I'm sure I was no match for Del in the pleasing-your-man department.

I lay on my stomach on the oakwood floor, resting my cheek against the cool wood. My body still throbbed with longing for my husband and that made me want to scream in frustration. The physical desire I'd always had for this man had slightly frightened me; it was too strong sometimes, too overwhelming. There were depths within him that I wanted to touch, to smooth away the hurt spots with my bare hands and take some of the pain into myself so he wouldn't have to bear the agony alone. But those places were also terrifying in their unpredictability, and like the coward I accused him of being, a part of me wanted to hand him and his complicated emotions over to Del with my blessings.

I lay on the floor with Scout next to me until the morning sun streamed through the window. It was officially Sunday. Our second anniversary and possibly the last day of our marriage.

A long hot shower and three cups of coffee managed to bring me to some kind of decent mood. Today was also my best friend's wedding shower and it would take every bit of acting ability within me to hide my true feelings.

I arrived at Miss Christine's Tea and Sympathy parlor ten minutes before Amanda. I wore tan wool slacks and an off-white silk cowboy shirt I bought especially for Elvia's shower and was arranging the party favors next to each china plate when Amanda breezed in.

"You're early!" she exclaimed, picking up one of the small mint green baskets I'd just placed. "These are great party favors!" She examined the leather bookmark, small box of Godiva chocolates, and silver heart charm.

"Thanks. I made a few extra just in case."

Within the hour, the shower was in full swing, the teahouse filled with the sounds of women laughing and talking. I realized that the music I'd chosen to play during the show, a combination of Bach and Tchaikovsky, two of Elvia's favorites, would never be heard. But my best friend was having a ball, her face flushed with pleasure and embarrassment, so it was a minor problem.

While Elvia opened her huge mound of gifts, I cruised from table to table to make sure everyone had enough to eat and drink. At Dove's table, she grabbed my arm and pulled me down into the empty chair next to her.

"Edna's gone to the ladies' room," Dove said. "Sit with

me a minute." She leaned over and whispered in my ear, "What're you and Gabe doing for your anniversary tonight?"

I looked her straight in the eye and lied my head off. "We're going out to dinner down in Morro Bay. I bought him a silver letter opener." That last sentence wasn't a lie. What I didn't say is I wanted to plunge it in his heart . . . or even better, in the heart of his ex-girlfriend.

Her face grew still, her pale blue eyes thoughtful. I could tell I wasn't fooling her a bit, but she wouldn't push me.

"That's good," she said. "Don't forget we're working on Elvia's quilt tomorrow afternoon."

"Yes, ma'am," I said and kissed her cheek, feeling like the biggest sinner in the world for lying to my gramma.

I managed to fake it through the rest of the shower, giving Elvia the day she so rightfully deserved. When she, I, and two of her brothers were loading her gifts in the back of the new black Lincoln Navigator that Emory had bought her, she pulled me aside and gave me a fierce hug.

"You are the best friend a person could ever have," she said. "Thank you for a perfect shower." Her voice caught in an involuntary sob.

"You've waited a long time, *hermana*," I said, hugging her back, letting the tears pricking at my eyes flow down my cheeks unheeded.

"Look at us," she said, laughing, when she saw my wet cheeks matched her own. "Getting sentimental in our old age."

"We'd both better wear waterproof mascara to your wedding," I said, sniffing.

"No kidding. I'll see you tomorrow. Oh, and happy second anniversary. Give my best wishes *tu esposo Gabriel*."

"Thanks, *amiga buena*. And give my cousin a hug for me."

After I had settled the bill with Miss Christine, adding a generous tip for her and José and thanking them both profusely for helping make the day perfect for my friend, I was finally free to relax my fake smile. It was two o'clock on the day of my second anniversary and I didn't have a clue what to do with myself. So I went back to the new house, changed into jeans and a sweatshirt, got Scout, and headed toward the folk art museum. There were still Maple's trunks to go through and maybe I'd come across some clue to what really happened between her, Mitch, and Garvey.

The museum was busy with artists getting back to work to restock their depleted inventories. Manuel caught me in my office while I was reading over the report he'd just laid on my desk. Our gamble with three booths had paid off, giving us the highest sales the co-op had ever had. The co-op's cut was almost seven hundred dollars—a four-hundred-dollar profit. Any kind of profit was worthy of celebration.

"Great job, boss lady," Manuel said.

"No, the congratulations go to you all," I answered. "Looks like things are finally starting to look up for the co-op."

He nodded, patted my shoulder, and walked away whistling, "Happy Days Are Here Again."

"For some people, anyway," I murmured and went out to the large room to work on the trunks.

It was only when the setting sun shined orange into one of the room's high windows that I realized two hours had passed. I glanced at the schoolhouse clock over a row of low cabinets. Four thirty-five. My hollow-feeling stomach told me that the few miniature chicken salad sandwiches I'd gobbled down at the shower had not been enough sustenance. Though I scorned myself for doing it, I checked my cell phone for any messages. There weren't any. Then again, what did I expect? What else did we have to say to each other?

I decided not to eat in town, afraid I'd run into either him or Del—or possibly both of them together—so I turned left on Lopez and headed away from downtown toward El Maguey, a small Mexican cafe where Jack and I often ate after we'd picked up an order at the Farm Supply. He'd loved their *pollo verde,* the only place in town that made it. I stopped eating there when he died, one more place where the memories we'd shared there were just too fresh and painful.

But right now, a big plate of *pollo verde* and some memories of easier, happier times seemed just the right antidote for my blue mood. When I passed by the old Mission Cemetery, a thought occurred to me and I made a quick U-turn on the mostly empty stretch of upper Lopez Street. I wanted to see Garvey Sullivan's grave.

It was now dusk. Blue time, I'd heard Isaac call it—a photography term. Right as the sun went down, but before you completely lose the light. A time when the best pictures are taken. There is a lavender gauziness hovering over everything, an almost physical presence to the air that makes it easy to imagine that there is more than just the dimension we are living in, that there are, indeed, battles fought and deals made among principalities and angels and with God Himself, and that if you just stared hard enough into the haze, you'd catch a glimpse of flashing swords and dragons breathing fire.

The old Mission Cemetery was the only Catholic cemetery in San Celina. It lay across the street from San Celina's main cemetery, where Jack and my mother were buried. I'd been to this cemetery only once as a young teenager when Elvia's grandfather was buried.

I drove under a huge black wrought iron archway. I stopped to read the small sign posted at driver level.

Old Mission Cemetery was first located inside the Santa Celine Mission quadrangle. On August 12, 1878, a law was passed by the city council prohibiting burials within the city limits. After several extensions the present cemetery was opened on November 2, 1878. Some tombstones indicate earlier burials and these were probably moved from the original Mission location.

There are people buried here who had no tombstones. Information regarding these burials is located on the map available at the cemetery office. This map shows the location of all burial plots, with and without tombstones, by section, row and number. This includes both mausoleums. This cemetery is under the direction of Mr. Joseph Martinez of the Monterey Diocese, Monterey, California.

The cemetery itself was stark and almost treeless. Most of the grave sites were gravel covered and lined with low, concrete borders. Late afternoon shadows shaded the tall white monuments, giving the faces of the marble angels an almost living countenance.

I drove straight to the small cemetery office, hoping it would still be open and someone could direct me to Garvey's grave. Though this wasn't a huge cemetery, it would take me a couple of hours to search for it on my own.

"Stay," I told Scout. "I won't be long."

Inside the office, a sixtyish Hispanic woman in a flowered print dress was watering a bright green philodendron in a brass planter shaped like a sleigh. She jumped when I rapped softly on the door frame.

"I'm so sorry," I said. "I didn't mean to startle you. But is this where I get a map to the cemetery?"

She smiled at me and set down her plastic watering can. "That's all right. I'm just not used to getting much company. I have a map right here, but the cemetery closes at dark." She glanced out the window. "Which looks like it will be in about fifteen minutes. Can I help you find somebody?"

"No," I said quickly, not exactly sure why. "I'm sure I'll find who I'm looking for on the map."

She handed me a map, an alphabetical listing of the cemetery occupants, and a one-page history of the cemetery written by the San Celina County Genealogical Society.

"I won't throw you out," she said. "They close the front

gates, but there's a back way out on Fair Oaks Street that's always open." She gestured me to the window, where she pointed out the road leading to a small side street. "I'll be here until five or so. Let me know if you can't find who you're looking for."

"Thank you. I won't be long," I promised. "And I have a flashlight."

"Just be careful," she said. "The paths are a little tricky to walk. Lots of little potholes and uneven spots."

"Thanks, I will."

Out in my truck, I found Garvey Sullivan's name on the alphabetical listing. Section five, row three, grave site number one. I located it on the map, a large corner plot, and in less than five minutes, I was standing in front of the Sullivan family plot.

It was marked with a large white cross at least four feet tall with a three-dimensional lily of the valley carving trailing up the length of the cross. Two stone angels holding swords guarded each side of the cross. One angel was missing the tip of his wing. Only Garvey's last name was carved in relief—SULLIVAN. Underneath were the names of his father, his mother, and Garvey and the dates of their births and deaths. Nothing else and no one else.

And lying at the base of the cross, one almost dead long-stem red rose.

I picked up the dry flower, and its petals were caught by the evening breeze and scattered at my feet. My heart started beating faster in my chest. Who had left this rose? Garvey Sullivan had been dead for fifty years and had had no family living here in San Celina for a long time. Someone, though, still remembered him, and I knew if I found that someone, another piece of this puzzle, maybe even the solution, might be found.

I jumped in my truck and drove back to the cemetery office. The Hispanic lady was just locking the door when I rushed up.

"I have a question," I said.

"I'll try to answer it," she said, pocketing the key. "But

I've only worked here for three years so I might not know the answer."

"There's a plot at the northeast end, the Sullivan family. It has a white stone cross with two angels guarding it. I found this at the base of it." I held up the dead rose. "And I was wondering . . ."

She gave a small laugh. "Oh, the lady in black's delivery."

"What?" The lady in black? Could it be . . . no, it was impossible . . .

The woman laughed again. "I'm sorry. There's not actually a lady in black who puts a rose on Mr. Sullivan's grave. That's just one of our little jokes here. You know, like the lady in black who visited Rudolph Valentino's grave for so many years."

Disappointment enveloped me. I should have realized it wouldn't be so easy. "So, what do you mean, her delivery?"

"Well, the story is that for as long as anyone can remember, a red rose has been delivered once a month to that grave. Regular as clockwork. I could have told you that if you'd told me who you were looking for."

I tried not to sound too eager. "Who delivers it?"

She shrugged and opened her black purse, tossing the ring of keys inside. "Mission Floral downtown is all I know. They have a couple of regular monthly orders like that. As for who pays them, I guess you'll have to ask them."

"Thanks, I will."

As I suspected, they were closed by the time I drove back downtown. And they were also closed Mondays. There was not even an emergency number to call so it looked like I would have to wait until Tuesday to find out any information about this mysterious mourner. Could it be Maple? But if she'd been doing it for years, why hadn't a police officer traced it back to her?

I spent the rest of the evening at the new house reading one of the few books I'd brought with me, a book by

Gerald Haslam called *Workin' Man's Blues* about the history of country music in California. The phone didn't ring once. What a difference from last year on this day when Gabe and I celebrated our first anniversary with a drive up the coast for a romantic dinner, then two nights in a cabin in Big Sur. I touched the necklace he'd given me, which I wore every day under my flannel shirts—a simple platinum horseshoe, the chain extending from the open ends of the shoe so the luck wouldn't run out. Part of me was tempted to take it off, but it had become such an accustomed feel around my neck, I couldn't.

The next morning after checking with Elvia to see if she needed any emotional support or errands done and hearing all was running smoothly on the wedding front, I decided to take Dove's advice and go talk to Mac about questioning Oralee. I called his office, knowing that Monday is the traditional minister's day off and managed to pry out of his very protective assistant that he was out at the Martinez ranch practicing his team penning.

The Martinez ranch was only a short half-hour drive away near Santa Flora. At the big ranch house, Maria Martinez, a woman I'd known for years through the Cattlewomen's Association, directed me to the corrals out back of the house.

"Come back by for a cup of coffee when you're through," she said. "I want to show you my ideas for an opportunity quilt for the Women's Shelter auction. Got some great horse fabric in Paducah last year. Besides, I just baked three cherry pies and we'd better grab us a piece before the men get in here."

"You've got a deal," I said.

Out back, a crowd of ten or so men were perched on the pipe corral's upper rungs cheering Mac on as he and his huge bay stallion, Peck (short for Peckerwood, which, not being the most appropriate name for a minister's horse, he'd shortened to assuage the delicate sensibilities of some of his more straitlaced church members), did their best to steer one last recalcitrant calf in with his penned buddies.

A man on the fence called, "Give it up, *padre*! The calf wins!" The men sitting on the fence cheered and hooted.

Mac yanked off his brown Stetson and slammed it against his muscular Wrangler-clad thigh.

"Dang it," he yelled. "I'd best be keeping my day job, I guess."

The men laughed again, two or three spit, then razzed him some more.

"Hey, guys," I said, walking up behind them.

They all nodded and said hello. Most of them I knew by sight and name, the ag community getting smaller and smaller every year.

"Hey, Roberto," I said, greeting Maria's husband. "I've got a question for the *padre* here. Can I borrow him a minute?"

Roberto, a tall, lean Hispanic man with a salt-and-pepper handlebar mustache, said, "Why not? He obviously ain't no kinda cowboy so hopefully he'll be better at ministering to his flock." A wide grin punctuated his words.

"I heard that," Mac said, riding up to us. "You all can kiss my patootie. Peck's too distracted by those mares over in the barn. Definitely living up to his name."

Roberto winked at me. "I do believe patootie is minister-speak for ass. And I believe the padre may be putting his own feelings on that old horse of his. What do you think, Benni? Believe our young reverend over there is as horny as his horse?"

Mac's widowed and celibate state had been a source of humor among his fellow ranchers since he'd returned home and taken over as First Baptist Church's minister. He'd grown up branding and riding with most of them, so he was given no mercy despite his ecclesiastical status.

"I believe I don't even want to go there," I said, slipping my hands in my back pockets.

Mac took a little more kidding as he swung off Peck,

telling them all what they could do with their suggestions by the curve of his upper lip.

"Oh, man, better watch out. He's giving us the Elvis sneer now," an old cowboy said, spitting a long brown strand of tobacco juice two inches from Mac's size thirteen cowboy boots.

Mac looked at me, a huge grin on his face. "You know what the only trouble with *some* Baptists is? They just didn't hold them under long enough."

The men roared in laughter. It was obvious he was well liked by these men, many of whom attended his church on a semiregular basis.

"Walk with me," Mac said, leading Peck away from the still laughing men. "We can talk while this old fleabag cools off."

"This won't take long," I said. "Dove just suggested I talk with you about this . . . thing I'm working on."

"No problem," he said, looking down at me from his six-foot-four-inch height. His gray eyes were calm and soothing. "I'm done for the day anyway."

We walked down the road toward the trucks and horse trailers. Behind us, the men cheered on Roberto as he attempted to pen the same calf that had escaped from Mac.

Mac laughed and scratched his horse's warm neck. A former Baylor tackle who'd turned down the pros to serve a more demanding coach than any in the NFL, he'd come back to San Celina shortly after Jack died. I attended his church sporadically at first, but had become more regular in the last few months, something he teased me as being one of his more successful spiritual accomplishments.

He was a hometown boy, six years older than me, someone I'd known all my life. Someone I'd even had an adolescent crush on when I was twelve and he was eighteen. Since that time we'd both been married and widowed and I'd remarried. At thirty-six and forty-two, we'd developed an appreciation for our friendship and I could even, occasionally, think of him as a spiritual advisor. That is, when I wasn't teasing him about past peccadillos

such as the time he and my uncle Arnie, his best friend
in high school, were caught by the vice-principal reselling
his grandma Oralee's beer for a substantial profit to their
fellow football players.

"So, what's up?" Mac asked.

I told him a quick version of Maple and Garvey and
what I believed about Maple. "Dove said Oralee might
know something about all this and that I should ask you."

"Why not ask Grandma herself?" Mac asked, his broad,
handsome face perplexed. He tied Peck loosely to a ring
and started unbuckling his saddle.

"Dove said she was only talking to you these days."

Mac's face remained confused as he hefted off the saddle and blanket and shoved them into the trailer's small
equipment locker. "I don't know what Dove's talking
about. Grandma Oralee is doing fine. I saw her yesterday.
Just go on over to the retirement home. She'd be tickled
to see you."

I chewed on my bottom lip and rubbed Peck's cheek.
Why had Dove sent me to Mac then?

"Anything else going on?" he asked, his voice casual.
He took out a well-used curry brush and with practiced
strokes cleaned off Peck's sweat and dirt-encrusted back.

I couldn't meet his eyes. Dang that Dove. She was
making sure I received spiritual advice whether I wanted
it or not. I shrugged. "Not much. Elvia's wedding been
keeping me busy."

He continued currying Peck. "Wasn't yesterday your
anniversary? Second, right?"

I nodded and didn't answer. He would remember since,
after our Las Vegas elopement, he'd married us for a second time five days later to appease Dove's spiritual re-
quirements.

"So, what did you two do?" He grinned. "Remember,
I'm your minister. I want the G-rated version."

I gave him a halfhearted smile back. "Oh, you
know . . ."

His face grew concerned. "What I know is you since

you were a knock-kneed kid. And your expression tells me something's wrong."

I started to answer, then choked. I shook my head at him dumbly.

"Here," he said, handing me the curry brush. "You clean off old Peck here and I'll just rest my bones." He sat down on the trailer's bumper and looked away from me.

I started brushing Peck's wide back, and with each long stroke, the story gradually came out. By the time I'd finished, Peck's coat was gleaming, his eyes rolled back from the sheer pleasure of my touch, and there were tears in my eyes. Mac never uttered a single word until I held the brush out to him.

"Let's take Peck for a drink," he said.

Down at the small creek that ran alongside the Martinez's long driveway, while Peck drank deeply, Mac asked, "So, what do you plan on doing?"

"What can I do?" I said bitterly. "Seems like he holds all the cards in this game."

Mac patted my shoulder. "I think you might have an ace or two."

I didn't answer.

"You knew this marriage wasn't going to be easy. You and I discussed that at great length, if I remember correctly. Of course, that was *after* you'd already married him."

"I know." I was going to leave it at that, not wanting to hear any "I told you so's" but couldn't resist adding, "But I expected stepchildren and ex-wife problems, maybe even some old Vietnam stuff, but I never expected him to say he might still be in love with someone else. What could I do to prepare for that? I feel so stupid. This is so unfair. If he didn't love me, he shouldn't have married me."

Mac stroked Peck's shiny flank. The horse lifted his head and sniffed at the air, his ears twisting like little antennas. "He loves you, Benni. Take my word on that. This is just a little burp from his past."

"Burp! More like an extended beer belch." Then, I couldn't help giving a small laugh. "Could we have managed to find a grosser metaphor?"

He laughed with me. "You know, he married *you*. That says a lot. I've seen a lot of variations on male-female relationships and I've come to one simple conclusion. If a man is willing to be legal partners with a woman and make her the beneficiary of his life insurance and all that he owns, *that,* my dear friend, is trust and that is a lot of what real love is about. You can certainly love someone without trusting them, but I'm not entirely certain you can trust someone without feeling love for them."

"That's kind of a practical way of looking at love," I said.

"Real love, *mature* love, is as much practical as passionate," he said. "It's not just the Song of Solomon, it's also First Corinthians 13. Pretty easy to understand. Very concrete adjectives and verbs. 'Love is patient, is kind, is not proud, not easily angered, keeps no records of wrongs.' "

"Right, easy as eating pie," I said.

He raised his eyebrows. "I didn't say it was easy to do, just practical."

I sighed, embarrassed by my snappish tone. "I'm sorry, Mac."

He put a huge arm around my shoulders. "You're hurt, angry, confused. All of that is perfectly human. Have you prayed about it?"

My voice was a whisper. "I'm too pissed off to pray."

He gave a small chuckle. "It's okay, God can take you being angry. How about I say a quick one right now?"

I nodded. He started before I could even bow my head and close my eyes.

"Lord God," he said, in his beautiful, deep bass. "Like you heard, Benni's real angry now, at Gabe and at you. Help her find her way to peace. Help Gabe do what is right. And help this woman who has come between them find peace also, just somewhere other than San Celina, if you don't mind. But most of all, help us trust in your mercy and your wisdom. We ask that you work this all out because the people involved sure aren't doing that good a job of it. Thank you. Amen."

I echoed his amen.

"Anything else?" he asked, squeezing my shoulders.

"No, thanks. I do feel better even though nothing has changed."

"Good," he said. "After my poor showing in that corral, I was hoping that those yokels weren't right about my ministering abilities. Keep me informed, okay? And I'll keep you in my prayers."

"Thanks, Mac, I will."

"Oh, and do go by and see Oralee. Who knows, she might have some information on that case you're working on. If you find out anything new, I'd be curious to hear about it."

"Sure thing."

I spent a half hour or so shooting the breeze with Maria, eating a piece of her excellent cherry pie and giving her my input on the opportunity quilt that incorporated local ranch brands in the log cabin pattern. Then I headed toward Oak Terrace Retirement Home, a facility perched on a hill overlooking the road out of San Celina to Morro Bay. I found Oralee in the sun room polishing a pair of red cowboy boots.

"Wow, those are pretty fancy," I said.

"They're a pain in the ass is what they are," she replied, holding one up in a gnarled hand. "Show every little mark. Mac bought them for me." At the mention of her beloved grandson's name, her tanned old face broke into a big smile.

"I just saw Mac," I said. "He said I should come by and see you. I've got some questions about the war years."

Her face lit up and I glanced at the clock above the stone mantel. I would have to steer this conversation with great care or I'd be here all day listening to World War II recollections. It took me only a few minutes to explain to her what I wanted to know.

"I never thought she did it," Oralee said. "She was a real fine lady. That Mitch was a rich, spoiled brat who managed to wiggle his way out of serving his country. I doubt he'd have thought twice about stealing his best friend's girl, maybe even killing him if the circumstances were right."

"Except a person can't be stolen from someone else," I said. "She wasn't a horse or a cow getting rustled. She would have had to go along willingly."

By the expression on Oralee's face, I could see I'd struck a nerve, but she was never one to back down. "She was a good woman. I'd bet my ranch on it. If there was any killing, she didn't do it. And as for running off with him, well, I never cottoned to that theory either. I saw the way she looked at Garvey when they went to some of the Cattlemen's balls. She loved that man. She wouldn't hurt him."

I sighed and thanked her, though I really wasn't any farther along the path of knowing the truth than when I'd arrived an hour ago. We chatted a little longer. I filled her in on all the latest gossip with the Cattlewomen and in Dove's life and wedding plans.

"I'm sure looking forward to that wedding, wherever it ends up taking place," she said, with a pleased cackle. "Maybe I'll wear my red boots."

"Dove would purely love that," I said. "I'll let you know where they land as soon as I know."

I spent another three, unfruitful hours visiting the women of Oak Terrace's Coffin Star Quilt Guild, of which I was an unofficial member. You had to be at least seventy-five to be voted in, but I was given honorary membership so they'd have someone to thread their needles and bring them new fabric for their stashes. They'd all remembered the scandal. Of the now thirteen members who remembered the incident, the split was ten in favor of Maple, two undecided, and one who thought she was definitely guilty.

"It was the top story in the local paper, right there next to Hitler's shenanigans," said Thelma Rook, who had once owned the largest feed store in San Celina. "But I never did quite believe it was as simple as the paper implied. The *Tribune* never mentioned Mitch Warner, of course, so most of us heard about that through the grapevine."

"I noticed that when I read the articles at the library," I said.

"Well," Martha Pickering, Thelma's roommate and best friend, said, "I think she was a nice little country girl who just got in over her head. She and I rolled many a Red Cross bandage together and she just plumb didn't have it in her to murder anyone."

"That seems to be the general consensus," I said. "Except for Constance Sinclair and Vynelle Williams." I'd just been in Vynelle's room ten minutes before and she was the one dissenting viewpoint, which I was trying to listen to with an open mind like a good historian should.

"Oh, that Vynelle," Thelma said, shaking her head primly. "She'd find fault with Saint Joan of Arc. Then again, she and Constance ran in the same crowd once upon a time before Vynelle's husband embezzled all that money from the bank. She's *still* trying to get back into the good graces of this town's so-called social elite even though they dumped her like a load of manure twenty years ago."

Vynelle had been as dismissive and certain of Maple's guilt as Constance, but with no real concrete reason why. I assumed it was, again, a class issue, as well as an envy one. The trouble was I was only getting people's feelings and suspicions, no real evidence. That made finding who'd been sending those flowers all those years even more important.

"Thanks a lot, ladies," I said, hugging them both.

"You've been a big help. I'll keep you up on what's happening with it."

"You do that," Martha said, taking one of my hands between her two warm, wrinkled ones. "And bring us some yellows and oranges for our fabric stash next time, you hear? It's getting on spring and my mind's working on a quilt of mums."

"You got it, sisters," I said. "Talk to you soon."

It was already one o'clock so I dialed Dove and let her know I was on my way to the ranch to work on Elvia's quilt. We had only five squares left to quilt and time was running short.

At the ranch, I made myself an egg salad sandwich and ate it while I watched Dove stitch on Elvia's quilt. It had turned out more beautiful than we'd hoped. It was as special for me as I knew it would be for Elvia and Emory because of all the hours I spent quilting it with Dove.

"You're eating that sandwich in a right leisurely manner," she commented dryly, holding up her needle to the quilting lamp, the better to thread it. She scoffed at fancy needle threaders, claiming if people ate enough carrots, they wouldn't need them. Her eyes narrowed as she sought the needle's eye. We were sitting in the family room right off the kitchen, where the scent of baking zucchini bread filled the air with the smell of allspice, nutmeg, and cinnamon. Outside, a light February rain had started, tempting me to kick back and take a nap after I ate, not finish Elvia's quilt.

"Quit your bellyaching," I answered, pushing Daddy's recliner back one notch just to show her I wasn't in a hurry. "I'll finish when I finish."

"Where you learned to sass like that, I'll never know," she said with absolute sincerity.

Isaac walked into the room just as she uttered her last comment, gave a small chuckle, and winked at me.

"She's serious," I said, smiling at him. "She thinks I got it from someone else."

"No comment," he said, leaning down to kiss the top

of her snowy head. "At least until we get hitched, then all bets are off."

"Ha, ain't that the truth," Dove said, grinning.

They gave each other an adoring look.

"Okay, you guys, save it for the honeymoon." I pushed the chair upright and joined Dove on the sofa. "Let's finish this old horse blanket."

"*Now* she wants to work," Dove said.

"What did you say the name of this pattern was again?" Isaac asked, pouring himself a cup of coffee from the coffeemaker.

"Steps to the Altar," I said, threading a needle. "It's a pretty easy pattern, but Dove and I really liked the name and we wanted to make Elvia something other than the traditional Wedding Ring."

He nodded, his face solemn. "Steps to the Altar," he repeated. "Very appropriate. But take it from someone who knows, the steps to the altar are easy, it's the steps to a marriage that are hard."

Dove studied Isaac's face for a moment. "That," she said softly, "is about the truest thing I ever heard spoken."

"I'll be down by the creek," he said. "There're some egrets feeding there and I want some pictures of them."

"Dinner's at six," Dove said. "Don't be late or I'll throw it to the pigs."

Isaac's old face grinned. "She would too."

I laughed. "I wouldn't worry too much. We don't have pigs."

After he'd left, Dove and I settled into a rhythm that we'd developed over the years of quilting together, an easy balance of talk and breaks every so often to stretch the kinks from our legs and fingers. Some of our best conversations had come about when we were quilting, especially when she'd forced me to quilt as a teenager. The combination of having to concentrate on a physical act and the inability to look at the person while you were talking had enabled Dove and I to discuss delicate topics without too much pressure and emotion.

At first, I mostly listened as she talked about this book she'd just bought that had chapters and chapters of unusual weddings and wedding spots.

"In Las Vegas, you can have a Star Trek wedding, a King Arthur wedding, or even a Godfather wedding complete with a fake attack by rival mobsters."

I raised my eyebrows at that one, but didn't say a word.

"I'm kind of partial to the Beach Blanket Bingo wedding package, though," she continued, her eyes on her stitching. "Two muscle men would carry me down the aisle on a surfboard to any song I'd like. I was thinking the Beach Boys' 'Wish They All Could Be California Girls' would be about right. I think I've lived here long enough to qualify for that, don't you?"

Okay, that one made me giggle. "You aren't serious?"

She shook her head. "Just wanted to see if I could get you to smile."

"So you did," I said, giving her a half smile.

"I mean in your eyes."

I bent my head back over my square. "I'm fine." But I knew I wasn't fooling her a bit.

"Did you go see Mac?" she asked.

"Yes."

"And?"

"And I'm fine."

There was a moment of silence, then I couldn't stand it. "Gabe thinks he might be in love with someone else," I blurted out.

She never dropped a stitch. "Go on," she said.

I stopped sewing and poured the whole story out. By the time I was done, tears were flowing down my face and I could barely talk.

Dove got up, fetched a clean embroidered tea towel, and handed it to me, patting me gently on the back. "It's going to be okay, honeybun. It's just a little hitch in the rope."

"Hitch! Try a big old slip knot that gets tighter and tighter every day. Geeze, I want to kill him. Not to mention her! I wish I'd never met him. I truly do. What a total loser. What a jerk. I hope he ends up toothless and impotent. And I hope she, I hope she . . ." I just couldn't think of something bad enough. "I hope she develops canker sores the size of Kansas. I can't believe I've been sitting around moaning and groaning about this. Let them have each other. It's just what they deserve. I was fine before he came into my life and I'll be fine long after he's gone."

She let me rant and rave for a good ten minutes. The flat-out anger dried my tears so I tossed the tea towel aside. When, like an old-fashioned windup toy, I'd finally ran out of steam, she spoke in a clear, calm voice.

"You two can survive this, you know. Sometimes in a marriage, one person has to be the stronger, the more forgiving. If you're together long enough, it evens out. Trust me, honeybun, a marriage can even survive one of the partners thinking they are in love with someone else. Usually, those feelings aren't real, they're just something hurting inside that person."

I gazed at her in misery, my anger dissipated and replaced now by an overwhelming sadness. "I've done the best I can, Gramma. I've been the best wife I know how to be. I know I've failed in some ways . . ."

"This is not necessarily something you could have prevented," Dove said. "This is old business that he never took care of when he should have. And business like that tends to come back to bite us in the butt. Trust him, Benni. Trust yourself. Trust that you and he were meant to be together. And if he wants forgiveness, give it to him. In the long run, it will make you both better people."

My temper flared again. "Trust him! You *are* kidding. Dove, you're not *hearing* me. He told me he thought he might be in love with another woman. Shoot, maybe he's always been in love with her. Maybe I was the mistake. Trust him? Right now I trust him about as much as I would a rattlesnake. For all I know, they're in bed together as we speak."

She *tsked* under her breath. "My hearing's just fine, young lady. And I'm telling you, I doubt what he feels for that woman is love. This I do know. He's an honorable man. He would never cheat on you."

Anger melted back into misery. "You don't know that for sure."

"No, not for sure, but I trust *my* instincts and they say he's suffering over this as much as you. He'll come around. And just remember one other thing. There's not a one of us that can't be tempted in that way and lots of others. It's not the temptation that does us in, it's the giving in to it that seals the bargain with the devil."

I shrugged, feigning indifference, though I knew I wasn't fooling Dove a bit. "Right now, I'm not sure I care whether he gives in to temptation or not."

Her eyes gave me a disbelieving look over the top of her glasses.

I sighed. Not only was I losing my husband, but I was obviously disappointing Dove with my reactions. "Did anything like this ever happen to you and Grampa?"

She nodded, her eyes growing hazy with memory. "It's not that unusual. Sometimes a person thinks they want this, that, or the other when what they really want is just not to feel bad inside. And it might take them a while to figure out that all those things won't heal that longing inside. That you got to face the fact you have the longing, then let God fix it."

"So when Grampa—" Before I could go any further, my cell phone rang. It was Joan Sackett from the police department.

"Hey, Benni, I've got some information for you."

"Great!" I said, fumbling around for some paper and pencil. "What did you find out?"

"That old cop I saw at the festival called me back with Bob Weston's phone number. Believe it or not, he doesn't live far away. Up around Jolon."

Jolon was a very small town about seventy-five miles north near the San Antonio Mission in Monterey County.

The mission was the only one located on an active military base—Fort Hunter-Leggitt. I'd visited the mission once for a high school history class field trip.

"What's his story?" I asked.

"He must be in his late seventies, early eighties," she continued. "He was one of the detectives who worked on the Sullivan murder. I gave him a call and paved the way a bit for you. Seems like a nice old guy. Pretty talkative once he was convinced I was really a cop. I flirted with him a bit so he'd let me interview him for the department's oral history project. Can you imagine the untold stories knocking around in that man's head?"

I took down his number and thanked Joan profusely for getting back to me so quickly. Then I called the number. Mr. Weston answered on the third ring.

"Mr. Weston? This is Benni Harper. Joan Sackett of the San Celina Police Department said she—"

His voice was strong and blunt as a brick. I would have known he was a cop without ever being told. "Yes, yes, young woman. I was just on the phone with her. Tell me, is she married?"

"Uh . . . divorced, I think."

"Fine, fine. What about you?"

I hesitated a moment, then said, "Married."

"You sure?"

I cleared my throat. "Absolutely."

"Hmp," he answered as if he already knew everything that had taken place between me and Gabe. I bet he'd been a good detective. "So, when do you want to meet?"

"As soon as you can," I said.

"How about tonight? The Hacienda Restaurant at Hearst's old hunting lodge? Know where that is? It's the Monday night steak special. Two top sirloin dinners for nine-fifty. I'm not averse to a woman buying me a meal, by the way. How's six o'clock sound? I don't want them to run out of lime sherbet. It's my favorite."

"Of course," I said, a bit unnerved by his shotgun

approach. "I'll meet you there. Did Joan tell you my husband—"

"Is the chief of police. She did. I've heard about him. Fine police officer, I'm told, even if he did sell out to management. Cares about the ranks. Not too full of himself. Too good-looking, they say, which is never a plus in our business, distracts the females too much, interferes with investigating except on the rare occasion when you can use it. But there you go. We all have our crosses to bear. Joan said you wanted to discuss the Sullivan mess. Been a long time since anyone's wanted to know about that. Don't know if I can help much. Will your husband be joining us?"

"No, it's just me. I'll explain my involvement when I see you, Mr. Weston. Six o'clock is great. Thank you for seeing me on such short notice."

"No problem, missy. Old man like me doesn't get to have dinner with a young woman too often. Looking forward to it. And you tell that Joan that I'll be calling her."

"I sure will," I said, smiling in spite of myself.

"What's that all about?" Dove asked when I got off.

I explained the latest twist in my search for the truth in the Sullivan murder.

"That man will have some interesting stories, no doubt," Dove said. "And who knows? Maybe he'll give you something you can use."

Since it was only three o'clock, I continued working on the quilt until four. We had only one square left, which Dove assured me she could finish tonight. "You get on the road. And keep that cell phone with you. That's a lonely drive out to The Hacienda. Me and Isaac went there a while back for some real good prime rib."

"It's two-for-one steak night apparently."

"Well, then, eat up. The protein will make you feel better."

As I gathered up my jacket and purse, I turned back to Dove, determined to hear the whole story of Grampa falling in love with someone else. I wanted to know how long it took her to forgive him, did she feel differently about him, did she ever regret not just kicking his butt out.

"When Grampa fell in love with that other woman," I said, "how long before you and he . . . before things were okay?"

She looked up from the last square she was quilting. I knew Dove. She was superstitious, though she would deny it. She would deliberately drop a stitch in this square so, like the Amish, she would not insult God by attempting a perfect quilt. I could have told her there were plenty of dropped stitches in my squares. Not unlike my life.

Her white eyebrows went up slightly. "Who said it was Grampa?"

20

BENNI

ON THE DRIVE out to The Hacienda I marveled at how my gramma could still surprise me. I didn't have time to find out the details about this other man she'd thought she'd loved, which was probably why she didn't mention it until I was ready to leave.

"We'll discuss it someday," she said, walking me to the door. "Just remember it was your grampa who understood what true love was. He waited for me until I came to my senses. And for that, he owns a piece of my heart that no one else ever will." With that statement, she kissed my cheek, bopped me on the butt with her palm, and told me to get along, find out the truth about Maple Sullivan, and bring it on back to her. She needed a good story to take to the next historical meeting.

The shadows were growing long when I made the turn off Interstate 101 for The Hacienda. I passed an empty guard shack, the only indication that I was now on military property. It had been a rainy winter and the hills were a brilliant green dotted with yellow ground clouds of wild mustard and Bermuda buttercups, a flower whose stems tasted sour when you chewed them, somewhere between lemon and lime. The early rain guaranteed that feed would be abundant this year. Not one car passed me as I drove into the hills dotted with white clusters of early popcorn weed. A diamond-shaped yellow-and-black sign flashed by on my right—TANK CROSSING—reminding me that this wasn't just an ordinary country road.

The Hacienda Restaurant and Lodge was located near a group of obviously military buildings. Though I'd lived in San Celina most of my life, I'd never come to this restaurant in southern Monterey County. I didn't even remember these buildings from my school field trip. I drove up the small hill to the mission-style lodge and parked next to a Monterey County Sheriff's car. Once in a spacious courtyard covered with flattened grass, I followed a couple who appeared to know where they were going. We passed under one of the archways and had a choice of two glass doors. The left went into the restaurant, the right into a cocktail lounge, which was just starting to fill with people. The couple chose the restaurant and I followed.

The restaurant was one large room lit by rustic, octagon-shaped chandeliers resembling wagon wheels. The high-beamed ceilings and adobe walls echoed the mission theme. Greco-style painting with a slightly Native American and Mexican motif edged all the deep windows and the archways leading to the kitchen and the small-windowed back room that seemed to serve as the salad bar. Above this archway, there was, incongruously, a lighted bingo board. Behind the entry an elaborate mural had been painted of the early military history of California. In calligraphic lettering it announced:

The Military Come to the Providence of California.

While I waited behind the couple, I picked up a brochure with The Hacienda pictured on front. The buildings were designed in 1929 by Julia Morgan, a close friend of William Randolph Hearst and the designer of the infamous Hearst Castle. The rooms in the lodge were originally built for the workers of Hearst's vast cattle ranch and were also used to provide Hearst's myriad of friends with a "ranch" experience including barbecues, dances, and impromptu rodeos. The brochure claimed the ranch had enjoyed visits from Clark Gable, Spencer Tracy, Herbert Hoover, and other celebrities and politicians. Now it was a semisecret spot for birders, hikers, and vacationers looking for an inexpensive, low-stress hideaway.

The couple was seated and I moved forward. "I'm meeting someone . . ." I started to tell the ponytailed waitress.

"Yeah, Mr. Weston. He's already got a table. Over there." She pointed across the wide adobe-colored room. A gray-haired man wearing a pale blue sports shirt stood up and gave a quick wave.

"Thanks," I said and headed toward him, weaving through the already crowded room. The tables were simple Formica-topped restaurant tables and the chairs armless, padded highbacks with teal-colored cushions.

"Benni Harper?" The man pulled out my chair. He was about five-six with a straight-backed, military-style bearing. His blue shirt was without a wrinkle and his thin gray hair short and tidy. He smiled widely, revealing a perfect set of dentures that seemed a little too large for his mouth. Blue-gray eyes that reminded me of Gabe's gave me a brief once-over in a gesture that was in every cop's permanent repertoire.

"Yes. Mr. Weston?"

He gave a small chuckle and helped me scoot in my chair. "Humor me, young woman, and call me Bob." He sat down across from me. "This is a big deal for me, you know. Don't get many phone calls from the ladies anymore. Spent the last two hours primping."

"Now I find that real hard to believe," I said, instantly charmed by his honesty. I just hoped he'd be as forthcoming with his knowledge of the Sullivan murder.

We ordered our steaks and shot the breeze a little while, discussing the history of these buildings, how he liked living in a town as small as Jolon, how I liked being a cop's wife.

"My dear Beth," he said, his lined face going soft in memory. "God rest her soul, she had the patience of a saint. Takes that to be married to a career police officer. I don't know how she put up with me all those years." His eyes grew teary over his salad.

I touched the top of his rough hand. "I'm sure it was worth it to her. She must have loved you very much."

He gave a brusque nod, embarrassed by his emotional lapse. "She always claimed to."

Halfway through our steaks, I managed to steer the conversation to the actual reason I was meeting him. He talked about the Sullivan murder with a reluctance that I suspected had to do with the frustration of remembering an unsolved case.

"I never thought she did it," he said, chewing his steak carefully.

"Why's that?" I tried not to sound too eager. I wanted his honest opinion, not just someone who would tell me what I wanted to hear.

He paused for a moment and sipped his iced tea. "Now, that's a good question. I don't really know why. I suppose if you held a gun to my head, pardon my analogy, and made me explain myself, I'd have to say it just wasn't in her."

Playing the devil's advocate, I said, "She was pretty darn smart. You must have read some of her newspaper articles. Maple Sullivan was more than capable of planning a murder."

"Now, I didn't say she wasn't *smart* enough. I mean she wasn't hard enough. I saw the crime scene. That took someone who had a cold heart and a strong stomach. He was shot in the temple. Bullet went right through the cheekbone and blew his left eye plumb out. The person who did that calmly walked away and left him there. I don't believe she had it in her to do that."

"On what basis?" I asked, setting my fork down. The medium-rare steak in front of me suddenly lost its appeal. "Had you ever met her?"

"Nope," he admitted. "But she was a woman, after all."

I bit the inside of my cheek to keep from blurting out a protesting squawk. Waiting until the urge passed, I said, "A woman is perfectly capable of being that calm and calculating. And of murdering someone."

He grinned at me. "You one of them women's libbers?"

I studied my fork, then looked him straight in the eyes. "If being a women's libber means I believe women are just as capable as men of cold, calculating behavior, then I guess I am."

He chuckled, speared a large piece of dripping meat, and shoved it between his lips. "Now don't go getting your knickers in a bundle. I'm not sure I agree with you. Women certainly can be mean and cruel, but in my long years of watching the human race, I'd say men got 'em beat ten to one."

"Maybe," I hedged. "But you still haven't given me a concrete reason why you think she didn't kill her husband."

"You know, I got the distinct impression when we first spoke that you didn't think she did it."

"I don't, but I want to be fair. It's important to find out the truth even if it proves what I don't personally want to be true."

He nodded, chewing thoughtfully. He placed his knife on the plate and tented his fingers, thinking before he answered. "You'd have made a fine detective, young woman."

I smiled at him. "Thank you. Now, tell me why you don't think she did it. Give me some concrete reasons why *you* don't think she killed her husband."

He held up his right index finger. "One, when women kill, they tend to use poison, not guns. Especially during the era we're talking about. Might be different now, but back then, with all the research I did, women poisoned when they wanted to kill." He held up a second finger. "Two, she was afraid of guns. I mean, she had one of them phobias. There's a name for it, can't recall at the moment. The old brain isn't as quick as it used to be. But she wouldn't even allow them in the house. I contacted her parents back in Kentucky to confirm it and it wasn't just something she told people to set the whole thing up. She really was scared to death of firearms of any kind, had been since she was a little girl. They told me that before they even knew Garvey Sullivan had been shot." He held up a third finger. "Three, she didn't stand to inherit much. Not until she gave birth to their first child. Signed a document stating that if the marriage didn't work out and there were no heirs born, she'd get a flat ten thousand dollars and all the personal items he'd given her. One of the first prenuptial agreements, I gathered. His father talked him into it, and apparently, she went along. She wouldn't have gained much by killing him."

"Ten thousand dollars was a lot of money in the forties," I pointed out.

"Not compared to what she'd gotten if she'd stayed."

"Yes, but it could be the start of a new life."

"Say, one with another man? Yes, I thought of that and that's exactly what I think happened. I said I didn't think she killed her husband. I didn't say I thought she didn't know something about who did. I think Mitch Warner and Garvey Sullivan got into an argument about her affections. Mitch perhaps asking Garvey to let her go. Garvey refuses. A gun appears and someone is killed. In this case, Garvey. Mitch and Maple flee and another domestic murder is left unsolved. They might have been rich, but I've seen that same scenario played out hundreds of times in my career. Mark my words, this was two fellas fighting over a girl, a story as old as Adam."

"So, how come the papers made it sound like the police thought Maple did it? Is there something you're not telling me?"

He snorted with derision. "Of course the newspapers would make it look like she did it. That bird cage liner was partially owned by the Warners. All my opinions and conclusions were tossed aside."

"Of course," I said, sighing. "What was I thinking?" I pushed my plate of half-eaten steak aside and rested my elbows on the table. "Let me tell you something I found out and see what you think." I told him about the rose delivered monthly to Garvey Sullivan's grave.

He shook his head, his mouth turning down as he listened. "Now that's a curiosity. How long's that been going on? Deliveries must have started after the case had been relegated to the inactive file or I would have tried to trace it. If someone had reported it, that is."

"I don't know," I admitted. "That's what I'm going to try and find out tomorrow. Tell me, what did happen to the case files on this?"

He dabbed his mouth with his teal-colored napkin. "Don't really know. I imagine somewhere along the line someone just threw everything out. Town the size of San Celina's not going to have the manpower to have one of them old case units. There were a lot of unsolved cases that got pushed aside once the war was over. A lot of people did things during that time they didn't want known, and if they had the power to cover them up, destroy evidence of their crooked dealings, they did. Everyone wanted to start fresh in the fifties, leave the sadness of the war behind." His blue-gray eyes bore into mine. "You'll let me know what you find out? It would be nice if this case could be put to rest before I join Beth, you know?"

"Of course," I said. "I'll call you if I find out anything new."

He walked me out to my truck and shook my hand warmly before opening my door. "It's been a pleasure, Mrs. Harper. Tell that husband of yours that he'd best keep you. You're a good'un."

I gave a half smile at the irony of his statement, considering the situation between me and Gabe, and thanked him again for taking the time to see me.

"You take care, Bob."

"Will do. Drive careful now," he replied. "Lock your doors."

On the drive back, I went over in my mind what new information I'd gleaned from Bob Weston. The most significant was Maple's fear of guns, which had never been mentioned anywhere. That was a piece of information that would have probably been in the case file had it still existed.

At home, Scout was overjoyed to see me and we had a nice long walk downtown even though it was past ten o'clock. The streetlights glowed a soft gold on the sidewalks, and twice I stopped and chatted with other downtown residents out for a stroll. I would have enjoyed living this close to the center of town. I couldn't help wondering where I would be living six months from now.

The next day I was waiting outside Mission Floral at 10 A.M. when they opened.

"Wow," said the young college-age girl unlocking the door. "You must need some flowers bad." She grinned at me with a mouthful of silver-colored braces.

"Actually, I have a question about a possible customer of yours."

She walked behind the counter and punched some numbers in the cash register. "You'll have to ask my mom about that. She owns this place. I just work here part-time when I'm not in school."

"When's your mother due in?"

"Around noon."

I sighed. "Okay, I'll be back."

I decided to kill some time down at Blind Harry's, find out what was going on with Elvia and Emory. It was hard to believe it was only five days until their wedding. It didn't surprise me that she wasn't there, but out taking care of another of the millions of details a four-hundred-guest wedding required.

"Would you care to leave her a message?" Mrs. Langcroft, one of her assistant managers, asked. She was a retired children's librarian who couldn't resist the lure of working with books.

"No, thanks. I'll call her on her cell phone if I don't run into her somewhere."

I was on my way downstairs to buy a café mocha and a newspaper when I spotted Sam restocking books in the mystery section.

"Hey, stepson," I said, going over to him. "How's it going?" I gave him a smile and a light punch in the arm.

He looked at me as if I'd just swallowed a live spider. "How can you be so cheerful?" His astonished facial expression turned hopeful. "Did you and Dad make up? Is that woman gone?"

I must admit I was speechless for a moment. Though I'd certainly had plenty of marital tiffs with Jack, and since we lived on his family's ranch, which bordered the Ramsey ranch, thereby guaranteeing more than our fair share of comments and opinions by both sets of families, I'd never had to discuss a spousal argument with a child, step or otherwise.

"Uh, no," I stuttered. "We're still . . . working on it."

He swore colorfully, calling Del names out loud that I only called her in my mind.

"*Shh,* Sam," I said, pointing to our proximity to the always crowded children's section. "Don't worry about this. Your dad and I will work it out."

"Yeah, right," he said bitterly. "Just like he and my mom did. What an asshole he is. He talks about *me* keeping it in my pants, *me* being responsible. What about him?"

For the second time in thirty seconds, I was without words. I stared at his angry face, trying to choose my words wisely. Whatever happened between me and Gabe, I truly didn't want his fragile relationship with Sam to be destroyed.

"Sam, your dad's in a really . . . tough place right now."

"More like a really stupid place."

I held up my hand for him to stop. "Sam, whatever he

does or doesn't do with me, the truth remains that he loves you and wants the best for you. This . . . thing with Del caught both him and me by surprise. I . . . I'm sorry for whatever problems this woman caused with you and your mom, but try to see your dad's whole life, the whole of who he is and not just the mistakes he's made. He's been a good father to you in so many ways. Sam, he loves you more than he loves his own life. I promise you that."

He shoved a handful of books into an empty space. "How can you defend him when he's being such an asshole? I don't understand that. Why don't you want to just kill him?"

I looked up at Sam's agonized face. "Truth?"

He nodded emphatically.

I took a deep breath. "Okay, truth is, I do want to kill your father. There are moments when I regret ever having met him. And frankly, if there were a way I could hold Del Hernandez's head under water until she was blowing bubbles, I would."

"So why don't you? Why don't you just go kick her ass? Tell her to get lost." He clenched his fists.

I thought about that for a moment. Why didn't I just go and confront her? Tell her exactly what I thought about her and her actions.

"Because I have too much pride, Sam. I'll never let her see how much she's hurt me. I refuse to give her that power. It's one thing to let your father see it, but I'll be darned if I'll let her have that satisfaction. *That's* why. And the reality is I have to let this thing play out the way it's meant to be. I can't make your father want to be with me, any more than you can make someone be with you when they don't want to be. I love your father, but I'm only fifty percent of this marriage."

"But I don't want you to stop being my stepmom," he said in a low voice.

I squeezed his muscled biceps. "Oh, Sam, that's one of the nicest things anyone has ever said to me. I don't want to stop being your stepmom either, but if it comes to that, remember, you and I will always be friends."

"Really?"

I nodded, wishing I could erase the sad look off his face. Wishing I could freeze my own heart into not hurting so much. In that moment, I hated Del with all my being for bringing this pain into my life, into Sam's life. And I hated Gabe for allowing it to happen.

His face did not look entirely convinced. "I hope you're not mad at me for telling my mom. She said she talked to you."

"Not at all. Your mom's a very special woman. You treasure her, okay?"

"Okay. I guess I'll see you at the wedding Saturday."

"You bet."

I went downstairs and tried to forget about Gabe and Del and the whole mess my life was in while I drank my café mocha and read today's *Tribune*. Two hours finally passed and I was back at Mission Floral. The owner had come in a few minutes ahead of me.

"She's in back," another young girl told me. This one looked to be about fourteen and had a bright green streak down the side of her black hair.

I made my way to the back of the store, where a woman in her early fifties was working on a huge funeral wreath of white gladioli and gold mums. A radio in the background played our local oldies station. Herman's Hermits was singing about Mrs. Brown's lovely daughter. The woman turned to face me. Her platinum-streaked black hair was pulled up in a messy topknot. A white stick dangled from her unpainted mouth. She pulled out a red Tootsie Roll Pop and said, "Can I help you?"

"I hope so. I'm Benni Harper. I talked to your daughter this morning."

She held out a dirt-stained hand. "Janet Nicholson. I own this place. She said something about you wanting to know something about one of our customers."

I quickly explained my story. She listened, moving the sucker from one side of her mouth to the other. When I'd finished, she took it completely out of her mouth and shook it slightly from side to side.

"I'm sorry, but our records are confidential. There's obviously some reason why this person wants to remain anonymous and I should honor that."

"But this is very important—"

"So's my reputation. If it gets out that we give out information about our customers, think of how that would make us look."

"But—"

"Sorry." She turned back to the white-and-gold funeral wreath.

Back outside, I kicked the ground in frustration. How else was I going to find out who was sending those flowers? The thought that Maple's actual address was as close as Mission Floral's records in physical distance but out of my actual reach made me want to bite through a steel bit.

An idea came to me as I was unlocking my truck's door and I headed back downtown. If anyone could help me, she could.

Amanda Landry's law office was located above the Ross Discount Department store downtown. Inside its expensively decorated Kentucky-colonial-home-style waiting room, I begged her receptionist for a minute of her time.

"Two minutes tops," I said. "My name is Benni Harper. I'm an old friend."

"She's with a client," the receptionist said in a cool, professional voice. She was a woman in her late sixties who had the look and manner of someone born drinking from a silver baby bottle. Amanda had just hired her, which was why I introduced myself. She'd get to know me eventually, as this wasn't the first time I'd cajoled Amanda into letting me use her investigator's prodigious Internet capabilities.

"Would you care to wait?" She pointed to the cordovan leather sofa.

"Absolutely," I said, sitting down. "Thank you." Etta James sang a sad, he's-left-me song in the background.

Fifteen minutes later when I was well into an article in *Southern Living* on plantation house restoration, Amanda walked into the reception area.

"Benni, girl! What a surprise!" Her voiced boomed across the compact reception area. "Have you met Sara?"

"Sort of." I held out my hand. "Nice to meet you."

"How do you do," the woman said in a quiet, elegant voice. Her handshake was firm, but her skin soft as a newborn kitten's.

"I just love her," Amanda said, giving the woman an enthusiastic one-armed hug. "Has only worked here a month and already knows me like a book."

"Do you have a few minutes for Ms. Harper?" Sara asked, her delicate face a pale pink from embarrassment.

"Oh, shoot, Sara," Amanda said, gesturing at me to follow her. "I always have time for my favorite cowgirl. Benni's an old friend."

"I'll remember," Sara said, smiling graciously at me.

Inside Amanda's office, she quickly filled me in on Sara. "Just between you and me and the hitching post, she's a client I represented back in Alabama right before I left. Criminal trial. She was the defendant."

"What'd she do?" I asked.

"She blew away the asshole of a husband who'd been beating her senseless for thirty-two years. She served her three years and was released completely destitute. Her son, a real chip off the asshole's block, abandoned her and she had no marketable skills. I sent her the money to come out here and work for me."

I smiled at Amanda. Rich from her deceased daddy's ill-gotten gains as the crookedest judge in Alabama, she continued to use her money in ways like this, helping people who needed a hand up.

"You're a good woman, Miss Mandy," I said, using her housekeeper's nickname for her. The blues-singing, very hunky male housekeeper she was still contemplating falling in love with.

She made a scoffing gesture with her hand. *"Pshaw,* as my mama used to say. Sara's the best thing I ever did for myself next to hiring Leilani."

"And Eli," I said, grinning. Eli was her housekeeper.

"We're not going to go there today," she said, grinning back at me. "So what can I do you for?"

"I'm in desperate need of Leilani's services." Like I'd done so many times in the last few days, I quickly told Maple and Garvey's story and how far I'd gotten in my investigation.

"What possessed you to attempt this right before Elvia's wedding?" she asked, leaning back in her chair and laughing.

I shrugged. "It just sort of happened. Obviously, there's no real hurry except that if these flowers are being sent by Maple herself, well, I'd love to get a chance to talk to her while I can."

She leaned forward and picked up the phone. "Let me see what Leilani can dig up." After relaying to her the scanty information I'd discovered, she hung up the phone. "She said to give her about fifteen minutes."

"She's amazing," I said.

"Amen, Sister Benni," Amanda agreed.

We chatted about Elvia's wedding and again debated the wisdom of Amanda dating her housekeeper, who we were both sure was interested in her romantically, and though the feeling was definitely mutual on her side, the possibility of losing him as a housekeeper was a real consideration. We still hadn't debated all points to death by the time Leilani knocked on her door.

Leilani was a former San Celina police detective and investigator for the district attorney's office. A soft-spoken, satin-skinned Samoan woman with depthless eyes that dared you to lie, she was a whiz at computers as well as, according to city police legend, the toughest female cop the force had ever seen. If there was any way for me to get that address over the Internet, Leilani would know how to do it.

"Hey, Leilani," Amanda said. "You remember Benni." She nodded wordlessly at me. I waved hello.

"Mission Floral doesn't seem to do anything by computer," she said. "I'm guessing they still do bookkeeping the old-fashioned way."

"Darn," I said. "That means unless I break into their offices and riffle through their files, I'll never find this woman's address."

"Don't give up so easy," Amanda said. "Any ideas, Leilani?"

She held out a sheet of paper. "This is the best I could do. I checked the records, and Janet Nicholson has owned Mission Floral since 1978. Before that, it was owned by a Mr. and Mrs. James and Clara Downey, who'd owned it since 1939. Clara Downey died three years ago, but Mr. Downey lives in Templeton. Here's his address and phone number."

"Great!" I said, standing up and reaching for the paper. "If the deliveries started before Janet Nicholson owned the shop, he might know something about them. It's a long shot, but who knows?"

"That's exactly what I thought," Leilani said.

"Leilani, again you save the day," Amanda said, beaming. "Thank you kindly."

Leilani nodded at both of us and left.

"Thanks, Amanda," I said, giving her a hug before I left. "See you this Saturday at the Mission."

"Wouldn't miss this wedding for all the roux in New Orleans," she said.

It was now one o'clock, and though I knew I should grab something to eat, I was too excited about the possibility that this Mr. Downey might have Maple Bennett's—or whatever she called herself now—address.

I sat in my truck and dialed his number on my cell phone. It took a little talking before he agreed to meet me at a cafe in downtown Templeton.

Templeton's ode to the West was obvious in the painstaking consistency in its main street buildings. Once an authentic cowboy town, it was rapidly becoming lined with upscale bistros and wine stores. Though the Templeton stock auction down the road was still as authentically Western as anyplace in Montana or Wyoming, the town of Templeton itself was succumbing to the Central Coast's invasion of fringe-wearing, Ralph Lauren–clad stockbrokers and dot.com executives who wanted a rural experience without too much manure smell and accompanied by a nice crisp Chardonnay.

Mr. Downey was waiting for me in a back booth at The Lett's Dine Inn, a small cafe that appeared to still be in the pancakes and chicken fried steak category rather than crepes with lemon zest and steak Diane. I recognized him from his candid description over the phone. "I'll be the eighty-two-year-old geezer wearing a scraggly mustache, a cue ball head, and a red-checkered hunting jacket."

"Mr. James Downey?"

"That's my name last time I checked my driver's license." He gestured to the bench seat across from him. "What'll you have?" He gestured over at the waitress, who yelled out, "Be right there, Jimmy."

He grinned. "So, you're looking into the Sullivan murder, eh? Land sakes alive, that was a long time ago. Why're you interested in that old tragedy?"

Yet again I told the story of my involvement and interest up to and including Janet Nicholson's refusal to share the information of the flower buyer to me this morning and how Leilani came up with his name. During my explanation, we were interrupted by the waitress, who took our orders—a grilled cheese sandwich and bowl of tomato soup for him, a BLT for me.

"So," I said. "I was wondering, since you and Mrs. Downey owned the store before they did, maybe you'd remember something about this person and their order."

"So you think this Maple Sullivan might have been the one sending the flowers?"

"Maybe, maybe not," I said. "But it's really the only lead I have to work on."

The waitress brought our food and for a few minutes we concentrated on ketchup, salt, pepper, and Tabasco sauce. He took a small bite of his grilled cheese, chewed it slowly, then said, "What do you plan on doing with her if you find her?"

That stopped me cold, my sandwich halfway to my mouth. That was something I honestly hadn't considered. All I'd concentrated on was finding her and talking to her, finding out what really happened if she'd tell me.

"You're married to San Celina's police chief, aren't you?" Mr. Downey asked.

I nodded, not bothering to ask how he knew that.

"So, would you feel obligated to turn her in seeing as she's still a suspect in her husband's murder?"

Again, that was something I hadn't even thought about. So I did for about thirty seconds. "No," I said firmly. "I just want to talk to her. To be honest, I don't think she did it."

He ate a spoonful of soup, looking up at me as he did. "What if she did?"

This was getting much more complicated than I'd anticipated. To be truthful, deep inside I never thought of any of these people as still being alive. It had been more like a puzzle to me, a quest of sorts. If I hadn't desperately needed something to keep my mind off the possibility of my own marriage disintegrating before my eyes, I'm not sure I'd have pursued it this far.

If she *was* still alive, the fact remained, she was wanted for questioning. What was my duty as a citizen in that regard? Since I hadn't had any time to contemplate the moral and ethical ramifications of it, I fell back on my standard procedure.

"When I come to that bridge, I guess I'll just have to trust my instincts," I said weakly.

He nodded as if he understood. "I reckon you'll make the right decision, young woman." He pushed his half-finished lunch aside, reached down next to him, and pulled three stained green ledgers up and placed them on the table. "Me and Clara sold the place in the late seventies just like your friend told you. We'd owned it since 1939. Ran it on a shoestring all through the war. Kept all our own handwritten records in these ledgers until 1978 when we sold it to Janet Nicholson. We had a part-time accountant those last couple of years and he started sending out real bills and recording them in his own system. He'd give us a monthly statement all typed up nice and neat. That's what went with the business when we sold it to Janet. She didn't want our old ledgers, said they weren't of any use to her. Clara and I kept them because they were kind of a record of our life during that time. We used to go through them when she was still with me and remember all the people we'd arranged flowers for."

He opened the ledger sitting on the table. "The first request for the rose to be sent to Garvey Sullivan's grave came on May 10, 1952. After that, we'd get a money order once a year for the exact amount a dozen roses would cost plus our standard delivery charge times twelve. Got it regular as clockwork until we sold the place."

"Did the person leave a name?" I asked, trying to keep my excitement from grabbing the ledger from his hands.

He ran his finger down the ledger. "Only once, I remember. Oddest thing. It was long after that first request. Right around 1977. They wrote it on the money order, but it made me wonder if it wasn't someone new and they weren't thinking about being traced. Then they must have realized what they'd done and never did it again. But we recorded it that first time." He turned the book around for me to read.

"Mrs. Albert C. Smith." That was all it said.

I sighed, trying not to be too disappointed. The chance of me finding her by this piece of information was minute, to say the least.

"No address on any of the entries?" I asked. "Not even a city?"

He turned the ledger back around, grinning at me. "Now, I was waiting to see if you'd ask that. As a matter of fact, me and Clara were right curious about it seeing as we remembered the murder and all and we suspected that this Mrs. Smith might be Maple Bennett Sullivan."

"You did?" I pushed my sandwich aside. "Why didn't you go to the police?"

His lined face hardened. "Because we don't think she did it. Lived here in this county all my life. Eighty-five years last month. And there's one thing that's as true as the day is long, there's people in this county who made a lot of money off other people's back-breaking work, there's people in this county who've done bad things, terrible things, but never had to pay for them because their grandpas weren't nothing more than robber barons stealing from the Indians and the Mexicans and the Japanese and the Chinese and whoever else they could plunder. The Warners and the Sullivans had some good people in their families, but they had more'n their share of bad apples. I think poor little Maple Sullivan got in way over her head and took the fall for that Warner boy, who was too dang cowardly to even fight for the country that made his family rich. And his daddy and his cronies made sure she appeared to be the one who pulled the trigger when anyone who'd ever met her knew that she wasn't that kind. Me and Clara done lots of business with Maple Sullivan and she was the sweetest, kindest lady you could imagine. You know, she gave us all her milk rations for a year when our Janie was a little one and the doctor said she had weak bones, that maybe extra milk might help her. And we weren't the only people she'd helped, not by a long shot. Besides, why in the world would a woman who'd killed her husband risk getting caught just so she could put a flower on his grave? That's an innocent woman, I tell you." He cleared his throat wetly. "No, sir, they weren't going to hear about her from us. Not by a long shot."

All those years they protected her whereabouts. It was amazing. I couldn't help but wonder what Bob Weston would think about all this.

If, a little voice inside me said, you tell him. He is, after all, a police officer, retired or not. He might still feel duty bound to turn her in and let justice run its course. Another moral decision I'd have to face sooner or later.

"Did you ever talk to her?" I asked. "Were you *certain* it was Maple Sullivan?"

He pulled his sandwich back in front of him and picked it up. "No, we never talked to her. And we weren't absolutely certain it was her, but who else would it be?"

"There wasn't any indication in the ledger of an address."

"No, there never was a return address, but we did notice the postal mark. Guess she trusted us enough not to give her away. She was taking a big chance, especially when we sold the place. We wanted to let her know, but there was no way to get in touch with her. That Janet was new in town, fresh from Colorado. By the time we sold the store to her, Maple Sullivan's story was old news. We just told her she was a relative of Garvey Sullivan's who made this request every year. She didn't even question it."

"The return address," I reminded him.

"Oh, yes, the postmark. It was Idyllwild, California. Out there near Palm Springs up in the San Jacinto Mountains. We looked it up on the map. Always meant to take a trip there when we retired but then Clara got sick. Heard it's a real pretty little mountain town, but I really couldn't tell you."

21

❖ ❖ ❖

BENNI

I WAS SO excited I could barely sit still. I managed to finish my lunch and chat with Mr. Downey without giving in to the urge to rush out the door and run for a phone. After insisting on paying for his lunch and after multiple promises that I'd let him know whatever I found out, I drove home in record time. Though my cell phone tempted me, I held back the urge to pull over to the side of the road and use it. This conversation was definitely not one I wanted to conduct over an uncertain cell phone connection.

My high hopes were smashed to gravel when there was no listing in Idyllwild for a Mr. or Mrs. Albert Smith. I stared at the phone in irritation. Did I really expect it to be that easy? I could go back to Amanda and ask to use Leilani's expertise again, but I wanted to use up all of my own resources first. Amanda was a wonderful and helpful friend, but I didn't want to overstay my welcome. I'd give myself the rest of the day, and if I couldn't come up with something, I'd throw myself on her mercy one more time.

My laptop computer was at the folk art museum so, taking Scout with me this time, I headed there, intending on spending the afternoon searching the Internet myself for any Albert C. Smiths in the general vicinity of Palm Springs and Idyllwild. After checking my California atlas, I searched every possible combination of Albert C. Smith I could think of in the Internet phone books including any within a fifty-mile radius of Idyllwild. None of the phone numbers turned out to have people even remotely connected to Maple Sullivan. Or at least that's what they told me. I was sitting back in my chair, feet propped up on my desk, frowning at my gray screen when the phone rang. It was Dove.

"Hi," she said. "Did you get me a good shower gift? It's tonight, you know."

"I remember, and yes, I got you a—"

"Don't tell me! I want it to be a surprise."

I'd bought her a red silk nightgown from Angelina's. It would be a surprise, all right.

"How are things going with the wedding plans?" I asked, afraid of her answer. I had good reason to be.

"I was thinking Caveman," she said.

"No way," I answered. "I look terrible in animal skins."

"Skydiving?"

"Get someone else to be your matron of honor."

"Roller coaster?"

"They make me queasy, you know that."

"Hot air balloon?"

"Better not. Since Gabe is best man and I'm not feeling too kindly toward him right now, I might just push him out of the basket."

She didn't laugh.

"Hey, that's a joke," I said.

"My wedding's not a joking matter." Her voice went an octave higher with what sounded like panic.

"Dove," I said, trying to keep her calm and me from screaming in frustration. "I truly, truly think that getting married to you in a plain old church is about as much excitement as Isaac can handle."

"But I want it to be special," she whined, sounding for

all the world like me when I was sixteen and begging for a lower-cut prom dress than Dove thought proper.

"You're going to have to decide soon."

"Don't pressure me!" she cried and hung up.

Desperately needing some caffeine after that little scene, I was rummaging around in the refrigerator of our small kitchen looking for milk that wouldn't curdle when it hit my cup of coffee when Edna McClun walked in.

"Hi, Benni. How's the cataloging going?"

"Hey, Edna. It's . . . going."

"Well, no hurry, but . . ." She gave me another bright, encouraging smile. She must have been a drill sergeant in her former life.

"I'll be able to work on it more steadily after this Saturday," I said.

She nodded. "Weddings can be distracting. See you tonight?"

"Sure," I said. "I'll pick up the cake in a little while and take it over to the restaurant." I gave up looking for any milk. I'd drink my coffee straight.

"Oh, I can do that," she said. "It's over at Stern's Bakery, right? I have to go by there anyway. And remember, you don't have to hurry with Maple Sullivan's cataloging. Just be ready to give a little report on your progress at the next historical society meeting. I think we're all a tad curious about what you found in those trunks."

"You got it, Edna," I said with a false smile, which in a matter of seconds turned into a real one. Her mention of the historical society gave me an idea. If anyone knew the nitty-gritty about a town and its citizens, live and deceased, it was the people who belonged to these organizations.

Back in my office, I set my coffee on my desk and called Information for the number of the Idyllwild Chamber of Commerce, jotting it down on a note pad. I opened the atlas and found Idyllwild, figuring out it would be at least a seven-hour drive from San Celina. Before I could call the Chamber of Commerce and ask if there was a number for a local historical society, Hud walked through the doorway.

"Hey, ranch girl," he said. "What's new?" He was wearing a plain white T-shirt with a smudge of dirt on the front and dark blue Wranglers. He carried a sheet of paper.

"Not much. Are you working on the trunks?" I asked, gesturing at the paper in his hand and casually closing the atlas, hoping he hadn't noted the page.

"Yes, ma'am." He dangled it in front of me before walking over to the credenza and slipping it into Maple Sullivan's file. "And I've just finished my first trunk. Unlike some people in this room, I have been working real hard on this project." He turned and pointed at the atlas on my desk. "Goin' on a trip?"

"No," I said, meeting his direct gaze. "Just doing some paperwork."

He smirked at me. "You do not have a face made for poker playing. What have you found out about Maple Sullivan?"

I kept eye contact, determined not to appear suspicious. Mr. Downey's questions about what I would do if I found her and she admitted to killing Garvey resounded in my brain. I thought I knew Hud well enough to know that his cop instincts would override his historian instinct and he would insist on reporting her whereabouts to someone in authority. Not to mention what a feather it would be in his cap to solve a fifty-year-old crime. He wasn't going to find out a thing about where she now lived from me. At least until I could talk to her first.

He flopped down in one of my black vinyl and metal visitor chairs. "You have found out something! And you're trying to decide how much to tell me." His smirk turned into a grumpy expression. "I thought we were a team on this. You said we'd share information."

"I will as soon as I get some."

His face still irritated, he leaned over, grabbed my full cup of coffee, and took a swallow.

"I hate it when you do that," I said.

"That's why I do it," he replied, making a face.

I picked up a small stuffed horse sitting on my desk and threw it at him. It hit the cup of coffee, spilling it across the front of his white T-shirt.

"Holy shit!" He jumped up, dropped the almost empty cup, and tore the coffee-soaked T-shirt off over his head.

I sat in my chair and laughed . . . the coffee wasn't *that* hot . . . until he had his shirt off. My laughter instantly stopped as I stared in shock at the five raised horizontal scars spread across his tanned chest. I recognized their origin, having a small similar one on the back of my right leg, which had been inflicted by my uncle Arnie when he was a stupid fourteen-year-old boy messing around with a bull whip.

I stood up, my eyes traveling from the scars into his brown eyes. Their emotionless depths told me nothing. "Hud . . . I'm sorry . . . I . . ." My eyes dropped back down to his scars.

"Forget it," he said in a gruff voice, mopping at his chest with the balled-up T-shirt.

"We have T-shirts in the back," I said, rushing out of the office, my face flaming, slamming the door behind me. I ran down the hall and into the supply room, grabbed one of the large black folk art museum T-shirts we sell in the gift shop. When I came back, he was standing in front of my small window, his wide, muscled back to the door. The scars reached all the way around him, like some kind of endlessly cruel embrace. He turned when he heard me walk in. I forced myself to keep my eyes on his face as I softly shut my office door.

"Here," I said, holding out the T-shirt. "No charge."

He reached for the shirt and I stole another glance at the scars. They spanned his chest and just the thought of a whip tearing into human skin like that caused my throat to tighten.

"Go ahead, take a good look," he said, his voice cool.

A sudden urge came over me to reach out and run my

hand over them, to try and soothe the emotional pain these old physical wounds must still carry inside this man. I fought the urge, sticking my hands deep into my jeans pockets.

His voice was quiet and dispassionate when he said, "Only permanent thing I ever got from my dear ole daddy except for my ten-million-dollar trust fund."

If anything could distract me from the pale pinkish scars to stare back into his face, that was it. "*You* have ten million dollars?"

He gave a cynical laugh and pulled the T-shirt quickly over his head, covering his old wounds. But now, every time I looked at him, I would know. And he would know I knew.

"You ever heard of Brooklin Oil Company?"

I shook my head no.

His shoulders moved slightly, shrugging into the shirt. "Guess Texas business isn't all that important out here in the Golden State. Brooklin Oil was incorporated by my great-granddaddy. Isn't actually an oil company anymore. Merged with Chevron a-ways back and my daddy retired to his two favorite hobbies, golf and bopping college cheerleaders. When he retired, he reluctantly threw me my share and told me to get lost. Kind of like he did my mama." He gave me a half smile. "Who, by the way, really is Cajun."

I couldn't help asking, "When . . . when did your dad do . . . ?"

His eyes turned almost black at the memory. "I was thirteen years old."

Involuntarily, I gave a small gasp.

He continued talking as if he hadn't heard my reaction. "To his credit, it was the only time. When I tried to get between him and my mama, he gave me a choice, me or her. I thought myself a man. He made me stand there and prove it. Of course, me and mama left after that."

"The police . . . did you . . . ?"

He shook his head no, giving another cynical laugh.

"Benni, my dad is worth almost a quarter of a billion dollars. What police department is going to arrest him for beating his wife and kid? After that, we left to live with my pawpaw and mawmaw Gautreaux in Beaumont, my mama's parents. Well, I did, anyway. Mama started with the hospitals. She kinda never lived with me after that."

"Hospitals?"

He looked at me for a long moment, then said in a slow, patient voice, "Benni, my mother is pretty much crazy. She took so many beatings from my dad the doctors think it might have done something permanent to her brain. She lives in a fantasy world where the memory of . . . well, where it's just a whole lot happier than in her real life. Sometimes, I can't blame her."

I looked down at my coffee-stained floor, studying the tips of his black cherry–colored boots, trying to hide the tears pooling at the back of my eyes.

"The stories about your mother . . ." I said in a low voice, still not looking up.

"She reads a lot and then takes what she reads and assimilates it into this really wonderful history. She honestly believes she's done all those things."

His voice softened into almost a whisper. "I know it was cruel to tease you about her, but it was just my stupid way of coping. I really do love her. Actually, she's real happy in her fantasy world. Happier than most of us, truth be told."

I swallowed over the thick saltiness in my throat. How did this puny little planet that God created manage to hold all the cruelty human beings were able to invent?

He stepped closer, took my chin, and lifted my head. His fingers felt warm on my skin, calloused like Gabe's, but with a different texture. He stroked my chin with his thumb while we stared at each other for a long moment.

"It's okay, ranch girl. It was a long time ago. I haven't seen my daddy in twenty-five years. But I'm sure proud that you care enough to choke up about it."

We continued staring at each other, our breathing becoming slower, deeper. If I didn't do something quick, the next step would be his lips on mine. And at that moment, I craved the taste and feel of his mouth more than anything I'd ever wanted in my life.

But my life was already screwed up enough without adding that complication. And it was wrong, no matter how much I wanted it. I turned my head, breaking the fragile emotional thread connecting us.

"Dang." His laugh was as low and intimate as if we had kissed. "But, darlin', that *is* a first and ten. No denyin' I'm in the game now."

Embarrassed by my momentary weakness and annoyed at his confident tone, I backed away and took refuge behind my desk. "I've got work to do. Like I said, the T-shirt's on the house. I'm sorry for spilling coffee on you."

"No problem," he said, still smiling. "It was *almost* worth it. Now, are you going to tell me where you're heading off to? I'm assuming it has to do with Maple Sullivan. Remember our promise to share information."

I stuck my hands in the back pockets of my Wranglers and lied through my teeth. "I'm not going anywhere."

He shook his head and grinned. "Lordy Mama, you are so cute when you lie. Did you know your right eyebrow gets this little twitch every time you tell a fib?"

My hand flew up to my face. Geeze Louise, he was right. "Get out."

"When are you going?" he asked.

"Goodbye, Detective," I said.

"Is it dangerous? Will you at least tell me that?" His expression looked genuinely concerned.

"No, it's not. I promise." I held up two fingers.

He studied my face for a moment, then finally said, "Okay, you're not lying. Just call me if you're going to do something the least bit dangerous, okay? Promise."

"Okay," I said, without a twitch.

Before I had time to move back, he stepped closer and stroked my cheek with the back of his hand. "You be safe, ranch girl." Then he turned and walked out of my office whistling softly under his breath.

It took me a minute or two to regain normal breathing. This situation with Hud was rapidly moving beyond my control. In that moment, Dove's words about any of us being tempted came back to me in a flood. Remembering about how much I'd wanted to kiss Hud—was I really any more innocent than Gabe?

I filed that confusing dilemma in the back of my mind, turned my scratch pad over, and dialed the number of the Idyllwild Chamber of Commerce. I asked the woman who answered if the town had a historical society.

"Why, we surely do. The person to talk to would be Arlene Rivers," the woman said. "She's president this year. What was it you were looking for?"

"Genealogical research," I said off the top of my head. "I'm tracing family trees." That wasn't exactly a lie. I was sort of tracing a family tree, just not mine.

"Oh, isn't that the most addictive thing?" the woman said, laughing. "I got started on mine when my son hooked me up to the Internet and I've gone back sixteen generations. It's a disease, genealogy. And for the life of me, I don't know what I'm going to do with all this information. My son couldn't care less."

"It is addictive," I agreed. Just to cover all bases, I asked her about Mrs. Albert C. Smith.

"Oh, I've only lived here two years," the woman said. "Me and my husband retired here from Riverside. The name doesn't sound familiar, but I'm sure Arlene could help you."

"Can I have Ms. Rivers's phone number?"

"Certainly, but it's Mrs. Rivers. She's eighty-two and doesn't like being called Ms. She's a spry one, lived here since she was a child. Always makes a homemade angel food cake for the historical society meetings. Whips the egg whites by hand, mind you, which she never forgets to tell us." She read the number to me. "You tell her that Betty Juniper down at the chamber said you were okay.

She'll talk to you. In fact, you may have to plumb hang up on her once she starts to gabbing."

"Great, thanks."

I dialed the number, and after six rings, a faint voice answered.

"Hello?"

"Mrs. Rivers? Mrs. Arlene Rivers?"

"Yes, who's calling?"

I dropped Betty's name and gave her my genealogical search story. Then I asked her about Mrs. Albert C. Smith.

Her voice came on a little stronger. "Albert Smith? He's dead."

"Oh, I'm sorry," I said. "But I'm actually looking for his wife."

"Lily? She's dead too."

I leaned back in my chair, disappointment flooding through me. I'd had such a good feeling about this lead.

"Her sister's alive, though. You want to talk to her?"

I sat forward and grabbed a scratch pad. It couldn't hurt. "Sure, what's her sister's name?"

"Thelma. Thelma Jones. Isn't that something? One of them married a Smith, the other a Jones. I think that's really something." Her laugh cackled like water on a tin roof.

"It is funny," I said. "Do you have a phone number?"

Her voice instantly grew sharp and suspicious. "Who did you say you was again?"

I patiently explained my story of searching family roots and how Betty from the Chamber of Commerce said I was okay.

She gave a snort. "That Betty's red hair is dyed or my name isn't Arlene Rivers. But she seems a good egg so I guess it would be okay. Let me go get it. Now stay here. Don't go away."

"I won't."

After almost five minutes she finally returned. "Sorry about the wait," she said. "It was downstairs and these old bones don't move as fast as they used to." She read off the number, then made me repeat it back to her.

"Thanks, Mrs. Rivers. I really appreciate your taking the trouble to help me."

"Oh, no trouble. Why, I think looking for your roots is something to be encouraged. My family came to California . . ."

After another fifteen minutes of hearing her family's trials and tribulations starting with the Gold Rush, I was able to pry myself away from her. I felt guilty, knowing she was probably lonely and craved conversation, but I couldn't wait any longer to call this Thelma Jones and see if she had any information about Mrs. Albert C. Smith and the flowers delivered to Garvey's grave.

I dialed the number and another elderly lady's voice came over the phone.

"Mrs. Thelma Jones?"

"Speaking."

Before she thought I was a phone solicitor, I hastily explained how I had got her name and gave her my genealogical story. There was a long pause before she answered.

"What is it you want to know?"

I hesitated a moment, not sure exactly how I should phrase it. Finally, I just decided to tell the truth . . . or at least part of it. I told her about cataloging Maple Sullivan's trunks, about my discovery of the flowers, and my curiosity about them. I left out any mention of the crime and hoped she didn't know anything about it.

"Oh, isn't that interesting," she exclaimed. "You know, I'd wondered for years why I was sending flowers to that family's grave."

"You're sending them?"

"It was in my sister's will. She left money specifically for it. Her instructions were clear. Send an unsigned money order once a year to this florist with a note saying it was for the Sullivan plot. There's enough for three more years, then it runs out."

"Did your sister know Garvey Sullivan?" I asked.

"Oh, I don't think so. They weren't actually from her. Apparently, it was something *she* was asked to do. She told me that right before she passed away five years ago. Breast cancer, poor thing. It was a slow going for Lily, so we had a lot of time to talk and plan. Organized as the day is long, my Lily. Always was, even as a little bitty girl. Used to fold her doll's clothes away neat as a pin. Loved to iron Daddy's cotton handkerchiefs."

"Who asked her to send the flowers?" I said, trying to get her back on track.

"Why, her dearest friend, next to me, of course. Marybell Knott."

"Marybell Knott," I repeated.

"She died about eighteen or so years ago," Thelma Jones continued. She gave a great sigh over the phone. "So many of my age are gone now."

I silently echoed her sigh. At least I wouldn't be faced with the dilemma of turning Maple in.

"A lovely lady. A bit of a recluse, but always willing to help out at church. She wrote our historical society newsletter for almost thirty years. Real clever with words. Even wrote a play once we all performed. It about broke Lily's heart when Marybell passed on. Oddest thing. She got breast cancer too. What're the chances of both of them dying from the same disease so many years apart?"

"Was Marybell married?" I asked. "Did she have children?"

"No, she was what we all used to call an old maid. She seemed to like her life, though. Worked as a waitress at the Red Kettle Cafe here in town for as long as I can remember. When she finally had to retire because of her arthritis, more than one person in this town mourned. No one could waitress like Marybell Knott."

I was excited. Deep in my heart, I believed I'd found Maple Sullivan. She'd even returned to her roots and worked at the only skill she had next to writing. But I needed real proof.

"You know," Thelma Jones said. "If it's Marybell

you're interested in, I've got a box of her things stored in my garage. It's been there since my sister died. I looked through it once, just a bunch of old letters and a few knickknacks. You're more than welcome to look through it. Frankly, I'd be tickled if you hauled it away. I've got more than enough junk of my own."

My heart jumped. Maybe there'd be something in there that would prove she was Maple Bennett Sullivan.

"When would you like to come by?" she asked.

I glanced down at my desk calendar. There was no way I could do it today with Dove's shower tonight, and Friday was out since it was Elvia and Emory's rehearsal dinner. It was at least a seven-hour drive to Idyllwild from San Celina. That was without the traffic I'd most likely hit going through Los Angeles. Unless I wanted to wait until next week, which I didn't, there was only tomorrow.

"How about tomorrow?" I asked. "Early afternoon?" I'd probably have to spend the night, but the way things were with me and Gabe and how busy everyone was with the weddings, no one would even miss me. I'd be back in plenty of time on Friday for the rehearsal dinner.

"That's fine with me. I have my bridge club in the morning, but I'm free after the noon hour."

After getting directions to her house, I hung up, so excited I wished I could get in my truck and leave this moment. But I still had Dove's shower to get through tonight. Right now, silly games and jokes about marriage were the last thing I wanted to hear, but this was a special time for Dove and I'd already ruined it enough by telling her about Gabe and me. Tonight, I swore to myself, I'd be as chipper and entertaining as a USO performer.

I spent the rest of the afternoon working on the trunks and doing some long-neglected paperwork in my office. A little before five o'clock, I headed home and changed into a new pair of Wranglers, a white snap-button cowboy shirt, and my good Tony Lama black boots. When I reached the restaurant where Dove's shower was to be held, there were at least thirty people there before me already chowing down on the spicy buffalo wings, cheese and vegetable platters, tiny tri-tip beef sandwiches, and potato salad. I loaded up a plate and joined Elvia and Amanda at a back table, where we giggled and laughed at the antics of some of our town's most respected senior citizens, who could, apparently, party down with the best of them when the occasion called for it. Dove, sitting at a front table of honor, was roasted brilliantly by her long-time friends and I found myself forgetting my problems for a little while and having a great time. They even managed to cajole me, Amanda, and Elvia up to the stage to sing with the karaoke machine a pathetically mangled version of "My Guy." The irony of the song's words certainly wasn't lost on me.

About nine o'clock we young ones all decided to call it a night since Amanda had court in the morning, Elvia was due for a last bridal fitting, and I made some vague reference to some work down at the museum. In reality, I wanted to leave San Celina at about 4 A.M. since I had no idea how bad the traffic would be going through Los Angeles.

I went up to the front table and gave Dove a big hug. "It was the most fun wedding shower I've ever gone to."

"Good to see you smiling," she whispered in my ear. "Things'll work out. Trust me, honeybun."

"I do, Gramma."

"Well, I want you to be the first to know I've decided on a wedding spot. And it's really, really special."

I braced myself. Lord, I prayed, please don't let it involve anything with extreme heights or fire. Or snakes. Or any kind of wild animals. Or . . . Then I couldn't help myself. I had to try one last time.

"Dove, it will be special because he's marrying *you*. No theme wedding or crazy wedding spot will make it any more memorable. He loves you. You love him. *That's* what makes it special."

There was a long silence. Then she laughed and said, "Before I was so rudely interrupted, I was about to say that I've decided . . ." She paused a long moment, torturing me.

I made a face at her.

She laughed. "I've decided that you've been right all along. I booked the church for three weeks from Saturday and we'll have the reception at the ranch."

I hugged her again. "Gramma, I'm so glad."

"Don't be too happy. I'm putting you in charge of the reception."

"I'll send out the invitations as soon as you write me out a list."

Relieved that Dove's wedding was finally settled, I said my goodbyes to Amanda and Elvia and headed across the street to the municipal parking lot.

When I was putting my key in the lock, I heard a voice call my name. I turned and saw Del walking toward me. She was dressed in tight Levi's, a pair of black dressy boots, and a form-fitting white cotton blouse. We wore almost the same outfit, just interpreted in completely opposite ways. Obviously she had a free night since Gabe was at Emory's bachelor party.

"We have to talk." Her voice was curt, demanding. Her cop's voice.

I looked around to see if there was anyone watching us, but the parking lot was empty. This was bound to be unpleasant and I preferred not having it bandied about by the local gossips.

"About what?" I asked, trying to sound cool and in control. I leaned against my truck and crossed my arms over my chest. The urge to smack her across the face was just too tempting.

"I think you know."

I studied the tips of my boots, deliberately taking my time answering. I reached down and flicked off a leaf stuck to the toe of my left foot, making her wait to hear my reaction.

"Delilah," I finally said, straightening up. "What in the world is there for us to talk about? You want my husband

and you're doing your level best to get him. He'll go with you or he won't, it's that simple. You and I have nothing to discuss."

"I *will* get him back," she said, her voice rising slightly, an edge of hysteria causing her nostrils to flare. "He loved me first. Long before he even knew you. I took him before from Lydia and I can take him from you."

I shrugged, pretending indifference, even though I felt like throwing up. She had broken up Gabe and Lydia. No matter how inevitable Lydia had said their marriage's demise had been, the truth was that Del had dealt the final blow. Could she do that with me and Gabe too? I honestly didn't know.

A sudden calm came over me, and for once, I didn't feel like an awkward kid, a tongue-tied adolescent who couldn't find the right words to say, who felt like everyone knew the rules of the game but me. For once, I felt in control. I looked straight into her eyes.

"I was the first woman he ever loved," she said, more than a hint of desperation in her husky voice. "He told me he never loved Lydia. They only got married because she was pregnant. He loved me first. He told me that."

"Maybe he did," I said softly. "But isn't the real question who he'll love last?"

I didn't wait for her answer. I turned, got into my truck, and drove out of the parking lot without even once looking back in my rearview mirror.

22

BENNI

THAT NIGHT, ANXIETY about my marriage problems and excitement about finally discovering what had happened with Maple Sullivan caused me to toss and turn in my sleeping bag, watching the moon through the bedroom's window move like cold molasses across the sky. Finally, at 3 A.M. I gave up trying to sleep, packed an overnight bag, put Scout's traveling water and food dishes in the truck, and set out for Idyllwild.

As I had expected, four hours later, I hit bumper-welding traffic in Los Angeles, but once I inched through that, it was an easy drive. I followed the freeways until I came to Highway 74, which wound through the palm tree–lined retirement community of Hemet and started up the mountain toward the town of Idyllwild. Though I'd taken four breaks for both me and Scout, by this time, my eyes were crusty from fatigue and concentrating on unfamiliar roads and my hands were stiff from gripping my truck's steering wheel.

We passed over the San Jacinto River and began steeply climbing with each turn, a shallow creek bed to our right, the sheer face of the mountain to our left. The two-lane road twisted unpredictably, giving no relief to my aching shoulders. Scout hung his head out of the window, his nose quivering at the scent of wild rabbits, coyotes, and squirrels. Around one corner we caught our first glimpse of pine trees covered with snow. I hadn't expected snow and I mentally kicked myself for not calling and checking on the roads. But Idyllwild was, at the most, five thousand feet and there hadn't been any rain all day so I hoped the roads were clear. A fork in the road gave me a choice of Idyllwild or Palm Desert. I veered left and soon came to a small sign: IDYLLWILD, POPULATION 2200, ELEVATION 5303. WELCOME TO AMERICA'S CLEANEST FOREST. I passed the Idyllwild Arts Camp on my left and in minutes found myself in the middle of the compact mountain town.

There was just enough snow to make it look like a Christmas card. Snow frosted the roofs of many of the shops, most of which sported a cabin motif. A huge fort-like structure housing more shops engulfed the center of town, and after a quick driving inspection, I decided to ask about a room at the Idyllwild Inn, a motel and cabin complex in the middle of town sitting next to one of the town's crowning glories, a chainsaw-carved totem pole topped by an American eagle.

Again, I kicked myself for not putting this trip off until after Elvia and Emory's wedding and doing a little research into places to stay. I didn't even know if they'd allow dogs. I checked my watch—a little before noon. Even if I had only an hour-long conversation with Thelma Jones, and drove straight back home, I'd still get there at the earliest 9 P.M. That was if I didn't fall asleep on the road and kill myself or someone else. No, considering the amount of sleep I didn't get last night, it would be better if I spent the night. And I didn't have a lot of time to look for someplace to stay. I'd have to take my chances with the Idyllwild Inn.

"I'll be right back," I told Scout, who whined to get out, his nose still vibrating at the new smells. A blue jay jumped from limb to limb in the tree next to our car, scolding us with loud squawks. Scout barked in frustration and pawed at the window.

"You'll never catch him," I said, giving him a rough scrub on the head. "Now, behave. I want to secure us a place to lay our heads tonight and you need to appear to be well trained." He licked my hand and barked at the jay again.

The snow made a satisfying crunching sound under my boots as I walked toward a huge carved gray squirrel holding a sign saying IDYLLWILD INN. Trying not to slip since my leather-soled boots were not the best shoes for snowy weather, I picked my way up the steps to the office part of the old house, praying they'd take dogs. Luck was on my side today. Though they didn't allow dogs in their theme rooms, a double row of rooms I'd seen from the parking lot, they did allow them in their cabins back behind the office. I rented a studio cabin with fireplace and drove to it along the snow-crusted paths at the back of the pine-covered complex. I quickly checked it out—bed, table, chair, stone fireplace, tiny bathroom. Everything I needed. I dumped my overnight bag on the bed and turned on the heat to take the chill off the small room. Then I took Scout for a quick walk, studying the town map I'd picked up in the Inn's office.

Thelma Jones's street was only about a half mile away. When I got back to my cabin, I called her on the phone and was told to come right over, she was fixing a pot of tea right that moment.

She lived in a tiny, woodframe house set back on a spacious tree-filled lot. Wooden lawn ornaments of chipmunks and bears lined her stone walkway. Though it was still February, a three-leaf-clover flag celebrating the coming St. Patrick's Day fluttered in the breeze and there were no less than five wooden windmills situated throughout the yard. Obviously her husband or somebody owned a fancy jigsaw and knew how to use it. The lot was thick with trees though you could easily see her neighbors on both sides, one a post and beam cabin that appeared unoccupied, and the other filled with children having a snowball fight in their front yard.

I watched them for a few seconds, tempted to join. Before I made it halfway up the walk to her blue-shuttered house, the front door opened. Thelma Jones, wearing a red chenille sweater and black pants, waved at me. Her thin gray hair was pulled back in a ponytail with a red bow.

"Let your puppy loose in the backyard," she said, pointing to a side gate. "It's fenced. Then come on in the side door. I'll be in the kitchen."

I thanked her, then went back to my truck to fetch a grateful Scout. He bounded across the wide, unsullied expanse of snow in her backyard, both his ears straight up in pleasure. I laughed out loud at his excitement. This was obviously a dog who had never seen snow before. He immediately spotted a chattering squirrel, chased it up a pine tree, and then stood at the base of the tree barking with joyous abandon at the unimpressed rodent.

"Have fun, boy," I said, opening the windowed door to the side of the house that I assumed was the kitchen.

Inside Thelma's kitchen, decorated with a cherries and chicken theme, I introduced myself and sat down across from her in the red-and-yellow-painted breakfast nook. She poured me a cup of tea and offered me a chocolate chip cookie still warm from the oven.

"Thanks," I said, suddenly ravenous. I hadn't eaten breakfast and it was a little after 1 P.M. All the coffee I'd consumed since 3 A.M. was starting to jangle my nerves. Food was exactly what I needed.

"So, you're looking into Marybell Knott's life," she said, settling down across from me. She pushed the plate of cookies closer to me.

"Yes," I said. "What do you remember about her?"

While I drank three cups of tea and ate four cookies, Thelma told me what she knew about Marybell Knott. How she'd come to the small town of Idyllwild back in the forties, how beloved she'd been by the longtime residents of "The Hill" as they called Idyllwild, how Thelma and her sister, Lily, had both nursed Marybell through her last days.

"She never spoke of where she was from, whether she had family or not," Thelma said, her watery green eyes focusing on the wall behind my shoulder. She absentmindedly tapped her small teaspoon against the thin china cup. "She had a slight Southern accent, you know. So me and Lily always guessed she was from somewhere in the South, though she'd never speak of her past. She went to church faithfully every Sunday. As strong an Episcopalian as you could ever want. A dear, dear lady." She looked at the brass-framed picture of Marybell and her sister, Lily, a photograph she'd fetched from the living room bookshelf.

I studied the face of this elderly woman standing in front of a decorated Christmas tree, trying vainly to see anything about her that would suggest she was Maple Sullivan. The eyes, maybe? Her mouth? Were those her cheekbones behind the sagging, slightly chubby skin of a woman in her seventies? I couldn't be sure. The only picture I had of Maple was when she was in her twenties.

"Do you have any younger pictures of Marybell?" I asked.

She shook her head no. "This is one of the few we had. She hated having her picture taken. Said she wasn't at all photogenic. She'd always be the one volunteering to take the pictures."

"So," I said, sipping yet another cup of tea, trying not to rush her yet wanting desperately to take the box of Marybell's possessions and go through them piece by piece in my little cabin. "You said you helped your sister nurse Marybell. Did she . . . at the end . . . was she . . ." I swallowed nervously, then just blurted out, "Did she have any last words?"

Thelma sighed. "I wasn't with her when she passed on, Lily was. I was down the hill on a senior citizens' trip to a matinee of *Oklahoma*. Lily was beside herself, as you can imagine. If Hugh hadn't been there, why, I think Lily would have just collapsed."

"Hugh?" I asked.

"Hugh Laramie. A dear man. Reminded me a lot of Marybell, actually. Reserved, a bit of a loner, quite religious himself. Like Marybell, he never missed a service at the Episcopal church. For years he owned a little leather shop downtown before his hands got too full of arthritis to work. Made belts and wallets and key chains to sell to the tourists. His shop was even featured on one of those travel shows—that Huell Howser fellow. We always wondered about him and Marybell, if there wasn't something going on. But if there was, they hid it well. Of course, at the end, when she asked for him, we just wondered all the more. But by that time, it didn't matter. All that mattered was we'd lost her."

Thelma's eyes teared up and she reached into the sleeve of her sweater for an embroidered handkerchief. She dabbed at her eyes with the wrinkled cotton. "Then we lost Lily, which about did me in. Me and Hugh shared a lot of tears during that time. We surely did."

"This Hugh Laramie," I said. "Is he still living here?"

She nodded. "Yes, over on the other side of the Fort. You know, that big log building in town. He's got a house over by the arts camp."

"You said he was the last person to talk to Marybell before she died."

She nodded again. "Lily said he was in there for a good long time. Over an hour. When he left, she went back to sit with Marybell, who was kinda slipping in and out because of the pain medicine, and then Marybell just squeezed Lily's hand. Lily went out to the living room, and when she came back to check on her an hour or so later, she'd passed on." Thelma gave a small sniff and dabbed at her nose. "Guess Marybell just had to say goodbye to Hugh. Whatever they had together, she wanted to talk to him last. That tells you something right there."

I set my half-eaten cookie down and asked, "Do you think Hugh might talk to me?"

"I don't see why not," she said. "Let me call him. But first, let me show you her box."

She took me out to the single-car garage and pointed to a pasteboard box on a low shelf. "Go ahead and put it in your car," she said. "I'll go give Hugh a call and see if he'll talk to you."

I lugged the box to my truck and slipped it in the bed. Resisting the urge to go through it, I hurried back inside to find out if this Hugh Laramie would see me.

She was on the phone in the kitchen. "She's right here," she said into the receiver. Then she handed it to me. "He wants to speak to you."

"Hello? Mr. Laramie," I said. "I'm Benni Harper."

"Thelma told me you wanted to speak to me about Marybell Knott."

"Yes, if you're not too busy."

"Come by at six o'clock," he said, his voice so soft I had to press my ear to the receiver to hear him. "I'll talk to you then. Thelma will give you directions."

"He said he'd talk to me," I said, hanging up the phone. "And that you'd give me directions to his house."

After writing the easy instructions on a piece of notebook paper, I thanked Thelma profusely and went to get Scout.

Thelma stood on her back step and asked, "Will her things be part of your museum up in . . . where was it you said you were from?"

"San Celina. If I have a say, they will." And, I thought, if they are truly Maple Bennett Sullivan's possessions. "Are you sure you want to give them to me?"

She waved a hand at me. "I'm an old woman with more than enough of my own junk. When I pass away, they'd just be given to the Goodwill or sold to a junk dealer. Just as well you have them as strangers."

"Thank you," I said. "Take care."

It was only 3:30 P.M. so I had a while to wait before

my meeting with Hugh Laramie. I went to a small grocery store a couple of blocks from my cabin and bought some dog food, a roll of paper towels, a loaf of bread, a package of bologna, a small jar of mayonnaise, and a couple of Cokes. I was hungry even after the four cookies, but I didn't want to take the time to go to a restaurant. I wanted to see what was in that box.

After drying off Scout's feet and legs as best I could with the paper towels, I poured him some dog food, made myself a sandwich, and opened the pasteboard box marked MARYBELL on the side.

There wasn't much to see. A lot of letters and cards, which I scanned to see if any were connected to San Celina. They were all from people here in Idyllwild. There was a redwood box of junk jewelry, some crocheted doilies, a couple of teacups, a pale pink scarf knitted from angora yarn, a worn King James Bible, once white leather but now butter-colored with age. The Bible held no confessional letters or indications that she'd once been Maple Sullivan. After I'd spread everything out on the double bed, I patiently went through it again, believing in my heart that she hadn't completely abandoned who she'd been. Something was here, somewhere in this meager box of possessions she'd left behind.

I went through each piece of jewelry, felt inside the three handbags that were in the box. Nothing. I sat at the small brown table and finished my sandwich, chewing it in frustration. She was a smart woman, if Marybell had indeed been Maple, and had completely covered her tracks. What now? All I had left was Hugh Laramie.

After putting everything back into the box, I set my travel alarm clock for five forty-five and lay down on the bed. Fatigue made every blink of my eyes feel like sandpaper against skin. It seemed only seconds before the alarm jarred me awake. For a moment, I was disoriented, not remembering where I was, why I was there. I splashed some cold water on my face, took Scout out for a quick walk, and then left him inside the cabin with strict instructions to be good.

Hugh Laramie lived in a small stucco house on a lot surprisingly barren of trees. Unlike Thelma's house, his place was extremely plain, almost spartan. A single pine, at least thirty feet tall, grew in front. I walked down the recently cleared sidewalk to his pale blue front door. He answered after two knocks. He appeared to be in his late seventies with a full head of white hair and the shiny reddish complexion you often see on people with Celtic blood running through their veins. Even though he was slightly stooped with age, he towered over me at least a foot.

"Mr. Laramie?" I held out my hand. "I'm Benni Harper."

He took my hand in both of his, patting the top of my hand gently. They were warm and soft, and for some reason, I instantly felt soothed.

"Yes, yes, come in, young lady. I have some peppermint tea brewing. Do you drink tea? I made it with bottled water. I know how you young people hate tap water."

"Thank you," I said, stepping into his overly warm living room. "Peppermint tea would be wonderful."

"Make yourself at home," he said, pointing over at a threadbare brown sofa. "I'll go on now and get the tea."

I took off my jacket and laid it down on the sofa. The room was as undecorated as the outside of his house. The sofa, a maple rocking chair, a small television, a couple of end tables, and a coffee table. The walls were bare except for the far wall, where an impressive collection of crosses and crucifixes, about thirty or so, hung. I was studying them when he came back into the living room with a tray filled with tea items.

"My only indulgence," he said, nodding at the wall of crosses. "Been collecting them since I was twenty years old. My favorite is that Navajo one." He pointed to a silver-and-turquoise cross to my left. "The man who made it for me died of liver cancer. Last thing he ever made.

Lloyd Yazzi. Good man. God-fearing man." His blue eyes clouded with memories of his friend.

He gave his head a small shake and gestured at me to take a seat on the sofa. After fussing with the tea and offering me a plate of pale sugar cookies, he leaned back in his rocking chair. "So, you're wanting to know about Marybell Knott."

I nodded.

"Why?"

I looked into his pale eyes, and for some reason, for the first time since I'd started on this quest, I felt compelled to tell the whole story, completely, without any lies or evasions. I don't know what it was about this man, but whether he wanted it or not, as he slowly rocked in his maple chair, he received the real story, including everything that was happening between me and Gabe, me and Hud, and how I realized that I wanted desperately for a happy ending to everything, especially Maple's story, even though I knew that was probably an impossible wish.

"I guess," I said, "what I really want is to know she ended up okay. That she had a good life. I don't believe she killed Garvey. I don't know why, but I just don't." I set my teacup down and leaned forward, resting my elbows on my knees. "Mr. Laramie, I have a feeling you have what I need. Was Marybell Knott really Maple Sullivan? Did she have a happy life? Can you help me?"

He stopped rocking and stood up. "I have something to show you." I stood up to follow him, but he gestured at me to sit back down. "No, stay here. I'll get it."

When he came back, he carried a small box. He sat down next to me on the sofa and handed it to me. I opened the box and pulled out a small silver locket.

"Oh," I said, my exclamation a small sigh. I knew what this was and what I'd find when I opened it. A picture of Garvey Sullivan. The picture that she'd gently complained about in her letter, the one where he wasn't smiling.

I looked up at Mr. Laramie. "How did you . . . I . . . I don't know where to start. Did you know who she was?"

He clasped his large, soft hands in his lap. "Not for many, many years. To us here, she was Marybell Knott. She was a waitress at the Red Kettle and belonged to the historical society. She loved cats and was very clever with words. Back in the sixties, she wrote a Christmas play for the children at the church that was so popular we've done it every year since."

"Were you and she . . . ?" I didn't know exactly how to say it.

He gave a sad smile. "A couple? Oh, no, we were only friends. Dear, dear friends. We felt comfortable with each other. Never felt like we had to chatter away when we were together. That says a lot about a friendship, the ability to be quiet together. Had a lot in common, the two of us, though we didn't find out how much until the end of her life."

"What do you mean?"

He pointed at the wall of crosses and crucifixes. "I was a Jesuit priest. Left the priesthood when I was forty, back in 1965. Moved here and started my leather shop."

I smiled. That explained why I found him so easy to talk to. He was trained in listening to people's deepest feelings.

As if he were reading my mind, he said, "It's a long story why I parted from the Catholic Church. Wasn't the Church's fault. It all lay within me. I've been happy with the Episcopalians. All the same God, as far as I'm concerned." He looked at me silently for a moment, then said, "I've never told anyone else but Marybell that I was a priest. Until now."

"Maple Sullivan converted to Catholicism when she married Garvey," I said.

"I know."

I held his steady gaze and said in a low voice, "Mr. Laramie, I need to know what happened to Maple."

"Even if you can't make it public knowledge? Even if it would be her wishes that the history books remain as they are?"

That stopped me. I had assumed from the beginning that whatever I found out, unless she was still alive, would fill out the story of her life, would set the record straight. I never thought about what she might have wanted known about her . . . or not known. I assumed that the truth would always be the most important thing.

"I don't know," I said honestly.

"I'll tell you and then you can make up your mind. Everyone who's involved with this is dead now. No one can be hurt, but memories are funny, precious things that many people guard like gold. Sometimes, even if we reveal the truth, people still don't want to change their memories."

"That's awful," I said. "The truth should always be better than a lie."

"Ah, but it's a fallen world we live in, my dear."

"So, what is the truth about Maple Sullivan?"

He twisted around, arranged a pillow behind his back, and proceeded to tell me the true story of Garvey Sullivan's death.

23

BENNI

"I TOLD MARYBELL . . . Maple . . . a few years before she died that I'd been a priest," he said. "She laughed and said she'd guessed it a long time ago. She was no dummy. I asked how she knew and she confessed that she'd been a Catholic for a short, happy time of her life and she missed it. I didn't ask her at the time why she'd left the Church, just as she never quizzed me about why I left. Our ability to let the other have their past without insisting on knowing it was what made our friendship so special. We both had things to hide, things we were ashamed of, for good reasons or not, and we never forced the other to reveal more than they wanted."

He folded his hands across his stomach. "The day she died, she asked Thelma to call me. I guess she suspected the end was near. She wanted to make a confession, get absolution, receive the Holy Eucharist. I told her she knew I couldn't officially perform Extreme Unction, but she said that we were both a couple of rogue Catholics and that perhaps God would grant us mercy and forgiveness in our attempt to do what is right. I agreed with her and heard her confession, prayed with her for forgiveness, and

gave her my blessing, such as it was." His old blue eyes
grew watery at the memory. "Since it wasn't an official
confession, I don't think it would hurt to tell you. Whatever judgment God has rendered has already been done.
Whether you tell anyone or not about this is up to you.
Frankly, it will feel good to get it off my chest. You were
right, she didn't kill her husband, Garvey."

"I knew it!" I burst out, unable to control myself.
"Mitch Warner? Did he—?" I started.

"No, Mitch didn't kill him either. Mr. Warner helped
Maple make her fresh start and was a good friend to her.
He lost as much as she did when they ran away that day
except he had a rich, powerful family to help him start a
new life in Mexico. For years she received checks from
him until she told him that she was doing fine, that he no
longer was responsible for her. About three years before
she died, she said she got a letter from a woman named
Maria down in Mexico City who claimed to be his daughter. Said she found her address among his things and
wanted Marybell to know he'd passed away. Heart problems."

"So who killed Garvey Sullivan?" I asked, trying not
to grab his arm and shake it.

"He did," Mr. Laramie said, his voice sad. "He killed
himself."

Then it all made sense. "Maple discovered her husband's body," I said, "called Mitch, and between the two
of them, they made it appear as murder."

I looked at Mr. Laramie in amazement, stunned by the
enormity of Maple and Mitch's sacrifice.

"They did it so he could be buried on sacred ground,"
I whispered.

He nodded, his eyes closing for a moment. "She knew
how much that meant to him, to his family. She said without him, she had no life there anyway. And Mitch was
the kind of friend any of us can only hope and pray we
have."

Why hadn't I seen it before? All the references to Garvey's sadness, his disappearances, his time in San Francisco. She'd taken the blame for his suicide so he could lie next to his family throughout eternity.

Hugh opened his eyes. "That, among other things, is one of the reasons I left the Church. It's changed so much these days. Now, many of the priests would, out of kindness to the families, look the other way, allow the person who commits this heartbreaking act against himself to be buried on sacred ground. Suicide is a touchy subject in the Church. I've always believed that we cannot be damned when we commit acts we do not realize we are committing. Of course, only God can truly know the heart of a person. In Garvey's case, he was an extremely depressed man, had fought it all his life. After his death, Marybell said all those trips he made to San Francisco made sense to her then. He was seeking medical help. All those weeks he'd stay at the ranch and not want her to visit him. He tried desperately to hide his mental illness from the world and from his wife. One night, apparently, his sadness became just too much."

"His father never knew," I said.

Mr. Laramie shook his head. "No one did, except Mitch Warner and me. And now you."

I sat back against the sofa, feeling completely drained. "If I tell the truth, even to clear her name, her sacrifice would be for nothing."

He shrugged. "I doubt that the Church would throw his body out of the family plot, but she told me on her death bed that she never wanted anyone to know what had happened to him, that she wanted his memory to remain as a good, Catholic man. The good, Catholic man she knew he was."

"Even if it meant she lost her whole life."

"Even then."

I sat there for a moment, stunned. Then I remembered something. "Mr. Laramie, there was a baby blanket in her things. Did she ever tell you anything about a baby?"

He nodded, exhaustion softening his flushed face. "She

told me the baby died two days after it was born. It was a little boy. He only weighed four pounds. It happened right before she moved here. She was living in Riverside at the time. Their son is buried in a grave there." He closed his eyes briefly, then opened them. "Maple is buried down in Hemet. And I believe, though they were separated in life, they are all together now, Mrs. Harper, resting in God's embrace. I truly believe that."

I nodded in agreement. "Thank you for telling me her story," I said, standing up. "You can trust that I will honor Maple's memory, her sacrifice."

He laid a hand on my shoulder and gently patted it. "I know that, young woman. I sensed that the minute your hand touched mine. Go with God, my dear. I'll be praying for you and your own troubles. And trust in the power of love. As you've seen, it's more powerful than we humans truly realize."

Back in my cabin, I made a fire and sat in front of it staring at the flames until they were nothing but embers. Would I have ever been able to sacrifice what Maple had for love? I wasn't sure. Right then, I wasn't even sure what love really was. Was it, as Mac pointed out, truly wanting the best for that person, sometimes even protecting them from themselves, being patient and kind and forgiving? I had no idea. Finally, I set my alarm for 6 A.M. Then, too tired to do more than crawl under the covers, I fell asleep in my clothes, my hand touching Scout's head as he lay on the floor next to me.

After I got up and packed, I dropped my key off in the slot in the office's front door and started for home. I pulled over once for coffee and once for a taco in Ventura. In spite of the two traffic jams in Los Angeles and the San Fernando Valley, I reached San Celina at 3 P.M. I had an hour to take a shower, get dressed, and drive to the mission for Elvia and Emory's wedding rehearsal.

I was only five minutes late.

"Where have you been?" Elvia said, when I met her in

the bride's room. "I've been trying to call you all day and only got your voice mail."

"I guess I forgot to turn my cell phone on," I said, hugging her. "I'm here now. How're you doing?"

I patiently listened to all her last-minute woes about napkins and hand-decorated truffles and the mixup about the cake filling, saying all the proper things and making all the sympathetic noises. But my mind was on Maple Sullivan and what I would or wouldn't tell Hud. I'd already decided only seconds after hearing Mr. Laramie's story that I wasn't going to make the story public. Maple gave her life to hide her husband's secret—who was I to throw all of that away?

Gabe and I barely glanced at each other the whole rehearsal. When Emory and Elvia stood before the priest and pretended to say their vows, I felt as if I would be sick. I swallowed hard over the cold stone in my throat.

A couple of times, Emory gave me an odd look and finally asked, "Is everything okay with you and the chief?"

"We're fine," I told my cousin, patting him on the shoulder. "Just stressed out over this move. You know how irritating escrow can be."

He nodded, his face not entirely convinced.

"Now, stop it," I said, punching him gently in the arm. "You have a wedding and a honeymoon you've been waiting twenty-five years for. You just quit worrying about me."

He grinned. "Sweetcakes, I never thought this day would come."

I gave him a full-on hug. "I know, kiddo. I know."

After that exchange, I went over to Gabe and asked him to come out to the Mission garden with me. His followed me without a word.

"Look," I said, before he could speak. "We're doing a real poor job of hiding our problems here, and my cousin and my best friend deserve better than that. I'll fake it if you will, okay? Just for tonight and tomorrow. Then we'll let the chips fall where they may. Deal?" I made my voice as cool and dispassionate as I could. If I could, I wasn't going to let him see how much I was torn up inside. I wasn't going to let anyone see it.

Apparently I was successful. His bottom lip stiffened under his mustache. A sure sign he was upset. Had Del told him about our encounter? At this point, I didn't care. All I wanted was to get through this wedding without falling to pieces in public.

"Deal." His voice was cool. He turned and walked back into the church.

At Daniello's Trattoria, a new restaurant out by the mall, Emory had rented the whole back room for the rehearsal dinner. A string quartet played softly in the background as we ate lasagna and eggplant parmesan.

Gabe and I did our best to pretend as if everything were normal between us. I think we succeeded as I didn't get any troubled looks from either Emory or Dove, the two people who knew me best.

I was passing by the restaurant's bar area on my way out to my truck when I heard Hud call my name. He was sitting on a black leather barstool at the end of the small, but elegant mahogany bar.

"How was your trip?" he asked.

I slid onto the barstool next to him. "Fine."

"Do you have anything to tell me?"

I studied his face for a moment, the responsibility of what I knew weighing heavily on my conscience. Hud was first and foremost a police officer. This was an old case, but it was still an unsolved homicide. Would he feel duty bound to report what he knew to someone in authority?

"I don't know," I said.

He twirled the golden brown liquid in his old-fashioned glass, then took a sip. "But you know what happened."

I nodded yes.

"You're afraid I'll feel obligated to tell someone, right?"

I nodded again.

"And what was told to you was told in confidence."

"Sort of."

"They gave you the discretion to tell who you wanted."

I bit my bottom lip. Hud was a good detective.

He tipped back his head and drained his glass, setting it firmly on the bar in front of him. The bartender looked at him in question and he shook his head no. "I got to give it to you, ranch girl, you are a loyal one. You're not going to tell me, are you?"

I shook my head no. "It's not that I don't trust you—"

"Except that you don't trust me."

"You're a cop," I said. We both knew what I meant.

"That, darlin', is where you are wrong. I am not nor ever have been first and foremost a cop. Someday, you'll realize that."

I didn't answer because I didn't know what to say. To be honest, I just didn't know him well enough to know if he was bullshitting me or not. So I couldn't take the chance.

He smiled sadly, reached inside his tweed Western-style coat, and pulled out an envelope. "If I ever need a secret kept, I'll sure remember that you're the one to tell. Found this while you were on your travels. Somehow, in all Garvey's careful hiding, it wasn't destroyed."

I opened the envelope. It appeared to be a unfilled prescription from a Dr. Samuel Crowther in San Francisco. The date scribbled on it was two weeks before Garvey's death. I could barely make out the word, it was so faded, the handwriting so bad.

I said in surprise, "Lithium?"

"It appears that something caused Garvey not to fill this prescription in San Francisco. He came back to San Celina and two weeks later he was dead. All his books on Abraham Lincoln make sense now. He was trying to find out how he coped with depression. Of course, it wasn't called that back then. Back then it was called melancholia and there was only two ways to treat it—shock treatments and lithium. I'm guessing neither worked for Garvey Sullivan. I'm guessing he killed himself, and Maple and Mitch covered it up."

I didn't say a word, but I knew by the expression on my face that he knew he was right.

"The thing I can't figure out," he said, truly perplexed, "was why would they do that? They both threw away their lives to protect his reputation. That is unbelievable. And stupid."

"Not stupid," I said. "And not to protect his reputation. It was so he could be buried next to his mother in the family plot in the Mission Cemetery. It was so he could be buried on sacred ground."

Hud stared at me, his dark eyes angry. He and I had tangled about God before and I could tell he wanted to say something. I braced myself for his tirade, then was surprised when he just inhaled deeply and gestured at the bartender for a refill.

"Want something to drink?" he asked me.

"No, thanks. I have to go home and get some sleep. Big day tomorrow."

"Oh, yes, the wedding of the century."

"Are you going to tell anyone about what you discovered?"

He thanked the bartender and took a sip of his drink before answering. "What do you think I should do?"

"I can't tell you that."

He set the glass down, reached over, and took my hand. My first instinct was to snatch it away, but his anguished expression kept me from it.

He covered my hand with both of his. It made me feel warm and protected. Something I hadn't felt in the last week and a half. Something I wasn't sure I'd ever feel again.

"I think we should let these poor people rest in peace," he said, "even though I cannot come close to understanding why two people would throw their lives away so someone else can be buried in dirt that is the same as anywhere else. See, ranch girl, I do have a heart even if I am a cop and a Texan."

"I'm still trying to decide what's worse," I said, laughing in relief. Maple's secret would be safe.

He brought my hand up to his lips and kissed it gently.

"Hey," Gabe's baritone boomed from behind me. "Would you mind taking your lips off my wife's hand?"

I jumped at the unexpected sound of his voice and instinctively pulled my hand back. Hud held it tight a second before letting go.

With slow deliberation, he looked up at Gabe, a lazy smile on his face. "With a great and sorrowful reluctance, Chief Ortiz. With a great and sorrowful reluctance."

Then he stood up, touched two fingers to his forehead in salute, and sauntered right past Gabe, big as you please. The shocked expression on Gabe's face was worth every irritating thing Hud had ever done or said to me.

"What was that all about?" Gabe demanded. "Isn't he that sheriff's detective you dealt with last September with the Norton homicide? What was he doing kissing your hand here where everyone can see? What in the—"

I held up my hand for him to stop. "For someone who has been living in a glass mansion this last week and a half, you're not in any position to throw even one pebble. *Not one single pebble.* See you tomorrow." I breezed past him and didn't look back.

In spite of all the turmoil between me and Gabe, I was sure I would sleep deeply that night, probably because I was just so exhausted. And maybe because I'd found a bit of peace about Maple and Garvey. Though I wasn't sure where my own marriage was heading, I was glad that my belief in the person I thought Maple to be and the love they'd shared had not been a product of my imagination. I couldn't help wondering how different it would be now with all the drugs and therapies they have for depression, if maybe he'd have ended up living a long and happy life. Maybe they'd have had children and grandchildren and the house would never have turned into a historical landmark but had remained a real home with birthday parties and Christmas celebrations and anniversaries.

On the drive back to the new house, I forced myself to think about the possibilities. Maybe Gabe would leave me. Maybe he would go with his first love, Del Hernandez. But he'd always remember me as the woman in his life who didn't beg him to stay. If he stayed, it would be his choice. And if he didn't, I would survive as surely as I'd survived Jack's death. I loved him. I wanted him. Although the thought of never again running my hands down his warm back, counting his ribs with my fingers, feeling his hardness inside me, his lips on the back of my neck, my breasts, the inside of my wrist, was almost too painful to bear, I knew I would survive. I'd experienced love twice in my lifetime. For that, I would always be grateful.

24

GABE

GABE STOOD IN the bar and watched Benni walk away from him. Seeing another man look at her with such naked longing ripped at his stomach like a bullet through flesh. That man—what was his name, something Hudson—was in love with her as surely as Gabe was his father's son.

"And what did you expect, *mijo*," he could imagine his father saying. "Do not think that a good woman is left alone for too long. There are too few of them, and the smart men, they know it. You have always been too greedy, Gabe. How many times do I tell you? *Quien todo lo quiere todo lo pierde.*"

His father's words blared through his brain like a siren. *He who wants everything will lose everything.*

Did Benni realize how this man, Hudson, felt about her? Had she fallen in love with him? Had Gabe screwed up the only relationship in his life that had ever brought him peace? His mind burned with turmoil. He wished he could reach inside his brain and scoop out with his bare hands the sections that had brought about all of this.

In minutes he was out at his car, cursing under his breath at its sluggish carburetor. It was time he got rid of his Corvette, maybe give it to Sam. Maybe it was time to buy a new car to go along with his new life.

Whatever new life he had left.

At Del's hotel, she answered the door on his first knock, her face lighting up when she saw him.

"I knew you'd come," she said, opening the door wider.

"Go home," he said. "Don't come back. Don't ever call me again."

Her coffee-colored eyes darted around him, as if she expected to see someone behind him prompting his words.

His heart beat faster. Is that what she thought? Did she think he was that easy to manipulate? Is that the appearance he gave to her? To everyone else? Shame and anger heated the back of his neck.

"She talked you into going back to her," she said, spitting out the words. "She jerked your chain and you responded. What a good boy you are. What did she do, call your mama? Did your mama tell you to go back to your smug little wife? And here you are, doing just what you're told. What a good little Mexican boy you turned out to be."

He had never been tempted to hit a woman until now. His hands deep in the pockets of his trench coat itched with the desire. But he wouldn't. That wasn't the type of man he was, that he'd ever been.

In that moment, he was overcome with shame for the part he'd played in this game. For how he'd used Del to make himself feel better, feel an illusion of excitement and youth, for just a split second in time. After this, he would call Father Mark. It was time. Time to let all of this go. Time for reconciliation. God would forgive, Mark had assured him of that. He could only hope his wife would show the same mercy.

"I'm sorry, Del," he said, his voice kinder this time. "I should have never hurt you like this. Go home to your family. Have a good life. Find someone to love."

Her voice cracked with anger. "You're a fool, Gabriel Ortiz. Do you have any idea what you've lost? Do you?"

"Yes," he said. "I'm afraid I do."

25

BENNI

THE WEDDING WAS . . . well, I just don't have the words for it. Gorgeous, perfect, the wedding of Elvia's childhood dreams. Santa Celine Mission was filled with the scent of roses and lilies and lavender. I cried when I walked down the aisle ahead of Elvia and saw my cousin's beaming face. I cried even harder when Elvia floated down the aisle gripping her father's arm as if it were the only oak tree standing in a hurricane.

When they repeated their vows after Father Mark, I glanced over at Gabe. He looked so impossibly handsome in his tuxedo. The tears that flowed from me at that moment had nothing to do with the wedding and everything to do with the passion I still felt for this man, the desire I had for him both physically and emotionally. It would not be easy to let him go. Though Jack had been my first love, the love of my youth, Gabe was definitely the love I had wanted to be my last. Both were special. Both had changed my life irrevocably. I would never be the same woman I was before either of them loved me. And I did not regret for one moment giving either of them my heart.

I touched Maple's locket that, at the last minute, I'd

exchanged Gabe's necklace for. Somehow, I knew she'd understand how I felt.

When Elvia and Emory were introduced as husband and wife, I suspected every tissue in the audience was soaked. Señora Aragon was the only one not crying. Her face had a smile that, as Daddy would say, reached clear around to the back of her head. I could already hear her voice nagging at Elvia about having a *bebé*.

It was most certainly a day filled with tears, both happy and sad, though I doubt anyone could tell the difference in me. At least, I hoped they couldn't. Gabe and I gave all the appearances of being a happily married couple. It wasn't as hard as I'd thought it would be. I just remembered the good times we shared and pretended it was then instead of now.

At one point in the reception, located at a local hotel, we caught each other's eyes and he came over to me.

"We need to talk," he said in a low voice.

"Not now," I said curtly. I'd managed to maintain a mask of marital harmony this long and I wasn't about to get into an argument with him during the last moments of Emory and Elvia's wedding celebration.

"When?" he asked, his blue-gray eyes dark with emotion.

"I don't know"

"I told her to leave."

I stared at him, not certain how his words made me feel. Relieved? Victorious? Angry? Did he really think it was that simple? He had to know that damage had been done to our relationship, possibly irreparable damage. And I wasn't sure whether I was ready to dissect it all yet. I shrugged and walked away.

A half hour later, Father Mark caught me alone at the punch bowl.

"You know," he said, sipping a glass of pale gold punch. "I am not betraying a confidence when I tell you that man would die for you." I guessed by his compassionate expression that he knew about me and Gabe.

I couldn't look him in the eye. Was I ready to forgive Gabe? Truly? And was I willing to accept the part of this that was my fault? That was even a harder question. "I know."

"Love is not so easily found these days that we can toss it away without a fight," he said, his voice edged with a sadness that made me wonder about his own past.

"Thank you, Father," I said, not willing to discuss it right now. I was still too confused. But I was glad for one thing. That Gabe wasn't alone. That he had someone to confide in. "Thank you for being there for him."

"Despite his flaws, Benni, he is a good man."

"Yes, Father, he is," I agreed. "He is a very good man."

After all the toasts had been toasted and the last piece of cake eaten, we finally saw the newlywed couple off in their shiny black Lincoln Navigator, decorated with a psychedelic rainbow of tissue flowers compliments of Elvia's seventeen nieces and nephews. They were heading off to Aspen for a three-week honeymoon in a mountain top chalet loaned to Emory by a friend. Her dream honeymoon to the Caribbean was not to be since my cousin still had not overcome his fear of flying. By the look on Elvia's face, a chalet in Aspen would be just fine.

"Go, be fruitful and multiply," I told her as I helped her change into her pale blue cashmere going-away suit.

She rolled her eyes. "You and Mama. She's already making the signs." Elvia moved her arms as if she were rocking a baby.

"And this surprises you?" I asked, laughing.

Right before Emory stepped into the decorated car, I hugged my cousin hard. "You'd better take good care of her. She's the best friend I've got." Before he could protest, I added, "Best *girlfriend*."

He kissed my cheek and whispered in my ear, "People can live happily ever after. You always told me that and now I believe it."

Tears pricked my eyes. "You will. You'll live happily ever after."

It was almost 6 P.M. by the time I drove back to the new house and had changed into jeans and a sweatshirt. The rain that had been threatening to dampen Elvia and Emory's day finally broke out of the black clouds in an angry torrent.

Exhaustion was not the word for what I was feeling. It was more like I was completely depleted of feeling. I'd put Maple's box of possessions along with her diary in the back of the closet under the stairs. Her story would go with me throughout my life, a testament to one person's true love for another.

I was just opening the refrigerator to get some milk to make myself hot chocolate when the doorbell rang. Its full, pleasant chime echoed through the still empty house. It was a chime I could have grown to love.

Gabe stood in the doorway, still dressed in his tuxedo, water dripping from his hair and trench coat. With all that had happened, his striking looks could still take my breath away. He would never know what it felt like to be just an average person, a person no one ever looked twice at walking down the street. He possessed the privilege that came with physical beauty. And yet, he was, as Father Mark asserted, a good man. A good man whom I happened to love.

"We need to talk," he said.

I didn't open the door wider. "Yes."

"I don't want to lose you."

I didn't answer. What could I say to that?

"*Querida*, please," he said. "*Lo siento.* I am so sorry. I want you. I love you. Please, let me come home."

I gripped the doorknob, suddenly angry at how easy he thought it would be. "How do I know that's what you really feel? That you won't change your mind tomorrow when some other woman wanders in from your past? How do I know for sure?" I asked, knowing as I said it that there was no simple answer to my questions. No guarantees for anything in this world.

His face twisted in pain. "*Escucha a mi corazon,*" he

said, taking my hand and placing it on his chest. "Listen to my heart."

I pulled my hand back and hesitated, deciding. It was moments like this, I knew, that changed lives forever. Inhaling deeply, I did the only thing I knew was possible for me. I stepped back and opened the door wider. A sound like a sob caught in his chest and he stepped through the doorway, stumbling over the unfamiliar threshold, falling toward me. And with every bit of strength left in my tired arms, I caught him.

26

GABE

SHE HAD FORGIVEN him. Though his first wish would always be that this last week and a half would vanish from time, that Del had never come back, that his past had never intruded into this tentative and fragile life he had built, Benni's forgiveness was the second wish and he was grateful it was answered.

That evening after he'd showed up at her door—*their* door, she would later correct him—and she took him back, as they drank the hot chocolate she'd made, she told him the story she'd been given by the ex-priest who lived in Idyllwild. After he'd heard about Maple's sacrifice, he pulled Benni to him and held her until his arms stopped trembling.

"What a lucky man," he'd said.

"She was lucky too," she answered, her pale face without a trace of artifice. "Loving someone that much. That's a blessing too."

"Will you come with me to the Mission?" he asked later. "I want to light a candle," he said. "For us. For thanks."

"Light one for Maple," she said, "And for Garvey."

As they walked downtown through the rain to Mission Santa Celine, down the dark, silent streets of San Celina, he grasped her hand tighter, leaning close to catch a scent of her hair, the sweet and smoky green apple smell of it, a smell he would crave to his dying breath.

Inside the Mission Church, it was cold and empty. The spring rains had driven even the most faithful home to their warm fireplaces. The high ceilings caused their footsteps to echo and fly through the rafters like darting sparrows. She sat down on the second pew, sliding over far enough for him to join her when he was finished.

He knelt with one knee in front of the altar, crossed himself, and kissed his thumbnail, his heart pounding hard in his chest, feeling like he'd run down the aisle toward the sad, tortured face of the slain Christ.

"Forgive me," he murmured, staying on his knee a moment before rising. He turned to the row of candles at the side of the altar and slipped some bills into the box. He lit a candle first for himself and Benni, in gratitude for her open heart, for deliverance from his own demons. Then a candle each for Maple and Garvey and their son.

"Descanse en Paz," he said, his words a small breath of sound in the old church. "Rest in peace."

Then he joined his wife in the pew and they sat for a long time gazing at the painted altar, at the flickering candles, the heat of each other's hands their one warmth.

She had forgiven him. This he knew, though there were times for many months afterward when she glanced at him with a tentative expression. Then, like a hummingbird, it would be gone. He asked Father Mark about it one time, about the ability for one person to forgive another. If forgiveness depended on fickle hearts like his own, God help them all.

"Only God is capable of all-encompassing forgiveness," Father Mark told him over fettuccine Alfredo. "What we humans do, to badly mangle what the apostle Paul said, is like looking through a glass darkly. We forgive, then take it back over and over. But eventually, if our hearts are truly humble, God grants us a very close facsimile."

He took a sip of Chardonnay and smiled at Gabe. "Sanctification, the working out of our being more like God who created us, takes us our whole lives, Gabriel. Benni loves you, my friend. How or why people love is something even that wise old homeboy Solomon never could figure out. Just accept the miracle and be grateful."

Later that night, after he and Benni had come back from the Mission to their new house, they made love. She came to him openly, without hesitation. And though their moving together started gently, tentatively, toward the end, he lost himself in her, in a desperate and fearless passion that left them both breathless and filled, tears wetting their cheeks.

Afterward he curled around her, encircling her with his body. As her breathing slowed, her compact body twitching every so often as she fell toward sleep, he forced himself to stay awake, savoring this moment, trying to make it last a fraction longer. Once she gave a great start, awakened herself, then turned her head to look at him, her eyes filled with fear, not knowing him for a moment. Or perhaps knowing him and still being afraid.

"Querida," he said softly, not wanting to startle her further. "It's only a bad dream. Go back to sleep."

The knowledge of who he was flooded back into her face and her eyes fluttered and closed.

"A bad dream," she repeated and laid her head down on the pillow.

"Sí, mi corazon, a dream."

He curled around her again, cradling her body to his. Before he fell toward sleep, he sent up a prayer to the God he would never understand and whom he had no choice but to follow.

"Protect her," he whispered to the shadows. "Protect us all through this long, dark night."

Turn the page
for an exciting preview of
Sunshine and Shadow
the upcoming Benni Harper mystery by
Earlene Fowler

Prologue

March 18, 1995
Saturday
Dove's Wedding Day

"ARE YOU SCARED?" I asked my gramma Dove as I pinned the delicate spray of baby's breath around her smooth white hair, arranged today in an elaborately braided bun. She had sent everyone away but me, her matron of honor and oldest grandchild. Her bright lupine blue eyes were glassy with excitement.

We stood in the pastor's book-lined office at San Celina First Baptist Church. Muted conversation and laughter seeped through the thick mahogany door to the sanctuary. In ten minutes she would walk down the church's center aisle clutching the solid right arm of her oldest son, my father, Ben Harper. The church, built a hundred years ago of smooth gray and tan stones dug from the hills of San Celina County, was filled to almost law-breaking capacity with five hundred people, including friends and neighbors, her children, grandchildren, and great-grandchildren. They were all excited for this momentous and unexpected occasion to commence.

"So, are you?" I asked again.

Dove turned away from the round mirror we'd hung next to the picture of Jesus praying in the Garden of Gethsemane to stare at me with solemn eyes. "Down to my very toes," she said.

"Isaac loves you," I replied, picking a speck of black lint off her lacy, sky blue dress. Isaac Lyons, world famous photographer, five-time-married man-of-the-world, had fallen face-down-in-love with my gramma from the first moment they met.

"Love isn't always enough," she said flatly, her still obvious Arkansas accent slightly slurring the words. She fingered one of her deep blue sapphire earrings, Isaac's engagement gift.

I pondered her words for a moment, knowing what she said was true. "But sometimes you have to take that chance. Sometimes love is all you have."

Her ample chest rose and fell in a sigh. "Maybe so."

"It must be weird, getting married after all these years."

Dove was seventy-seven years old and had been widowed since she was forty-two.

"Thirty-five years I've done as I've pleased." She turned back to the mirror, critically eyeing her reflection. With a wetted finger, she smoothed down a stray piece of hair.

I looked at her reflection in the mirror, rearranged a small piece of baby's breath. "Isaac won't try to tell you what to do. He knows better."

She smiled at herself. "Yes, he does." Then her face turn soft with what seemed like sadness.

"Are you thinking of Grampa?" I asked.

Her eyes dropped, revealing the delicate blue veins on her eyelids. "How did you know?"

"I thought about Jack when Gabe and I got married." Jack was my first husband, my high school sweetheart, who was killed three years ago in an auto accident.

Her eyes came back up and caught mine. "Both times?"

"Yes." My second husband, Gabe Ortiz, and I had

eloped to Las Vegas, but were married in a second cere-
mony in this very church a little over two years ago. "But
especially when I was married here. Jack and I spent so
much time here." My own reflection showed a thirty-
seven-year-old woman in a round-collared peach dress,
reddish-blond hair pulled back in a French braid. I'd worn
my hair up when I married Jack, in dancing curls that
took a can of hair spray to hold in place.

"I am thinking about your grampa."

"You still miss him."

She ran a finger under one eye, uncomfortable with the
mascara she was wearing. "You know how I feel. He was
my first love."

I slipped my arm around her shoulder. The stiff lace
tickled my palm. "Remember standing in this room with
me when I was getting ready to marry Jack? Daddy was
so nervous. He still smoked then and I think he had ten
cigarettes in ten minutes. He reeked of tobacco when we
walked down the aisle." I wrinkled my nose.

We both laughed. I had been nineteen, full of hope and
excitement, bubbling over with youthful arrogance. Now
I can look back and savor those carefree times, as brief
as they seemed now. Perhaps we're given those perfect
moments to sustain us through the hard times that inevi-
tably come as we maneuver through this life on earth.

"Your daddy is pacing outside the door right now," she
said. "He told me last night that he hopes all the women
in his life are settled for a while, that he was tired of all
the romantic intrigue."

I grinned at her in the gray-tinted mirror. Part of my
smile was hidden by a clover-shaped dark spot in the silver. "He needs some romantic intrigue of his own." It
would be hard to imagine my father in love. He'd been
widowed himself for over thirty years.

A soft snort came from her pale pink lips. "I'll leave
that to you."

From behind the wall we could hear the muffled sound
of organ music. The door to the sanctuary opened and

MacKenzie "Mac" Reid, our minister, walked in. His six-
four, ex-football-player figure seemed to fill the warm
room.

"How're we doing, ladies?" he asked, grinning widely
from behind his bushy chestnut beard. Forty-three and a
widower himself, he was thrilled that Dove had found
someone after all these years. "Means there's hope for
me," he told us at the rehearsal dinner last night.

"How much time does she have left before walking the
plank?" I asked, grinning back.

He glanced at his black sports watch. "Five minutes.
Looks like everyone's here." He took both of Dove's
hands in his massive ones and gazed down at her with his
gentle, pewter gray eyes. "Sister Ramsey, are you ready?"

There was a small moment of hesitation, then a strong,
"As ready as I'll ever be, Brother Mac."

"Then I'll see you out there."

After he left, I grabbed her hand. "I'm so happy for
you. It's about time you had someone of your own."

Her eyes grew misty. "Maybe this isn't the right thing.
Time is so short. One of us will have to survive being
widowed again. Isaac has lost three wives to death. I've
lost your grampa. I don't know if I want to go through
that again." Her normally booming voice was low and
afraid. It was a voice that had soothed me and scolded
me, threatened me and praised me throughout my life. "I
don't know if I can."

I paused a moment before answering, wanting to comfort her, wanting to help her through this dilemma as she
had helped me through so many sad and difficult times in
my thirty-seven years. She'd essentially been my mother
since I was six years old and my own mother died of
cancer. Without hesitation or complaint, she'd uprooted
her whole life in Arkansas and moved to the Central Coast
of California to help Daddy raise me as well as run the
Ramsey ranch. She deserved this happiness.

I held her cold hand tightly, trying to transfer my
hand's warmth to hers. "Remember when Jack was killed

and so many people were telling me that I was young, that I could still find someone, that my life wasn't over, that I shouldn't give up?"

She clucked under her breath. "People never just say they're sorry. Always got to be giving advice."

"Remember when I finally blew up and yelled at you that I was sick of people telling me what I should or shouldn't do, that I never wanted to love anyone again, that I never, ever wanted to suffer the pain of losing someone again? You listened to me rant and rave and then told me that I didn't have to, that I could sit in my room and do nothing for the rest of my life if I wanted and that you'd support me in that decision and would always love me and never nag me to do anything else."

Her pink lips turned up in a smile "I lied. I did eventually nag you to start a new life."

"Yes, but not at first. You let me wallow, you let me *grieve*. You gave me the gift of time. That was what I needed. Time to get used to my new life, a life that didn't include Jack. I had to get used to that life before I could even think about having a life with someone else."

She glanced up at the clock on the wall. Its ticking seemed like a tiny, insistent voice telling us time was running out.

"I know, get to the point. My point is, if you want to ditch this marriage and run back to the ranch, I'll drive you. My truck is right outside. I'll support you in whatever you want to do and I will love you no matter what. Just like you always have me. But first, tell me truly, how do you feel about this man?"

She sighed again. "I've had a long time to get used to a life without your grampa."

"Yes, you have."

"His passing tore my heart to shreds."

"Yes, I know." I continued to hold her hand.

"But I didn't fall apart."

"No, you didn't. Ramsey women don't fall apart. You've told me that more than once."

"We had us some wonderful times, me and your grampa. Oh, honeybun, I wish you could have known him. He had the most beautiful singing voice. He was always a'singing, when we'd pick cotton and beans, when I was going through labor to have our babies, when they'd get the colic and couldn't sleep. I knew he'd died when he was chopping wood because he quit singing in the middle of a song."

She sang softly, "Blessed assurance, Jesus is mine . . ." She stopped, swallowed hard. "He stopped right there and I knew something was wrong because he never stopped singing in the middle of a song, not in all the years I knew him."

The outside door opened and Daddy stuck his head in. "Dove, we need to get out to the front of the church now. It's time."

The sound of the organ thrummed through the office walls. I could just make out the melody—"We've Only Just Begun." Dove had always loved the Carpenters.

"One last time," I said. "How do you feel about Isaac?"

She looked directly into my eyes. "He pure out gladdens my heart."

I squeezed her hand gently. "Then it's time, Gramma."

For a moment, her pale blue eyes widened and she grasped my hand so tightly I almost winced. "Don't leave me."

"Not a chance," I said, leading her to the door toward my father. "Not until I deliver you safely into the arms of the one who loves you."

"And then?" she asked, her voice reedy with panic.

"Then I'll stick around to make sure he's treating you right. Just like you always have me."

With that, she let go of my hand, straightened her spine, and stepped over the threshold, the old Dove restored. "Then let's get this marriage on the road."

EARLENE FOWLER

The Agatha Award-winning series featuring
Benni Harper, curator of San Celina's folk art museum and amateur sleuth

FOOL'S PUZZLE   0-425-14545-X
Ex-cowgirl Benni Harper moved to San Celina, California, to begin a new career as curator of the town's folk art museum. But when one of the museum's first quilt exhibit artists is found dead, Benni must piece together a pattern of family secrets and small-town lies to catch the killer.

IRISH CHAIN   0-425-15137-9
When Brady O'Hara and his former girlfriend are murdered at the San Celina Senior Citizen's Prom, Benni believes it's more than mere jealousy—and she risks everything to unveil the conspiracy O'Hara had been hiding for fifty years.

KANSAS TROUBLES   0-425-15696-6
After their wedding, Benni and Gabe visit his hometown near Wichita. There Benni meets Tyler Brown: aspiring country singer, gifted quilter, and former Amish wife. But when Tyler is murdered and the case comes between Gabe and her, Benni learns that her marriage is much like the Kansas weather: bound to be stormy.

GOOSE IN THE POND   0-425-16239-7
When Benni finds a dead woman lying facedown in the lake, dressed in a Mother Goose costume, her investigation takes her inside the Storyteller's Guild. There she discovers that Mother Goose was telling more than fairy tales—she was a gossip columnist who aired the kind of secrets that destroy lives—and inspire revenge...

SEVEN SISTERS   0-425-17917-6
When trying to unravel a feuding family's tragic past, Benni uncovers a shocking pattern of tragedy—and stitches a hodgepodge of clues into a very disturbing design.

ARKANSAS TRAVELER   0-425-18428-5
Soon after arriving in Sugartree, Arkansas, where she spent many childhood summers, Benni discovers that there's something sinister brewing in this usually peaceful small town...